MADNESS IN LIBERIA

BY ANTHONY FABIANO

I0565872

Escrire

A FICTION IMPRINT FROM ADDUCENT

TITLES DISTRIBUTED IN

NORTH AMERICA

UNITED KINGDOM

WESTERN EUROPE

SOUTH AMERICA

AUSTRALIA

MADNESS IN LIBERIA

BY ANTHONY FABIANO

ISBN 9781937592837 (PAPERBACK)

JACKSONVILLE, FLORIDA

PUBLISHED IN THE UNITED STATES OF AMERICA

DEDICATION

To my lovely wife, Teresa - for all of your hardship, troubles, and anxiety while I was deployed to Africa and combat zones in my military career. You are a wonderful mother, friend, and soulmate.

Acknowledgments

I would like to thank all 54 members of the joint United States military mentoring team that deployed in January 2010 under Liberian Defense Sector Reform. I would like to offer sincere gratitude to the following individuals, in order enlisted first as they are the most important.

Master Sergeant Philip Dover, U.S. Marine Corps

Gunnery Sergeant Steven Phillips, U.S. Marine Corps

Gunnery Sergeant Ryan Benedict, U.S. Marine Corps

Staff Sergeant Daniel Reschke, U.S. Air Force

Major Will Markham, U.S. Marine Corps

Major Arthur Ayo-Aghimien II, U.S. Air Force

Major Tyron Neal, U.S. Marine Corps

Major Tim Bracken, U.S. Army

Captain Greg Dandeles, U.S. Air Force

Captain Labarron McBride, U.S. Marine Corps

Captain Matt Sanderson, U.S. Army

CHAPTER 1

The female Mossad operative had been in deep cover for over four months. She held the sniper rifle close to her chin and pulled the trigger. A puff of air emerged from the weapon, the noise suppressed by the eight-inch silencer. The three targets were head shots. She remained still in the dense brush until after nightfall. She slithered from the sniper's nest and inspected her targets for any intelligence. Francesca Waszey, a Lieutenant Colonel in the Israeli Defense Force, was considered by most as the world's deadliest assassin. She mastered her craft. The Hezbollah camp was along the Marshall River, deep within Liberia – a nation torn by war, ungoverned, and infiltrated by terrorists. Francesca took photos of the dead faces, one unrecognizable as she blew half the head off with a single shot. Her mission was simple – kill as many Hezbollah as possible wherever they hide in the world. She made notes in her ledger and added the three scores tonight to the thirty-two kills over the past three weeks. Francesca was focused and driven to avenge the death of her mother from a Hezbollah terrorist car bomb in Tel Aviv. She was a young girl at the time and committed her life from that point to kill.

Major Tom Russell, U.S. Marine Corps, had heard stories about lost souls who opted to live in the African bush - men who distanced themselves from civilization. Men who gave up on the world and craved isolation. Perhaps, they sought self-imposed exile forced by the continuous onslaught of media, the unrelenting waterfall of ten-minute media updates. Russell had heard about men who ventured off into the wild unknown within the dark African continent. Bodies found years later on the floor of some bamboo hut. Skeletons wrapped in a weathered garment. No burial performed.

When he heard that his contact would be a British seasoned colonel who lived in the African bush, Russell's mind raced with thoughts. Russell had no previous experience in Africa, not even a five star safari. Russell had only read about the impact of the African bush. Would he encounter a man possessed by the horror caused from living outside of any resemblance of western civilization? Would this man be coherent? Would he find someone similar to Kurtz from Joseph Conrad's *Heart of Darkness* who struggled with demons?

1

Russell watched the road that led them into Liberia, a nation brutalized by fourteen years of civil war that left over 400,000 dead and one million displaced out of a population of three million. Russell looked behind at the other vehicle, which followed. The vehicles were seasoned, each over 200,000 miles driven. The Freetown motor pool sergeant informed Russell the vehicles operated better with age. Signs on the vehicle doors stated IMATT with horizontal stripes of green, white, and blue that resembled Sierra Leone's flag. IMATT stood for International Military Advisory and Training Team, which was forged by UN agreements after Sierra Leone's brutal civil war. Brigadier General Canteberry of Her Majesty's Army oversaw IMATT and was assigned to mentor the new Sierra Leone army. Russell liked the British General as he was direct; to the point.

The vehicles bounced around the road that was filled with deep holes, up to several feet wide at certain points. Russell felt the bumps and wondered if his intestines would bounce out of his mouth from the hard jolts. The motor pool sergeant informed Russell that the air conditioner had not worked in over a year. Another hard jolt ripped into his body. Russell wondered if it could get any worse.

Russell shifted his position to glance into the side mirror. Bags were loaded onto the top of both vehicles. He looked over to Captain Lewis Stone, another Marine officer, who drove. Stone's grip was tight. His massive forearms grappled with the unbalanced road and absorbed the constant shock. Stone was a mammoth sized man at two-hundred-forty pounds and nearly six and a half feet tall. There was not much this Nigerian-born man could not physically accomplish. He played outside linebacker at Oklahoma University and had a shot at professional football. However, his true calling was military service in hopes of someday avenging his father's death.

Stone's father was an oilman who routinely traveled back and forth between Nigeria and America. During one of Nigeria's tumultuous years in 1994, the Stone family was sent to live in Oklahoma under the protection of a close friend. His father remained in Nigeria to negotiate with the newly formed government and would not pay protection money to a military junta that had seized power. On a dark street in Lagos, Stone's father was executed. News traveled at tortoise speed and four months passed with no word. Stone's mother took the news hard and died unexpectedly of a broken heart during his junior year at Oklahoma. Stone's mother never told him about the trust fund that awaited him. He found out after her will was read, but he did not want any of it. The money remained untouched by a prestigious Zurich law firm.

Russell was pleased that his team was on the move. He was glad to get out of Freetown with all of his team's gear packed tight. Along with Captain Stone, his team included two Marine Corps Gunnery Sergeants, otherwise known as Gunnys. Rozelli and Rageone, both reservists who had day jobs as NYPD cops assigned to First Police Plaza, lower Manhattan, a short distance from Ground Zero. Both served with Russell in Iraq and were hand selected for this mission. Everyone wore civilian clothes as Brigadier General Canteberry told them to remove anything that looked military. Beards were allowed, and the Gunnys started a competition for who would grow the best goatee. Russell had not shaved in several days and disliked the small beard growth.

The UN weapons embargo restricted weapons within Liberia's borders. Only knives less than five inches were allowed; however, many Liberians ignored the mandate and their weapon of choice was the machete. The long sharp blades were everywhere, and many carried them in the open. Each Marine concealed a sixteen-inch Special Forces knife under their shirts, regardless of what the UN embargo stated. Russell knew they needed self-protection. He felt naked without a pistol strapped to his leg and a rifle on his shoulder, as he possessed in Iraq. Within the vehicle, they concealed four wooden crates that contained a high-powered Soviet sniper rifle, four Uzi submachineguns, and a satellite communication antennae. The weapons were seized by IMATT and could not be traced. The sniper rifle was reconfigured for long-range targets during night operations. High-powered night vision scopes were added. In Freetown, each team member fired several hundred rounds for familiarization and proficiency. Rozelli shined as the best sniper.

Along the dusty Sierra Leone roads, large transport vehicles passed and kicked up dust. The dry season left everything bare. Russell looked out the window and saw dead bushes that littered the landscape. Small quaint villages, compilations of mud and grass huts nestled up against the main road. Stiff branches that reached into the road struck the vehicles and wreaked havoc on vehicle paint. Summer in West Africa arrived in the calendar year and March was the hottest point. Russell was amazed at the heat and cursed the lack of air conditioning. He looked out the window. Nothing moved, not animals, not people. It was too hot. Russell bent forward to look out the windshield. The large transport vehicles took up the entire road. The previous white canopies were weathered by the dirt and heat, yet Russell could read the overly stated large UN signs. Four more trucks passed. Russell counted. His instinct derived on the harsh Iraqi roads forced him to count. It was instinct. Eighteen UN trucks had passed on the way back toward Freetown. He heard UN forces would depart Sierra Leone and leave a few military trainers under IMATT and Brigadier General Canteberry's control. These vehicles were part of the UN's final pullout from Sierra Leone.

Russell contemplated how he got to Africa. Colonel Jack Crevace called Russell on New Year's Day. At first, Russell thought it was a joke as he had a good relationship with his mentor. Russell and the rest of the team first met Crevace in Baghdad early 2004 and they all deployed two more times to Iraq together. After the last deployment in 2006, Russell went back to his civilian life in Seattle and remained in the Reserves while Crevace took an assignment at the newly formed Africa Command in Germany, assigned as lead Strategic Planner. Crevace was in need of a specialized team to insert quickly into Liberia. Russell, Stone, Rozelli, and Rageone were at the top of the list.

After the call, Russell was on the next flight out of Seattle toward Europe. He landed in Charles De Galle Airport, took a train to Berlin, drove a rental car to Belgium, took the next flight to Ghana, and jumped on the UN-chartered flight to Freetown. The rest of his team did not have as much travel difficulty. They met in Quantico, Virginia, and Crevace flew them to London on a coordinated US Air Force flight. They waited a full week to catch a British Air Force flight to Freetown. However, Crevace wanted Russell in Africa immediately and Russell complied. He spent ten days getting briefed and organized while his team waited. Back in Seattle, Russell had no animals; not even a plant depended upon him. He tossed away the restaurant leftovers and dismal scraps of food. Nothing kept him in Seattle, not even a girlfriend.

Russell looked at his notes and read the Accra Peace Agreement signed by the three Liberian warring factions in August 2003, just a few years prior. Several internal UN reviews lamented the Disarmament, Demobilization, and Reintegration (DDR) of the former Liberian army. Charles Taylor's military was categorized as thugs, murderers, and rapists. One of the comments Russell read stated that the nation's donors were concerned over the DDR concept to integrate former child soldiers back into Liberian society. The report outlined how over 13,000 former combatants and over 30,000 weapons existed in Liberia. Most significantly, the former child soldier was without much hope of employment – creating an atmosphere ripe for Al-Qaeda recruitment. A British report revealed the flow of UN personnel into Liberia under UN Mission in Liberia (UNMIL). A staggering 14,000 UN troops were deployed, more than enough to maintain stability, or so everyone thought. Russell concluded it was incredible irony that he would cross into Liberia on Doctor Martin Luther King Day, 16 January, a holiday not just for celebrating the most significant civil rights leader but also a testament for Doctor King's accomplishments. Russell pondered what Doctor King would have to say about the violence Liberians endured at the hand of child soldiers.

Russell wondered if Liberia would be able to sustain peace. For the past three years after Charles Taylor went into exile, Liberians had lived under the protection of the UN; however, war criminals were not brought to justice and roamed free. On this day and with respect to Doctor King, the newly elected Liberian President Ellen Johnson-Sirleaf took the oath of office in a ceremony to match the coronation of any royalty. African, European, Chinese, Japanese, and American dignitaries attended the most heavily guarded presidential ceremony in the history of West Africa. Sirleaf became the first female ever to be elected president on the Africa Continent and many associated with Charles Taylor wanted her to fail. Some wanted her dead.

Russell thought of the impact on the brutality of Liberia's latest civil war. He looked at the binder of photographs that displayed horrific scenes, gruesome still images of death. Inside his notebook cover, Russell read the anonymous quote the British General asked him to inscribe: *"Doped up soldiers robed in the spoils of war – dresses, wigs, construction helmets, and swimming goggles – fired on civilians and rival factions with equal disdain."* The shock and savagery of the Liberian civil war captivated the world in the worse possible way. General Canteberry showed him satellite images of suspected mass graves. No one knew the exact number of dead. Estimates ranged from 250,000 to 400,000 killed during the fourteen years that encompassed two major civil wars. No one will ever know the actual number, yet the magnitude was etched everywhere. The one thing the British General confirmed was the mass exodus of biblical proportions as one million Liberians departed the war zone, out of a population of just three million.

Six more hours had passed without a rest break. The timetable had to be kept for the rendezvous at the Liberian border. The huge holes in the narrow road forced slow speed. Russell adjusted the time, space, and distance measurements in his head. At first, he had difficulty while he converted the kilometers, but within moments he mastered it. The border post had to be crossed by noon before it closed. There existed a four-hour window to allow vehicles to pass before the mass exodus of refugees. Traveling on the roads had to be completed in daylight hours due to bandits. From the Sierra Leone-Liberia border, it would take another seven hours to reach their camp. If they arrived past noon, they would spend the night on the Sierra Leone side of the road, unable to pass over the bridge that connected the two nations. Russell looked at his watch relentlessly.

"There," Russell said, "Border checkpoint straight ahead." As they approached the bridge, Russell observed the river was over two-hundred feet below. The bridge rattled as they rolled on the forty-year old structure.

Across the bridge was Liberia, a land devastated by some of the most brutal maltreatment humans had ever experienced. Russell saw the oversized Liberian flag as it fluttered in the breeze. The colors of red, white, and blue were draped across the flag, similar to the United States. The big difference was one big white star which rested in the center of the blue background. Russell recalled how Liberians viewed themselves as America's fifty-first state, as freed slaves had formed the nation. Below the Mano River cascaded and divided Sierra Leone and Liberia.

Halfway across, Russell viewed the silhouette of a man who stood near the small shack that served as the Liberian customs building. The man wore a tan bush hat, obsessively large Russell thought. Next to the man was an African, about the same size.

"Welcome to Liberia, lads." shouted the tall, slender white man, "I'm Colonel Kitson and this is Ike." His appearance was impeccable with creased brown slacks and a bleached white dress shirt. The African named Ike was very muscular and toned.

"Thank you, let me introduce you to my team," Russell said as he gave a halfhearted salute from the brim of his bush hat. The colonel looked at him with a quirky lip and wondered why he was being saluted in civilian clothes.

"Let's hold off on pleasantries as we need to get moving. It will take about seven hours to get to the camp and we don't want to be caught out in the open at night," he paused, "if you know what I mean."

Russell gazed at the Liberian crest plastered on the shack's wall and read the inscription, 'The love of Liberty brought us here'. He thought how much death and mutilation came to Liberia during the recent civil war after the freed American slaves came back to their ancestral African land; so many with hopes and dreams shattered.

Ike and the Liberian border guards talked for what seemed too long until Kitson became frustrated and took over the discussion. Within a minute, the team's passports were stamped.

"You lads keep close." Kitson informed the team as he exited the border post. It was only two hundred kilometers from the border to the British camp that resided within the Firestone Plantation.

The Liberian roads were far worse than what Russell observed on the other side of the border. The vehicles bounced in the deep ruts. All of a sudden, Kitson's vehicle in front swerved, not a little, but a lot. There was a tremendous shift of the wheels to the left of the road over higher ground. The vehicle plowed through several brown, dried bushes and came to an abrupt stop. Ike climbed out of the vehicle, picked up the animal - what looked like a dead rodent - by the tail and placed the carcass in a trash bag. Russell did not know what to think as Ike went out of the way to run over the animal. Within a moment, the convoy lurched forward again. The roads spewed clouds of earthy red dust.

Russell read his notes. He understood the historical context for Africa as major European powers - France, Britain, Portugal, Germany, Belgium, Spain, and Italy - carved out borders as they fought for control of Africa. Imperialism started with the first white settlers who searched for rare minerals with complete disregard for the indigenous populations. Belgium's King Leopold II became one of the most notorious and brutal imperial masters who helped coin the phrase 'long sleeve or short sleeve' that determined how high someone would have their arm chopped off. Liberia did not have an imperial master as the bedrock of independence was cemented with the arrival of freed American slaves. Liberia was left alone from European colonization as it declared independence in 1847.

Russell was exalted when he read the antiquated sign weathered with age, 'Welcome to Firestone Plantation, 1929'. He recalled that the Firestone Corporation had signed a ninety-nine-year lease. They did not enter the Firestone Plantation but instead took a detour down a trail that Russell could not even believe was an actual road. The vehicles bounced violently from the deep intrusive ruts in the dirt road. Abruptly the British Colonel's vehicle stopped, and the African man got out and waved his arms in the air. As Russell's vehicle approached the small hill, he saw a man in a large dug out hole with a bamboo reed roof. Inside was a machine gun, which pointed down the road. The vehicles entered the compound, which the previous tenants, the Liberian Black Berets, had disbanded. Since the Liberian government needed money and assistance, the British were able to secure the camp for minimal costs.

"You can put your kit in that bungalow." Kitson directed. "The others bungalows are open for your men." Kitson pointed toward the crumbling cement buildings with plywood windows and added. "We can all meet in one hour for dinner."

For several hours, the American team spread out and inventoried equipment. Each knew what they packed in the land rovers, yet their years of military experience forced them to re-examine all of the gear and weapons one more time. Communication gear was loaded into Stone's bungalow and a satellite dish was quickly assembled. Russell made a quick call back to Germany on a satellite phone to inform Colonel Crevace that the team had arrived.

Kitson welcomed the Americans to his bungalow. He was pleased with the renovations and small scraps of furniture that Ike rebuilt. He showed several paintings that he purchased in the local village, scenes of a better time in Liberia. At dinner, they dined on a well laid out meal of African vegetables, fruits, and an unknown meat dish. The meat dish was covered in dark brown gravy and no one could tell what it was.

"What's that?" asked Rozelli in his thick New York accent as he pointed to a bowl.

Ike waved his finger in the air and professed, "tn sumthin nat far u." The new arrivals had no idea what Ike said, yet understood the context of his statement. Rozelli took that as a challenge, plastered the chunk of meat on his plate with the sauce, and eyed the other Marines in a daring fashion. The bowl was passed to the other Marines and each followed suit. Mouths nearly blistered; eyes swelled; and tears flowed as the volatile Liberian pepper sauce went down. Everyone was in instant pain, everyone except for Captain Stone of Nigerian descent. Stone smiled as he watched the other members of his team as they grappled with the spicy fire.

"What kind of meat is this?" Russell inquired.

"Bush meat," replied Ike with a big smile, "Ey ranin dover."

"One does not see many animals walking around Liberia." Kitson interjected. "War took care of that. Everything that could walk or crawl was eaten." The guests understood and enjoyed eating the possum that Ike ran over a few hours prior.

As night fell, Colonel Frank Kitson Jr. of Her Majesty's Army walked out onto his veranda and overlooked the Black Beret camp. He was proud of the camp's reconstruction with limited resources. The guard towers and fence-line were a far cry from what he built in Northern Ireland, yet would work. He knew what security was needed to protect the camp.

Colonel Kitson served Her Majesty well for the past thirty-two years, many more than he ever thought since attending the Royal Military Academy at Sandhurst, the British equivalent of West Point. On one occasion Kitson retired; however, a call from the Prince of Wales brought him back to service in Afghanistan and subsequently West

Africa. Kitson's father was a well-respected general whose reputation loomed over him. Colonel Kitson's adolescent years were spent in Kenya, where his dad served during the Mau Mau rebellion. Kitson learned firsthand the struggle between good and evil. As a British soldier, the young Kitson served in Eritrea when Ethiopia threatened to invade and the Sudan where he held dying infants in his arms as disease decimated the refugee camps. But it was his time in Norther Rhodesia as a Second Lieutenant that made him a legend.

Kitson sipped the gin and tonic and remarked to Ike, "I say it will be nice to have guests for a while. Don't you agree?"

"Ya, bossman." Ike called Kitson bossman. The British Colonel did not like being called bossman; however, he understood Ike's affection that he had a job, a roof, and food. Ike did not know how old he was but guessed that he must be fifty as his skin was wrinkled. Ike was Mandingo, a member of what was once one of the most influential tribes in West Africa. Ike was raised in a small village called Foya in Lofa County about ten miles from the intersection of Liberia, Sierra Leone, and Guinea. Lofa County was the northeast part of Liberia and witnessed many cross-border raids. Ike had not returned to Foya for seven years ever since his family and half the village of 400 were brutally killed by child soldiers. Babies were crushed under rebel boots. Women were sexually assaulted. Ike was shot four times, yet he managed to live as he crawled out. After three days, he snuck back into the village. His family was buried in a mass grave by villagers who survived the onslaught. Ike had nothing left and limped toward Monrovia. On a rainy day over a year ago he helped a white man whose vehicle slid into a ditch. The white man, Kitson, offered him a job on the spot.

"Make sure there are no snakes in the compound tonight." Kitson said as he pointed toward the bungalows and smirked. "I would hate for our guests to be bitten on their first day." Russell's team had received the brief on Liberia that the country teemed with some of the most poisonous snakes in the world: king cobra, bush viper, and of course the black mamba. The black mamba was an extremely aggressive and territorial snake, the most feared in Africa. Black mambas were actually grey on the outside but were named for the black inside their mouths. Black mambas struck fear in all Africans. Typical snakes were six to eight feet, yet some had grown up to fourteen feet. The mix of neurological and cardio-toxic venom was deadly. If bitten, death arrived in four hours without administration of anti-venom. Inside Liberia, there were six doses of snake antivenin locked in a UN safe. As Ike marched off to do his task, Kitson continued to sip his gin and tonic, a favorite drink in Africa to ward off malaria.

Young chimpanzees shrieked as the last glimmers of daylight sparkled. There were five chimps in the compound. Kitson found them for sale on the Monrovia streets. Wires nooses were hung around the chimp's necks. Kitson purchased the chimps for forty dollars each. Lucy was the biggest and caused the most trouble. She grabbed plantains, a local banana, off the kitchen table before Ike had a chance to fry them into chips. Ike watched Lucy as she caused mischief. By the time the chimps would become three years old, each would be four feet tall, two hundred pounds, and be able to tear the face off any sized man. Ike liked Lucy, yet he knew he would have to let her go someday.

The sound of the Brussels Air 747 on final approach to Roberts International Airport broke the chimp's chatter. The landing pattern was above Firestone Plantation as to avoid any shots by rebel forces that held out capture. Flights expanded to four times a week and Kitson watched the aircraft as it lowered its landing gear. Kitson sat back in his chair and wondered who was on this flight to help Liberia get back to normalcy. After the plane passed, Lucy and the other chimps continued their nightly chatter for another hour.

In the morning, the American team, except for Captain Stone, had extreme bouts of dysentery. Russell looked outside of his bungalow and saw the British colonel doing his daily exercises. Stone was beside him and lifted a bar attached to concrete blocks. Stone kept up with the British colonel's robust pace. Russell felt beaten from the hot pepper sauce, yet he rounded up the battle-tested Gunnys out of the bathroom. They proceeded to join the rest in the morning heat. After the Americans warmed up, Kitson took them on a five mile run that reached deeper into the rubber tree groves. Ike drove in front to make sure no snakes sat on the trail to warm their scaly outer skin in the morning sun.

Russell felt severe stomach pains, yet he hung in. American pride was at stake. He pushed his body to keep up.

CHAPTER 2

The Firestone Plantation seemed to be on the other side of the world compared to the harsh life inside of Monrovia's city limits. In the greater Monrovia area, over 600,000 Liberians congregated to forge an existence. Monrovia was formed on a peninsula and became the capital in the late 1800s. In the 1950s, Liberia was the talk of West Africa as well-dressed civilized gentlemen and women walked along manicured streets. Beautiful marble sculptures occupied the exterior facades of government buildings. The University of Monrovia was respected as a place of intellectual thought. Since Liberia was not a European colony, the spread of Pan Africanism in the 1960s to bring rule back to Africans did not tumble Liberia into chaos as witnessed in many other African nations. For over a century, Monrovia thrived. Liberians experienced higher standards of living than most Africans that was until massive unrest eroded the tranquility as two civil wars raged from 1989 to 2003.

The Cape Hotel remained the most luxurious hotel in war-torn Monrovia as it was minimally impacted by the rampant and unchecked pilferage. The Cape Hotel was located near the US Embassy, which had Marine security forces for protection. At one point during the last civil war, rebels shot directly into the US Embassy compound from abandoned buildings. The Marines were forced to move out into the city to secure higher ground, which helped protect the Cape Hotel from looters. However; the Marine protection ended as the US Embassy was evacuated yet again and the Cape Hotel had to depend upon its own security. With eight full-scale evacuations, the American Embassy in Liberia remained the most evacuated embassy in US history. Security forces from South Africa and Angola were hired to protect the hotel.

Directly in front of the Cape Hotel was the finest beach in all of West Africa. Crystal blue waves crashed onto the shoreline. The soft sand melted underneath bare feet. Palm trees were naturally everywhere, swaying in the breeze. Scenic sunset views made everyone believe that this could be a Hawaiian beach. The steep rock cliff walls that protected the embassy helped form a small hamlet cove. On this morning after the presidential inauguration, the Cape Hotel had a lot of activity. The newly elected Liberian president hosted a vibrant party in the main dining room and cleanup continued. A luncheon with the newly appointed Cabinet Ministers and many dignitaries to include the US Ambassador would occupy the entire restaurant. A majority of West African leaders and dozens of foreigner diplomats remained in Monrovia in hopes of privately meeting with the new president. The hotel's guests spoke numerous languages and the Cape staff worked hard to keep up with all of the demands.

Tareek Najaf managed the daily operations at the Cape Hotel. He was Lebanese by birth and made sure everyone knew that he was Druze and not Hamas or worse, Hezbollah. The Druze sects were mountain fighters and fiercely opposed to the more radical Lebanese elements. During the 2003 fighting in the mountains that overlooked Beirut, Hezbollah fighters moved into his village as the Lebanese Christians fled their positions. Hezbollah fighters believed Tareek's village supported the Lebanese Christians and opened fire with anti-aircraft canons used as direct fire weapons that demolished all of the village's buildings. His mother, sisters, wife, and beautiful baby girl Marsa were killed instantly as their home collapsed. Tareek heard the news in Beirut and could not get out of the city no matter how hard he tried. All the roads were blocked and occupied by fighting factions. Hezbollah pounded the area with artillery. Lebanese Christians fought back. Hamas suicide bombers unleashed their terror in the streets. Beirut was in chaos. The closest he got was fifteen miles. His neighbor kept what was left of the bodies in a barn for three days, but eventually could not wait any longer due to the smell. His neighbor buried Tareek's family in one grave. Not being able to bury his family tore at his soul.

Tareek had boarded a ship and sailed to West Africa along with many other Lebanese who sought refuge. He and arrived just weeks before the start of the last Liberian civil war. Tareek's uncle Anwar owned the Cape Hotel for the past ten years. Uncle Anwar purchased the Cape Hotel between the two civil wars at an extremely discounted price. Tareek kept a picture of Marsa in a medallion locket around his neck and repeatedly kissed the medallion throughout the day. Silently, Tareek recited a prayer for his lost family.

Tareek looked every bit the charmer with his native brown Middle Eastern skin and slender figure. He exercised every day. As a thirty-five year old man, he had the abdominal muscles of someone half his age. He was smart enough not to run in Monrovia or he would have become a hood ornament for one of the speeding out of control taxicabs that littered Monrovia. There was no right of way on Monrovia streets, just complete driving chaos. At the Cape Hotel, he swam every day to keep conditioned. He installed a full gym in the basement that he used daily. Tareek was taller than most Lebanese, at six feet even. He liked that he could look many of the foreigners in the eye. On this day, he wore a white cotton suit that enhanced his dark complexion.

The Cape Hotel was the oasis in the war-ravaged capital city Monrovia. The city had no power grid and lacked an adequate sewage system. Two massive generators cycled on and off and kept the Cape Hotel powered and more importantly air-conditioned. The hum of these monstrous generators took time to get used to and became hypnotic. The five thousand gallon water tank on top of the hotel was filled every day by UN trucks - every hotel and embassy received support from the UN as there were no commercial solutions as of yet. Raw sewage overflowed from broken clay pipes that were inlaid decades before. Many Liberians utilized buckets to relieve themselves or they snuck onto the beach at night when no one watched. Empty, vandalized and mostly crumbling buildings polluted Monrovia's landscape. In every nook and cranny, Liberians endured, resilient in the face of fourth-world living conditions. Liberians had a special link to America as the nation was formed by freed slaves. However, brutality and war's savagery tested their convictions. Military coups became the norm. Children were recruited to fight. Many were given hallucinogenic drugs.

The Cape Hotel became the primary outlet for many of the foreign contractors. The emergence from civil war brought hundreds of independent contractors to work for the plethora of international aid organizations. Foreign languages were abundant in Liberia. The cost for professional services of independent consultants ranged from a few hundred to several thousand dollars per hour. On top of the daily cost was the need for UN security. UN personnel occupied an old hotel on the other side of the former Presidential Palace at a negotiated price with the new government of Liberia whereby the terms were never revealed.

All of the costs were borne by the international community with the United States paying the most.

Tareek walked toward the pool and watched several French women enjoy the warmth of West Africa compared to Europe's winter. European style swimsuits tightly gripped several French women who walked in high heels around the poolside. Local good looking Liberian men were hired as cabana boys. They quickly moved from one guest to another. The somewhat plump, older American men huddled under the screens for shade. In January, the African sun was brutal. Tareek looked crisp in his perfectly pressed white cotton suit. For afternoon wear, he removed the tie, yet he looked as much a professional hotel manager as anyone in Liberia. The new razor crisp barb wiring on top of the protective cement wall that ran the perimeter of the pool glistened in the late morning sun, as did some of the white semi-nude bodies.

Tareek motioned to one of the cabana boys and requested freshly squeezed lemonade. He checked the booking sheet that he kept in a leather brown folder. Reservations for the week were ninety percent. For each room, he charged two hundred dollars, as there was limited competition. The presidential ceremony treated him well as he doubled prices for the event. Every guest paid in cash so he did not have to worry about illegal or stolen credit cards. Cash was king in post-war Liberia, especially US greenbacks. The use of credit cards was widely discouraged as fraud was very commonplace. Everyone carried cash.

Tareek's first payment was not to the government of Liberia that taxed a thirty-five percent standard rate. No, the first payment each month in the amount of two thousand dollars was made to Hezbollah for protection, which tore Tareek's soul apart as he blamed them for the death of his family. Hezbollah had a strong hold on many Lebanese who lived outside of Beirut. Fear and intimidation tactics were rampant.

The remaining profits were reinvested into updating the hotel. New beds, fixtures, tables, and linen arrived in forty-foot containers from Cyprus. The rooftop piano bar received a full makeover that was needed after the front door received a direct RPG rocket shot, which blew the doors out and plastered the walls with shrapnel. Outside of the kitchen's back door, there was a shallow grave containing five security guards Uncle Anwar paid to stay and guard the Cape Hotel when the rebels attacked and infiltrated Monrovia. He moved the bodies to a proper cemetery and placed a luxury pool in the exact location.

When Tareek arrived, he brought with him a strong surveillance background. In Beirut, Tareek had worked for a security company that provided high-end listening devices and video surveillance for major hotel chains to guard against suicide bombers. He installed high tech equipment throughout the Cape Hotel that was unnoticeable. Entry and exit points, hallways, public areas, and entire exterior were under constant surveillance. Reservations were confirmed in advance and each occupant had their passport photocopied, scanned, and matched to known international criminals tracked by Interpol.

As he watched the dignitaries mingle at the bar from his security camera, Tareek triggered several listening devices to listen. Majority of the leaders from the thirteen West African countries that comprised the Economic Community of West African States (ECOWAS) were present for President Sirleaf's inauguration as the 24th President of Liberia. Nigeria's president took the entire top floor of the Cape Hotel for his entourage. Tareek had to make room and evicted several foreign aid workers who had signed six month lodging agreements. He paid for their vacation trip to Paris.

Tareek had his ear to the ground on all of the underground news. He heard there would be a large shipment of cocaine passing through the airport. Without a doubt, he knew Rajik Nabee would be involved. There were six Lebanese families who controlled most of Liberia's commerce. Rajik was the manager of the casino at Coconut Grove Resort and sought to make his fortune in more sinister ways. Tareek despised Rajik who he believed was linked to Hezbollah. Trained in Libya and expert in demolitions, Rajik believed that he was a freedom fighter; however, he learned quickly how to make mountains of money smuggling weapons. He served in several important assignments during a recent Israeli incursion three years ago, was wounded, and sent to Liberia to recover from his injuries. Many of the Lebanese freedom fighters were sent to West Africa for rest and recuperation. Tareek had heard the FARC, the Colombian drug cartel, needed a new route to ship large amounts of cocaine. West African countries that emerged out from under civil war became the perfect recruiting ground for newly appointed Ministers and hard-core criminals who have committed some of the worse war crimes in recent memory still eluded capture. Rajik was someone no one trusted.

The hotel's pool was the center of activity later in the afternoon as many sought to cool off. One lady caught everyone's attention when she passed from the cool crisp water to her lounge chair. Francesca was athletic and trained in martial arts from an early age. Her muscles were toned, and she walked with a purpose. The smooth silky texture of her skin and attractive physique made men around the pool cringe with excitement. She always wore a full piece bathing suit much to the chagrin of the ex-pats who keenly watched her. The full swimsuit covered a scar that taught her a valuable life lesson on how not to trust anyone. The blast had sent a piece of shrapnel along her left side but luckily did not damage any major organs. Francesca was listed on the hotel registry as a doctor from Barcelona. If Hezbollah operatives knew her true identity as a Mossad operative, she would be dead.

Tareek walked down to the beach and inspected the lounge chairs and the sand that his workers raked five times. The sand was perfect. The American Embassy was perched higher on the hill next to his little beach cove that he converted into one of the most relaxing beach spots in Monrovia. The ambassador's residence was the closest building and security patrols were constant near the pleasant little beach cove paradise. Seabirds gently drifted in the warm salt air drafts and watched for any specks of food abandoned by hotel guests. Fresh beach towels were laid out on the lounge chairs and the umbrellas opened to protect the foreigners from the vicious January sunshine. While the northern hemisphere chilled, West Africa's weather was beautiful and topped ninety degrees with clear skies. He sipped his fresh squeezed lemonade and eyed a usual problem twenty feet away from the yellow rope, which extended from the road to the ocean. A local man squatted and displayed his backside. His large rear protruded from scraps of clothes as he loomed over the hole he made in the sand to relieve his bodily waste. The smell would not have drifted far enough to reach Tareek, but the sight definitely turned his stomach. He motioned to several of his security guards. The man ran and jumped in the waves to clean himself. Toilet paper was a much sought after commodity. The security guards yelled and chased the local man off. Tareek mumbled to himself about living in a fourth world country and tossed his lemonade out. It would be one of those days.

CHAPTER 3

The Marines spent the day running through the obstacle course that resided outside the Black Beret camp. Ditches were dug and log walls constructed to enhance the already challenging obstacle courses. The last group of Liberians had occupied the remote camp over eight years ago. As Charles Taylor tried to hold onto power, he assigned some of the Black Berets to Presidential Guard detail. Taylor did not trust his own secret service and feared an internal assassination plot. The Black Berets were transitioned into the Liberian Anti-Terrorism Unit (ATU). The ATU was controlled by Charles Taylor's ruthless son Chucky. The ATU became known as death squads as they killed hundreds without any fear of reprisal or prosecution. The Black Berets were one of the few military units under Charles Taylor that emerged from the fourteen years of civil war with honor. The tightly knit group of soldiers worked closely together. The Black Beret leader was Colonel Marzah who refused to help keep Taylor in power. Taylor was not pleased and ordered his extermination. Colonel Marzah's nickname was 'zigzag', which he received his notoriety as he dodged over fifty shots during the 1996 assassination attempt on Charles Taylor. As with many of the Black Berets, Colonel 'zigzag' Marzah remained in hiding. As a patriot for Liberia, he supported Charles Taylor's removal, yet he did not trust the new Liberian government and definitely not the UN. Too many false rumors circulated on the Black Berets, fabricated by the ATU. From the hillside shack he occupied inside Firestone Plantation, he watched the camp he used to command, still afraid to come forward.

Sweat rolled off the four Americans as they navigated the obstacles. The four Marines pushed through the vegetation that overgrew the obstacle course. Afterward, they grabbed packs loaded with forty pounds of rocks and started a ten-mile hike. By late morning, they were physically spent. They were not accustomed to the hot humid conditions. It was a cold January winter back home and Russell could not believe he dragged himself out of Seattle, halfway around the world to sweat like a pig in West Africa's heat. As he returned to camp, Russell saw the British Colonel on his porch. He relaxed out of the sun. In the background, Russell heard Nina Simone blaring from loudspeakers anchored to the top of the porch roof. The Gunnys headed for the showers while the two officers approached the British colonel's bungalow.

"Can we join you Colonel?" Russell asked. The British Colonel gave a nod to a chair. "This is quite a camp you have." Being security conscious, Russell already checked the perimeter and noted the high tech surveillance video scopes, guard towers with armed security, several sandbagged bunkers, and what appeared to be an electrified fence going around the four-kilometer base.

"Indeed," Kitson said as he looked at his new guests. He did not have many guests in the past fourteen months as he established Her Majesty's forward observation post in Liberia. Majesty's government was very concerned with the progress made in Sierra Leone and even more concerned about the instability in neighboring Liberia. Violence endured from savage cross-border attacks. Drug-induced children joined the rebels and blatantly shot anything that moved. Rapes were so common that nearly every female within Liberian and Sierra Leone witnessed or were exposed to this brutality. Lawlessness ruled.

"Let's talk about the mission." Kitson said in a direct manner. "Your formal orders are on the computer." He pointed toward the communication building, which was the most fortified building in the compound. Antennas jutted out of the roof and several satellite dishes pointed to the heavens. "The orders did not say much but appears to give you the latitude to get the job done here. More detailed instructions have been provided in several other instructions." He looked around to make sure none of the Liberians were in close ear shot proximity. Even though the British fully vetted the Liberians with the aid of MI6, Kitson remained cautious. "General Abbdas is the target for a snatch and gab. He was one of the most vicious officers under Charles Taylor and was directly responsible for the murder of over two thousand civilians."

"Sounds pretty easy, go in and take him out." Russell remarked with a slight laugh in his tone.

"Not so easy, as he has not been seen in years. He lives in Sapo National Forest surrounded by four hundred hard-core murderers." Kitson lifted his gin and tonic for a long sip. "General Abbdas is planning his own insurgency and using the money from the sale of blood diamonds to finance it."

"Sapo?" Russell inquired. "Where's that?"

"Sapo is in a remote area south of us. It had some of the most pristine jungles in West Africa and home to some of the rarest animals in the world that was until Charles Taylor's regime fell and all of his hard-core thugs moved in."

"Tell me about the blood diamonds?" Russell asked.

"Liberia has not been known for having diamond mines. The large amount of diamond exports in the past decade came from conflict diamonds coming across the border from Sierra Leone."

"Is that is why Britain is involved?" Russell pried further.

"You are sharp." Kitson looked at Russell and added. "They said that about you and your dossier is pretty compelling."

"I have a dossier." Russell responded flatly. "I'm nobody."

"Perhaps, but we do not take chances as your American intelligence may. Our MI6 is very thorough." Kitson remarked.

"So if I understand this. I have four guys including me"

"You will have six. There's a Nigerian general tasked with forming the new Liberian army. He has offered two US trained Liberian Lieutenants who seem very competent."

Stone turned his head quickly when he heard Nigerians were in Liberia training the new military and asked, "There's a Nigerian general in charge?"

The British Colonel leaned in closer and said, "He could be a general in anybody's army", in case there was a doubt in their minds on his ability to provide good officers for the operation.

"What's this new Liberian army?" asked Russell.

"The UN mandate will expire in few years and the forces will leave. Liberia will need an army to keep long-term security. Your embassy has worked hard to get qualified officers to the states for training."

"Ok, but I need to evaluate them before deciding," Russell stated and Kitson nodded agreement. Russell continued, "So I will have a team of six that will penetrate a jungle canopy to snatch a war criminal general surrounded by hundreds of armed thugs."

"Heavily armed thugs who are war criminals." Kitson raised his finger to interject.

"How long do we have to get ready?" asked Stone.

"Not long, I read the summary of your training in Sierra Leone. You should do some more conditioning."

"We are all in good shape," retorted Stone, the combat veteran Marine and of Nigerian decent. His nickname was Captain America by his troops in Iraq. He led a communication team that assisted reconnaissance teams spread throughout Al Anbar Province in western Iraq. Several times, he was dropped off near the Syria and Iraq border with several others and instructed to monitor the foreign fighters who crossed into Iraq. He tracked long distances in the middle of the night and remained concealed all day long in the desert environment. Stone's assignment proved incredibly strenuous. His Nigerian heritage and bloodline provided him natural abilities in the hot desert.

"Not for this mission, you are not," corrected the seasoned African expert. Rhodesia taught the British Colonel well. His experience as a young, aggressive officer in the bush taught Kitson life's most important lesson – humility. In 1979, then Second Lieutenant Kitson deployed for a year to the war-torn country that was not only changing its name from Rhodesia to Zimbabwe, but was also coming to grips with horrific aftermath of viral carnage. Thousands laid dead everywhere and many white settlers were butchered on their farms and hung from hooks in their barns, dangling as vultures picked apart the corpses. In those early days of his military career, Kitson saw more death to last a lifetime.

Lieutenant Kitson was tasked to capture weapons and have the rebel leader acknowledge the peace accord established by Rhodesia's white autocratic ruler, Ian Smith. British troops attempted to curb the violence. There were fifteen British soldiers under Lieutenant Kitson's command. As he walked around the platoon's perimeter, Kitson instinctively knew they were watched. The next day Kitson dressed in his finest officer uniform and walked unarmed three hundred meters out from his safety net; sat down with the table and chairs he brought; and waited. In the middle of the table, he placed two cups and a pot of her countries finest tea. Several hours passed in the blazing African sun, yet he did not move - would not move. Kitson sweated profusely, but he did not show the slightest discomfort. The setting sun blinded him from seeing the four hundred heavily armed rebels approach. The leader laid his pistol on the table. Second Lieutenant Kitson motioned for the rebel leader to sit and they spent a moment in the setting African sun sharing tea. What the young British officer did not realize was a photographer traveled with the rebels. Two days later, his mother was horrified to see front page London Times, *'Young British Officer Captured Rebels with Her Majesty's Finest Tea'*. His father, the general, was not amused at his son's reckless behavior. The young officer was not ashamed for what he did and probably saved the lives of his men. Regardless, all was forgiven by his father when young Frank Kitson was bestowed with the Queen's Medal for bravery.

"We did the obstacle course." Russell replied. "What else should we do to prepare for the mission?"

"In Africa, it is not just the body conditioning," Kitson paused, "But the mind. You are going to witness things in Africa that you will never see again in your life." Kitson continued. "Tribalism, barbaric ritualistic killings, witch doctors, and murder and rape on a scale you will never see in ten lifetimes. Human life does not account for much in Africa, not like western societies."

"I understand that this is mostly a counter-insurgency operation." Russell interjected.

"True, but nothing like you may have seen in Iraq or Afghanistan." The educator continued. "You must know that no two insurgencies are the same, especially when it comes to Africa."

"We studied insurgencies at officer-training." Russell tried to explain, "We even have a good manual on small wars"

"Where do you think you got that from? The tenants of your small wars manual were based in the bananas wars but based upon principles of Charles Callwell."

"Who?"

"Charles Callwell served in the Boer wars at the turn of the last century. He wrote the first small wars manual. The main principle of any counter-insurgency doctrine is human-centric operations. You must at all costs protect the populace. Counter-insurgency operations are extremely labor intensive."

"I understand. It's not a simple packaged war where everybody knows who the bad guys are." Russell reflected on his own warfare. His senses became attuned to every movement. Seconds seemed like minutes as everything moved in slow motion. On 10 February 2004, the military vehicle convoy he traveled drove into downtown Iskandariyah. As the vehicle turned the corner, a massive bomb exploded at the police station and explosive flames erupted down the street. Fragments cascaded across the hardened vehicle's outer shell. In the explosive fog, Russell jumped out of the vehicle to help and saw scraps of bodies, people who gathered for a community meeting that he was late for. When he could muster the courage, he asked the local Iraqi Police Chief what he would do now and to his surprise the Iraqi told him that he would be back to work tomorrow. Over two hundred and forty Iraqi civilians died that day from the explosion.

"What you witnessed in Iraq highlights how politicians are discouraged by body counts." Kitson stated as a matter of fact. "Insurgencies are fought among the populace - in the streets – the neighborhoods – even in mosques." He paused for a moment and added. "Everyone is impacted."

"We had a lot of foreign fighters," responded Stone, who served near the Syrian border while Russell oversaw the other half of the specialized team in Baghdad.

"That is why you must do a census to know who you are fighting against. Contrary to how you Americans think, you cannot kill everyone."

"True, but we can take out a lot of the shitheads who rejoiced when planes crashed into the Twin Towers," retorted Russell.

"Spoken like a true yank." The British Colonel paused for effect. "My father served on many assignments in Africa. He told me something Jomo Kenyatta shared with him."

"Who?"

"Jomo Kenyatta." Kitson observed the puzzled look on the Americans. "The Mau Mau rebellion in Kenya?" Kitson asked and added. "Lord, what do they teach you in America?" After a few sips of gin and tonic, he continued. "Mr. Kenyatta told my father that in Africa, war comes on the back of the fastest horse, but peace comes on the back of a turtle."

"I understand," Russell replied. "Violence is an easy means to achieve results."

Kitson poured several gin and tonics and lifted his in a toast and said, "Good for the mosquitoes." Kitson continued, "We need to get some raw intelligence on what is going on within Sapo."

"The mission?" Russell asked and Kitson nodded.

"If we can remove the finance fueling the insurgency," Kitson paused and looked at the two new arrivals into the country, "Liberia may have a shot at peace."

"What about removing the head of the serpent?" Russell referred to the murderous former Liberian officer that they would be hunting.

"Will not work." Kitson said. "If you recall Patrice Lumumba in the Congo." Russell gave him a quizzical look. "I really need to spend some time teaching your men counter-insurgency operations in Africa. Patrice Lumumba was Prime Minister in the Congo after independence from Belgium. He was murdered by Belgian officers. Lumumba's death did not end the Congo insurgency. Assassinating a leader may make him a martyr." Russell nodded in agreement. "An insurgency leader must be removed and made to look like he quit."

"Snatch and grab?" Russell asked. Kitson nodded agreement. "And we are some of the best at that." Russell replied.

"Good." Kitson looked at his watch. "Looks like it is almost dinner."

"Please excuse us Colonel," Russell said politely, "We need to clean up." As they walked back toward the bungalow, Russell saw Ike thrust a large stick underneath the structure. Ike stood up, pointed to the signs drawn on the door of Russell's bungalow, and spoke something. Russell had no idea what Ike was saying. Ike sensed that and took his time to annunciate. Ike was named after Dwight D Eisenhower. His full name is Dwight Eisenhower Wayalah. Education levels in Liberia were not very high but Ike was smart. He could not read but he listened well.

Ike took his time speaking. "In Liberia, u die cause u cursed to death."

"You mean hexes?"

"Ey donno means." Ike replied.

"Voodoo?"

"Ya, ya, voodoo. Witchmen cum fur u when u cursed." Ike's eyes grew large when he spoke. "U gat yar bones in Iraq?"

"What? I do not know what you mean."

"Bones, yar bones, u gat em?"

"I'm sorry what does that mean."

"Ya, ya. Bones tis killin tith yar hands." Ike raised his large hands in the air.

"I understand." Russell said.

"U gat yar bones in Iraq?"

"If you see a young man racing to you on a motorcycle would you shoot?"

"Ya, bad men."

"Well it is hard to know who your enemies are."

"Ey donno."

"In war, there are many levels of warfare from guerillas to insurgents to full spectrum kinetic operations." Russell wanted to take back his words as he saw the quizzical look that came over Ike's face.

"Guerillas, ya. Lots em har." Ike pointed to Lucy and the other chimps screaming away in the trees.

"Not monkeys, guerillas, Charles Taylor's men."

Ike waived his hand in the air and said. "Bad men. Heart men cum far yar heart n eat it while u sleep." Russell walked into his bungalow and wondered the horrors Ike must have witnessed.

Russell recalled pictures of the atrocities in Sierra Leone of child soldiers standing on top of mutilated bodies and reaching into the chest cavity to pull out the hearts. They wanted to gain from the death of their enemy. Child soldiers took large bites out of the hearts that were beating only a few moments before. The blood from their victim's heart flowed down the young tender faces and jubilation erupted with shouting and unison dancing and singing. The weapons were too heavy for some of the weaker, less mature child soldiers to hold up above their heads so they used both arms.

Dinner was delicious. Several bottles of wine flowed at dinner and of course the compulsory glass of aged scotch afterwards. In the past several days, Russell consumed more alcohol than in the past six months. As he stumbled back to his bungalow, he saw the Gunnys still living it up on the porch of the British Colonel as they shared stories and jokes. Being from New York and city cops, the Gunnys had great jokes to share. As he crashed on the bed, Russell fought again with his mosquito bed net and ripped it off the ceiling. At this point, he did not care about malaria mosquitoes. He just wanted sleep.

The Cape Hotel resembled a beacon of light as darkness approached. Large spotlights illuminated the compound. Throughout Monrovia, central power distribution did not exist as the wires were looted and power plant destroyed. There was only generator power for those who could afford the generator and exorbitant fuel costs. For many Liberians sunset meant the big light in the sky would be turned off shortly. As the foreign guests enjoyed sunset drinks on the Cape Hotel veranda, Liberians scrounged for food. For most Liberians, the work of the day helped purchase an evening meal. A good portion to include children would have only small portions of rice or unsold fish that sat in the sun all day long. However, their plight did not bother the dozen or so NGOs and contractors who stayed at the Cape Hotel. They snacked on appetizers and cold beers as they watched sunset.

Francesca stood on the balcony atop the Cape Hotel off the piano bar. The warm seaward breeze flowed off the ocean at just the right angle to send her dress up just slightly. At least half a dozen heads turned quickly to catch a glimpse of her toned legs as she walked across the room. The after-dinner crowd was rather large for a Tuesday night. She laughed to herself as she thought how every day in Liberia seemed like it was the weekend. In the four months she had lived at the Cape Hotel the party scene had definitely picked up. She would use the drunkenness of men to her advantage.

Several Chinese diplomats walked quickly through the crowd as more of them arrived for a private dinner party with several German railroad consultants. Over the past six months, the Chinese Embassy staff tripled and the new embassy compound opened last month in time

27

for the new presidential inauguration. The Chinese Embassy put on a fantastic opening event with all of Monrovia's high society in attendance to include the president-elect Johnson-Sirleaf. The only problem occurred when the Chinese ignited an elaborate fireworks display and forgot to inform the locals who ran for cover as they thought war had started all over again.

China remained greedy for its own internal expansion and viewed Africa as its new colony, ready to strip all resources from her at a deep discount. China's reach extended to Liberia's neighbors as well. Guinea held over forty percent of the known world's reserve of bauxite which was the primary ingredient for aluminum. The only way to get it to a port was by rail through Liberia. A railroad did not exist but the Chinese were willing to invest hundreds of millions to bring out billions in profit. To get the railroad, the Chinese made concessions. One of the high-ticket items was to build a new Liberia University in Carrysburg, which was forty miles outside of Monrovia and deep into the hinterland. Liberia received the Chinese two-step. China agreed to build a new Liberian University but would not pay for professors. The only thing the Chinese never really cared to explain to the Liberian officials was who will instruct the new students, the future of Liberia. A beautiful facility remained vacant, except for local security guards and several Chinese who watched over their propaganda masterpiece. Two oversized flags waved in the breeze, one was Liberian and the other was Chinese. Additionally, a Chinese mining company had just signed a five-billion-dollar iron ore concession contract with the government of Liberia for the prized Ventte Mountain. Americans and NGOs told the Liberians that they could not trust the Chinese, yet the sight and sounds of heavy earth moving equipment repairing roads and building the University outshined realism. Worse, the pockets of some Liberian government officials were filled with Chinese gratitude.

Tareek worked the crowd of contractors, consultants, and diplomats like any professional musician would strum a guitar. He was a natural at making everyone feel at ease in this war-torn country. He always had the latest intelligence about UN movements and the hunt for ousted members of Charles Taylor's regime. The new face to this Cape Hotel party scene had been the some of the newly appointed Ministers of the Liberian government and he sought each one out individually. Tareek saw several newly arrived Russians talk with the Deputy Minister for Commerce. The Russians were eager to start drilling offshore. A Russian company had discussions with Liberia on potentially working together to develop the newly discovered vast oil and gas fields. The Russians came in full force to negotiate directly with the government of Liberia, and they were fortunate to already have elements of the Russian mafia in place in case discussions went south. Tareek noticed the close discussions and eyed the center candle piece he made sure was emplaced. He chuckled slightly as he would have the full transcript within an hour.

In the far corner of the room, Uncle Anwar talked with six older Lebanese men who represented the families that had an economic strangle hold on Liberia's commerce and development. Tareek glanced over at the heated conversation between Uncle Anwar and Ghasson. Ghasson was considered the godfather for the eighty thousand Lebanese who resided in Liberia. Ghasson could be a shoe in, impersonator for Telly Savalas. The fabled Kojak lollipop was replaced by a Cuban Monte Crisco number ten. The cigar smoke floated above the men and Ghasson pointed his finger into Anwar's chest. Tareek did not place a microphone on the table out of respect, but now wish he had.

The mass of foreigners at the roof top piano bar represented everything that was happening in Liberia. The Lebanese made large investments to make a home away from Beirut. The Japanese worried about the future of the Firestone Plantation. The Germans worked with UN Food Program and combated theft. The French tackled literacy and no functional schools. The Dutch were concerned about where the five malaria bed nets disappeared to. The Russians chased oil deals and illegal lumber. The Chinese went after any rare earth mineral they could extract. And the Americans sat back as "Big Brother" to Liberia and watched the chaos unfold, unable to stop the locomotive. To add to the madness in the post-war reconstruction, the UN's embargo on weapons had been ineffective as a Hezbollah gun runner set up shop.

Everyone present at the piano bar enjoyed the open-air warm breezes from the balcony that provided a romantic feel to the room. The dark mahogany tables, safari paintings, and antique African decorations gave a nostalgic feel to the piano bar. Strands of 'As Time Goes by' rang off the center piano. These sounds were mastered by an elderly Liberian who used to play in a Liberian military band for the former President Charles Taylor. The foreigners called him "Play it Again Sam" as no one knew his real name. Mostly, they called him Sam.

Francesca walked across the room toward the bar. She eyed the crowd. Elder gentlemen from America stopped talking and opened their mouths to witness the passing of this stunning lady. The cocktail dress was not revealing by any means, yet the elder men could tell she was muscular and toned. Her long brown hair gingerly moved across the small of her back. Several Lebanese men turned as she approached the bar. Francesca smiled and ordered champagne. The men spoke in Arabic and would not suspect the stunning lady to know what they had discussed. Francesca leaned toward the conversation to eavesdrop. As she leaned in closer, she heard about the arriving plane tomorrow night. The Lebanese men continued to talk about the money that they would make off of the flight. They had no reason for concern in speaking Arabic in Liberia and in front of the Europeans, except tonight they stood next to an Israeli Mossad agent.

CHAPTER 4

West African sunrise brought immediate heat. The late January sun was brutal and ripped moisture from the earth. After more than a few cups of coffee, Russell and Stone ventured up to the camp's communication building to read their orders. They held their heads as they walked out into the blistering heat, and it was only eight in the morning. The level of intoxication from numerous gin and tonics, dinner wine, and the compulsory aged scotch nightcap gave them severe hangovers. A local guard on Her Majesty's payroll resided behind the desk. The metal door was marked communications room and had a drawn antennae just in case the locals working in the compound could not read. The guard motioned for them to enter the room. Russell did not forget the explicit instructions by his host to stay away from the front door as it was rigged to explode. The bookcase was opened, rested at a forty-five degree angle and revealed the concealed entrance. They ducked their heads and entered the room. Immediately, Russell saw the wires coming off the main door that ran underneath the building. The room was relatively large, fifteen feet by eight feet. There were no windows. Underneath the floorboards rested two thousand pounds of explosives triggered to detonate on either forced entry or remote eight-digit code access by transmitter that stayed on the British Colonel's nightstand. Russell questioned his paranoia, but did not want to say anything.

Kitson sat at the table and looked through a jeweler's glass into a large rough diamond. The stack of rough diamonds on the table was a small mound. Russell wondered how much they were worth. Without looking up, the British Colonel sensed the presence of their inquisitive eyes. "Have you ever seen rough diamonds before?" Kitson held the pigeon sized egg rough diamond for each one of them to look at. The British Colonel pointed to the small pile of rough diamonds on the table. "These are leftovers from the Sierra Leone conflict. The RUF used to smuggle these into Liberia during the war to sell on the open market. More problematic is Al-Qaeda now uses blood diamonds as currency to wage their war."

"How much is there?" Stone inquired.

"About three million pounds worth." He pointed to the open safe and he clarified, "that's about five million American dollars."

"Jesus."

"Believe me, Jesus or any type of God left this land a long time ago. People sold their souls for these diamonds." Kitson picked up the diamonds and started to place them in small black velvet sacks that would be used at any high-end jewelry shop, which took Russell somewhat by surprise. "Hopefully this will keep you focused. A lot of people have suffered just to get this diamond here to this point."

"How big is this?"

"About forty carats I would guess." Kitson responded. "I really do not know much about diamond quality and size."

"I do." Russell had a momentary flash back to the Manhattan lower east side jewelry shop where he spent several hours and days looking at diamonds for his fiancé. He was scared about what she would say. He thought Kristin may say yes but coming from high society of north shore Long Island and living in Oyster Bay for most of her life except four years at Harvard for undergrad, she was isolated in the most expensive lifestyle America had to offer. He did not care what she had or did not have, he was in love. It was neither the condo her father paid for while attending Law School at Columbia nor was it the trust fund that bothered him. It was her father's condescending remarks about how she could do better. Understandably, Kristin's father worked hard to become partner in Krager and Stern, one of the most prestigious merger and acquisitions law firms in Manhattan and probably the world. Indeed, Kristin's father made more money in one year than a Marine major would make in a lifetime of military service. Russell spent weeks researching all the aspects of diamonds and most importantly his price point. Sounds in the rest of the room brought him back to reality.

"What are these?" Stone asked as he picked up a tusk, "Ivory?"

"Indeed." Kitson looked at the pile of tusks in the wooden box. "Illicit ivory sales are making their way into Liberia now. We caught five ivory poachers a few months ago as they headed toward the Chinese work camps." They looked at the British Colonel with inquisitive look. "The Chinese use ivory for medicinal purposes. Along with all of the other foreigners who want decorative ivory, many animals are in danger."

"What did you do with the poachers?"

"Ike took them to the local police station." He put down a piece of ivory and looked them both in the eyes. "They were released. Ike found them smuggling again two weeks later."

"In Nigeria we had problems with poachers until the military opened fire." Stone said a matter of fact. "Then we did not have problems anymore. The animals were safe."

"In Liberia, animals used to be killed for food, but now the ivory is worth a great deal." Kitson pointed to a map on the wall. "The Chinese have a sensational appetite for ivory. There are large work camps in the north." Kitson showed photos of the endangered small West African elephant that was much smaller than its cousin on Serengeti. However, the ivory tusk were just as sought after, especially with very little conservation in post-war-torn Liberia. "Four elephants were butchered last week." Kitson was visibly upset. "Their carcasses were left to rot in the sun." Kitson pointed toward the box. "Ike tracked the smugglers in Monrovia's black market district and retrieved them."

"This one still has blood on it." Russell said. "What did Ike do with them?" Russell asked. Kitson gave him a glazed stare that answered Russell's question on the final disposition of the smugglers. Justice was pretty much non-existent in Liberia, yet retribution was plentiful. Russell was disgusted at the photo and instead of throwing the tusk into the large wooden box, he gently placed it down. Since he arrived, Russell had not seen one large animal walk freely in the vast openness of Firestone Plantation. Many endangered animals such as the West African elephant had been illegally slaughtered.

The communication room was equipped with several high-powered satellite radios along the far wall. The British Colonel walked over to the main table. Several maps were spread open with pins placed at varying points around the country. A large area on a map was circled and words Sapo written in large letters. He passed the folder with the official orders to Russell.

REL TO USA AND GBR

The top of the document was marked classified. He knew the marking REL that the contents could only be released to those military members from the United States and Great Britain.

//SUBJ//STABILIZATION OPERATIONS IN LIBERIA
1. OPERATION PROTECT LIBERIA is hereby enacted.
2. At most haste, guard any individuals or documents that may be used against members of Charles Taylor regime in international court for CRIMES AGAINST HUMANITY.
3. Keep former members of Charles Taylor regime from establishing an insurgency.
Signed//Chip Grasson//GEN//CDR US AFRICA COMMAND

Each of them read the document several times. None of them have ever operated at this level. They remained silent as they tried to comprehend the mission.

The British Colonel left his guests alone to exam the documents and to discuss the mission. More importantly, he did not want to give the impression the British Government, Her Majesty, or any British officer endorsed the insane American plan. He knew they would be walking into a den of fire as more than a thousand rebels hid in the jungle. Each heavily armed and waiting for the chance for the next military coup. For many, the crimes and atrocities committed during the latest civil war meant they could never return to Monrovia or their villages. Wanted fliers had been distributed by the UN and to date there were over two hundred and forty members of the former Taylor regime on the most wanted list for crimes against humanity.

"What the hell does this mean?" Stone asked.

"It means we are open to operate in Liberia." Russell replied. For the next several hours, they poured over the maps, satellite imagery, aerial photos, and heat signature graphs of rebel camps, phone recordings, and local surveillance documents. The most compelling document was the dossier MI6 developed on General Abbdas, former Chief of Staff for Taylor's army. During the Sierra Leone civil war, he went back and forth over the border bringing truckloads of weapons and ammunition. On the return trip, he brought an ammunition box filled with rough diamonds. The general regularly visited the RUF leaders at the riverbed camps in northern Sierra Leone. He saw the workers sweating in the daylight, chained together. Their blood and the blood of their families flowed throughout Sierra Leone to fuel the RUF's insurgency. Blood diamonds easily moved across the border with the assistance of Charles Taylor's government and General Abbdas personal efforts. When Charles Taylor had problems, the RUF leaders were more than happy to loan him several hundred brain washed, bloody-thirsty child soldiers. The funneling of blood diamonds kept the cycle of violence going.

Russell and Stone spent the rest of the day going over the pages of documents. Never of them had ever planned a mission at this level, almost a CIA type mission to infiltrate a vastly superior enemy. They spent nearly four hours developing and analyzing several courses of action. They needed the general alive and more than likely, he would not go easily. Stone fetched the Gunnys to review the mission orders.

"Are you kidding me...sir?" injected Rageone while Rozelli nodded his disapproval. The Gunnys had known each other for nearly sixteen years and could guess what the other would say. The two Marine Corps reservists were New York City police officers and could smell a shitty assignment a mile away. Both served on the NYPD Hostage Rescue Team and were tasked out to the FBI's elite Counter Espionage Unit. In the aftermath of 9/11, both wanted to do more than rescuing kidnapped victims. Rozelli heard about the new FBI team that would operate out of 26 Federal Plaza in downtown Manhattan. They would get a lot of travel, kill or capture some global terrorists, and maybe someday pay back the bastards that took down the towers. They had been recruited into the FBI's team and it did not hurt a former Marine ran the Counter Espionage Unit and another former Marine, James Kalstrum, was Director, FBI's New York office. Even though New York had the largest FBI office outside of Washington, D.C. with five thousand agents and support staff, Director Kalstrum knew a majority of the former Marines and when he received a recommendation to bring aboard some of NYPD's finest, he jumped at the chance. Neither Gunny had worn a police uniform in five years, but they were still allowed to operate in the Marine Corps Reserves. Both volunteered to go to Iraq and that is where they operated under Russell as part of 34th Interrogator Translator Team responsible for snatching and grabbing High Value Targets (HVTs) in western Iraq, mainly Fallujah during most of the 2004 brutal house-to-house fighting.

"A snatch and grab would work, but we will need to make a harness to carry him out," injected Russell trying to get control back for his plan. He respected the Gunnys and would not want anyone else in a difficult situation. However, he also knew when a mission sounded like a potential death sentence. On more than one occasion during the fight for Fallujah, he and his Gunnys were recipients of less than stellar thought-out plans that had them going into an area with overwhelming foreign fighters and told to either grab or terminate an insurgent leader.

"Ok, but he is not going to leave willingly," Rozelli replied. "We will need something to knock him out," he stopped for a moment, "drugs probably the best as we could kill him with a hit to the head."

"Concur." Russell said.

"I don't like the infiltration plan. No offense to you," Rageone turned to Stone, "but we are some of the whitest folks in this country. They will see us coming a mile away."

"That will be the hardest part. We should send a recon team out," inputted Russell.

"Boss, regardless that I am black, they will still know that I am not from here. I may look Nigerian and sometimes talk like I am from Lagos, but I would get more scrutiny."

"Good point. We can use the Liberian Lieutenants." Russell said. "They should be able to get in."

"How about Ike?" Rozelli asked. "You should hear his stories about the war and what he did." Russell did hear from the British Colonel about Ike's near suicide mission into Sierra Leone to get revenge. Ike did not know exactly who was responsible for attacking his village and killing his family. He knew it was RUF rebels. Ike tracked for five days into Kono district of Sierra Leone. He walked along the riverbed at night, slept during the day until he found the blood diamond camp. RUF soldiers employed kidnapped men, women, and children to pan the riverbed for diamonds. The few kidnapped women who survived torture and mutilation were cooks and bedroom slaves. In the early morning hours as early rays of sunlight gave him enough to see his target, Ike pointed the AK47 and opened fire. He cycled through four magazines and when his ammunition was spent, he picked up a RUF weapon and sent more lead into the still bodies. Rage filled his face and he gave no sympathy as he looked down into the faces of mere children. Regardless they were RUF. In Ike's mind, they all needed to die. The blood diamond workers crouched in fear and wondered if they would receive the same fate. Ike waived his arm in peace for them to leave.

"I can ask the Brit." In their own circles, the Marines commonly referred to the British Colonel as simply the Brit.

"We only have one chance. With the four of us, Ike, and the two Lieutenants, that gives us seven. Four will carry the harness, one on point, one in rear, and one as suppressing fire with the machine gun." The other Marines nodded at Major Russell's final order. The mission was set and preparations needed to begin.

At the Cape Hotel, the vibrant sun and cool water in the pool set the stage for a vivacious afternoon pool party and a feast for the foreign guests. The beautiful lady who everyone believed worked for Doctors Without Borders did not stay for the pool party and walked the Monrovia streets. From old glass bottles to plastic jugs, everything received a second life in Liberia, as was the case in many developing countries. War left very little for those who stayed. There were only so many ships that can off load supplies and far less trucks that could move the goods around. Everything had a value. The large empty Club beer bottles were used for old oil and sometimes gas. The plastic bottles once used by foreign visitors and discarded were used to carry brownish well water to families.

Three hundred years ago, West Africa was the main hub for moving slaves, ripped from their tribes to the colonies to feed the growing agriculture progress in the Americas. At the chance to return, only a small fraction of freed slaves made the journey back to West Africa. And contrary to belief, only a smaller few made it back to West Africa during the America's Civil War. The society of West Africa has been adversely impacted by the 1700s African slave trade and still recovering. The Congo people were stolen from tribes of the Congo River region and brutally beaten along the journey to West Africa for release to America.

In the spring of 2003, rebels controlled majority of Liberia and fired directly into Monrovia. Charles McArthur Taylor wore a military uniform and five stars of a general, trying to resemble the great General Douglas McArthur that was his middle name. The Economic Community of West Africa States (ECOWAS), the United States, and Great Britain put significant pressure on Charles Taylor to step down. For months he refused. On his last day with big bands and fanfare, he quoted Doctor Martin Luther King "we are free at last". He worked his own deal for political exile in Nigeria; however, some of his most vile soldiers remained to operate out of Liberia. All of West Africa was impacted by Charles Taylor's ruthless intervention and atrocities. One million Liberians went into exile out of a population of three and half million. Official death counts remained unknown as mass graves littered the countryside. Estimates ran as high as four hundred thousand and as low as two hundred and fifty thousand dead. For those Liberians who remained, mortal hardship became the norm.

In Monrovia, sweat poured off the young men as they pushed steel carts containing at least six hundred pounds of water in large plastic containers of odd shapes and sizes. All held in place by makeshift ropes attached together, frays of rope lingering outside of the main line waving. If a few more frayed, the rope would surely break and send water containers across the pavement. Wheel barrels became the primary means of goods transportation. Russell heard that a wheel barrel union had formed. The most interesting aspect he noted was each wheel barrel contained only one specific commodity such as shoe polish, shampoo, sandals, cooking pots, hundreds of non-essential items that Liberians craved. Everywhere there was commerce, yet no taxes on the goods exchange. By UN mandate and the large overhead five billion foreign debts ran up by Samuel Doe and Charles Taylor, the new Liberia government could not operate a budget deficit. The little money brought in paid what they could. There was nothing extra for the majority of the citizens who resided in the second poorest country in the world, only in front of the Democratic Republic of the Congo.

The Monrovia streets were active and the long legged beauty moved briskly between the shops. The amputees stood in the street trying to block the way of foreign shoppers for handouts. However, when they saw her approach in a demanding manner the amputees limped to the side. Cloaked in dagger and intrigue had been her staple for more than eight years now. After initial military training, as all Israelis completed to include females, she entered Tel Aviv Medical University. She was fortunate to receive approval to study abroad in Barcelona for two semesters and was pleasantly surprised that the Israeli Defense Force (IDF) extended her stay so she could become a doctor. Several months later, she found herself as the cleaner on her first mission outside of Paris that turned bad. In Barcelona, she learned proper Spanish and mannerisms. She was always on guard, a similar mental fate for many Israelis who believed they were surrounded by many neighbors who wanted nothing better than eliminating the entire Israeli population.

Meanwhile at the Firestone Plantation, the Marines inspected their equipment multiple times. They snuck out the concealed entrance in the communication building and joined the British colonel on the veranda. Ike prepared gin and tonics.

"It is amazing that such a beautiful place can be so screwed up." Kitson said as he admired the sunset.

"From what I've studied, war's savagery has always plagued this continent." Russell added. "I call it Europe's failed colonial policy." Putting the blame on Europe raised the British Colonel's curiosity and the surprise expression on his face showed he was taken aback. Russell continued, "If you ever look at the Mercator map you will see a big Europe and a little Africa that is part of the arrogance of the colonial Europeans. They carved out colonies with little care."

"Our empire was vast, but we brought civilization here."

"How can you bring civilization, when it already existed?" responded Stone, the Nigerian.

He could tell the British Colonel was getting frustrated with him. "We brought government organization, education, infrastructure," but he was cut off before he could finish.

"But at a price," retorted Russell.

"Indeed, the price was paid in blood." The two remained silent for several moments, as they both knew the ultimate price soldiers pay as politicians make woefully ill-informed decisions. "I wonder how Africa would have turned out without colonies."

"Some still call Liberia America's colony." Russell said.

"I would be honest. I did not know Liberia was formed by freed slaves being sent back from America," Rozelli replied.

"Liberia was already here before then, but it was not called Liberia." Stone said as he knew the history. "Every freed slave returned to Liberia became known as Congo people. Most of the slaves came from the Congo river area, hence Congo people,"

"I was raised a good portion of my life in Kenya." Kitson said. "My father was in the military." He withheld one key point about his father being Sir General Frank Kitson, who became one of the premier authorities on counter-insurgency. "He lived a lot of his life fighting small wars all over Africa. He was respected by the governments he helped stabilize and he was feared by his enemies."

"You must respect your father greatly," Russell said.

"I do. Our army is much smaller than America's and everyone knows you. Some enter the military for the family name sake and cannot lead a tourist to the tower of London." Kitson laughed at his own joke and added a serious point. "My father was a great officer." After a few moments of reflection on his life, he turned to his guests and asked about their parents.

"My father was murdered in Lagos when I was ten years old." Stone said. The blunt remark almost held in the stillness of the night air. Alcohol opened his thoughts. "Someday I will find those responsible and they will feel my wrath." In the dim light, Russell could see the flow of several tears. Each finished their drink and bid each other goodnight. Russell walked back to his bungalow and saw Ike check for snakes.

"Lock yar doors. Heartmen cum far u, no matter tif yar good or bad." Ike said trying to put a scare into the new joins. The primeval worship of the occult started in West Africa and migrated toward Caribbean countries in the late seventeen hundreds with the slave trade. Voodoo, witch doctors, eating live hearts, and evil worship stated in

West Africa and was still practiced, but it was all now under the surface. There were no visible signs around Monrovia for witch doctors or stores selling chicken feet. Many government officials have attended occult gatherings as a rite of passage for the society. The older elite Monrovia high society conducted worships in their mansions. All of the newly arriving Congo people into Liberia found it shocking that such practices and beliefs were still profound in government circles, but these newly arriving Congo people felt the pressure of attending gatherings.

Russell walked around the perimeter of the camp. He pulled out the forty carat rough diamond and held it up into the light coming from the spotlight near the main gate. The milky white nature of the rough diamond is very light and a lot of the light from the lamp passes. He did not know clarity or quality, but he could tell the diamond had a pink tone. All he needed now was for his former fiancé to see him standing in the middle of a war-torn country holding a large conflict diamond. He imagined Kristin's father telling her, "See I told you, you are so better off not marrying down to his level." He remembered Piping Rock Country Club on Long Island that summer day. He should have told Mr. Vanderheuse to go to hell and see what Kristin would have done. If she left with him, than he knew that she was the one and they would be happily married no matter what the fifth generation Anglo-Saxon had to say. Perhaps, Kristin should have stood up to daddy, but she would not. Her life was easily paid for and laid out in front of her. The yearlong fling with a Marine was intense and pissed her dear daddy off to no end.

Kristin's older sister Margaret was more direct and to the point. She told Russell that his love affair with Kristin would '*alienate*' her from the rest of the fifth generation family. In the terms of Long Island speak, the word alienate meant she would be cut out of the will and family fortune. He left that alone. Several weeks later over coffee in their favorite West Village jaunt, he asked her how much her inheritance was. She told him that her trust fund was worth ten million dollars. Her father was from very old money. The Vanderheuse family already had a seat at Long Island society's table for over a hundred years. Russell concluded that if both daughters each had over ten million in trust funds that her father must be worth at least thirty million. He was far off, keeping in pace with the other Long Island old money, the tightwad

Vanderheuse fortune was pegged at over sixty million. Russell laughed as he possessed a forty-carat rough diamond, an untraceable diamond. He did not know what the precious gem's value would be, but speculated several million dollars. For a moment, he had temptation. He put the rough diamond back in his pocket to remind him why he was in Liberia.

At the Coconut Grove Resort casino, the room was full. Many locals did not gamble, as free drinks were the norm for those who could get the nod to walk in. In the casino backroom, there was a ten thousand dollar buy-in for poker. The dealers were all females from Peru and they were stunning. The dealer's short revealing neckline was hypnotic to the gamblers close to her. In the back of the casino was the unofficial poker room that Rajik started without the knowledge of the resort owner who lived in Philadelphia and visited only once a year. Very few won against the house at the poker tables as the dealers were specially selected. The money won and lost in the backroom helped Rajik launder counterfeit bills. Outside, a line of extremely beautiful local women waited for Rajik to pass and approve as nightly girlfriends. He only allowed the most absolutely drop dead gorgeous to enter. He walked back and forth and chose only four out of the fifteen to enter. One of his guards sprayed each with perfume. Four girls were selected and they entered the back door. Rajik had a full house at the casino and it was not even midnight yet. Several of the foreign gamblers already bet big and lost bigger. A Chinese manager who worked at the iron ore camp bet heavy on the roulette wheel. With each spin of the wheel, he made over two thousand dollars in chips. He had already acquired nearly twenty-two thousand dollars. Rajik watched him for moment and motioned for one of his thugs to keep a closer watch. If he won more, Rajik would follow him outside for an ambush assault. One of his specially trained Peruvian girls came up to the man and gave him a laced drink that immediately declined his performance. In several turns, he lost everything. Rajik was satisfied and went to the bar to meet his contact.

"What time does the plane land?" Rajik asked.

"We should expect them around midnight," the Colombian corrected himself, "perhaps two in the morning. It is very difficult to know head winds and speed." The stripped out 727 would carry only four, two pilots and two to refuel during the midflight from Bogota.

"Good."

"Is the air control set?"

Rajik looked over to the poker table and could see the sweat drip off the forehead of the Minister of Defense, a man connected Liberian all the way to the Presidential Palace. "We are covered."

Francesca listened intently to the ear piece that had a line of sight to the poker table. As she walked past, she had placed an empty glass on the table that possessed what looked like an ice cube. The Mossad operative rubbed the back of a Canadian surgeon who she met earlier in the day. They talked all night about serving with Doctors Without Borders and the sixty-two-year-old man thought he was getting lucky tonight. Francesca cozied up to the older man, nearly twice her age as she watched the faces at the poker table. She kept close to her date as to avoid any possible contact with any of the Lebanese. Her identity must remain an absolute secret.

CHAPTER 5

Driving toward Monrovia from the Firestone Plantation, Ike swerved around a yellow cab that was stripped to the frame. Russell thought it resembled an IED hulk, familiar to what he had witnessed in Iraq. For a moment, his mind thought of Fallujah. Russell looked out the window from the back seat, grimaced, and grabbed the handle grip on the vehicle ceiling. As they passed the IED looking hulk, nothing happened. He relaxed his grip. Traffic patterns and controls in Monrovia were non-existent as cars drove into traffic head-on. Vehicles swerved at the last possible moment to avoid collision. Speeds were excessive. Vehicles barely hung together with parts scavenged from many different types of vehicles. Tires were bald. Liberians were aggressive drivers. The threat from death in a vehicle collision was real and it did not take long for Russell to realize that he was in danger. His thought of an accident was compounded by the fact of inadequate medical care in Liberia's dilapidated hospital. Foreigners and locals both knew that patients who went to Monrovia General Hospital usually die.

Reminders of the most recent civil war lingered in the midst of the city's skyline. The tallest building in Monrovia was the Hotel Dukor. It resided on the cliff overlooking the area called Mamba Point near the Cape Hotel and US Embassy. Off to the right was an area called West Point, which was continuously portrayed in international media showing the disgusting living conditions. Tin rusted roofs clung together to protect over two hundred thousand in a one square mile area. The other tall buildings in Monrovia were two nearly adjacent twenty-story apartment buildings. From the distance, Russell could look straight through the insides. The interior guts of plaster walls and windows removed, stolen as spoils of survival in a brutal conflict. With no economy during the obscene fighting, money was made by stripping anything and everything in sight. These two apartment buildings were victims. On the side of the farthest apartment building that overlooked the bridge to Monrovia were large holes, deposits of high velocity metal shells fired from 106 millimeter recoilless rifles mounted on pickup trucks that did heavy damage. The smaller freckles of 7.62-millimeter rounds from AK47s dotted the cement, but the heavy impact of direct fire artillery did the real damage, leaving lasting scars.

Signs of progress emitted from the dozen radio transmission antennas of all sizes, which jutted from the rooftops. Yet no one lived within these buildings. It had been three years since the end of the last civil war and there remained no clear delineation on who owned what property. Historical records of real estate ownership were set ablaze. Many property owners died during the fourteen brutal years and many more left Liberia. There existed a colossal problem with the property ownership registry. Metal sheets formed the fences around these apartment buildings to keep squatters out; however they found means to enter. Squatters utilized barren buildings, made walls from any form of wood, metal, or scrap they found. Buckets were used for human waste or they climbed up onto the top of the building to relieve themselves. From the rooftops, the flow of sewage during the rainy months. For the most part, Liberians within Monrovia city limits made homes wherever they could. Windows were boarded with scraps of wood and makeshift screens erected to provide some ventilation. Many buildings did not have a roof that forced residents to reside on the lower floors. For the less fortunate, they endured the harshest of living conditions.

Inside of Barclay Training Center, nicknamed BTC, existed the headquarter buildings for the Ministry of Defense and the reformed Liberian army. The United States spent close to two hundred million dollars to form the new army of almost two thousand soldiers. To limit future potential military coups, top quality Liberian officers underwent training in Quantico with the Marine Corps. Russell admired the large murals that spread across the walls. The pictures depicted a friendlier military, one that did not commit atrocities.

At the front gate of the BTC compound, Kitson and Russell watched guards check the vehicle and identification cards. The guards looked suspiciously at Ike and would not allow him into the compound. Kitson and Russell got out and walked the five hundred feet to the army headquarters. Two SUVs in front of the military headquarters building were haphazardly painted green and brown in a camouflage scheme.

Four Nigerian soldiers stood in the doorway with AK-47s strapped across their chest. They neither smiled nor acknowledged the foreign guests. Russell followed the British Colonel and took a hard look at the AK-47s. He recalled the last time he saw this type of weapon was in Iraq. At the general's office, a Nigerian jumped to his feet and from his interaction with the British Colonel, Russell surmised this was the military aide. Within a minute, they entered the general's office.

"My friend...greetings." A very large man, near three hundred pounds, with a muscular build on his six foot-five-inch frame walked from behind his desk with his right hand outward. Major General Abdu Abdurallah smiled and warmly greeted everyone. The British Colonel mastered a handshake that took seven moves and finished with a relatively loud snap of the fingers between the two men. The British Colonel spent several minutes to introduce Major Russell based upon what he read in his dossier. Russell did not know how to shake hands like an African, but tried and failed. The Nigerian general laughed and slapped him on the back. After twenty minutes of introductions and pleasantries, they shared intelligence on the UN's progress keeping the peace. The talk shifted toward the Sapo mission.

"I know this man" The Nigerian said as he pointed to General Abbdas in the picture. "He came to Nigeria when Taylor was still in power trying to buy weapons from us."

"Is he dangerous?" Russell inquired. Looking at the epaulets and trying to understand the rank, he added "Sir."

"Yes and he has company." The Nigerian general said and he added, "Koroma is with him." Russell recalled what the MI6 reported. Johnny Paul Koroma was a fugitive from Sierra Leone indicted in 2003 by the Special Court in Sierra Leone. He had been charged under Article 3 of the Geneva Convention for crimes against humanity, employing child soldiers, sexual violence, rape, young girls kidnapped for sex slaves, and boys abducted as fighters. Koroma appointed himself a general in a ceremony to rival a royal coronation. Koroma led the Armed Forces Revolutionary Council (AFRC) and partnered with the RUF as a military junta against President Kabbah and captured Freetown for ten months before a local force backed by the UK that sent him into exile in Liberia. There he received Charles Taylor's protection. Recent reports had Koroma meeting with Al-Qaeda in Mali and Niger as he tried to sell the pounds of blood diamonds he smuggled out of Sierra Leone. Koroma left with over three hundred RUF hard-core murderers and many child soldiers. Koroma's precise location was not known, yet rumors had him living in Lofa County in northwest Liberia.

"Here are the only photos we have." The Nigerian general pulled out a shoe box filled with all types of photographs. Most of the photos were over four years old.

"There are many bad men still in Liberia." Kitson said. He pointed to a man in one of the photos next to Koroma. "This man is Rashad Mansuray. He trained in Libya and Syria and was recruited into Al-Qaeda. He was in the RUF and absolutely deadly. MI6 believes he has established a new avenue for blood diamonds to support Al-Qaeda."

"We got to get these guys," Russell said.

"We operate in unusual circumstances here. The UN does many good things but they are also how you say, handicapped." The general gave a wide smile and nod to Kitson as they both knew what needed to be done. "Charles Taylor is safe in exile in my country, and he can never come back to power. However, this is Africa and many strange things happen here." The general leaned closer to Russell. "There are evil men still here who want to bring back the old regime," He pointed at each of his guests and put his large hand on his chest, "and we cannot let that happen."

"Can the UN help?" Russell inquired.

"You will find my UN friends have a hard time taking care of themselves." The Nigerian general laughed at his own joke. "Three years have passed since Taylor was forced out and many thugs still operate in Liberia freely."

"Such as in Sapo?" Kitson retorted.

"Yes, Sapo. There is a place that was once beautiful and now thousands of rebels tear everything up looking for gold." The general continued, "These men have no honor, many are war criminals."

"Sending a small team should work to capture Abbdas and Koroma." Russell informed the senior officers. Kitson looked at him and nodded in agreement.

"True." He held up two folders and passed them to his guests. "I have two fine Lieutenants." The bios on Second Lieutenants Davidson Forleh and Prince Johnson III were impressive. Forleh attended Officers Candidate School in Rwanda while Johnson attended in Sierra Leone. Both attended the prestigious Marine Corps Basic School in Quantico, Virginia. For six months, they were heavily trained in small unit's skills and leadership.

"Koroma has a Hezbollah contact." Kitson interjected. "MI6 believes he is up to something big," said the British Colonel as he reflected on the report he read several weeks before, "that is the only reason he would come out of hiding."

The Nigerian general continued, "You need to remember that these men can never go home. Most have taken bush wives and started families." Russell heard about bush wives, or should they say young women kidnapped, raped, and held in captivity for years forced by fear tactics to remain. The Nigerian general passed him a map that listed UN ONLY on the top. He did not want to ask where he got it from, as he knows there are many Nigerian senior officers on the UNMIL staff. The general pointed toward the lower left of Liberia. "There. Sapo is where they are. Sapo National Forest quickly became the dumping ground for degenerates and murderers after the war." Charles Taylor's thugs moved out of Monrovia and hid in Sapo.

On the other side of the BTC compound, Deputy Minister of Defense for Operations, Adolphus Urey did not know whom to trust. As an outsider from America, he was part of the new Congo people who migrated back to Liberia. The term Congo people came from the freed slaves returning from America. These twenty thousand or so freed slaves formed the foundation of Liberian society. Local tribesmen called them Congo people as most of their parents or grandparents were captured from the Congo river valley and sold into slavery in Freetown or Accra. Fast forward one hundred and eighty years, a new breed of Congo have returned to Liberia. During the fourteen-year civil war, nearly a million Liberians escaped war and a good amount journeyed to America, mostly Philadelphia and Baltimore area to escape with their lives. The intellectual drain from Liberia continued as war raged. For most, they hoped they or their children could return someday to reinvigorate Liberian society from despair. Many of the new Congo people had not stepped foot into Liberia for nearly a decade.

Deputy Minister Urey was born and raised in Liberia but attended college in America at George Washington University. His father owned a palm tree plantation and harvested palm oil that was profitable enough to send his only son to America. The plantation was in Robertsport, far from the violence that engulfed Monrovia. His father knew that his family were targeted based upon what little wealth he possessed so his father sent his mother and three sisters to live in Maryland with relatives. For the first few months, the regular phone calls and weekly letters kept them in touch, but then there was silence. No word came for months, not even from the workers on the plantation. The lack of information crushed his mother more than anything. No one knew if his father survived the widespread murdering. As a thirty-five year old, Adolphus was one of the youngest Ministers in the entire newly formed Liberian government; courtesy in part to his family name, and more importantly that he volunteered. As the new government started to form, President Johnson-Sirleaf reached out to many of her distant relative and exiled Liberians anxiously waiting for the previous regime to topple and transition under UN mandate.

The Deputy Minister looked at a note sent to his office. He crumpled and tossed it into the trashcan. He was stupid that one night, drinking heavily, and gambling in the casino backroom. When the stakes were raised, he tried to bet against the house and lost big, nearly eighty thousand US dollars. What he should have known was Hezbollah had the game rigged. The Deputy Minister reviewed the deed to his father's three-hundred-acre plantation. He heard millionaires from America snatched up waterfront property all over Liberia at a fraction of the price. Property was cheap as not many resort developers were unwilling to venture into war-torn Liberia. The note demanded Urey to pay the debt with interest or suffer the consequences.

Over a hundred miles away from Monrovia, Sapo National Forest claimed over seven hundred square miles of pristine jungle. Five years before, animals were abundant, but that was before several hundred former fighters moved in. Along the river bed that crisscrossed the middle of the camp there were dozens of former child soldiers working. The riverbed provided ample gravel to sift for gold that could be sold to Lebanese in Monrovia. Small businesses emerged in these camps - bars, restaurants, gambling parlors, and houses of ill repute. Word of the gold spread in the exile ranks.

General Samuel Abbdas set up his headquarters within Sapo. He walked out of the mangled building that now served as his home. It was far cry from the conditions he was accustomed to. He looked out over his balcony at the disturbance below near the water pump. One of his men was getting a little too friendly with one of the bush wives and she did not want anything to do with him. The commotion started as a shouting match and escalated when she mustered the courage and spat on him. The child solider slapped the woman who was much older than him in the face and carried her off. A normal day's activity Abbdas thought for an army in exile. He looked at several of the maps sprawled out across his lap. The freedom fighters as he called them were the worse part of Charles Taylor's death squads. Mutilation, disfigurement, and all types of ruthless abuse were common to them during the civil war years, but now in exile, they sat and waited for word. The bag of rough diamonds rested on the table, a small amount but would fetch fifty thousand dollars on the black market. The continuation of this army in exile depended upon the illegal sale of diamonds smuggled from Sierra Leone and any extortion money from those who dug for gold.

The only item General Abbdas carried into Sapo was a small metal box filled with presidential documents. General Abbdas had strong ties with Charles Taylor and worked alongside him during the siege of Samuel Doe's Presidential Palace. Abbdas was a sergeant in one of the death squads. He was there when Prince Johnson took a knife to Samuel Doe's chest and thrust it into the deposed president. Abbdas checked and made sure Doe was dead. As a trophy, he mutilated one of Doe's ears. Soon after, Taylor rewarded him by appointing him a major. Abbdas gained more power and became the most corrupt officer in the Liberian military. Taylor personally tasked Abbdas to manage the flow of illegal weapons to Sierra Leone that helped sustain their brutal civil war in exchange for blood diamonds. When Charles Taylor did not have enough troops to fight the rebels, he sent Abbdas to recruit and train child soldiers from Sierra Leone. The main point of training demonstrated to the child soldiers how to properly inject heroine in their veins. In the last year of his regime, Taylor appointed Abbdas as Chief of Staff whereby he controlled the entire Liberian army, nearly five thousand strong.

Abbdas looked down at the map and squinted in the afternoon sunlight to see where he could send the next raiding party. Could he risk going back into Guinea or loot Cote D'Ivoire towns or would he be bold enough to enter the mouth of the tiger. Over a thousand Nigerian professional troops were camped within Monrovia to protect the new government. He did not look up when one of his bush wives arrived. Sumarka brought a delicious lunch for him and left it on the table. His troops were watching him so he knocked the plate off the table and onto the floor. Sumarka did not blink an eye and immediately went to clean up the mess. The troops laughed. Waiting a few more minutes, he looked up to his troops and said, "We will wait until the rainy season to attack Monrovia." Sumarka was still cleaning up the mess and heard the dismal projection of the next attack in Nimba County. "The rain will conceal our movements." Abbdas stated with confidence.

Russell departed BTC compound pleased with the Nigerian general's offer to add two Liberian officers to his team. If the Lieutenants were half as good as the file stated, they would be a valuable addition. Russell contemplated the mission as Ike drove them away from the military area, back into the Monrovia slums. The Sapo mission would require a considerable amount of integral planning and they needed intelligence on what to expect in the dense jungle. Few reports existed and the aerial photos highlighted near impassable terrain.

Several streets from BTC, Ike stopped at the only high-class market in Monrovia called Abu Jabbi, which of course was owned and operated by Uncle Anwar who actually won it in a poker game from Ghasson. As soon as they stopped, half a dozen amputees crowded around the vehicle and asked for handouts, which they called "small, small". Russell smiled and gave a nice greeting as he pushed past them. As Ike went into shop, the British Colonel and Russell walked the streets.

The central shopping district was gutted by looters during the civil war. The once vibrant stores possessed an eerie chill as the front facades were ransacked. Farther up the street was an abandoned place of worship, or so Russell thought. The windowless church erupted with song, children's voices could be heard in joyous revolt of the terror surrounding them every day. Voices vibrantly attacked the evil that once had a strangle hold on their country. Evil would not be tolerated anymore, not for today, tomorrow, or their lifetime. The church goers sang in defiance and rejoiced. Fear remained, yet it was nothing like the rampant fear of death and devastation during the bloody civil war.

On the corner of the street, a man stood still. No one recognized his problem until he attempted to cross the street. Russell watched as the man dragged his left leg, limp from probable torture. Another unfortunate victim of a brutal civil war was permanently scarred. His foot was perpendicular to the direction he moved forward. It was the most comfortable way to move his limped appendage. The knee did not work as it was smashed with some type of instrument and the foot crushed by a truck tire as he was held down and repeatedly run over. Laughter from the child soldiers who held him down still echoed in his mind. He could not remember any faces, but he plainly remembered the laughter. Russell wondered if the man ever received proper medical attention. If he did make it to one of the major refugee camps in neighboring Guinea, the camp's medical staff was probably so overwhelmed that they told him amputation was the only means. Or perhaps, he held out in the bush, saved by some family, nursed back to health the best that they could do.

The complexity of the ruthless warfare left many fighting for sheer existence. In all-out guerilla warfare there is no safe ground - no magic place to say you could not touch me. Thousands perished. Many more thousands lived with the haunted dreams. Russell was amazed at the gravity of the situation as he recalled the statistics on the two Liberian civil wars. More than four hundred thousand lives were lost and over a million citizens went into exile. Families were torn apart. The world did not respond to Liberia's call in time of need.

As Russell walked along the devastated street, he thought of the posh conditions on Long Island. The Piping Rock Country Club was one of the most exquisite private clubs on Long Island and in the midst of the fabled Gold Coast. Kristin, his girlfriend, was a rebel within her family. The thought of her being with a military man, regardless if he was an Annapolis graduate and officer, did not mean much to her family. In her families mind, she was trolling. Kristin's father was blue blood, fifth generation and could trace ancestry back before the American Revolution. And for the most part, his ancestors supported the British in the American Revolution and reported on George Washington movements around Long Island. Russell got obnoxiously drunk at the annual Fourth of July festivity, the main staple of the Piping Rock Country Club summer program and informed everyone how Mr. Vanderheuse's ancestors were traitors. He felt uncomfortable wearing a coat and tie to a pool party. The blue blood crowd lounged on the vast patio surrounding the manicured country club. No one swam in the crystal blue pool. Every male was wearing a jacket and every lady a flowing summer dress. Some wore large hats that looked like small umbrellas on their heads. Of course, all had top of the line, very expensive sunglasses. Russell did not fit in here, not now, not ever. Russell remembered what Kristin's dad said to him, "Tom, you know when I was scuba diving in Thailand, by the time I went down and came back up I was down over one million dollars in the market."

Russell, who had only a few hundred dollars to his name at that time, did not care and replied, "But those were paper losses."

"Tom, have you ever had a loss in the market."

"Mr. Vanderheuse your idea of a loss and mine are totally different." The father looked at his loving daughter and slightly smiled, confirming that his little precious, the youngest of three daughters was far too good for this Marine officer.

As they drove back to Firestone Plantation, Russell looked out the window and saw shirts and sports jerseys from all over America. The names of long retired NFL or NBA stars cover their bodies. There are many shirts that showed a family reunion that happened over five years ago. The Roberts family reunion in Atlanta was not very popular as there were over ten shirts of the same design seen on the same day. Perhaps a family tragedy, bad economy, or bad weather curtailed the Roberts clan from getting together. Most all of the Liberians had no idea who the person was, and they do not care. The clothes were courtesy of numerous churches and large donation organizations in America. What the donors never saw were the sale of these pile of clothes at the port of Monrovia to Lebanese who purchased the entire bundles. Local women were hired to wash and dry each article of clothing. Men who pushed wheel barrels stood ready at the port exit to purchase the goods and start the long journey that ferried the merchandise across the bridge to the center of Monrovia. Trucks, covered in soot from diesel exhaust sat idle as piles of clothing were moved to Red Light district for sale.

"Are we cleared hot?" Rozelli asked immediately.

"Indeed you are," Kitson said. "You can pick up the two Lieutenants in the morning."

"Good, we need to get them in shape quickly," retorted Rageone.

"You should be watchful as Liberians are darn good athletes."

"Roger sir, but combat is combat." Kitson smiled and walked off as if he was hiding something.

"What's on the docket for tonight?" Rozelli asked.

In a comical tone, "You are all excused, but we officers have to go and mingle with the Nigerian general tonight."

"Maybe we can hit the casino tonight?" They had heard about the party scene at the Lebanese operated casino and it was tempting.

"Not yet," Russell quickly injected, "Let's remember no one can be trusted and everyone is collecting intelligence on us."

Russell, Kitson, and Stone arrived at the Club beer factory and were met by five armed private security guards. Names were checked against the night's access list. Mirrors were used to view underneath the vehicle for explosives. Inside the complex, there were six buildings: one large building housing the Club beer factory and five residences for the executive families. Each building possessed five-bedroom, five bathroom residences with its own service entrance. When the Nigerians arrived in Monrovia to install peace under the UN security mandate, the owner of the Club beer factory met with them and asked for protection. The agreement provided a cost-free house for as long as the Nigerians remained. External security and protection from the all of the emerging criminal activities were taken care of by two hundred Nigerian heavily armed soldiers. Along the exterior wall were several watchtowers over fifteen feet high.

As the three officers entered the general's private quarters, he singled out Stone, "Greetings my brother. I have heard you are from Nigeria."

"Yes general. I was raised near Badagry."

"Was your father a fisherman?"

"No sir. My father worked in oil production."

"The name Stone is not Nigerian."

"My mother changed our last name when we moved to America. My father died when I was young."

"What was your father's name?"

"Dangote." Immediate silence came across the room. Others who were not paying attention to the general's conversation immediately turned their heads. Russell looked suspiciously at Stone. "My father came from a distinguished family." Stone replied to Russell. To say the least thought the general. Aliko Dangote was the first native African billionaire. He started the Dangote Group thirty years ago and now employed over twelve thousand Nigerians as the largest single employer in that country. On the latest Forbes World's Richest Aliko Dangote's wealth was estimated at three billion. Russell walked around the room looking at several large photos on the wall. General Abdurallah was in all of them in full uniform with large shinning medals, something out of a former Ugandan President Edi Ammine home movie.

"General, who is this in the picture with you?" Russell asked as he pointed to the main photo hung in the middle of the room.

"Ah, that is my good friend President Obasanjo." The Nigerian general stated with a smile. "He promoted me to general in this photo."

General Abdurallah had a lot of exposure to the American military over his thirty-year career and he immediately liked Major Russell and Captain Stone. He directed the two younger officers toward the libations at the bar. As he exited from his private chamber, the Nigerian general held up a vintage bottle of French Rothschild and showed the British colonel who quickly nodded consent. For a Muslim, he did not burden himself with strict religious compliance in his own home. Among friends he enjoyed the first, second, and third bottle of fine wine he purchased at the recent European Union's West Africa Peace Summit in Paris. As the senior military officer in Liberia, he shared the Peace Summit's table with the newly elected Liberian President Ellen Johnson-Sirleaf. He never served under a female leader as it was not a custom in Nigeria, but from the start he liked President Ellen's spunkiness and drive. After assuming command of the new Liberian army, he met the old guard of general officers and several Ministers who served under the previous Doe and Taylor regimes. One stood out. Lieutenant General Dubar proved the voice of calm and reason for many years.

When Master Sergeant Samuel Doe walked the five hundred meters from BTC to the Presidential Palace with thirty armed thugs, he caught President Tolbert asleep and executed him that night. The next day, Doe got on the national radio and proclaimed himself president. Later that same day, he arrested the entire cabinet. The legislature was disbanded and the key cabinet members, mostly possessing the last name Tolbert were lined along the rear wall within the BTC compound. A younger Ellen Johnson, who served as Minister of Finance at the time, stood alongside twelve other cabinet members awaiting their execution. General Dubar talked a voice of reason into his former Master Sergeant Doe who he now had to salute and call Mr. President. With Dubar's help, Ellen Sirleaf was spared death and lived in prison for nine months. She remained isolated and existed on a diet of fish heads and rice. General Abdurallah comprehended the historical context that haunted Liberian politics and society, demons reached from the past and vendettas were not forgotten. He was smart enough to tap Dubar's support for the new Liberian army.

As the military aide rang the dinner chime, the officers entered the dining room to see fine china and drink goblets on the table. The Nigerian enlisted soldiers wore formal white jackets with red sachets around their waists. As they found their assigned name placard and sat down, the military aide offered prayers in both Islam and Christianity. After they pronounced amen for both prayers, the guests were served fresh fish, roasted large snails in pepper sauce, stewed casaba, and rice balls. Small bowls of Liberian hot sauce were placed by each plate to temp the bravery of the guests. Russell looked over to see Stone submerge his face into the incredibly spicy hot pepper sauce and he drank it up. Damn Nigerian thought Russell. He did not dare try the Liberian pepper sauce. He speared a large roasted snail the size of a baseball with a fork and chewed the meat. Russell gummed a snail that chewed like leather. The pepper sauce that surrounded the snail penetrated the leather meat and ignited Russell's mouth. He hastily grabbed for water, spilled his water glass, and gulped down the glass of wine. The meal exploded in his mouth and felt worse in his stomach.

Driving back to Firestone Plantation, Russell needed to think about something besides his stomach's turmoil. He broke the silence, "I did not know much about Nigeria before coming here." Russell said. Lagos has over eighteen million residents with very few high-rise buildings. Nigeria's population exploded to nearly one hundred and fifty million. At the same time, Nigeria became an economic powerhouse. As the world's twelfth largest oil producer, significant new wealth plagued Nigerian society as seventy percent lived on less than one US dollar per day, well below the poverty line. Only a small portion held the vast wealth.

"Have you talked to your relatives in Nigeria?" Russell asked.

"Not in years." Stone replied. "My uncle wanted me to work in the family business. I don't know."

"What kind of job?"

"I would be appointed Vice President of Operations in my uncle's oil division." Stone said as a matter of fact.

"Wow. That must carry one heck of a salary."

"More than you could imagine." Stone said softly and added after a short pause, "More than I would ever want to deal with."

"Maybe you can stop there after this mission." Russell said.

"Perhaps." Stone said. "Outside the capital of Abuja is Zuma Rock. Someday I will take you there to climb."

"That would be nice." Russell missed climbing. Right now, he should be back in Seattle working on his mountaineering skills. The calls were constant during the Pacific Northwest winter as amateur climbers lacked sense and tried tackling Mount Rainier. However, now he was on hiatus in the dreadful humidity of West Africa summer.

The turmoil started in Russell's stomach and migrated toward his intestines. The roasted snails with pepper sauce caused an unbearable pain. The hour and half ride back to the camp tortured him. He held off the worse bowel movement ever in his life. The thirty minute bowel event in the latrine nearly put him to sleep from exhaustion. He crawled into his rack with exhaustion and discovered a mosquito bed net neatly hung again. He brushed six dead white mosquitoes off the net. Majority of white mosquitoes carried malaria. He recalled the British Surgeon in Freetown lecturing his team that regardless of what medication they take, they would contract malaria if bitten by the white mosquito. Russell curled up from the severe abdominal pains and crashed hard for the night.

CHAPTER 6

The morning sunlight coupled with Lucy's screams outside his window awoke Russell. He had planned on a run, but he just could not get out of bed. For the next three hours he did not move - could not move. The previous night's dinner injected a ferocious sickness into his body. Cramps, muscle aches, and sheer agony encompassed him. He grabbed an intravenous bag from a medical kit, punctured his forearm, and set up a ringers lactate drip into his arm. Just before lunch, the Gunnys knocked on his door. One look at their leader, and the Gunnys did not chide him. Those roasted snails in pepper sauce were near lethal to Russell and crippled his movements for the foreseeable future.

The rest of the team was on the move. Stone followed Ike in the second vehicle while the Gunnys split up between the vehicles as added security. Doors were locked in case of a potential stop. In Monrovia, mobs formed and occupants were pulled from vehicles and robbed. Monrovia driving scared Stone who had learned how to drive in Lagos by the time he was fourteen. The Gunnys were used to patrol car driving in the streets of Queens and the Bronx, yet Monrovia was worse. In Red Light district, the sides of the road were crowded with all sorts of vendors. From old glass bottles to plastic jugs, everything received a second life in Liberia, out of necessity. The last civil war left little for those who remained. There were few ships that unloaded supplies and far less trucks that moved the goods around. Everything had a value. The large empty Club beer bottles were used for old oil. The plastic bottles once used by foreign visitors and discarded were now used to carry brownish water to families. Four brand new large green harvester trackers sat idle. The massive farm equipment was a donation from an American aid organization who failed to do any homework on Liberian crops. Wheat could not be grown in Liberia. The large green harvesters remained silent for the over ten months and became landmark symbols for many of the foreigners who got lost in the city.

At the BTV compound, the Liberian Second Lieutenants had their gear packed and staged at the main headquarters. Stone looked at the two men who did not seem much. Both were typical Liberian size, about five and a half feet tall and one hundred and fifty pounds. Stone could tell they were muscular but he would not know how well until they got out into the bush. After introductions, the vehicles were loaded, Lieutenants split between the vehicles.

"How did you like TBS?" Stone asked. TBS was the Basic School, which was the Marine Corps officer-training program in Quantico, Virginia. Commonly TBS was referred to by graduates in other terms such as Time Between Saturdays, The Big Suck, Tenacious Bold Scary, and many other names not fit for the general public.

"Good," relied Lieutenant Forleh, "except I did not do well on the final PFT." PFT was the Marine Corps physical fitness test consisting of twenty dead hang pull-ups, one hundred crunches in two minutes, and three-mile run in eighteen minutes. "Somebody beat me."

"What was your time?"

"Fifteen fifty." The Liberian officer said.

Stone and Rozelli turned to the backseat. "Are you kidding me, sir?" asked the Gunny. Lieutenant Forleh smiled. Any thought that these Liberian men would not be able to hang was quickly put out of their mind. Completing the three-mile course after the pull-ups and sit-ups in under eighteen minutes would be impressive. Completing the three-mile course within sixteen minutes was extremely rare.

"Who beat you?" Stone inquired.

"Lieutenant Johnson." If Liberia had an Olympic team, these two officers would definitely be on it for track and field, thought Stone.

About a forty-minute drive southward from Monrovia was the town of Marshall. Rajik liked Marshall because it existed along a nondescript river. Liberia had dozens of inland waterways that reached out toward the open ocean. The more discrete rivers provided a natural hideaway for those who did not wish to be found. The uneven, broken up road heading to Marshall discouraged many tourists. Dugout canoes from large old logs rested along the riverbank. Liberian men labored hard in the canoes as they traveled up and down the river. Old men had the upper body physique of men half their age. The river thrust the small boats toward the ocean and the only means to move upstream was by sheer strength.

Rajik sat on the floating dock in a large cushioned lounge chair. The overhead awning provided much needed shade. On the shore, there were four buildings and a large boathouse. Rajik looked at his private ledger that he kept hidden at the Marshall compound. He spent eighteen thousand dollars to renovate and construct the compound. Up and down the river, Lebanese families had built camps to provide an exit strategy if another military coup occurred. Many Lebanese were unprepared during the last civil war and ran for their lives. Many lost fortunes. Since land can only be owned by Liberians, the Lebanese bribed locals to give up their homes along the water.

Over the past two years, Rajik had skimmed several hundred thousand dollars from the casino, but he knew it was not enough. To get out of Liberia for good he would need a considerable amount more. In addition to smuggling weapons into West Africa, Rajik branched out into other illegal activities. Rajik muscled his way into becoming the primary hawala representative for Hezbollah in West Africa. Hawala was the underground money transfer network for terrorists and Lebanese criminals. The stakes were high for those who mule the run in and out of countries and even higher when they disappear without making final payments. Families were often victim to repercussions. Rajik murdered several hawala mules for their money, blamed it on them for embezzling, and murdered several of their family members as repercussion to maintain a state of fear. No one would dare take action against Rajik.

The six Lebanese families that ran a majority of the businesses in Liberia would be pleased if Rajik disappeared. The Lebanese community had over eighty thousand residents, and between the six family leaders they knew just about everything going on. No one was brought into Liberia unless approved by a vote of the family heads. Ghasson was appointed the main figurehead for all of the Lebanese and regularly met with the new Liberian Ministers. Allowances were paid to several Ministers in the form of regular dinners and exempt bar tabs at the Cape Hotel. The perks provided to the new government Ministers were just in case to keep good business relations, especially if the UN ever pulled out and gave Liberia back to Liberians.

Rajik came to Monrovia on recuperation from a gunshot wound he obtained during the last Israeli incursion into the Gaza Strip. After he noticed the instability that haunted Liberia, Rajik saw considerable opportunity. At the casino, he opened a backroom for the high-stakes gamblers. Young pretty local girls were inspected every night and got the privilege to drink free. The VIP backroom had its own private bar, comfortable lounge chairs, large bathroom, and of course private gaming tables in the center of the room. If any of the girls became too drunk, they were sent out the back door and roughly handled. Rajik's thugs would not punch them in the face but had been known to give several kidney shots hard enough to make blood appear in their urine. Rajik knew he would never get in with the good graces of the six Lebanese families who wanted to be more kind and friendly to the Liberians. Rajik would gladly abuse, corrupt, or kill a Liberian to garner more wealth.

On the Marshall River, canoes passed Rajik's floating dock and headed up river. Local fishermen paddled hard against the current to bring fish to market. The locals did not wave or look at the man many in the Marshall area feared. Sometimes late at night screams emitted from the boathouse. Rajik fumbled through the ledger book and estimated he needed two million dollars to get out of Monrovia permanently. The one absolute thing he learned in Beirut was he could not just walk away from Hezbollah. His recuperation from the wounds was over and he heard his local commander in Beirut has asked when he would return. He knew how much Ghasson and the other Lebanese despised his tactics and it would be only a matter of time that either he would get a bullet in the back of the head or shipped off against his wishes back to Beirut. Rajik knew his departure would have to be abrupt.

Back at the remote Firestone Plantation camp, Russell started to move around his bungalow. He struggled toward the couch in the small family room, felt dizzy, and dropped his body hard on the bug-infested couch. He did not care about the mold smell or the little baby black spiders that roamed all over the cushions. The mother spider must have recently discarded her interior hold of babies. Hundreds of them were on the move. Russell did not care; he needed rest. His mind raced back to his past. Russell had walked in the presence of audacious wealth.

It was the summer just before the 9/11 terrorist attacks and he was in the Hamptons, specifically East Hampton village. His Columbia MBA class pitched together and rented rooms at several large homes, which proved a cost effective way to make a summer fling in the Hamptons affordable. Bunk beds were the norm as if a throwback to summer camp days. Each individual rented bed space in a room for a set number of weekends, rain or shine did not matter. It was only for the weekend starting on Thursday as earliest arrival to Monday morning. It did not matter if you had a wife, girlfriend, or a hookup, each guy paid for her. Same held true for any buddies. It was the same summer a documentary film crew interviewed several members of the Hilton and Rockefeller pedigree who were shocked how people can share rooms. Russell was shocked at the distorted Hampton's lifestyle of the quaint village and rows of billionaire summer playground beach cottages. Parents believed their perfect children would become the next Hamptons elite. Education did not matter. Only a last name or trust fund mattered in this bizarre community social network.

Russell's mind raced back to that summer in the Hamptons. He thought of the wild parties and chance encounters of being in the same bar as a Hampton celebrity, yet never breaking into their secret society. Now, what he saw in Liberia made him humble as a human being ever could. Humble that he was not one of these victims of carnage. Humble that he was born and raised in the freedom of America. For generations, military service has taken the most obnoxious, undisciplined, poor or rich snob and forged them into something. Humility was something he learned in the humid summer days along the water at Annapolis and in the woods of Quantico. Humility was carved in his skull during the violent street-to-street fighting in Fallujah and a massive explosion in Iskandariyah that he witnessed. He was far from the Hamptons. After what he saw in the streets of Monrovia and what he had experienced in Iraq, he could never go back as the same man before 9/11. He committed himself to never visit again in his life the perfectly aligned East Hampton village streets. He knew 9/11 would not change the Hamptons; nothing would, not even present day Liberia.

Russell focused his eyes in the bungalow and mustered the energy to walk to the kitchen for water, but there was none. Days started to mingle into one another. It had been over a month since Russell departed the snowcapped mountains that surrounded Seattle. He had been down hard over the past three days, really unable to function properly. The nightmares ensued and were compounded from malaria medication. Nightmares of Iskandariyah encapsulated his mind. Ike came running in the middle of the night on several occasions after he heard screams. The flashbacks to the destruction in Iskandariyah haunted Russell. The scream of Iraqis dying seemed so real in his mind. Body parts in the street, sheer carnage erupted across all of the buildings, and the smell of burned flesh clogged his senses and forever burned into his mind. Iskandariyah would always be in his thoughts.

The afternoon air was still and humid, nearly noxious to breathe. There was no air passing through the Firestone Plantation. The wind was dead. The camp generator was dead too, the backup generator strangled to life. Ike shut it down as the emitted sounds became worse. The inside temperature of the bungalows was excruciating and forced Russell out. Ike was screaming some obscenities at the generator. The British Colonel sat on the porch and Russell joined him.

Russell pulled out some notes and he read them as he sat down. Gio and Mano tribes were from Nimba County, and they supported Charles Taylor. Taylor wanted to kill Doe, but he had Prince Johnson, whose name had nothing to do with royalty. Prince Johnson stuck a knife in the former president and killed him on 9 Sept 1990. Surprisingly, Doe became a favorite of Ronald Reagan and a regular visitor to America's White House. To make sure everyone knew the president was dead Johnson dragged his lifeless carcass around Monrovia and tied Doe around a monument. Some eyewitnesses reported seeing Prince Johnson pull out Doe's heart and take a bite out of it. Russell handed the British Colonel a copies of Johnson's service record. The letter heading stated, Armed Forces of Liberia, Office of the Adjutant General, Special Orders dated 24 December 1985, Second Lieutenant Prince Y. Johnson, service number CO-00877 hereby dismissed from active service for convenience of the Government 'for gross disrespect and insult offered the wife of the Head of State and Co-

64

Chairman of the People's Redemption Council'. Prince Johnson assignments were agent G2 section. His hometown was Gomaplay, Nimba County, Gio tribe, 5 ft. 6 in., 150 lbs., profession was typist, date enlisted 1 AUG 1974, period of five years, Johnson, Yeomi father, four dependents - no names provided. Russell wondered if the new Lieutenant on their team was a distant relative to this killer.

"It's amazing how everyone wants to kill everyone in power here." Russell said.

"Indeed." Kitson replied. "Your country just sent an armored car for the current President Johnson-Sirleaf."

"Why?" Russell looked surprised. "Are there death threats?"

"You never know. This is Africa." Kitson stated in a blunt manner. "There are too many vying for power and with the power there will be lots of money."

"What happens if Liberia has more offshore oil than Nigeria? Maybe our Nigerian general friend will be the new President of Liberia." Russell said in a joking manner.

"You jest. But make no mistake that Nigeria is the powerhouse in West Africa, similar to your role in NATO."

"I understand that now. So what is ECOWAS providing?" Russell asked.

"There is an ECOWAS standby force of roughly six thousand troops ready to move." Kitson said. Russell had heard about the ECOWAS standby force and the rumors of Nigerians who parachuted into Roberts International Airport during the last civil war. The Nigerians opened fire for twenty-four hours killing anything that moved. Seven thousand Nigerians entered Liberia and the body count remains hidden by the Nigerian government, estimates were two thousand wounded. In the fierce fighting, Liberia reported over ten thousand rebels were killed in the first week the Nigerians landed.

The sound of jet engines screeching into Roberts International Airport interrupted their conversation. The 757 wide body Brussels Airline plane from Accra, Ghana rumbled overhead as the flaps were engaged for final arrival. Direct approach remained over Firestone Plantation and far away from any rebels within Sapo. The flights became more frequent as more and more passengers ventured to Monrovia. Out of the three hundred and twenty seats on board over a third of the passengers were NGOs, contractors, and other do-gooders.

"With the UN's eight thousand troops, the fifteen hundred UN police, and this ECOWAS standby force, you would think this country would be more stable after five years." Russell said as he poured another round of gin and tonic for the both of them.

"Security is not something that comes easy. Having more police and soldiers will help, only if there is minimal corruption," Kitson responded.

"That's the same in any country."

"True, but you need to remember violence always wins," Kitson said and he added. "Extreme violence, now that gets folks attention."

"Doesn't look good for the home team." Russell quipped. Kitson looked at him with a contorted stare as he did not understand the comment.

"The Liberian police need a lot of help as well as the new military." Kitson said as he looked outward in the sky at the plane's exhaust trails. "They still do not know what they will call the new army. Some want to have a new name and others want to name it the Armed Forces of Liberia."

"What's wrong with that?" asked Russell.

"Everything is in a name. Not only were the rebels killing a lot of innocent people, so did the AFL." Kitson sipped and finished his fourth gin and tonic.

Russell remembered back to the reports he read on the formation of the new army. The vetting process has been extremely important to the success of the new army. Pictures were plastered around the soldier's villages and up to nine village elders interviewed. Only a few war criminals have been brought to justice. Witnesses had been reluctant to come forward out of sheer fear and death threats.

"Colonel, tell me about your time in Africa?"

"I served in Rhodesia" Kitson said.

"Do you mean Zimbabwe?"

"No I mean Rhodesia. It will always be Rhodesia to me." Kitson replied flatly.

"Ok, in Rhodesia, can you tell me about your service?" Russell instinctively understood the British officer would perhaps provide bits and pieces of information. He did not want to press him, yet he knew there was definitely an interesting story behind Kitson's service. Brigadier General Canteberry in Freetown made several references to the importance of having an individual with qualities of Colonel Frank Kitson, Jr. stationed in Liberia. Russell gravitated more and more to his newfound mentor.

"Indeed." Kitson replied and he continued. "In Rhodesia in 1979, I was a Second Lieutenant. After Ian Smith bungled the transition and repatriation of combatants, a few of us were called into the fight." Lifting to sip the gin and tonic he said. "Ah, that is good. As I was saying, a few of us had to talk to the combatants to ask them to surrender their weapons and enjoy peace."

"That must have been a shitty mission." Russell said. Colonel Kitson did not blink and showed the sign of a Zen master.

"The local tribesmen did not know what to make of us. We knew that they were out there watching us. There were only seven in my camp and we were completely surrounded by several thousand. With no guidance from headquarters, I made some hot tea and took a table out into the middle of the road about two thousand kilometers from our camp. I sat down and waited."

"What for?"

"Patience, I will get to that. I must have been sitting there for about an hour. The sun was getting lower in the sky as it was about four o'clock and in the winter month, it would be getting dark real soon. They were watching me. I had on my best uniform and smarted my boots."

"Smarted?"

"Cleaned and shined. Then I saw a pile of them come over the hill. They were the most magnificence looking bush warriors that I ever saw. Something you would read about in Zulu nation chronicles. I asked the chiefs to sit and have a spot of tea with me and they did. Unfortunately for me a photographer was following them to get their story and took a snapshot of me offering tea to this band of renegades."

"Were you armed?"

"No"

"You're telling me that you walked out two thousand kilometers away from your position, unarmed, to have tea with your enemy?"

"Not exactly. At that point in time, they were not my enemy as the war ceased hostilities when Ian Smith brokered the peace. But, yes I did walk out without my weapon."

"What did he say?"

"To tell you the truth, I really do not remember. I was so damn worried about being captured. But I did tell the rebel leader that the war was over. Now that I think of it, he actually seemed upset about it. I really believed he wanted to kill more of us."

"What did your family have to say about the mission?"

"It is funny to think back in those days we did not have the luxury of instant communication. My mother found out when she opened the London Times. On the front page was a large picture of me with the caption that peace was being made." They both laughed.

"What about your father?" Russell inquired. "The general?"

"My father was not pleased." Kitson said.

"Why was that?"

"At the time, my father was the Chief of the General Staff." The tone in his voice dropped off at the end and Major Russell took that as a strong cue to remain silent. More than five minutes passed as the British Colonel reflected on his father. He continued. "I did receive a lot of attention once the article hit the front page of the London Times."

"The general in Freetown mentioned you received the Queen's Medal. Was that for Rhodesia?"

In a low voice that sounded more humbling than anything, Kitson stated, "Yes, the Queen awarded me."

"Really?" The sign of gin and tonics started to show, especially since they have not even had dinner. Ike had not returned from generator maintenance and the silence from the generator house continued. Without power, dinner was definitely out of question. They both poured another gin and tonic.

"Actually, if you must know there are only six of these awards in existence. I granted the award in my will to my offspring." A few more sips. "It is funny to think how much attention I received and at such a young age."

"Did you ever meet Prince Charles?" Kind of like asking every American how is your president, can you tell him I say hello.

"Well I have met him several times. I taught his sons at Sandhurst."

"You schooled the Princes?"

"Right. I served with Harry in Afghanistan. His father wanted to make sure he was safe and asked me to deploy as an advisor and watch over him. Unfortunately, your American media vultures leaked the news that he was in Afghanistan so I had to curtail his tour of duty for his own protection."

"They did not help us in Iraq either. Terrorists got more information on how to best hit us by just turning on CNN."

"And now you have Al Jazeera English."

"My colonel in Fallujah told us all the time that Al Jazeera was the damn mouthpiece for Al-Qaeda." The British Colonel grabbed some more sardines and crackers. They munched on the snacks. Russell seized upon the opportunity to ask for more assistance. "Sir, if it is alright with you, I am going to need Ike."

"I thought as much." Kitson nodded his head in agreement. "Ike is very capable." The British Colonel never divulged information on Ike's background. "You need to remember one thing." He paused for dramatics to make sure his pupil listened. "In Africa, nothing is what it appears to be."

The Deputy Minister for Defense watched the UN guards with the blue helmets as they walked back and forth in front of the terminal at Roberts International Airport. He showed them his credentials and entered the secured area. Roberts International Airport had been under UN control for the past three years since it opened for international air travel. At first, the only security allowed was UN military forces and over time Liberian custom agents had been trained and the Bureau of Immigration and Nationalization was established. As the new Liberian military was formed, coordination between the Military of Defense, the Bureau of Immigration and Naturalization, and any other Liberian Ministry was non-existent. Donor nations signed up and sponsored only those entities by what funding they could support. As the global recession ripped wealth from Europe and America support faltered.

The control tower did not know about flight 8459. The plane passed along West Africa but not close enough to Lagos or Accra to be picked up on radar. The blind reckoning flying was aided by satellite GPS links in the modern cockpit. The pilot and co-pilot were nervous that was until the navigational aid beacon for Roberts International Airport registered. The co-pilot checked the fuel gage, and he was pleased that enough remained. The smell was unbearable from the fumes within the plane. He closed off the cockpit door as best he could with tape. In the back of the stripped-out Gulfstream 727, two FARC members sat next to six fifty-five gallon drums of aviation fuel. The only possible direct flight from Bogota to West Africa without landing required in-flight refueling. Since the Columbian drug cartel did not have military capable mid-air refueling, the next best thing was to strip out a plane and load up extra fuel drums.

The UN air traffic controller did not rise from his seat when the Deputy Minister of Defense walked into the control tower. He handed an approval letter signed by the Minister of Interior to allow flight 8459 to land. After he completed the final checks, the pilot received approval heading, altitude, and speed for descent. The runway lights were switched on. The last and only arriving flight of the day arrived and cleared out before sunset. Brussels Airways had been hesitant to fly at night in and out of Monrovia. In fact, the pilots were so nervous for security that they would not leave the plane. Fears over a potential hijack on the ground resonated in the European pilots' minds as they were used to flying into stable countries.

The Deputy Minister saw the lights from the control tower window. He remained in place until the plane landed and taxied to the opposite end of the airport. Rajik sped the SUV across the flight line. Within moments, the aircraft door flew open and two men gasped for fresh air. Rajik walked close to the cabin door and they could smell the fumes. The rubber hoses must have failed to keep a tight seal. The pilots emerged and were just as dizzy and near nauseous like the two FARC drug runners whose duty was to keep the plane fueled in-flight.

In the high grass, the female Mossad agent watched. Dressed in dark clothes, Francesca easily blended in the background. She skillfully cut and repaired the fence. Several identifiable markers signified the entry point. The night scope rigged on top of the sniper rifle was more than enough she needed to shoot a finger off of a man at three hundred yards and at five hundred yards she could put the specially made, fifty caliber round in the center of a man's chest. Francesca crawled over a hundred yards on her elbows.

The plane did not have any exterior lights, however with the assistance of the specialized night scope Francesca made out each individual. She carefully studied the pilots' faces. She aimed the sniper rifle on Rajik and sighted the scope on his head. As he turned toward her, she read three hundred and eighty yards on the scope. Francesca knew she could make the shot, but not tonight. She moved back to the entry point. After exiting, she repaired the fence. She passed the village called Smell Good But No Taste, which was named during World War II by local villagers who smelled the airmen cooking, but they were not allowed to eat there. She passed the makeshift buildings with tin roofs. No lights appeared as she moved. However, she sensed eyes peered out from the darkness within, and she sped up her pace.

Chapter 7

Russell crawled through the secret passage into the communication room. He felt better, yet he was not one hundred percent. He had lost over ten pounds in the past three days and vowed never to eat roasted snails in pepper sauce ever again. His mind now shifted toward the mission. Over the table, the Marines reviewed the 'bag and tag' plan again and again. Every time, a new point was made and more speculation and conjecture passed on what they would experience.

"We definitely need good ground intel on Sapo," injected Stone. He was a communication specialist, yet he definitely valued the need for raw intelligence.

"Absolutely," Rageone replied.

"What if we send Ike and the Lieutenants on advance reconnaissance?" Rozelli asked as he looked at Russell who did not look well still; however, he and the others knew that they had to defer any operational decisions to him. Even with his sickness, they trusted him. They trusted him to make the important life and death decisions as Russell did so many times in Iraq to keep them safe and bring them home in one piece.

"That would work." Russell considered the option. "Whoever we send would have to go deep cover."

Rozelli looked in the wooden crate of supplies and asked Stone, "Sir, how much surveillance equipment do we have?"

"We have some good gear," Stone opened the crate's lid and lifted out night vision googles. He placed communication headsets on the table. "We will not have secure comms. Everything we discuss will be in the open."

"Who is giving us the go ahead?" chimed Rageone.

"Colonel Jack Crevace." The room acknowledged the name. As part of the first team of Marines who deployed to Iraq in early 2004, Colonel Jack Crevace laid the foundation for a majority of the intelligence, the real intelligence, not the CNN, NSA, or CIA version, on how to seize, capture, and kill as many bad guys in the city of Fallujah. He was the primary architect around the plans to evacuate nearly thirty thousand civilians out of the city safely, but then they decided to hang four American contractors on a bridge in the center of Fallujah and the gloves came off. Without haste, Crevace enacted his plan that was not well liked by many of the senior generals, but in the end he saved as many lives being terrorized by the house-to-house fighting. Inside Fallujah, they were confronted by AK47 assault rifles, yet Crevace pursued his evacuation plan. Crevace had combat credibility. Russell and the others learned a great deal about patience and persistence from Colonel Jack Crevace.

"We will need better ground truth," Rageone replied. The years of experience as a New York City cop and his training as a member of the FBI's elite Counter Espionage Unit started to show.

"Agreed, let's send in a team," Russell directed.

"Captain Stone, should you go?" Rozelli asked. He had always been direct in his thoughts and even more direct in what he said. "You're the only one with the skin color to pull this off."

"No, I don't think that would be wise. Locals would definitely be able to pick me out as a foreigner. And if they suspect me as a Nigerian that will not go well as many of these rebels were shot at by the Nigerians during the civil war." Stone turned toward their leader. "Sir, I would recommend sending the Lieutenants."

"Can these two handle the mission?" Rozelli asked.

"From what I understand all of the officers coming to join the new army are much older and have more experience than what we would find in our military." Russell remembered the description of the vetting process for joining the new Liberian army. "I can ask the Brit if we can send Ike as well." He did not share his concern about Lieutenant Prince Johnson III possibly being related to the thug Prince Johnson II who murdered Samuel Doe. He needed to know for certain who to trust.

Lucy squealed as Ike took the bundle of plantains from her. She had been sneaking in more and more. Ike chased the monkey out of the open-air kitchen. Ike became more and more the lynchpin for all of the camp's operations. His heritage was Mandingo, descendants of ruling elite from the fifteenth century Mali Empire that stretched all over West Africa. As the decline of the empire occurred in the sixteenth century, Mandingos migrated from Mali to Guinea and then Liberia. Mandingos were Muslim and considered by Liberians as people who did not belong in Liberia, even if they lived in Liberia for generations. Ike had lived in the camp for nearly a year and had never felt more at home. The British Colonel had been very kind to him and promoted him to camp manager and his private cook. The other Liberian security guards in the camp feared Ike, not because of his close relation to the British Colonel but from the rumors about him as a ruthless fighter against the RUF rebels.

Russell gave the Gunnys assignments to develop an intelligence collection plan that comprised several dozen questions. He walked out of the communication building along with Stone. "I am feeling better. I need to get out of here." Russell and Stone made the hour and thirty-minute commute to Tubmanberg, which was the rebel headquarters during the civil war. Child soldiers were recruited to fight against Charles Taylor's National Patriotic Front of Liberia (NPFL). Tubmanberg was named after former Liberian president William Tubman who played a major role in modernizing the country. Harriet Tubman, the leader of the Underground Railroad, was a distant relative. Tubmanberg residents were proud of their ancestral ties back to the freedom train leader. Rebels occupied the area until a Nigerian army battalion landed at Roberts International Airport.

"What do you know about the rituals," Russell looked at Stone. "The killings?"

"Bad stuff happens here," Stone said. "You got to remember all of the voodoo stuff you have ever read about in Haiti or Dominican Republic." He paused for a moment and added. "That all started here and was exported." Ritualistic killings and the feeling of power over another living creature have been going on in West Africa for hundreds of years. Back to the early days of Zulu warriors coming to West Africa and inflicting mass murder upon local fishing tribes that it transcended into more ritualistic power struggle against evil. The voodoo and other worship practices of what some view as the darker world started in West Africa and fed its way to the Caribbean with the slave trade. For a long time, the practices continued.

"Is this about religion?" Russell inquired.

"No," Stone contemplated his next comment, "Problems with religion are based on generational hatred, mostly over land. In Nigeria, we have fighting between Christian and Muslim, but it is not a religious fight, as all of the so-called experts believe. There is a report in Lofa County about a Muslim daughter who wanted to convert to Christianity. She was found killed behind a police station. Parents were from both religions but that did not stop ritual killing."

Russell had read several reports on post-civil war economic reconstruction. Signs throughout Monrovia highlighted the point to pay your taxes to help Liberia move forward, yet the locals knew if they paid it went into the pockets of some government official. Wide distrust of the government existed. Taxes were at thirty-five percent and that did not include any bribes or protection needed, sometimes paid to the local police. Street merchants were not taxed, as they remained mobile pushing wheel barrels and carrying goods all over the city. Teachers remained unpaid from the government. Clean water was limited. Hence the immense reliance on foreign aid. The living condition had not improved since the end of hostilities. Household items that in many western countries were called necessities were considered luxury items in Liberia. Just having a clean plastic fork and spoon was progress.

Outside Robertsport in a remote field of casaba, the female Mossad agent crept like a lioness on the prowl. Francesca assumed a solid firing position. The recoil of the rifle against her shoulder was powerful and she grimaced at instant pain. A fifty-caliber projectile had significant force when pushed outside a shortened barrel. The special sniper rifle had a shorter stock for easier concealment, one aspect of a Mossad agent's primary objective. The sound was muffled by the silencer but was still loud enough to scare several large fruit bats overhead into flight. Without thought and with instant reaction, she knelt and withdrew the Desert Eagle pistol from her hip holster. Francesca replaced the six-inch barrel with a ten inch to provide more accuracy. The huge gun weighed over five pounds, yet she handled the gas-operated weapon effectively. She aimed at the two large bats and blew them out of the air as they zigzagged. The huge sound did not bother her as no one was within miles on the several hundred acre deserted palm oil plantation. She resumed her position on the ground behind the sniper rifle. The sticks marked out five hundred yards. The targets were large melons she had purchased on the side of the road. She moved large logs as a backdrop to keep the rounds from ricocheting. The small room concrete building was used for interrogations. It was down a small road that looked nothing like a road. Francesca pressed the gas pedal down hard and accelerated along path. She turned the wheel in the direction of Robertsport. Francesca stripped her fatigues and hung the loose sundress. Boots were replaced with designer sandals.

The small shops in Robertsport were packed with local art, woodcarvings, and decorative trinkets in the hopes of selling to foreigners. Francesca stopped at the regular shop she liked and purchased four necklaces. In case anyone asked about her, the locals would provide an update. She took her sandals off. The afternoon sun radiated heavily upon the beach and hot sand burned her feet as she walked toward the water. The waves crashed heavily on the shore and the water felt delicious on her feet. She walked in the surf and was followed by several young local boys who asked for money for schoolbooks. She received the same story each time about how they need books to write in. By the amount of money she provided, the locals could have purchased an entire library, but she kept up the illusion and was glad to give them money. Under a palm tree she relaxed in the shade and had her zoom camera ready. The waves were nearly four feet and gently rolled to the beach before crashing. The riptide currents were fierce and dangerous and the large rocks closer to the beach were even more dangerous. The beach was crowded with foreigners being pampered by locals. European men showed no disgrace wearing banana boat swim trunks and frolicking in the waves.

Robertsport had optimum surf conditions and the underground international surf community made the pilgrimage to Liberia. Some hoped to tackle the renowned ten-foot waves that erupted during the beginning of the storm season. Storms generated in West Africa formed the catalyst for the hurricanes moving into the Caribbean and America. Amateur surfers dared to attempt the small waves. Along the beach, a short girl from Georgia had a hard time carrying a large surfboard. She did not know how to surf but wanted to attempt the challenge. The waves crashed hard and fast, yet she was able to get out past the break. As she paddled faster into the ocean, she underestimated the riptide running underneath the crashing waves. On her first attempt to ever stand on a surfboard, she fell hard and fast. The toppling waves pushed her head onto the bottom and knocked her unconscious. The riptide pulled her limp body farther out away from the beach. The local teenage boys picked up the surfboard floating to the shore and pointed to the body. Most Liberians could not swim and the thought of trying to save someone in the water scared the hell out of the two teenage boys.

What surprised them was the movement of a large black man to the right of them. They watched the large man trample twenty feet into the surf line and dive into the water. Stone swam violently. For nearly twenty crawl strokes he did not take a breath. He quickly crashed through the first line of waves. He spotted the body and was there within fifty powerful strokes. He could see the light spots of blood on her forehead. From the shore, the crowd grew larger and several NGOs became hysterical. They pointed toward a black man; some surprised as they thought a Liberian saved the girl. The muscular black man drifted with the limp body as he swam sidestroke two hundred yards down the shoreline to veer away from the riptide. Once he believed he was far enough past, he kicked toward the shoreline and towed her limp body. Even though, she was only one hundred and twenty pounds it took every bit of his strength and he pushed his body to the limit. When he could finally stand he picked her up in his arms and ran toward the shore. Lifting his legs, he hurdled into the surf quickly as he did during tackling drills back in Oklahoma University on the football field. Captain Lewis Stone looked down once at this girl and thought she was the most beautiful woman he has ever seen before. Stone handed her over to her friends anxiously waiting on the beach.

Russell walked back with the two cold club beers he went to fetch and surmised the events. Several of the NGOs thanked Stone with big hugs. Under the shade of the palm tree, the battered surfer girl opened her eyes and regained consciousness. The crowd of NGOs around her administered first aid for the cut on her head. The two Marines clinked bottles in salute. Their plan of gaining the trust of the NGOs was moving along faster than either hoped. One guy with a ponytail told them about the bar they frequented in Monrovia called Wave Tops. From a hundred feet away, the female Mossad agent clipped a few dozen photos.

As Stone drove the vehicle back into Monrovia, Russell stared outside the land rover window. Once they were back within Monrovia city limits, Russell saw the extreme difference compared to Robertsport. A little girl no more than six squatted near a drain to relieve her bodily fluids. Men positioned in sewer holes dug out the dirt that had piled up by hand. Teenage boys hustled with anything that could move something: a wheel barrel, a cart, or young hardened backs. Mothers, no more than children themselves, carried little babies draped on their lower back nestled with a cloth wrap. On their heads were goods for sale and in their arms they carried more. Old men and women hobbling with age, yet still functioned, carried, and moved whatever needed to be sold. Wheelchair occupants, if you want to call the contraptions wheelchairs, labored to move along the busy sidewalk. Some contraptions were just pieces of steel and two ties linked together for movement and the occupants considered themselves lucky so they did not have to crawl. Their legs battered or taken during the brutal ravages of the last civil war. And on all of the faces were the daily despair that these occupants of a fourth world country tried to forge out a post-civil war existence. African civil wars became extremely severe and made the legendary Cambodian mass-murderer Pol Pot look like a Sunday school teacher. Liberians survived a deadly cat and mouse game of revenge killings, murder, ritualistic killings, rape, amputations, and all sorts of the worse perceivable human indignity ever casted upon a civilization. Horrifically, the shock wave was not short lived it lasted nearly fourteen years. Pain, anguish, and uncertainty hung like dark fixed clouds on their faces, begging for some semblance of hope for peace and stability.

From the time the two butchers Doe and Taylor occupied the Presidential Palace havoc rained upon the Liberian populace. Samuel Doe was a former disgruntled master sergeant in the AFL and concocted his plan in the troops' barracks. On a quiet night, he walked the five hundred meters up the hill to the Presidential Palace and shot Talbert. The rest of his family, mainly Ministers, were brought down to BTC and lined up along the back wall. There was no last minute pleading allowed as they were instantaneously riddled with automatic weapons fire. A few years later, Doe was shot by thugs who were aligned with Prince Johnson, a notorious murderer and basic scum.

The Cape Hotel was busy with government cars arriving and leaving. Guards dressed in black suits hid weapons underneath. They walked back and forth. Tareek's own security forces were not allowed to carry weapons but had small clubs just in case locals tried to rob a foreigner. Vibrant sounds emitted from the piano bar; well into the night. Locals loitered near the front entrance to hear the music and watched Monrovia high society enter the Cape Hotel. Rajik and Koroma walked together into the bar, and all eyes looked their way. Koroma had not been charged for war crimes, but everyone knew he was responsible for recruiting, training, and ordering child soldiers to kill. Cross-border attacks occurred. Rajik knew Tareek had been watching his every move. Rajik knew that he was not trusted and more than anything hated by the vast majority of the Lebanese families. Ghasson whispered to Uncle Anwar and he motioned for Tareek. The two talked quickly and Tareek departed. Other players, meddlers, and socialites in Monrovia ventured into the bar after a delicious dinner at Cape Hotel's main dining room. Some men wore sport coats and all of the ladies were dressed beautifully. Colonel Chan from the People's Republic of China passed an envelope full of money to Koroma. The Chinese government had been extremely interested in the threats to destabilize the new government and have paid both sides. From across the bar, several Russian mobsters raised a toast. They made a small fortune from illegal logging during the Taylor regime by bribing. Now, they had high hopes to bribe and receive logging concessions at discount prices form the new Liberia government. In the downstairs office, Tareek sat in front of the monitor for an hour and replayed the tapes again and again. Tareek could not make out what they said. Rajik and Koroma knew that everything they said would be recorded so they neither discussed the arriving flight tomorrow nor talked about the arriving prodigy who they believe could be the future of Liberia.

At the Black Beret camp, the Liberian Lieutenants and the Gunnys started early in the morning. They hiked for most of the day. The Gunnys wanted to test the Liberian Lieutenants. They had graduated from Marine officer-training school in Quantico, but the Gunnys had experience with Second Lieutenants in combat. Russell and Stone went out for a long run. The dirt road wound up and down small hills and they ventured deeper into Firestone Plantation. The rubber trees were angled after years of bark stripped to make the drain channel for rubber sap. The rubber trees looked majestic as he saw thousands lined perfectly in crisp rows. They ran uphill and continued on the road back toward the Black Beret camp. Russell had an uneasy feeling that they were being watched. From the deep brush along the hillside, Colonel 'zigzag' Marzah did not move from behind the trees. He was trained well by the US Army Green Berets at Fort Bragg. He could stalk and observe as good as any Green Beret.

Ike helped the Lieutenants inspect their gear as he knew how to operate deep in the jungle and what equipment would be required. The British Colonel told him to be prepared for the unexpected. Rageone and Rozelli spent several hours training Ike and the Lieutenants on the night vision goggles, scopes, weapons, and headsets. Once complete, the equipment was delicately wrapped and placed in old burlap bags once used for potatoes. Lieutenant Forleh was trained by Stone on the satellite radio that could easily reach the Black Beret camp in case of emergency. Russell was concerned and his anxiety showed as he watched the last of the equipment get loaded.

"Ike and the Lieutenants know the significance of the operation." Kitson said as he sensed Russell's uneasiness. He continued, "They will be alright."

"What happens if they are captured?" Russell inquired. "They will most likely be tortured and we will not be able to get to them in time." Silence ensued for a brief moment as both senior officers considered the worst case scenario. Both instinctively knew the brutality that occurred by interrogators who did not respect or observe the Geneva Convention or any thoughts of humanity.

"I told Ike not to be captured alive," Kitson stated. He choked up for a second and continued, "He's very reliable, but you are right we cannot be exposed. We need an alternate plan just in case."

"If they are seen, we can always pull them back and I can lead the Marines in." Russell contemplated a backup situation.

"We can't afford to lose you."

"Why, what do you know?"

"General Canteberry informed me at all costs you and your men are not to be seen." Kitson was very direct. "You must remain invisible. Our mission here is only known close hold."

"Do you think the Deputy Minister will give us up?"

"No, he wants a better Liberia." Kitson thought for a moment and added. "We can count on him to be on our side in the end." Kitson had a MI6 report that the Deputy Minister was being blackmailed.

At the Marshall compound, the morning sun provided a magnificent brightness to the river. The two Colombians who arrived on the flight from Bogota in the middle of the night liked the compound. However, the Argentine pilots were not pleased. After flying for more than thirteen hours continuously, they had to endure the toxic fumes from dripping fuel lines. Both pilots agreed the compensation package of twenty thousand cash for each trip was not enough, especially as they would start moving large packages of white powder treasure. Once large shipments of cocaine became involved, experience told them the risk level significantly increased. The pilots walked out onto the floating deck to see what the Colombians were so excited about. After they saw them laughing at the fishermen trying to paddle toward the jumping fish, they went back inside to rest more out of the heat. The return flight started in the middle of the night. They needed a lot more rest for the thirteen-hour return trip. To block out light, the pilots put blankets over the windows.

Chapter 8

At the BTC compound, the blades of grass sparkled in the morning dew as the sun radiated the grass. The line of nearly twenty young boys walked forward. Each one carried and swung a machete curved at the end for grass cutting. The Deputy Minister of Defense noticed their perfect struck form, almost as if they had rehearsed their swing all of their young lives. With the left arm brought behind each of their backs and giant wide arm movements along the course of grass, the young boys mowed the Minister's lawn. The grass had jettisoned long spouts out of the ground based upon the heavily fortified nutrients and tremendous rainfall. He laughed to himself that it took three days to cut the entire lawn, and the boys would be back at the beginning next week. The new lawnmower rested on the edge of the compound just near the tin shed. It was unable to make the final last thirty feet to the shed. The mower died from engine seizure due to lack of oil. No one bothered to push the dead mower out of the way under the tin shed.

Every time the Deputy Minister passed the deceased lawnmower, he laughed as this showed everything that was all wrong about Liberia. Someone within the Ministry was too cheap to maintain the lawn mower or they stole the money. The flock of local boys descended on the lawn making two US dollars a day and worked as hard as anyone could. The heat began to rise again and it was only nine in the morning. The boys sweated profusely, yet they did not require water breaks like most foreigners who devoured bottles of water each day. Liberians were conditioned to survive with less. In front of the main review stand, the team cut away the dense weeds. The adjacent bricks were marred by the machete's steel against the stone. The red, white, and blue painted bricks accented the Liberian flag, which rested above on the fifty-foot flag pool. No breeze moved and the heat decimated them, yet the young boys keep swinging. The Deputy Minister looked at the crumpled note. He did not know where to turn to. His father's picture rested squarely centered on his desk. He looked closely at his father's young face, a man with a large smile and a face filled with hope and vision. He remembered the promise he made to his mother to honor his dead father. The Deputy Minister knew he would not ask any of the

Liberian Police for assistance. He did not know how far the corruption ran; maybe others within the new government were blackmailed. He wondered how Rajik attained access to the flight line and was able to park a plane on the tarmac for days. His only option was to find the British colonel he had met last month.

Tareek greeted the four Americans as they walked into the Cape Hotel restaurant. As with all of the new arrivals to his hotel, Tareek took considerable interest in these four men. Several wore goatees, yet he knew instinctively by the look in their eyes that these men were military. Tareek motioned to Chad who slumbered over.

"Chad will serve you," Tareek said. Chad was another relative of Uncle Anwar. Chad was very incompetent. Regularly, Tareek yelled at Chad and pointed a finger in his chest that was filled with blubber and very little muscle. Even the Liberian staff laughed at Chad in his face. Regardless, Chad thought himself a lady's man and continually sexually harassed the female staff, which were all Liberian.

"What can I please you with?" Chad asked the Marines in his normal swirly voice. Rozelli looked at him and almost asked him if he was gay but held back. The four laughed as Chad departed to get some beers. Chad refused to return to bring drinks and ordered a waitress. The waitress was very good looking and was not pleased when Chad rubbed his hand on her backside as he directed her.

"What is your name?" Rozelli asked.

"Feeatu. My name is Feeatu." She smiled at them all. For a thirty-five-year-old woman with three boys who were now teenagers, Feeatu looked very fit. Liberia women never showed their age as most were forced to walk, carry, and work harder than men. Strenuous physical labor was the norm for many Liberian women.

"Where are you from?"

"My family is from Nimba County. I'm from there." She spoke relatively good English. The Cape Hotel had a mandatory language class for its workers to help them sound more American.

After a few moments, Tareek came back, pulled over a chair, sat down, and placed a piece of paper that had a headline labeled, '*Alphabet Soup*' in front of Russell. Underneath the headline was a list of international aid organizations: UNHCR, UNFPA, UNPCA, UNDP, UNICEF, WFP, CARE, USAID.

"I really do not know what they want to accomplish in Liberia." Tareek asked. "Do you?"

"We don't work with any of these organizations." Russell abruptly replied.

"Why are you here?"

"For the surf, we heard that there is great surfing here," Rageone said. He was able to grow more hair than all of them, especially as he came right from undercover work off the New York streets and did not have a military style trim. He put some greasy gel in his hair that was the scene on New Jersey beaches to make him look more bizarre. The dinner was good and again Stone stacked up his plate with Liberian pepper sauce. Stone taunted the others, yet no one took him up. Chad passed by and gave a slight laugh as he witnessed the Americans pass on the hot pepper. As they gave him a hard look, he slithered away. From across the room, Tareek listened to the conversation from the earpiece that received a signal from the microphone concealed in the candle. The conversation remained light and they did not discuss the upcoming mission. Tareek would not get any information from them today.

Francesca showed no emotion. Mossad training taught her to be cold. She walked pass the table of Americans toward the rear table in the corner. She placed her back against the wall and made contact with one of them. She could tell they were not the typical community activists or volunteers who came to Liberia. She suspected them to be US Special Forces and took several indiscrete photos. She was intrigued by them.

After dinner, the four Americans drove to the highest point in Monrovia. The wind blew fast and steady across the peninsula up from the port authority toward the Dukor Hotel rising on top of Monrovia. The 757 Brussels Airlines jet screeched overhead and descended toward Roberts International Airport. Russell looked at his watch and remarked out loud, "The plane is two hours late." He wondered what bundle of NGOs, contractors, and consultants would emerge from the plane to add to the chaos. Russell looked at the concrete poles at the former roof bar that long ago served Monrovia's elite before the first civil war. They needed to practice rappelling and the high walls isolated from view appeared adequate. Russell used the vision scope and looked at a vibrant bar on top of a nearby roof.

Wave Tops bar was set up as a refuge for the foreign surfer community and word quickly spread among all of the non-natives of the party spot. Bamboo logs covered the tin metal roof. A large crowd watched the majestic sunset. After the Marines walked up the five floors to the top of the building, they received a lot of attention entering Wave Tops - just as all new arrivals did. The Gunnys went right to the bar and ordered shots. Russell hoped the Gunnys would not create a scene or cause too much damage. Drunken driving rules were non-existent. Many foreigners staggered to their vehicles with black license plates and loaded into them. The black license plates signified diplomatic status. Stone carried his beer toward the balcony overlooking the crashing waves against the beach. He saw the short blonde girl walk away from the crowd of NGOs. She walked directly toward Stone with a purpose. The last time he saw her was on the beach after she nearly drowned.

"Do you know who I am?" she asked.

"I do," Stone said and thought to himself that he would never forget her face. "How did you know it was me?"

"My friend over there." She pointed and looked back at Stone. "She was there. I don't remember much of it."

"I guess you wouldn't. It must have been a bad hit," Stone paused for a moment and asked in a sincere voice, "Are you alright?"

"I'm ok." She stopped for a moment and looked closely at his deep brown eyes. "Can I ask you a question?"

"Sure."

"Are you Nigerian?"

"I am, but I am also American." Stone paused for a moment and asked. "How could you tell?"

"I work for the Peace Corps and spent two weeks at a conference last month in Lagos with a lot of aid workers. They were very dull."

"Sorry, I wasn't there."

"No that's not what I meant, stupid me. I'm just nervous."

"Why, why should you be nervous?"

"Talking to you. The story my friend told about this muscular man jumping into the waves to save me."

"What, was she surprised a black man could swim so well?"

"No, no, absolutely no. She was just so impressed. I, however, was unconscious and did not get to see your rescue." She smiled at Stone and touched his arm. Her tiny hand could barely cover his bicep, as she had to reach up. "Where did you learn how to swim so well?"

"I was raised in Oklahoma and learned to swim in my family's pool."

Russell came over when he spotted the conversation.

"Hi, are you going to introduce me?"

"Sorry, I don't know your name." Stone turned toward this short beautiful blonde.

"Britney, my name is Britney."

Stone smiled. He thought she looked as cute as a Barbie doll. "I'm Lewis Stone."

"I'm Tom Russell." She shook hands with both of them and continued to smile widely. Russell made a few jokes about the terrible heat, driving in Monrovia, and the food.

"So who are these guys?" asked her sister.

"Just friends."

"Friends of my baby sister must be approved by me."

"He saved me." Britney pointed to Stone.

"Thank you. I cannot be around all the time to protect and watch over her. My father had been very concerned with her Peace Corps phase but I convinced him that I had the situation under control here in Monrovia and would keep her safe."

"Really, so you are taking care of all of the thugs around here." Russell jumped at the opportunity as he could already tell he would not like this woman.

"We fight violence with peace and economic development."

"Spoken like a true NGO." Russell left off the nickname he gave to the NGOs like her as that was extremely impolite. She responded and he heard her talk, yet he did not care. Russell saw that his Captain was embarrassed by the argumentative discussion. Russell excused himself and met the Gunnys at the bar and shared a shot of Russian vodka. They were already on the fifth shot. Stone returned after he obtained a phone number for his little friend and drove the drunks back to Firestone Plantation.

The man who sat in first class on the Brussels flight that arrived into Monrovia from Kinshasa, Democratic Republic of Congo via Lagos did not want his true identity known. The name on his passport was not his. He wore a dread lock wig and baseball hat. He shaved his staple beard. He purposely went out of his way to alter his appearance. He was pleased no one recognized him. With his first-class ticket, the man passed quickly through Kinshasa security without anyone second-guessing his true identity. First class travelers were treated like royalty and did not receive the same level of scrutiny as coach passengers. Neither the security personnel nor anyone with the airline dared to disrupt a first-class passenger. It was a completely different mindset than Western or European security protocol. The traveler was equally pleased with his Liberian customs clearance. Along with the other first-class passengers, he unloaded the aircraft immediately and went to a special holding area where passports were stamped and he enjoyed a cocktail. As he got to the baggage carousel to retrieve his bags, he was not happy that he had to wait alongside locals who smelled. The baggage claim area was crowded with local men helping to grab bags for the arriving NGOs. No family members or others waiting for the arriving guests were allowed inside the terminal building. These men worked and sweated hard for a few dollars. Their smell irritated the man. He plugged his nose with cotton balls. As he walked outside, he removed the cotton and cleared his nostrils of snot right onto the floor. An older woman pushed past him, dropped to the ground, and kissed the cement. She did not care about the snot he just fired out of his nostril or the heat resonating off of the pavement nor did she care about the dirt. The taste of her native land drove an immense feeling of joy throughout her sixty year old body, another victim driven away by the civil war.

Koroma had spotted his contact immediately, not by his looks, but by the red velvet jacket he wore over his right shoulder as a prearranged signal. They climbed in the back seat of the first large black SUV and loaded the five large suitcases in the second vehicle. The tinted windows were refreshing to him as he looked out. He did not want anyone seeing him, especially the poor beggars who pressed up against the vehicles attempting to depart the airport. He despised them and if the date were three years ago he would have had them killed.

Koroma spoke to the driver and directed him toward Monrovia. The driver sped the vehicle at a blistering pace. Across from Coconut Grove Resort, the vehicles stopped at a metal gate. The horn sounded several times before a guard sloppily walked to the driver's window to inquire what they wanted. He looked in several times and did not give the appearance he really cared about his job. His shirt was pushed out of his pants and he looked like he was sleeping on duty. The new arrival mumbled how he would have had the guard killed if he caught him sleeping on duty. Then he thought maybe he would kill the guard anyways. The vehicles pulled into the Taylor compound and Charles McArthur Emmanuel Taylor, a.k.a. Chucky, was happy he was home.

Rajik had staged twenty of his private security guards at the Taylor compound with automatic weapons, something not seen in Liberia for the past five years since the UN moved in, yet Rajik knew he needed to show a sizable force to make Chucky feel secure. When Chucky walked into the room, Rajik rose and greeted him. The former commander of one the most ferocious group of murderers on the continent of Africa was very pleased to see all of the weapons. Charles Emmanuel was named after his father Charles Taylor. He earned his nickname Chucky as a brutal murderer similar to the Hollywood maniac toy killer that came to life. He held the same middle name of his father and like his father, Chucky thought of himself as a future general of Liberia. Chucky was raised in America, yet President Charles Taylor was more than happy to let his son take command of the Anti-Terrorism Unit (ATU), which were known as 'Demon Forces'.

The Taylor compound was directly across the street from the Coconut Grove Resort. Thick walls made from concrete blocked the view from the street. Rusted barbed wire draped over the top dissuaded intruders. A large steel door twenty feet long by ten feet high served as the only entry and exit point. His stepmother and Charles Taylor's present wife moved out of the country over a year ago. She was last seen in Paris living the high life as she sought divorce from Charles as he sat in exile. Koroma got the approval from Charles Taylor to move in and set up operations. Taylor waited in exile for word from General Abbdas that his rebel army gained strength. Koroma wondered if his former friend was insane enough to attack the UN or did he just want to bargain for power. Koroma wanted to negotiate land in northeast Liberia along the Sierra Leone and Guinea border. If they partnered together and scared the hell out of the UN, perhaps they could broker an agreement. He learned in the past four years since he was kicked out of Sierra Leone that any negotiation was possible, especially with the UN. The British were less willing to deal with him. Koroma feared charges in the international court for war crimes. He believed the British led the charge to indict him for what he did in Sierra Leone.

"What is the latest word?" Koroma asked. He poured two glasses to the rim with aged scotch. Chucky was pleased to see his father's library had not changed. Mahogany walls and large bookcases made the room appear very pleasing to his eyes. The twenty-foot high fireplace made out of stones remained untouched since his father was forced out of power. Chucky sat behind his father's English oak desk. It was over a hundred years old. In a London antique shop, his father paid sixty-five thousand dollars for it, all in cash. He recalled how strong his father felt about having a beautiful desk to feel respected and revered as an intellect.

"The enemies of my father are plotting against him. They are trying to extradite him."

"But the agreement said he could live in Nigeria. He should be able to stay in exile."

"The bastards in The Hague want to charge my father with training child soldiers in Sierra Leone. The Americans are gathering evidence and we must stop them." Chucky had another large scotch. Koroma could tell that he was already intoxicated. Chucky continued, "Here is where civilization began. Here is where Black Power can come back to rule Africa. We do not need westerners here to rule Africa."

"The man who is weak here will be a slave." Koroma responded

"Power must be taken." Chucky added. "We will take back Liberia and rule West Africa with an iron fist." He looked at a map on the table and drew circles around villages that he believed would support his father's triumphant return to power.

Chucky made sure no one saw him enter his father's master bathroom where he opened the safe under the hidden board within the sink. From the black canvas bag, he pulled out three stacks of one hundred dollar US bills. Each stack was five inches think. He walked back into the library and handed them to Koroma.

"Here's one hundred and fifty thousand." Chucky said. Koroma looked at the bills and rubbed his fingers through the first dozen bills and looked up. "Yes, you will need to launder them." Chucky added. Counterfeit US bills had been circulated throughout West Africa and every Lebanese storeowner in Monrovia was extremely suspicious of locals passing off crisp bills.

"I will have Rajik launder the money through the casino." Koroma said and left. Chucky counted how much counterfeit money remained in the black bag and he checked the private ledger. Chucky made sure he had access to his father's bank accounts in Switzerland before leaving Kinshasa.

The British Colonel received the call late in the evening. He gained his senses as he spoke with the Deputy Minister. Within a minute he was dressed and banged on Russell's door.

"I need your help with the Deputy Minister of Defense."

"Is it the Lieutenants?" Russell asked as he tried to wake up.

"No, Minister Urey just called me. There is a large shipment of cocaine flying into Liberia in a few days. Somehow he is caught up and needs our help."

"Why can't he go to the Liberian police or the UN?"

"It's complicated. We will need Captain Stone as well"

"Ok, let me get him." Russell did not even consider to attempt and awake the Gunnys. He knew each slept with a gun underneath his bed, and they were still plenty drunk enough to take a shot at him.

Ike drove the IMATT vehicle. He was visibly nervous as the British Colonel rarely ventured out at night, unless it was an emergency. Across the street from the BTC compound, Ike stopped the vehicle and reached underneath the seat for the two feet long machete. The dull sound of the blade coming out of the leather sheathe caught everyone's attention. Ike did not say a word. There was something in his movement that made Russell and Stone believe Ike knew how to handle himself in a difficult situation.

"Ike will go with you." The British Colonel turned to Stone.

"Understood." Stone replied. Both Kitson and Russell knew the importance of white people staying off Monrovia streets at night. As Ike and Stone departed the vehicle, and the British Colonel passed Russell a snub-nosed machinegun.

Stone went into the building. The sound was cacophonic. The vibrations of the music rattled the old brick. The windows were vacant from the church. Arcane voices shouted in no apparent rhythm violated the night. Screams of joy and harrowing voices amplified with stacks of speakers boxes. A hard line was wired to the power pole down the street to power the music system. No electric lights emerged from the windowless church, yet several hundred illuminated candles tossed shadows against the brick. A crowd of over two hundred packed into an area the size of a basketball court. A white face would have wrongly stood out in darkened crowd. An outsider would warrant unwanted curiosity and more than likely a knife into the side. Stone found the Deputy Minister in the corner. He was the only one wearing a business suit as he came right from work to the all night revival at the church. The Deputy Minister pointed toward the back door for them to talk outside, away from the blasting noise.

"There's a plane arriving from Bogota tomorrow night." The Deputy Minister shouted as he could not hear his own voice as his ear drums were nearly shattered from the blistering noise.

"Why are you telling us?" Stone inquired.

"The Colonel said you could help." The Deputy Minister abruptly stopped and looked around. He took a deep breath and talked softly. "They are blackmailing me."

"Who is blackmailing you?"

"The Lebanese."

"Who? Be specific."

"Rajik, the manager at the casino. He has hired thugs and they are brutal."

"Do you know the time?"

"Not yet." The Minister replied. "Rajik will inform me one hour ahead of time." The Deputy Minister was visibly disturbed. He had never served in the military for any country and took the job as a means to get back to Liberia in hopes of finding the truth about his father. The best way he thought of finding out about his father was becoming a member of the newly formed Liberian government. He would get access to files on the massacre that occurred at Robertsport. He needed to know what happed to his father, but somehow he was tricked by his large poker losses to become Rajik's puppet. He wiped his forehead with a cloth, sweat poured, and his breath picked up more. "What if they have guns?"

"We can take care of that." Stone spoke as he leaned in closer. "We got your back."

Several patrons of the all night revival came out for air and then ventured back into the loud darkened chaos. In the moonlight, Stone could tell the Deputy Minister was visibly disturbed. Ike did not speak a word but he could tell as well. Ike had witnessed more than enough death from war and could readily identify a man who had never been tested. After several more moments and discussion on the type of plane, how many men, the amount of cocaine, they broke up the meeting. Before departing, Stone put his large hand on the Deputy Minister's shoulder to reassure him that nothing would happen to him.

On the way back to Firestone Plantation, Stone relayed the meeting and added. "I sensed his fear."

"There is an old African proverb my father told me when I was a boy living in Kenya." Kitson thought of his father, a brilliant man who stopped the fighting during the Mau Mau rebellion. Kitson thought of the quote and spoke in a deliberate manner. "The meat that has fat will prove it by the heat of fire."

"Meaning what?" Russell inquired.

"One can only be tested in true combat." Kitson replied.

"The Deputy Minister told me how much he loved Liberia." Stone said. "He apologized to me for his mistakes."

"But we can correct them." Kitson said. "We can leverage him to take out a terrorist cell."

Across from the casino in the dilapidated Taylor compound, Chucky felt secure with the stack of weapons against the wall and grenades on the table. He sat on the couch and sloshed the scotch bottle toward his mouth and missed.

"Get me the guard at the entrance gate." Chucky shouted. Chucky's eyes were wide open, and he had a primeval look on his face. Chucky pulled a machete out of its sheath. "You think you can sleep on watch, not in my home." Chucky looked at the other guards and directed. "Hold him down." The guard squirmed and pulled away from the other two guards. "Hold him down." The guards knew he was serious as Chucky lifted the machete and swung it. The razor sharp blade struck the guard on the shoulder. Again he lifted the machete over his head and swung it downward. Chucky staggered from his intoxication. Again he missed the neck and struck the man's back. Chucky screamed foul words. "Hold him down." Chucky pulled the man's short hair. He could not get a good grip on his head and punched as he became more disgusted. He held the machete closer to the man's neck and took a smaller swing that struck the man's neck. The strike did not hurt the man, yet it drew blood. Chuck leaned back and fell on the floor laughing. He laughed for over a minute.

"You see," Chucky screamed. "I can cut you." Chucky's eyes flared open wide. Fear overcame the guard and he pleaded repeatedly for his life. Chucky laughed louder. After he sipped more scotch he stopped. "Hold him very tight." Chucky swung wildly and connected on the neck. Chucky fell over from the momentum onto the floor. Two feet away, Chucky looked into the eyes of the severed head that rolled.

CHAPTER 9

Ike drove the Liberian Lieutenants toward Sapo National Forest. The beat up truck rambled onward as volumes of smoke emitted from the exhaust pipes. The engine burned a tremendous amount of oil. Before they departed, Ike filled the engine with two quarts of oil; however he stopped three times to refill. They did not travel at night, as the headlights did not work. They motored toward Greenville, a small fishing village. By an inlet, the port had improved significantly. In the past several years, commerce had increased. Barges hauled goods from Monrovia because the roads in between were in such disrepair. The only road that connected Liberia zigzagged through the remote country and was dangerous. Ike parked the truck outside the city and they started to walk. The roads were also filled with locals walking, as few owned vehicles. Women carried overloaded baskets and jugs of water on their heads as they walked. Their pace unaffected by the juggling act. Motorcycles zipped past with three or four passengers jammed on back. Several white SUVs with UN logos passed. Trucks filled with illegally cut logs headed toward the port. Ike and the Lieutenants walked briskly for eight hours on the side of the single lane road. They arrived at Sapo National Forest main entrance by nightfall.

Within Monrovia, Russell wanted to research more about the last civil war. As their vehicle approached the Vamoma House along the famed Tubman Boulevard, Russell told Rozelli to pull over. Russell had read a dozen reports of the last days of the Taylor regime. The brutality was epic. The Vamoma House's location was the final line of defense for the protection of Monrovia. Rebels advanced fast and were barely held in place along the defensive line. Charles Taylor hid in the Presidential Palace while his depleted army dug in around this area. Taylor dined on fine meals and drank excessive amounts of his best wine as he cleared out the wine cellar. His troops had not been paid for nearly a year, yet they stood their ground against the advancing rebel army. In the closing days of the civil war, the rebels prepared for one last push toward Monrovia. Across the front line, child soldiers arrived along with 106-millimeter cannons jerry-rigged on top of trucks.

Russell recalled one report that stated Colonel Marzah had called the Presidential Palace and Charles Taylor would not take his call. Near midnight and under a perfect moon, Marzah informed his men that they would withdraw within the hour. Families in the area heard the withdrawal notice and lined up outside of the colonel's tent. Marzah told the troops to only take their weapons and ammunition, yet some tried to take more. A few were captured by the advancing rebels. The rear guard of ten soldiers were captured and never heard for again.

The entire area was saturated with rebels and Colonel Marzah chose a different route along the coast. Under a clear night, Marzah led over two thousand Liberians on what became known as the 'Great Retreat' down the beach. The column of troops extended for half a mile as they marched the twelve miles down the beach toward the BTC compound. By morning light, the final elements passed below the Presidential Palace and entered the large green gate where former President Doe executed a dozen members of the Tolbert family.

Across the brick face of the Vamoma House, the Marines placed their fingers into the large bullet holes. Russell knew these holes were made by large caliber machineguns. The RPG rocket holes were the size of his fist. Ricochets from smaller caliber AK47s were all over the walls. They climbed the staircase and looked toward the rear of the property. A new clothing factory was recently founded, a significant sign that Liberian women would not put up with abuse anymore. Russell made a mental note to see what NGO organization helped set this up and wanted to donate money.

Not far away at the Taylor compound, Chucky Taylor slapped the young lady across the face. She said something Rajik could not hear and evidently, Chucky did not like it. He hit her so hard that the force knocked her out of the chair. One of Rajik's hired local thugs already had her by the hair and dragged her toward the back door. Rajik brought over several more young girls to entertain Chucky. He wondered if Chucky was gay as kept beating the women he brought instead of playing with them. Rajik knew Chucky had a bad temper when he was drunk. As Rajik walked across the room, he saw the dried pool of blood on the floor and wondered what happened.

"Shipment's on schedule." Koroma said after he made sure that they were alone.

"Good, very good." Chucky said. "The cocaine can go to America and poison them." He paused for a moment and added "We will make nice money from the Colombians."

"Have you talked to General Abbdas lately?"

"General Abbdas has prepared the troops well." Chucky said as a matter of fact. Chucky had no idea how to train an army, especially an insurgency, yet he knew if the general gave his ragtag group of former soldiers alcohol, food, drugs, and bush wives that they would remain content in exile. "The plan is ready. Once the rainy season starts, we will make our move." Chucky thought for a moment. "When my father is ready to come back to power, we will have to move fast."

"Does your father know if any of the new Ministers will support him?" Koroma inquired. He did not want to be on the losing team again. Koroma barely escaped capture and imprisonment in Sierra Leone for crimes against humanity.

"They don't matter." Chucky shout back. "They are all new Congo people. They are more American than Liberian. When the shots start being fired, they will be on the first plane out of here."

"How will we get weapons?"

"Easy," Chucky replied. "We have made strong contacts with Hezbollah. Rajik can smuggle machine guns, rockets, and even a tank if we need it. My new helicopter will arrive soon on a container ship."

"The weapons are fine, but we need to take the fight to the UN and scare them out of here."

"I've thought of that." Chucky poured a stiff drink. "We need to make another Somalia." He tossed an old newspaper to Koromo and added. "Dead white bodies dragged through the street will scare the UN away. I know how Americans think and they are weak."

"How will we plan these attacks?"

"Al-Qaeda has mastered roadside bombs and we can have them train our men. There are piles of bombs all over that we can use. We will start war in the city streets right in front of the foreigners and the cameras." Chucky poured another scotch.

In Sapo National Forest, General Abbdas held the pistol against Sumarka's head. He wanted to pull the trigger but instead pistol slapped her hard enough to send her over the table. The baby tied behind her back screamed as she landed on the floor. Sumarka did not expect the hit alongside her head and landed partially on her baby. She untied the baby and ran off the porch. The general and his men laughed.

"The men are restless." His deputy said. "They want to kill." His deputy had served as a major in the infamous Black Berets and led multiple death squads over the years.

"Patience," General Abbdas said and he repeated himself. "Patience." He sipped a warm beer and added. "Soon we will attack." His officers warned him repeatedly that the men were restless. Abbdas worried his men were getting soft as they carved an existence in exile. Bars, restaurants, and the most important brothels existed under the jungle canopy. Bush wives had been taken, sold, and even traded. General Abbdas knew many of his men were HIV positive as no NGO came to Sapo to bring them condoms.

"How much gold do we have?" Abbdas asked.

"Over ten pounds." His deputy replied. "And we have plenty of diamonds."

"Koroma and our friends in Sierra Leone have kept us supplied well." Gold was abundant in Sapo along the ancient dried riverbed. The work was hard and anyone who came to sift for gold paid security to the rebels. The general was equally pleased with the flow of blood diamonds from the Kono district where the RUF kept small, secret work camps open. The general provided the slave labor from the children he captured during village raids. Anyone who ventured into Sapo searching for gold and did not pay protection found themselves heading toward the blood diamond camps in Sierra Leone. In Sapo, human life mattered little but gems and gold – they mattered greatly.

The date was 10 February. Russell looked at his watch. The two-year Iskandariyah anniversary shocked his senses. Every day, he pondered why he was still alive. The bomb that detonated the Iskandariyah police station ignited seconds before his armored vehicle turned the corner. He saw the fireball ride up the street and singe buildings. The burned smell of body parts blasted his senses, and he remembered the horrible scent as if it was yesterday. Russell wanted a drink, yet held off in preparation for the mission. He sat on the porch. The tin on the roof started to ruffle as gusts of wind penetrated Firestone Plantation, a prelude to what would follow during the rainy season. The breezes were steady at thirty knots and gusts come in that were at least twice as powerful. Several tin sheets ripped open and partially dislodged, and banged like a snare drum. The wind howled through buildings added to the weather orchestra. The change in weather came fast. He looked out over the camp. He thought back to Long Island summer and his former fiancé. When he came back from Iraq, he was uneasy. In Manhattan, Kristin joined him for lunch, perhaps she hoped they would get back together. Across the table, he could see the lingerie straps that lingered underneath her outfit. She had something on her mind and he was willing; however as they walked down 48th Street, a crane accidently dropped a twenty foot container over a dozen feet to the ground. The deafening sound forced him to take action. From his constant exposure to indirect fire, roadside bombs, and the Iskandariyah explosion, Russell's senses were on high alert. With brutal force, he tossed Kristin to the ground and covered her with his body. She screamed, yet Russell would not move until his mind brought him out of Iraq. The look on her face ended any thought of a romantic interlude. That was the last time he saw or spoke to his former fiancé.

"Weather changes here fast," Kitson said as he walked onto the porch. "When the rainy season comes, it gets ugly." Russell recalled how Liberia was the second wettest place on the planet. One weather forecast had projected twenty-two feet of rain would fall in a five-month period.

"How will that affect the Sapo mission?"

"It should be in our favor." Kitson said. "Liberians do not like bad weather."

"Will Ike and the Lieutenants be able to function?"

"Ike will. He is a seasoned warrior. The Lieutenants should do fine." Kitson raised his voice as a matter of fact. "They were trained in Quantico." Russell nodded agreement. 'Time Between Saturdays' or 'The Big Suck' have been common words associated with TBS, or as Marine officials call The Basic School, a six month program that tests physical and mental endurance of all new Marine Second Lieutenants. Unlike the other military services, all Marine officers are required to attend, endure, and prevail. Foreign officers got very few breaks and must be as hard as their American counterparts. Russell was pleased to have two Liberian officers who attended TBS, yet he did not know how they would act in combat situations.

The 727 Gulfstream jet started its final descent into Roberts International Airport. Two Colombians worked the jerry-rigged fuel lines in the back of the plane. One Colombian sat in the cockpit and rested a submachine gun across his lap pointed at the pilots. The Argentine pilots were pleased after returning from the last trip and the FARC would not tolerate any disgruntled employees so they placed an additional shooter onboard. The pile of cocaine reached the top of the airplane cabin's ceiling. The two Colombians in the rear of the plane were not permitted use of the laboratory at the front of the cabin. They were provided a bucket for the thirteen-hour flight. The smell was excruciating and they smoked cigars to combat the stench. The fuel drums rested next to them.

The Deputy Minister stood in the control tower and watched the UN air traffic controller. No flights came in the middle of the night and only one air traffic controller was required. The Deputy Minister handed over the thick envelope. Final approach was approved over the radio. From the flight line, Rajik, Chad, and Koroma watched pitch black skyline.

"What time will they arrive?" Koroma asked.

"Soon," Rajik replied. "Very soon." He handed Koroma a 45-caliber pistol. Everyone knew Koroma was responsible for directing hundreds of deaths in Sierra Leone and he was charged in international court for crimes against humanity.

"We can make good money from the Colombians." Koroma said. He was impressed with his plan to coordinate with the FARC and recruit Rajik to manipulate one of the new Ministers. Koroma needed money. He did not have the resources like the Taylor family. Koroma trusted Rajik, yet he would not trust any of Rajik's henchmen to provide security. The less people who knew would be best. The FARC promised three hundred thousand dollars would be delivered in cash after each flight. Koroma was pleased with the planning.

The Deputy Minister checked his microphone by speaking slowly and he heard the reply in his earpiece. Kitson sat in the back of the vehicle and worked the recording device. The Deputy Minister walked out of the terminal building toward the runway. Lights faded from the building, yet he saw the black SUV parked on the flight line.

"Where's Rajik?"

"He's not here."

"But I only deal with Rajik.'

"You will deal with me. I call the shots," replied Koroma as he looked down at the pistol exposed from his waistband.

"I do not want trouble." The Deputy Minister was scared. He trembled. Koroma sensed his fear and felt in control. Koroma rested a hand on the pistol.

Russell watched closely in the night vision scope. "Hold all shots," Russell spoke softly in the headset, "watch for more contacts." Two teams were split on both sides of the runway less than one hundred yards from the terminal. Rajik and Chad walked along the grass far away from any of the lights. In their mind, they were far out of sight from the Deputy Minister in case he tried something, but they did not count on the night vision scopes that followed their movements. "Two on the right, fifty meters." Rozelli spoke softly in the headset. The rest of the team did not respond, per protocol. If the threat was not identified, anyone of the shooters would have spoken.

The 727's final approach was fast and the plane landed quickly. The jet barely slowed to a stop when one of the pilots opened the door. The pilots wanted to get out of the plane, as they were very concerned about the submachine gun pointed at their backs. Koroma turned the black SUV's headlights on. Within a minute, the jet turned toward the vehicle. Koroma watched the plane lunge forward and abruptly stop.

"How much are you carrying?" Koroma shouted to the pilots as they emerged from the airplane.

"Four thousand kilos." The pilot looked back at the piles of neatly wrapped cocaine stacked in bundles. "It is very heavy."

"Do you have my money?" Koroma asked. The Columbian looked around and went back inside the plane. After a long moment, he handed Koroma a large black bag.

Russell felt adrenaline penetrate his veins, excitement not felt since Iraq. "Team one has the plane. Team two has new threat." Russell tapped Rozelli on the back and they moved toward the airplane. The sniper rifles with silencers were stretched forward in the ready fire position. Each held the night vision scope on the sights close to their eyes. They moved deliberately.

"New threat unknown." Stone said in the headset.

"Roger, take two loud shots toward the grass on my mark." Russell spoke as he moved forward closer. Loud shots meant to remove the silences. In another twenty feet, Russell and Rozelli would be in view. "Three, two, one, fire." Simultaneously, two high-powered sniper rifles erupted and penetrated within several feet of Rajik and Chad that sent dirt all over them. The sound caught Koroma off guard and he turned backward in the direction of the sounded. He stumbled and fell.

"Drop your weapons," Rozelli shouted as he approached the aircraft at a fast rate. He yelled, "On the ground." Rozelli repeated the command several more times, "On the ground. On the ground."

"Move, move, move." Russell shouted as he placed the barrel of the rifle into Koroma's chest. Koroma complied with the instructions and dropped his gun. The two pilots started to run and Rozelli placed two well-placed shots into their lower legs. Russell turned toward the shots and did not see the other Colombian emerge with the submachine gun. As he turned, he caught a flash out of his right eye and felt the warmth of fresh blood land on his skin as the Colombian's head exploded from the direct shot.

The female Mossad agent had become very proficient at the fifty-caliber sniper rifle, which was extremely powerful. Francesca looked into her scope again to make sure no one saw the location of the shot and her position. The Marines were orientated forward toward the flight line and did not expect a sniper from the opposite side of the runway.

"Shot fired, far side," Russell screamed in his headset. Riflescopes scanned the perimeter and nothing was spotted. Stone and Rageone held their position, as they did not know what the threat was.

For a moment, Russell thought that perhaps it was a missed shot aimed at him.

"CS grenade!" shouted Russell as he tossed the canister that contained CS gas into the plane's cabin. The sound and smoke filled the air. Spanish screams resounded from inside. As the two other Colombians climbed over the piles of cocaine and emerged from the airplane, Russell had them in his sight and was posed to fire, but he held back. He grabbed each one as they emerged and tossed them to the ground. Rozelli had handcuffs on the three suspects within thirty seconds.

"No further targets spotted." Stone said as he scanned the perimeter.

Like a lioness, the female Mossad agent moved backward slowly on all fours. She returned to the fence-line and crawled undetected back through the cut portion of the fence. After she was on the other side, Francesca ran fast into the darkness. No one saw her.

"Target, two hundred meters. Do I take the shot?" Rageone asked. He had the silhouette of Rajik in his crosshairs.

"No," Russell said. "Hold the shot," Russell grabbed a night scope and looked across the field and added. "From this distance, hard to tell if friend or foe."

Once he assessed the area was secure, Russell found the Deputy Minister crouched behind the SUV. Earlier, the Deputy Minister wanted a gun. By the expression on his face, Russell was pleased he did not give him a weapon. Within five minutes, the British Colonel was on the flight line with the truck. As they unloaded the cocaine by hand, they sweated substantially. The Deputy Minister was still frazzled and could not speak coherently. Kitson helped him get into the vehicle with the bag of cash in the passenger seat. Rozelli was already on the phone back to his FBI office at 26 Federal Plaza, New York. Kitson drove the truck toward the most secure place in Liberian, which happened to be the United States Embassy. As they approached Monrovia city limits, Rozelli had a return call from the New York Federal Prosecutor's office. The Colombian pallet riders and the two Argentine pilots would be charged in United States Federal Court based upon the FARC's plans to fly the cocaine to America. Koroma would be held and moved to Sierra Leone to face charges for crimes against humanity. Kitson looked in the back of the truck and watched Koroma. He has questions for him. The Colombians, Argentineans, and four thousand kilograms of cocaine were brought to the embassy. The Marine Security Guards had shotguns drawn and at the ready to fire. Everyone kept their weapons lowered and hidden, as they did not want to risk fratricide. The Gunny's had their FBI Counter Espionage Unit badges on the outside of their shirts.

Back at the airport, Rajik and Chad had run over a mile and slowed to a walk. Chad was out of breath and almost threw up. They walked along the backroads toward Marshall. Rajik did not speak the entire way. He was furious. Rajik retraced the steps over and over again on who double crossed him. The only person he thought of was a custodian at the Marshall compound. There was a local who took care of the beds, linen, food, and entertainment girls. Rajik told him to prepare a big party in celebration for a big shipment and maybe he sold out to steal the cocaine, yet the men at the airport were professionals, maybe former Special Forces. There were no Liberians capable of operating like these men. Somebody sold him out and Rajik was pissed. The sun started to rise as Rajik and Chad walked into the Marshall compound. Chad was exhausted and out of breath from the fast-paced walk. His flabby muscles were in pain as that was the most strenuous activity he had experienced.

"I know you set me up." Rajik wanted his answers and the Liberian camp manager was his current target.

"No, no...boss, wat u sayin."

"Tonight, they were waiting."

"Dunno wat u sayin. No, no. not ey."

"Then who?" Rajik shouted.

"Fam, ey hav fam." Rajik knew he had a family but that did not bother him. Rajik believed life was dealt with differently in Africa and the value was not very high.

"Take him to the boat and keep him out of sight." Rajik said. Chad did Rajik's bidding. Chad would always do Rajik's bidding, as he knew there was no fountain of wealth awaiting him at the Cape Hotel. Rajik had shown him something new and very powerful, a currency that he could never get from Tareek. Rajik taught Chad how to inflict the utmost fear into another human being.

Monkey Island was a twenty-minute boat ride down the river. The current pushed the boat at a rapid pace and made the journey very quick. Rajik turned off of the motors as he approached the backside of Monkey Island. No tourists were around and he was happy for that. NGO foreigners had heard of Monkey Island from the locals and word of mouth spread quickly. The locals took their little wooden boats to let the tourists see the chimps and take cute photos for their website postings. The chimps stayed out of the water as mortal instincts drove the fear of drowning into them. Rajik made Monkey Island something else. He made it his interrogation island.

Monkey Island was formed out of necessity. As with many things in war-torn Liberia, the first set of plans never worked out. As high rates of HIV and AIDS affected large populations of Africans, a German scientist established a research laboratory on the Liberian border near Guinea in Nimba County. A test group of twenty-five chimpanzees were injected with HIV and several experimental treatment drugs were used. No one ever knew of the project nor did they know about the side effects of the hormone experimental growth drugs would do to the chimps. Since the security situation deteriorated significantly, the German scientist tried to get several of his chimps evacuated. The Taylor regime had folded and waited for the UN to intervene. No international aid organization would help the German scientist. The only ways out were by charter airplane or walk out. The scientist could not afford to buy a plane and decided to take a temporary action. He hired a boat and found an island close to the Marshall River that he could temporarily leave his HIV experiment. On his next trip, he brought the metal cage to reintegrate the chimps together. The chimps were always held in separate cages and he wanted to make sure they did not become overtly violent toward one another, after all his future was tied to the anti-bodies growing inside these chimps. As the German scientist waded ashore inspecting the metal cage, he was not in deep enough waters and the growing young male chimp reached up with his right arm and tore his face off with one swing of his arm. His Liberian assistant was shocked and left his body there. The assistant believed bad juju came from the chimps. After arriving back at the Nimba County HIV Research Center, the assistant burned the compound to the ground, with all of the other twenty chimps inside. The wood sign declared: *A partnership for a bright African future to combat HIV.*

On the backside of Monkey Island, a five foot high steel cage with a small metal door rested in four feet of water. The tide was high right and Rajik knew conditions would be good for his interrogation chamber. His house manager was limp. Rajik kicked him to wake him up. Chad had done a good job with duct tape. Chad wanted to impress his new mentor. Rajik had positioned the boat with the stern to the metal door. The victim's limp dead weight required both of them to lift the limp body into the metal cage. Once inside, Rajik shut and locked the door with a large padlock. Without being told, Chad tossed water on the camp manager to wake him. When the man did not move, Chad sliced two large incisions into his legs. He screamed back to a coherent state of mine. Blood erupted. He screamed again.

"Ey no swim." The local man pleaded after he saw water underneath the cage.

"Don't worry." Rajik said. "The water will not come up any higher. If anything it will get lower, a lot lower," pointing to the shoreline, "and then, they will come." Rajik laughed and opened a beer. He pushed the engine into gear and moved the boat forty feet away and dropped the anchor. He picked up the radio and transmitted to the receiver he tied to the cage door. "Can you hear me?"

"Ya. Halp me. Ey no swim."

"Like I said, you will not have to worry about drowning." Using surgical tubing as a slingshot, Chad launched several balloons filled with pig's blood onto the shoreline. The blood smell helped lure the chimpanzees.

The first chimps that emerged were just curious, no more than three feet in height and probably females Rajik thought. After a few more moments, he watched several larger ones come forth sniffing around the shoreline. Rajik knew it would not take long. Standing on his back feet the silver back chimpanzee stretched his body almost six feet. He was massive and powerful. The local man looked at the large chimp less than fifteen away and let out a harrowing shriek. Rajik sat back and had another beer. Chad opened up some hummus and spread out a nice snack on the back of the boat. Rajik liked his new assistant. Rajik took off his shirt to sunbathe in the late afternoon sun. Chad did not as he was very self-absorbed by the size of his man boobs. They both laughed aloud.

"Do you want to tell me now?"

"Wat tha chimp doin?" asked the horrified local man who heard rumors about the wild, savage monkeys on the island.

"The chimps will tear you apart."

"Ey no wanna die."

"Tell me then. Who did you tell about the airplane?"

"Ey nat know bout plane." The victim screamed in the radio. Rajik could easily hear him from the boat without the radio.

"Yes, you do. You told someone about my Colombian guests coming."

"No, no, Ey nat know." Tareek saw the smaller monkey go near the cage and sniffed. The chimps sat for ten minutes and did not move as they watched their prey with suspicion. Rajik was hungry and tired. He waved goodbye as he started the boat's engine and started back toward the compound. He could not hear the man scream over the engine's sound. Rajik turned up the volume. The local man on the other end of the radio had a hard time trying to formulate words as his body was ripped apart.

CHAPTER 10

Sapo National Forest had a few old trails that were overgrown and barely recognizable. Ike and the Lieutenants walked for over three hours in the thick brush. The heat was intense and they sweated profusely. Movement was at a tortoise pace as they whacked a path through the jungle. At points, the thick overhead canopy kept the sun off of them, but the humidity was incredibly high. The Lieutenants swung the machetes like madmen and cleared a path. Each carried five extra sharpened machetes. Every twenty feet Ike placed small red infrared markers that Russell provided that would help identify the path at night. As the night settled, they moved back inside a small structure they built. As they rested, Ike saw several dwarves, small monkeys with human facial features and grey hair that extended like beards. The small monkeys screamed loud and shrieked throughout the night in a childlike scream that haunted them. They huddled inside the darkened cave and refrained from making a fire. Before sunrise, Ike woke the Lieutenants and they went down the makeshift path using NVGs to pick up the infrared markers. As they approached the end, they crawled forward, camouflaged themselves with palm leaves, and drew a map of the camp. They crawled further forward slowly to take photos. Armed men roamed freely, regardless of the UN weapons restrictions. Women and children carried water back and forth. The women skinned dead animals. The head of a smaller West Africa elephant laid on the ground, the ivory tusks were removed.

At the Black Beret camp, Russell walked the perimeter to double check security. He thought of the prior night's airport drug bust. The American Embassy purposely kept the US out of the news for the drug raid. The large pile of cocaine, two Columbians, and two Argentine pilots were on their way to New York on an Air Force cargo plane that arrived and departed before sunrise. Russell was pleased. More importantly, the British Colonel was pleased they got Koroma back to the Black Beret compound for questioning. The Gunnys started interrogation as Koroma was in shock from the arrest.

"You're a war criminal." Rozelli whispered into Koroma's ear. "You will not see the light of day again."

"We shall see." Koroma seemed confident. He thought he could beat any war crimes charges as he was never caught pulling the trigger and he was far too smart to put anything in writing.

"You will be charged for drug trafficking. And you will not be charged in Liberia or Sierra Leone. You will be charged in Federal Court in New York. It would be best if you told us what we need to know." Koroma did not speak. He knew that they had him. Drug charges would put him behind bars.

"Who are you working with?" They heard silence.

"What are you doing with the money?" They heard silence.

"Who else is involved?" They heard silence. Koroma held firm and said nothing. The small enclosed room was cleared of everything except for the wooden chair Koroma sat on. The exterior room in the outside hallway was blacked out with blankets along the windows and doors. Koroma's hands were handcuffed behind his back and his legs were duct taped to the legs of the chair. A bright light illuminated the room. Two video cameras ran concurrently. The Gunnys impressed Kitson and Russell on their interrogation tactics and skills, yet they were still getting nowhere and it would take time to break Koroma.

Both Rozelli and Rageone were New York City cops. Both served as Marine reservists with the Marine Corps' 34th Interrogator Translator Team. Both joined the FBI's elite Counter Espionage Unit. Their initial skills were taught by NYPD, honed with the Marine Corps premier 'bag and tag' team, and perfected with the FBI. Russell knew he was fortunate. The Gunnys started split operations from the beginning and switched roles of good cop, bad cop that kept Koroma off guard even more. Koroma was exhausted. He ate the food and drank the water provided and crapped his pants, the smell confirmed his anxiety. Over the next two days, the Gunnys alternated interrogation every two hours. After twelve hours, they cut Koroma out of the chair and he fell to the concrete floor. The overhead light remained on and Koroma could not tell if it were day or night. The Gunnys brought one item of comfort at a time and started with a mattress; followed by a blanket, a pillow, toilet paper, and a wash bucket. Each time, they asked more questions, reconfirmed previous statements, and solidified the intelligence.

"Give me a pen," Koroma directed after he was more than broken with little rest. He drew several diagrams, one was a hierarchy tree and the other was a map. "Here was the chain of command for the RUF. Here was my position." His name was placed four people down from the top and to the right. "I was the political officer for the RUF. I had nothing to do with the diamond camps." He pointed to the rough map he drew of Kono district. "Along the river here," He drew an x across the line on the map that represented the blood diamond camp he frequented. "This was where I went to get the diamonds." The Gunnys made notes.

"How many are at the camp?"

"Don't know." Koroma whispered. The Gunnys could tell he was exhausted and they kept pressuring the interrogation.

"Yes, you do. How many rebels are at the camp? How many prisoners?" Rozelli asked.

"How many?" Rageone pressured the prisoner. The Gunnys kept the pressure on him and pressed against him. "They are going to fry you," whispered Rozelli in Koroma's ear.

"No, no, no. I'll do jail time but no frying. I want a deal. A deal, you hear me." Koroma demanded.

"We can't offer you anything," directed Rozelli. "You are a war criminal. War criminals do not have rights."

"You cannot prove that I am a war criminal, a drug dealer maybe, but not a war criminal." Again Koroma pleaded.

"We don't care. We are not lawyers. We do not make deals. We do not negotiate. Regardless, you will rot in some prison. If you talk to us, we can make things easier for you." Koroma thought about that for several minutes and agreed to lay out the camp structure with GPS coordinates. He even provided a cell phone number for one of the diamond mules that carried the blood diamonds out of Sierra Leone. Liberia had no diamonds to speak of, yet next door, as the civil war waged in Sierra Leone, nearly a billion dollars' worth of blood diamonds were smuggled into Liberia. The blood diamond mules knew the cross-border routes better than anyone and the recently arrived large UN presence along the border had zero impact on stopping the flow of blood diamonds. Koroma was pleased with his confession, as he did not provide anything on Chucky or his father. Koroma believed in his mind if Charles Taylor came back to power, he could negotiate his release. Koroma knew the world feared Charles Taylor taking control over Liberia again and wrecking all of the hard work done over the past three years. Koroma felt confident his old friend would negotiate his release.

"Koroma laid out most of the blood diamond camp structure and several probable locations. He described how the mules carry the diamonds and who they broker with on Liberia's side," Rozelli said. "He's scared. I think he's telling the truth."

"We have actionable intel." Rageone offered. "We can move."

"Except we would be illegally entering Sierra Leone." Stone replied. "We need to be careful."

"How many rebels are at the camp?" asked Russell. He knew what was at stake, yet anger raged deep inside of him. Anger brought forward from the helplessness he experienced at Iskandariyah. He did not know if he could let this information fall to the wayside.

"Estimates vary depending upon time of year, right now is the best optimum time for the captives to pan for diamonds before the rainy season." Rozelli pointed toward the real Kono district map overlaid with Koroma's makeshift map drawing.

"How many?" Stone inquired.

"Best guess, thirty."

"How many captives?" Russell inquired.

"High end, I would guess max of two hundred." Rageone replied.

Russell took all of the information in from his Gunnys. He thought of the several hundred captive Africans forced into slave labor - men, women, and children - all living a horrible existence. Blood diamonds were farmed off the arms and backs of the slave laborers. From the repeated whips from long sticks, the captive's blood dripped into the muddy brown water. He did not have authority to operate in Sierra Leone; however, he had actionable intelligence that would be good for several more weeks before the rainy season.

"We need to brief the Brit." Russell said. "Tie all of this together and be ready this afternoon."

Russell read several UN reports on the internet that described the difficulty of the fledgling new government to take over security of Liberia. New Congo leaders tried to erase decades of problems, but they could not influence corruption. Corruption ran deep into the pores of Liberian society. The incestuous relationship between members of government continued even after the referendum on corruption. At one point during the Taylor regime, thirty percent of the population was employed by the government in one facet or another. Large scale capitalism projects had always been a taboo in Liberia, why would an individual or a company risk so much as the next military coup or corrupt government official would take everything away. The disparity in Liberia centered on those who could wield influence. Those few anointed members of Monrovian high society and some of the new Congo returnees have profited greatly from the generosity of the UN, America, and Lebanese taxpayers.

The Deputy Minister of Defense looked out his window at Defense Headquarters on the BTC compound. The empty Presidential Palace loomed on the horizon. His father worked there for two years as the Minister of Education before he went back to the palm oil farm in Robertsport. The family picture taken during better times rested in the forefront of his desk. He did not know his age in the photo when he was a little boy but estimated he must have been five years old. His father held his mother very tight and his two older sisters looked very pretty. The guard came into the office, "Sir, it is time."

"I want to thank you all for coming." President Johnson-Sirleaf stood at the main podium. "Today, we Liberians are proud for we have put a knife in the heart of drug running." The room was packed with reporters and Liberian National Police. "Last evening, our very own Deputy Minister of Defense risked his life to help put an end to Colombian drug runners. By his efforts, he single handedly captured four thousand kilos of cocaine worth over one hundred million US dollars."

From his sniper position, Rajik carefully watched the line of government cars depart. The president and her cabinet members departed with sirens flailing and lights flashing. The church rooftop did not provide the perfect coverage, but the position was elevated enough. The side street was under immense reconstruction and the only point was down the newly named UN drive. The shot ripped through the back window and blasted glass all over the Deputy Minister. He fell to the floor. Rajik left the rifle in place and ran across the roof toward the ladder. Rajik was on the ground and walked down the street as if nothing happened. The driver was injured and crashed into the stands. The Deputy Minister remained on the vehicle floor scared to death.

The Cape Hotel cabanas were crowded with dozens of foreigners who enjoyed the afternoon sun. It did not matter that it was the middle of the week. The foreigners were on their own work schedule and warm weather equated to beach relaxation. Tareek watched the Mossad agent as she walked to the beach umbrellas to relax by the beach. When no one watched, he approached.

"I heard a big drug bust happened last night." Tareek mentioned without looking at her directly. Tareeq had provided information on Hezbollah movements in West Africa back channels to Israeli intelligence. He now had a genuine Israeli agent to help him destroy the same terrorist organization that killed his family.

"My American friends are actively engaged." Francesca said quietly without looking upwards.

"Can you trust them?" asked Tareek.

"I don't know." Francesca contemplated the situation and continued. "Usually America and Israel work together, but in Africa I do not know." Tareek departed before anyone surmised that they were talking. A few minutes later, Francesca stood and walked toward the surf. Gently waves cascaded across her feet. She resembled one of the many NGOs who enjoyed the crystal blue waters. Francesca turned, looked at the sprawling US Embassy compound, and wondered what the heck the Americans were up to.

At the deserted Robertsport mansion, the single barrel shotgun was levied out the upstairs window as the vehicle approached. Everyone in the vehicle saw the gun's barrel pointed out the window and none felt uneasy, as they knew it could not do much damage. The Deputy Minister of Defense had barricade himself in the upper floor. Old remnants of wood were hastily nailed across the bottom and top of the staircase. He nailed the last of the boards to seal himself inside. After seeing who arrived, the Deputy Minister climbed down twenty feet on a knotted rope to exit the building. The one hundred and fifty year old brick mansion could sustain a minor assault. Kitson and Russell did not think the Deputy Minister looked very well.

"I may not stay in Liberia." The Liberian was frantic in his voice. "So much has been lost...so little gained." The Deputy Minister was visibly shaken. Russell took the shotgun and unloaded the weapon.

"You have a big difference." Kitson said as he tried to encourage the despondent man. "You owe it to your father."

Kitson remained with the Deputy Minister for the rest of the day. The two hundred acre former palm oil plantation resided along some of the best coastline in Robertsport. The mansion was completely gutted of all windows, plumbing pipes, electrical wires, and even some of the brick that was crushed to fill potholes on the main road. In the glory day of the mansion, he remembered fantastic balls in the main gallery ballroom. A twenty-foot crystal chandelier hung from the center of the room and mesmerized the guests. As a young boy, he would play throughout the house, running back and forth, as he chased his older sisters. The mansion was filled with laughter and joy. He felt more at home in the dilapidated mansion than anywhere else in his life. He came to Africa to make a difference not only for his family but for his native homeland. Indeed, he was part of the new Congo who had arrived in throngs to tell Liberians how to fix their country after fourteen years of civil war and a brutal Charles Taylor regime; however, many of the new Congo departed back to America to their safe lives.

"My father used to walk along here." The Deputy Minister spoke as he pointed toward the brick path along the top of the ridge that overlooked Robertsport beach. The British Colonel walked behind him. He let his friend lead.

"What happened to your father?" Kitson asked.

"No one knows. He just disappeared."

"Somebody must know." Kitson replied. They walked along the old brick stonework. Below in Robertsport, an old lady looked up toward the hill and was surprised to see men walk along the ridge. She went back to her toils of carrying a fifty-pound jug of fresh water balanced on her head. She used to work at the mansion, many years before. She stopped and looked back toward the men.

The Gunnys spent most of the day reviewing their interrogation notes, and they reviewed the tapes over and over again for several hours. When the officers returned, the Gunnys laid out an entire intelligence assessment on Koroma's interrogation to Kitson and Russell.

"Here is what we know." Rozelli said. "A blood diamond camp is located here. Rebel force estimates are fifty, captives number several hundred."

"Are you certain?" Kitson asked.

"Koroma seemed pretty serious and credible."

"That may be true. He knows that we have him." The British Colonel looked over the map and listened to the tape again several times. He looked at Koroma's facial expressions on the video.

"What are our options?" Russell asked.

"IMATT would be very interested in this information." However, the Americans knew the International Military Advisory and Training Team in Freetown had only twenty British military advisors.

"But will they act on it?" Stone asked.

"Doubtful." Kitson stated plainly. He looked at the Americans and sensed that they wanted to take action at the blood diamond camp.

After Koroma was brought out into the open, he smiled at the warmth of the sun. Koroma was pleased to see the sunlight. Ike and the Lieutenants were prepared for the long journey to Freetown. Koroma had been handcuffed, but he was relieved to be out of the cell. The hot shower and fresh clothes made him feel great. He knew if he was charged at The Hague he would be treated well. He knew the prison would be better than what he had seen in Monrovia and he did not have to deal with Chucky's psychotic personality. Koroma had a smirk on his face as the Gunnys placed him in the vehicle. Rozelli was surprised when Koroma said thank you several times. Everybody was outside to watch the vehicle depart. The Marines congratulated each other, yet the British Colonel remained silent. Ike drove with Lieutenant Johnson was in front and Lieutenant Forleh sat next to the war criminal. Ike looked in the rear view mirror incessantly. Lieutenant Johnson thought he was paranoid that they were being followed. At the Bo-waterside border checkpoint on the Liberia side of the border, the Lieutenants got out to deal with the border officials as they arrived in the afternoon after the border closed. As they walked inside, Ike slammed the vehicle in reverse and left the Lieutenants. They ran after him. Ike disregarded Koroma's repeated questions and kept focused on driving. Ike sped the vehicle as fast as he could on the primitive road conditions. By nightfall, Ike arrived back at his home village Foya. He had last visited the village eight years ago.

The Lieutenants called back to the Black Beret compound. The British Colonel went to go find his American guests.

"It looks like Ike is taking the matter of Koroma's disposition into his own hands." Kitson said pointedly.

"What are you not telling me?" Russell inquired. He was livid.

"You need to understand sometimes tribal justice rules in Africa." The seasoned British officer informed him.

"I don't understand. We have the Geneva Convention to abide by." Russell pointed out.

"Absolutely, in war we do as Western powers. In Africa where there are no identifiable enemies, the rules blur."

"They shouldn't." Russell now knew he had found what he had feared when he entered Liberia over a month ago. He wondered if the British Colonel had lost it.

"I do not condone Ike's actions." Kitson said. "Laws in Africa are not the same as in Western civilizations. Tribal laws are still prevalent in African society. Liberian police are considered corrupt. Criminals can pay their way out. Worse, if someone committed a crime against you, you are responsible to pay for their food while they are in prison awaiting trials. Remember the justice system was only started last month. Trials are backlogged by nearly a year. Quick and swift justice remains prevalent."

"That goes against everything the UN is trying to do here."

"Don't be so naïve, the UN has been here for a long time. If the UN really cared about getting Liberia back on track, there would have been more progress. Look at the surge America is doing in Iraq. You are putting resources against the problem. In Liberia, the UN has to deal with many donor nations to provide funding and each country has an agenda. For over two years, there has been too much bickering and little progress. Even your State Department has been divided on how to get the new military established. Your government has hired contractors to train the new army and equipped Liberia with more vehicles than they could ever use or maintain."

"All of that does not give us the right to have someone executed."

"We did not warrant any execution. Ike has taken upon his hands to make tribal justice. After being in Africa for many years, I understand why he did it." No other words were spoken.

In the summer of 1998, the village of Foya was vibrant. The villagers were predominantly from the Mandingo tribe and lived in peace. The men and women worked hard and forged an existence out of the mountain jungle in the northeast corner of Liberia near the intersection of Liberia, Guinea, and Sierra Leone. On a horrific day, the speakers emitted loud psychotic music. At first, they did not perceive the pickup trucks loaded with young boys as a threat. The young boys with RUF scrawled into scars on their arms opened fire before the trucks stopped. Smaller boys had a difficult holding the heavy weapons, yet managed to unload clips of ammunition into the wood huts. Ike tried to get back to his hut. He was shot several times. Some other villager dragged him away. Dead bodies littered the ground. Smoke emitted from the huts and clouded the tranquil mountainside. Women and girls were brutalized. Ike was wounded and crawled back to the village. He saw the man who ordered the attack. The boys laughed by the fire and shot up with heroine. A large bonfire ignited the night. Koroma leveled his AK47 toward a young girl and blew her head off. Ike watched as his little girl died. He passed out from the loss of blood. In the morning, the remnants of the attack shocked the survivors. Ike mourned his loss privately, buried his family, and walked away.

Ike beeped the horn loud as he entered Foya. The village elders arrived at the noise and were very pleased with Koroma's capture. Tribal rituals and retaliation meant more than the rule of law in the bush. Over the next three hours, the villagers built a large pile of wood and tied Koroma to the ten-foot post erected in the center. Villagers wore masks that have been passed down from generation to generation. They painted white clay along their skin in various forms. Koroma was stripped of all clothes and painted with white demon signs. Ike thought about cutting out his heart and taking a bite out of it, which was common practice to take possession of your enemy's powers. No, he concluded. Everyone wanted Koroma to suffer. As the fire ignited and illuminated the night, screams of joy plunged forward from previously depressed souls. Koroma screamed as the heat of the flame boiled his skin. The pain was excruciating and forced him into unconsciousness. Ike enjoyed the sight and hugged fellow villagers he had not seen in years. A large spread of food was presented in front of Ike as he sat next to the village elders. Young ladies danced to the sound of drums and screamed joyous sounds. For years, there was no joy, happiness, or redemption. On this night, it resonated in Foya. In one night, all of that came back. Ike sat proudly next to the village elders, men he revered as a young man. The village elders were nearly eighty years old and would not live much longer. For these old men to see redemption for the massacre that took place in Foya was an emotional bliss. Tears flowed down their eyes. Ike looked at the smoldering ash and could just make out the outline of Koroma's charred corpse against the pole.

Back at the Taylor compound, Chucky was intoxicated again and stumbled around the building. The rooms were his sanctuary as he could not be seen outside, not yet.

"Where's Koroma?" Chucky shouted. Several empty bottles of scotch rolled off the desk. Chucky was extremely intoxicated. The room was dark except for paper Chucky burned in the fireplace. A young local girl lay on the couch. Rajik did not know if she was alive or dead. He wondered if she were one of the regulars who frequented the casino, but he could not worry about her right now.

"He was taken." Rajik said. "The Americans knew about the drug shipment." He paused for a moment. "We were betrayed."

"Who did it?" Chucky screamed. "I want them dead." He tossed a bottle against the fireplace. Glass shattered and flew across the room.

"I plugged the leak." Rajik said proudly. He did not know that all of their conversations were taped when they met at the piano bar. No one knew that Tareeq provided intelligence on Hezbollah movements to the Israelis. No one would have guessed that the Minister of Defense would have the courage to reach out to the British. Rajik looked for the closest element of betrayal and found his local grounds keeper at the Marshall compound.

"Where is Koroma now?" Chucky asked.

"At the old Black Beret camp in Firestone. We believe the British are holding him." Rajik was informed by one of his contacts that Koroma was spotted in a vehicle near the Firestone Plantation.

"The British are viral scum." Rashad Mansuray said as he walked in the room. The seasoned Al-Qaeda operative just arrived in Liberia on a speedboat. "They are just as bad as the Americans."

"Koroma will bend." Chucky added. "He is weak." Chucky poured another drink. The others could tell Chucky was disgusted.

"We need to get the diamonds," Rajik said. He looked at the Al-Qaeda agent and wondered if he got in over his head. He had never worked with Al-Qaeda before, but heard how brutal they were against those who did not share their vision. Rajik wanted money, not to become a martyr. Rajik needed to get out of Monrovia, especially as he knew everything was about to heat up. He was not foolish to let Chucky's war become his own. Rajik was smart enough to stay on the outside criminal activity where no crimes could be charged against him.

"Yes, we want our diamonds back. Do you know where they are?" Rashad asked. Al-Qaeda had moved into West Africa with brutal force to take control of the illicit diamond smuggling. What senior terrorist leaders realized was the sensational appetite for illegal diamonds on the black market. Without the engraved serial numbers dictated by the Kimberly Accord, rough diamonds could easily move across borders and more importantly across languages as any diamond was a sought after commodity.

"No," Rajik said. "He hid them before we caught him trying to escape Liberia." Rajik put a photo on the table. "He did not give up anything when we tortured him. However, we have the wife under surveillance and she will take us to them," said Rajik.

"And then kill her," added Rashad.

"Kill them all!" pronounced Chucky. He looked at Rashad. "Take some men." Chucky pointed to the thugs Rajik left with him. "I want them dead...all of them dead." Chucky grabbed the pistol off the table and shot the girl on the couch who was already dead. Her body did not move. Chucky shot the corpse four more times. "I want Koroma dead. I don't trust him. He has no heart for pain. He will tell them everything." Chucky looked at Rajik and ordered. "Go kill anyone at the Black Beret camp.... Everyone must die."

Chapter 11

Russell loaded the old truck that the Gunnys got running with parts off the dead vehicles. They made sure the old UN sign on the door was completely peeled off. By no means, did they want to be associated with UNMIL. The number of UN white vehicles grew substantially over the past six months as a container ship unloaded several hundred. Liberians possessed beat up wrecks and kept their vehicles operational by any means, yet the UN drove new SUVs. The British Colonel was not pleased to see his guests depart. He warned them to be very careful in Monrovia, as they would be under constant surveillance. One slip of the tongue could put the mission in jeopardy. Russell had called Colonel Crevace in Germany and informed him that the team would take a few days of rest in Monrovia and more importantly would get the lay of the land. They drove a different route out of Firestone Plantation and stopped at Firestone village, which seemed like something out of a Joseph Stalin commune camp layout. The village was self-contained with school, hospital, electrical, coop vegetable gardens, and the store. The village remained relatively untouched during the two civil wars as the company paid off the rebel factions. Russell found the village arcane as if he had emerged from a time capsule back forty years. The school and houses remained untouched by the violence. The paint on the walls had not been updated for decades. A woman stopped, squatted, and relieved herself on the side of the road. She stood on the edge of the road's pavement as the grass was too thick and poisonous snakes occupied the thick grass. In front, there were a small group of cattle. Each cow had a thick chain attached to a hind leg, just in case someone tried to steal them. Russell laughed as he saw the cattle and believed if someone wanted the cow, they would cut off the hind leg linked to the chain.

After they arrived at the Cape Hotel, Russell turned toward the other Marines in the vehicle and spoke. "Gents, you need to remember that we will be under constant surveillance. Keep to the cover stories." Russell said sternly and he added. "Make sure to watch the booze."

"No worries," Rageone spoke. "We'll have them eating out of our hand." Russell had each one sit down and speak their cover stories several times. Each Marine rehearsed their portion of their cover story and ever one was linked together to sound reasonable. If any NGO happened to want check with the US Embassy, UN, or any other AID organization, their cover stories would be penetrated. The Cape Hotel rooms were magnificent compared to what they were used to for the past month. Stone went into each hotel room and scanned for electronic listening devices. He found several. In the hallway, he noticed video globes for all around surveillance.

"Tomorrow, we will get back to more training." Russell told the other Marines, more as a threat not to get too drunk. As he walked outside to scan the exterior security, Russell found a local teenager named Eric who was more than happy to wash their vehicle. Russell quickly discovered that Eric had only a fourth grade education level, which was very common in Liberia. In the heat, Eric worked hard as he carried buckets of water to wash the vehicle. Back and forth, Eric walked several hundred feet to the fresh water well. The young Liberian boy smiled as he had a job that day and his family would eat.

In the morning, Russell took his team for a run along the beautiful beach. The Marines ran down the beach toward the BTC compound. The large green and rusted door where President Doe tossed bodies on the beach loomed over them. They passed the vacant Presidential Palace. The temperature was blistering hot. The rainy season and much cooler weather was still weeks away. Dried lawns were everywhere. The Liberian earth waited patiently for the annual rainy season to arrive. Locals yearned for the cooler weather from the oppressive heat. In the meantime, the Marines observed locals who hauled gallons upon gallons of water in any type of sealed container. Makeshift pull carts were made out of lumber, metal, and old truck tires. Men pushed and pulled the pile of filled containers down the street. As the Marines passed, Russell noticed muscle ripped men who slowly moved the water jugs that weighed near a thousand pounds. Five men levied all of their muscles. They were toned and chiseled and could have easily posed for any body building magazine. They continued their daily exercise while the local men toiled hard to forge an existence.

Later in the day, the Marines took some time and went sightseeing. The stadium across from BTC was crowded outside and gathered their attention. A special soccer match was played for one legged players who were injured during the civil war. The teams of handicapped players were impressive. Stone cheered loudly as a football expert for both the American and the World's sport. The locals used vuvuzelas, long wooden decorated tubes. As the one legged soccer team scored, the vuvuzelas screamed high pitch sounds. The victims of war had not been idle and let their handicaps curtail them as they dominated the two legged soccer team. The Gunnys pointed out the fouls as the one legged team used crutches to sneak hits when the judges were not looking. Stone told them to give them a break, as they were handicapped.

Russell reflected on the crowd and how much pain they had endured. Russell thought of what the British Colonel told him on counter-insurgency operations in Africa. Russell's mindset had been predominantly kinetic operations, especially from his time in Iraq. However, Russell knew he could not take the Iraq and Afghanistan counter-insurgency models to Liberia or pretty much any other African nation. Russell was part of the Iraqi 'awakening' that led to a very successful counter-insurgency campaign in Al Anbar Province. In Liberia there was no identified insurgency in the midst of the populace. The only known insurgents waited in Sapo National Forest. Russell wondered if the Nigerians would send more troops back to Liberia to clear Sapo. Russell heard that Nigerians meant business and would kill every single person in sight if they had their way. Nigerians were known to shoot first and ask questions later.

Outside of the soccer stadium, lines of wheel barrels held single items for sale and the fast talkers waited patiently for the fans. Russell wondered why only single items were loaded in the wheel barrels. One contained shoe polish, another women's underwear, another shoelaces, another flip-flops, and many more contained single items. He wondered if people purchased from multiple vendors. It appeared like something out of a Twilight Zone episode that you can only buy one thing from one vendor. They quickly passed the stares of the makeshift market to get away fast.

Russell told Stone to drive toward the Hotel Dukor. The large deserted building looked over Monrovia. They ran the fifteen flights of stairs. At the top, Russell leaned over top of the edge of the rooftop and looked down over two hundred feet to the bottom. The inside wall concealed them from sight. As the tallest building in Monrovia and one that was relatively unoccupied by homeless squatters, the Hotel Dukor was the perfect selection. Three ropes hung over the wall and Rozelli was on belay at the bottom of the rope. The distance down the wall was too great to hear so each Marine had wireless earpieces and microphones. Russell could barely see the Gunny standing out from the wall as several trees blocked his view, yet he instinctively knew the Gunny had his back on the rope as his belay. Russell bent his knees and climbed into position perpendicular to the building. Russell rested for a moment as he secured the rope behind his back with his right arm, called the break. His left hand gripped the rope as he fed the line. He smiled at Stone and Rageone as he volunteered to venture down the wall first. He bounced, leaped simultaneously, and hit dirt within ten seconds. He ran away from the building that pulled all of the remaining rope out of the belt's harness ring. The rest of the team hit the wall and after each ran back up the fifteen flights of stairs. Local homeless men living in the scant, darkened empty rooms looked out into the darkened stairwell as grunts and groans from men who ran up the fifteen-story worth of stairs. After five evolutions, the Marines were exhausted. Russell paid the local security guard at the top of the building to watch one of the backpacks filled with a rope and several harnesses. The security guard was a former soldier and was happy to have the extra money.

After they piled into the vehicle, the four of them headed to the Cape Hotel. The dirt still clung onto their boots and sweat was stained on their clothes. Each of them smelled. The Cape Hotel was livelier than anything the Marines would have ever expected for a Sunday afternoon. Drinking afternoon cocktails along the beach were over a dozen foreigners, both men and women. The scene looked pretty damn good for the Marines. The Gunnys immediately ordered eight Club beers. They would not get caught dead drinking girly drinks with umbrellas, not even if needed for undercover work. And they did not want to wait for any replacements. They were thirsty.

The afternoon sun radiated on the tile pool deck. Umbrellas were pressed upward to shield some of the sun from the mostly white Europeans. The three local cabana men wore white shirts and blue shorts. They worked the crowd and were drenched with sweat as they rushed back and forth to get more cocktails. The Marines walked up to the pool and caught the attention of several of the female guests after they stripped down to their exercise shorts. They dove into the water to cool down. The beers started to flow freely and the fun started. The Gunnys started conversations with several French ladies that led into frolicking in the pool. Russell saw one of the girls standing at the other end and had a drunken idea to sneak up on her under water. As he dove into the pool and swam underwater, the heavy chlorine content forced him to keep his eyes closed. The Barcelona doctor stepped into the pool as the French lady departed. The pinch Russell gave on her backside caused the Barcelona lady to turn quickly. As Russell stood, he received the flat part of her hand across his face that nearly knocked him over. The sound of the slap resonated across the pool area and caught everyone's immediate attention. The Gunnys rolled over with laughter. The Barcelona doctor looked Russell in the eye and walked out of the pool. Russell's face was expressionless - stunned at the change of events.

Humiliated, Russell went to his room. The Gunnys still laughed as he walked away. Russell did not want to hear it. For the past thirty days, they have been together relatively constantly and he needed some space. He needed to clear his head on Koroma and did not know what to tell Colonel Crevace when he called, a conversation he knew was coming. The threat of Charles Taylor coming back to power was real. From what Koroma professed, Chucky was out of control and just as lethal when he led the ATU. Under his command, the ATU became known as the 'Demon Forces' for a reason as death and violence was inflicted on anything the ATU touched. Russell read one of the local Monrovian papers that touted the success of the Liberian undercover drug operation at Roberts International Airport. The commentaries regarded the Deputy Minister's actions as heroic and many commentators asked for him to consider running for president.

The sunset was perfect and the warm breeze off the ocean felt more like the Hawaiian Islands than Liberia. Russell walked along the terrace and admired the foreign women sipping cocktails under large umbrellas. One lady caught his eye.

"Can I join you?" Russell asked the lady who he believed was from Barcelona, yet she was Israeli.

"As you wish." She was curt.

"I wanted to say that I am sorry for earlier today." Russell replied. "I was a little drunk."

"And now?" She asked.

"Sober," Russell said. He paused. "Thank you. What is your name?"

"Names are not important."

"Well, I'm Tom" He paused for a moment as he was captivated by her eyes. "Can I ask what are you doing here?"

"I work for Doctors Without Borders" She added. "And you?" Russell had already asked around by paying off the Hotel staff to get all the information he could on her. No one knew much about her.

"I'm here as a consultant."

"For what?"

"Mainly to help the new government get up and running."

"Did you attend the presidential inauguration?" she asked. She wanted to know how connected this American was. She would make sure that Tareek reviewed video coverage to see if he talked to any of the US Embassy staff.

"No, I wasn't invited." He could not tell her that he just happened to be sneaking across the border from Sierra Leone at the exact time of the ceremony. "It must have been a good party."

"So I heard." She replied.

"You're very beautiful."

"So I have been told." She took a sip from her wine. "Beauty is within." She pointed to her chest area. She acted well and she was pleased with her performance. The grouper fish they both ordered was delicious. He passed on the Liberian pepper but was amazed when she did not. After a nice dinner and several glasses of wine, they walked up to the rooftop piano bar. Strands of piano music 'As Time Goes By' emanated throughout the room. A mid-size, athletic black man walked up to Russell and gave him a large hug. He whispered something in his ear and walked toward the exit.

"Who was that?"

"He is the one of the new Deputy Ministers." Russell was impressed that the Deputy Minister took Kitson's advice not to hide in fear. Two large local men stood behind the Deputy Ministers who had suits that did not fit, pistols bulged on their sides. Russell knew that these men were the new presidential guards and trained by the US Secret Service. Russell could tell these two were former military and wondered what they did during the civil war, as few were free of blood.

"Are you staying in Liberia long?" She asked Russell.

"Perhaps." Russell replied. "If I know your name, perhaps I will stay longer." Russell was mesmerized by her stunning beauty and gorgeous smile.

"Perhaps," She said slowly, "I will tell you my name."

"Maybe over another glass of wine." Russell said. He was trying to get themselves both drunk as he poured the last of the wine.

"Francesca." She said pointedly. "My name is Francesca."

Back at the remote Black Beret camp, the British colonel stayed up late and wondered if Ike would return soon. Kitson thought the camp felt excruciatingly empty. The Americans were gone, Ike was gone, and the Liberian Lieutenants went back to their barracks to visit with their families. Even Lucy was quiet, probably depressed that Ike left. Lucy had full access to the kitchen area since Ike departed and ate most of the plantains. After his fourth gin and tonic, Kitson cleaned up the kitchen and went to sleep.

The vehicles approached Firestone Plantation and continued through toward the Black Beret compound. Before the turn off in the road, the headlights were extinguished and vehicles stopped. Colonel 'zigzag' Marzah thought that was unusual. His camp was in perfect sight of the road intersection, and he was perplexed why the vehicles stopped. From the distance, he could not see well and moved closer.

Rashad pointed his AK47 toward the road and directed Rajik's henchmen to follow. They moved with hand and arm signals and no voice commands. Rashad was impressed by their tactics and heard that Rajik's thugs were trained in Libya. They moved at a quick pace. Rashad fired the first shot from his AK47. He was twenty feet from the guard and blew a large hole in the guard's chest. Volleys of fire opened up on the entire compound. Each building was ripped with multiple bullets and the intruders quickly gained entrance.

The British Colonel rolled out of bed onto the floor. Bullets penetrated the windows and sent glass everywhere. He reached up to the nightstand to grab the remote detonator. Kitson regained his senses and crawled to the window. He lifted his head to look out, but bounced down as more rounds hit his bungalow. He did not wait for the intruders to enter the communication building. Kitson pressed the five digit code and the detonator button. The explosion of two thousand pounds of explosives ripped the concrete block building into the air and illuminated the night. The explosive force knocked the intruders down. Kitson's bungalow was too close to the blast and the building's roof collapsed.

Rashad picked himself up and kept moving forward. He could not tell how many of Rajik's men were alive and he did not care. He checked the magazine and had only a few rounds left. He reloaded a full clip. He held his fire and looked for targets. Two of Rajik's men survived the explosion and fired indiscriminately. They gave away their positions. Within seconds, each fell as rounds penetrated their chest. Rashad still did not fire; he could not find the target. Five minutes passed and Rashad waited. He laid flat against the ground. Fire raged from the building's timbers that were not ejected from the explosion. The surrounding area was illuminated from the fire. Rashad gave up. Once on the dirt road, he ran to the vehicles and drove one away in his escape. Colonel 'zigzag' Marzah waited an hour as the fire burned down before he entered his old camp. He knew all of the shadow areas and best places to hide within the camp. After searching the buildings for several minutes, he found the British Colonel alive and carried him back to his camp.

Jazz music from the three-piece band resonated throughout the Cape Hotel from the roof top piano bar. Vibrant horns and a base guitar matched well with the piano. A local lady had a glamorous silver gown and sang a beautiful Nina Simone song.

"I'm not like your American girls." Francesca said. "I just don't walk to bed." She was out of practice with her Americanized English. As a teenager, she lived in Alexandria, Virginia. Her father was assigned to the Israeli Consulate in Washington, DC. Her father turned several high ranking military officers and several career government employees to provide secrets on the Palestinians and spy for Israel. She learned to speak American and learned everything about American culture. She was trained at an early age to witness how to recruit, train, and how to manipulate assets.

"What makes you think I am like that?" Russell understood what she said.

"I see you Americans and how you are with the local girls."

"That's not me." Russell said. They both looked over to the bar and just happened to be the time several American contractors were at the bar having shots of liquor. Within the hour, they would be down by the Cape Hotel gate looking for local young girls. The foreign contractors were happy to pay for companionship.

"There is something about you American Tom." Francesca sensed something about Russell. She knew how to size up individuals very quickly. She paused for a long moment. "I can tell you seek adrenaline."

"Nope, I'm just a romantic." Russell gave a horrible line and thought for a quick moment that he wished he had kept his mouth shut.

Francesca leaned forward and whispered. "I sense you are a dangerous man." She knew how to push any man's buttons.

"There is danger all around us." Russell looked across the room at several Russians and Hezbollah operatives eating fresh steaks from a butchered cow.

"And you can protect us?" Francesca inquired. She was a deadly killer and a seductive agent. The last thing she needed was a man to protect her. However, she needed information on the Americans and her scared persona would be helpful.

After another bottle of wine, Russell walked Francesca to her room. He thought about asking to go inside, but remembered what the British Colonel told him and more importantly what he told his men. But there was something about her, an intrigue that he had never found before. She had excitement written all over her forehead. He leaned in close, did not kiss her goodbye, and let the moment linger. She watched his romantic moves and pondered the idea of sending her right fist against his throat. Francesca used all feminine and sexual means possible for her intelligence collection, yet she never became romantically involved on a mission. She had no love life. She had no romantic flings. She would get just as much pleasure pointing a pistol below a man's waistline and watching him squirm. Just as she was about to lift a knee into his groin, he smiled and walked away. Tonight, both would sleep alone. Russell went to his room, crashed hard, and enjoyed not having a mosquito bed net that drove him crazy at the Black Beret camp. The continuous hum of the air conditioner killed off the pesky little vultures.

Tareek watched the close circuit camera to see if she would be able to lure the American into her room. He knew better not to put any video or listening devices into her room. Tareek knew she was deadly and would not cross her. Tareek watched the American as he walked back to his room. He had been very interested in the four Americans, especially as all of his listening devices had disappeared. These Americans did not appear the same as many of the NGOs that came to Liberia. In their eyes, he could tell these men were very familiar with violence.

Chapter 12

Big Carl was grotesque and overweight, even by American standards. His large belly hung far over his swimsuit. His age showed on his chest with large patches of grey hair. Empty discarded beers cans rested underneath his poolside chair. Two very young Liberian women, perhaps teenage girls around fourteen years of age sat on either side of him. Big Carl knew he got away with a pedophile crime that he would be charged with back in America. However; in Liberia, laws were hard to enforce. Big Carl was a contractor who supported another contractor that supported yet another contractor to train and equip the new Liberian army. Background checks were hard to unravel.

In West Africa after years of civil war, Big Carl took pleasure in the lack of law and got away with having an inappropriate relationship with minors. Civil law enforcement was practically non-existent. The young girls cooked, cleaned, and lived with Big Carl in a compound less than five hundred yards from UN headquarters. His apartment was large, filled with boxes of liquor and cases of Budweiser. Big Carl had a finger on the illegal trafficking of goods. He received a special government pass to operate in the port of Monrovia within the deserted Liberian Coast Guard base. Big Carl was obnoxious when he drank, which was often. His drunken behavior along with his relationship with two young locals isolated him from the rest of the contractors. He did not care. The money was better than what he had in Iraq working as a contractor.

Big Carl finished another beer, crumpled the can, and tossed it on the ground. He let out a large, disgusting belch. Across the pool, he watched several new arrivals at the contracting camp. The new arrivals looked at him with disgust, yet Big Carl did not care. He surmised that they would welcome him in a few short months when they wanted alcohol and companionship from young local women. He looked at his phone and saw a text message from Rajik that he had better return his call quickly. Big Carl struggled to get his fat body out of the chair and needed the assistance of his two young local helpers.

Back at the Firestone Plantation, Colonel Frank Kitson, Jr. knew he was in a bad situation before he opened his eyes. He remained still and did not move anything. He squinted and slowly regained consciousness. Out of the corner of his eye, he saw an older local man cook food over an open fire in the corner of the hut. He did not recognize him, but for some reason knew he was safe

"How long have I been out?" Kitson inquired as he attempted to sit upward. He groaned.

"Not long." Marzah replied.

"What happened?" Kitson asked.

"Bad men came for you."

"The explosion." Kitson remembered what had happened, "There was an explosion."

"I pulled you out." Marzah said. "The building collapsed on you."

"The guards? What about my guards?" Kitson was concerned.

"Dead," Marzah said softly. "All dead."

"Ike?" The British Colonel remembered and continued. "He wasn't there."

"Who?"

"Ike and my American guests. They were not there." His senses were starting to come back. Perhaps there would have been more trouble if the Marines were there and opened fire on everything.

"Lucky." Marzah added. "The explosion was big."

"Indeed." Kitson said as he tried to sit up. He recalled the two thousand pounds of high explosive TNT that he wired underneath the communication building. At the time, he did not believe that it was enough and wanted to link more into the explosive line, but ran out. The British Colonel sat up and then lay back down as he was still dizzy.

"Who are you?"

"Friends call me 'zigzag'."

"That's an unusual name."

"My rank is colonel. My last name is Marzah. I used to command the Black Berets. You were living in my camp."

"You worked for Charles Taylor?" Kitson asked.

131

"I did, but I surely did not partake in the same brutal murder tactics he and his demented son instilled." Zigzag handed his guest water and some food. He made rice and bush meat.

"My kit." The British officer said.

"What?"

"My gear, what about all of the stuff in my bungalow."

"I brought you here from the camp and have not been back."

"Ok," The British Colonel thought of his own gear selfishly and reminded himself that all the intelligence reports and communication gear would have been destroyed, but wanted to make sure. He could not move. He did not know this man. He needed Ike.

Robertsport held unbelievable beauty that lured Liberians for generations. The gentle rolling waves and ocean breeze held mosquitoes at bay. In the early 1900s, Robertsport was founded as a small enclave by the elite from Monrovia as a place to escape. Mansions and beach cottages were built all along the ridge. Restaurants and spas were built that catered to the elite Monrovia society. Men and women were dressed in their finest clothes. At night, they walked along the candle lit stone streets. A magnificent church and several schools were built. The village of Robertsport was the beacon of hope for the Congo people who ruled Liberia's economy, government, and society. They built something out of nothing and truly loved and enjoyed their beach retreat.

The majority of Liberia's civil war brutality remained away from Robertsport during much of the last two civil wars, except when the local business owners refused to pay protection to the NPFL, who were Charles Taylor's thugs. The NPFL fought against Samuel Doe's government. A younger Charles Taylor came to Robertsport to reason with the locals who still refused. Charles Taylor left the village and gave orders to the local NPFL leader, Major Abbdas. Up the hill on the ridge, the villagers were marched at gun point. Their movement was slow as they were all tied together. Families watched in horror and were held back by heroin addicted child soldiers with guns. Major Abbdas shot each with a pistol. As each one fell over, the chain of twenty men and women collapsed to the ground. There was no mark for the corpses buried under the large oak tree on the ridge.

The Deputy Minister overlaid a map of his father's palm oil plantation on top of a local map and placed it on the wall. He spent the entire day moving around the estate, but he had severe difficulty getting deeper into the palm grove as the roads were destroyed with age. He wondered how many squatters had moved into the grove and found remnants of wood huts, now decayed from the weather. He marked new roads on the map and drew grid squares divided into twenty acre squares. He did not know how much palm oil he could harvest, yet he heard many Liberians made good money from selling palm oil that could be used in all kinds of cosmetic products.

The Robertsport mansion structure was in relatively good shape. The slate roof remained solid over the years and kept the intense weather out from the rafters. The foundation was built on a solid granite ledge and had not shifted in the fifty years since the cornerstone was laid. His father built the mansion with local laborers over a four year period. Solid concrete walls were erected that would stand against the intense storms that arrived during rainy season. Hurricane force winds were common in the Robertsport area. The kitchen required a complete overhaul and the plumbing was aged and inadequate. The Deputy Minister hired a working crew of forty men to bring the mansion back to life. Trucks of supplies from Monrovia arrived and were unloaded. He interviewed and hired his own security staff. He counted out a stack of bills from the Colombian drug dealers and divided them into piles. He did not need to make an accounting ledger for his new business, as regulator and tax laws were very scarce. Eventually, he knew the Liberian Ministry of Finance would inquire on his profits, but there would be no thought on where he got the money. Many Liberians believed the new Congo people, mostly Americans were loaded. He laid out over seventy thousand dollars in the different piles and kept what remained in the bag. Several hundred thousand dollars made him an instant multi-millionaire. He did not care that it was drug money. He was going to make something out of the money. The church and schools needed major repair. Roads had to be fixed. And of course, he needed to find what happened to his father. If he became the ambassador of goodwill for Robertsport, he would hopefully reveal what really happened to his father.

In northern Liberia, the mountainside sun tried to penetrate the canopy near Foya village. The air was chilly compared to what Ike was used to in Monrovia and Firestone Plantation. Emotions came over Ike as he awoke in a straw hut. He walked outside and grabbed a blanket to serve as a coat. A misty dew haze hung over the village. Ike could make the burned pile of wood in the village center. He looked at the pile and saw Koroma's burned corpse rested against the center post. Ike walked down the road for twenty minutes and stood in front of a crumpled wall that was once his ancestral home. Not much remained for the brick home that he remembered as a little boy and as a father. Local villagers chipped away at the remnants. Ike recalled memories as a boy running and playing, but most of his memories were of his own family and the sheer joy his children brought to him. His wife worked hard and was loyal. Tears dripped down his face. He turned east and kneeled to pray. The Foya village elders hugged Ike as he came to bid farewell. He felt redemption. He felt pride. As he drove down the dirt path, children ran alongside him. As they waved and laughed, he thought of his own children who would never be young adults. The pain came back.

After a full day of driving along the primitive road that connected the northern villages to the coast, Ike arrived back to Firestone Rubber Plantation two days after the assault. Smoke remained in the air and hung over the Black Beret camp. Ike was shocked by what he saw and accelerated the land rover and crashed the gate. The metal fence fell on top of the land rover and bounced off. Ike slammed on the brake and spun the wheel. The vehicle slid to a stop in a half circle. Ike ran into the colonel's bungalow but could not find him. Everything was still, except for the chimps crawling along the ground looking for food. A mirror flash caught his eye; at first, he thought that it was a reflection of some trash but it continued. Ike climbed the hill and was faced with the end of a rifle pointed at him. The man motioned for Ike to go inside.

"Boss, boss. R u ok?" Ike was very worried.

"I'm fine." Kitson said. "The camp was destroyed."

"Boss, so sarry laft, so sarry." Ike was visibly shaken and the British Colonel placed his hand on Ike's arm to show that everything was going to be alright.

"Ike, you need to take me to the UN hospital." Ike knew where it was. No foreigners would go to JFK Hospital that was where Liberians went to die.

Ike brought his boss to the UNMIL hospital operated by the Jordanian medical team. He drove very fast and swerved in and out of traffic. The British Colonel pleaded for him to slow down; however, Ike did not slow. He pushed through the traffic lanes with a fierce vengeance. Horns did not help in Monrovia traffic as no one abided by any resemblance of traffic code. Ike did not waste time pushing the horn. He kept his foot on the gas pedal and braked only when he needed to slow slightly enough to swerve in and out of traffic.

Ike found Russell at the Cape Hotel. By time they arrived back to the UNMIL hospital Colonel Frank Kitson, Jr. was already gone. UN officials called in an emergency evacuation plane and the British Colonel was flown to London. Russell was extremely upset with himself as he chose to leave the camp. He had guilt syndrome and wondered if he had stayed would things have been different. Russell had Ike drive them to the Black Beret camp. As they approached, they saw a man searching in the rubble of Kitson's old bungalow. Ike motioned to Russell that he was not a threat.

"Who are you?" Russell asked and pulled out a large knife he had concealed under his shirt.

"Colonel Marzah. I used to command the Black Berets. This was my camp."

"What happened?"

Marzah pointed toward the hill. "From my camp, I spotted two vehicles and eight men. They came shooting and then a large explosion. I don't know what happened."

Russell knew why the explosion occurred. He inspected two bodies that remained on the ground. There were several more mangled corpses closer to the communication building, yet he could not bring it to himself to see them. Iskandariyah was still too close in his mind. He rolled one of the bodies over. Open eyes looked up at him and he closed the dead man's eyelids. Inside the jacket, he found a picture of Koroma. The man had no identification.

"Are you American?" Marzah inquired.

"Yes, U.S. Marine."

"I was trained in America at Fort Bragg. I spent over a year there once."

"Your English is good." Russell replied. "Why do you live there?" He pointed up to the hill.

"I like to watch my camp." Marzah looked across the destroyed buildings. "I miss my team."

"You served under Taylor?"

"I was forced to serve under Taylor."

"He's a war criminal." Russell said.

"I despised him for what he did to Liberia."

"Did you work with the ATU?" Russell read the horror stories of Taylor's infamous Anti-Terrorism Unit (ATU) and the brutality they inflicted upon their own people. He read that the UN considered charging anyone associated with ATU with crimes against humanity. He wondered if and when Liberian would be able to charge, arrest, and prosecute Liberians of war crimes. The entire Liberian Supreme Court and justice system required a complete overhaul.

"No, I refused to have my men work with those butchers. They were not soldiers, they were animals."

"What did you do when the UN came?"

"I ordered my men to turn in their weapons and sign the agreement not to pick up arms against the new Liberian government."

"You have a new president."

"Yes, she was the Minister of Finance before. She was saved from execution when Doe took over."

"You were there?"

"I was Doe's Lieutenant. He was my master sergeant. He always complained about pay and food. He complained about everything. He made threats against the Tolbert regime, but nobody took him serious. On one April night in 1980 when the rainy season started, he walked up the hill from BTC to the Presidential Palace with thirty thugs and found President Tolbert in bed. He shot him in his sleep. He sent a few men to the radio station and broadcasted the president was removed and the military was in charge." Russell recalled the insurgency doctrine that he studied. The first thing was to kill the president, usually in a public way, and the second was to take over the national radio station. "Doe captured most of the Cabinet members who were mostly Tolbert's and lined them up along the back wall within BTC. I ran to get General Dubar. He pleaded with Doe not to shoot. After an hour, Dubar agreed to support the new self-proclaimed temporary President Doe if he let Ellen live."

"That must have been pretty intense."

"Yes, it was. General Dubar was very upset with Doe and he almost got himself shot, but it was his talks with Doe that helped stop the massacre. After Doe executed the Tolberts, he was happy."

"Did you stay on?"

"I did. General Dubar brought all of us officers together and told us that we had to support the new elections. It really was not much of an election and Doe was elected easily. I went from one day telling Doe what to do and then I had to salute him."

"I heard Doe was a butcher."

"He was, worse than Taylor. In the basement of the Presidential Palace there were jail cells and Doe had his enemies captured and imprisoned. Before his cabinet meetings, he would take a prisoner out and have his guards cut out the heart while he was alive. Doe would take a bite out and pass the heart around. If the cabinet member did not bite the heart, he was shot. Several refused and were shot, or should we say fired." Russell knew that the child soldiers ate the hearts of their enemies as a means to capture their power.

"What did the rest of Africa do about Doe?"

"Nothing. Even America did nothing. Your President Reagan awarded Doe because he said that he would fight against the Soviet communists."

"I saw the photos of Doe at the White House."

"America kept Doe in power for a long time."

"Until Taylor came. What did you do when Taylor's NPFL attacked Monrovia?"

"I fought against them and then one day Doe showed up dead on TV and we had a new president."

"Prince Johnson killed Doe."

"Yes. I heard Taylor would not kill him so Johnson put a knife in Doe's chest and dragged his body to the center of Monrovia. He wrapped him with rope around a monument. Doe was still alive when the foreign camera crews arrived. Johnson cut out his heart."

"What did you do?" Russell asked.

"Like I have done each time there is a new government, I support the Liberian people. In African, governments come and go like the wind, but the people. The people they outlive government."

"I have been tasked with keeping Taylor from coming back to power." Russell stated pointedly.

"How are you going to do that?"

"He will be charged as a war criminal."

"The Accra Peace Accord said that he would not be charged. I did not agree with it, but it got Taylor out of Liberia before more bloodshed. I brought the army along the beach in the middle of the night to the safety of BTC. Taylor left us there to die. He never cared about us. He only cared about staying in power by fear, the fear of the ATU."

"You're right that Taylor cannot be charged as a war criminal in Liberia, but he could be charged in Sierra Leone."

"Interesting, that could work." The Liberian said.

"Will you help me?" Russell asked. Colonel Marzah nodded and motioned for them to follow him.

The Presidential Palace held information that Colonel Marzah needed. Russell called the Deputy Minister and informed him what happened at the Black Beret camp and requested admittance to the Presidential Palace. They loaded up everything that was not destroyed at the camp. Ike spent most of his time in the colonel's bungalow packing up everything. He knew if he left again nothing would remain as the locals would quickly overrun the compound and scavenge. Russell saw sparkles in the debris and surmised the bright reflections were diamonds. He touched the rough diamond in his pocket and made sure it was still there. Locals would have a sure bounty if they spent time shifting through the dirt and debris for the speckles of rough diamonds not destroyed from the tremendous blast. The communication building was completely destroyed. Russell inspected the American bungalows and grabbed everything that remained. The weapons, ammunition, night vision goggles, and headsets were locked in the safe. He carried bundles of equipment back and forth to the vehicle. He covered everything with a tarp; the safe was too heavy to take. Colonel Marzah raided the kitchen and packed up everything that Lucy did not break into and try to eat. There were three Liberian security guards dead, two intruders, and body parts for several more. Russell had no ambition to dig graves and told Ike to pay someone. He handed him a crisp one hundred dollar bill. He had no idea what the cost was and Ike told him that it was more than enough. They drove the land rover and took the intruder's vehicle that was left behind.

Liberia's Presidential Palace loomed over all of the government buildings. Over the past three years since it was emptied, weeds and shrubs have taken over the once manicured grounds. The fabled water garden with fountains and flowers was desolate. Everything was quiet. For years, Doe and Taylor occupied the Presidential Palace and wreaked havoc upon the Liberian populace. The new president moved down the street to the Ministry of Foreign Affairs. There was a fire several weeks before she took the oath of office. The electrical fire was reported as an accident and President Ellen was more than happy not to occupy the building that held so many ghosts and horrific secrets. The charged wires from the fire have since been removed and sold for the copper, nothing worth anything in Liberia stays put for long. Ike stayed with the vehicles.

"It's in the basement, a room that does not exist." He did not know what he meant and thought more of the superstitions that Liberians have placed on the Presidential Palace. Many Liberians believed it was haunted by the tortured souls. Russell followed him deeper into the basement, deeper into the haunted horrors of Doe's brutality. There were no lights, no windows. The small flashlights provided barely any light. Colonel Marzah turned several times and brought them into a large room.

"This room was where Doe executed his enemies," Colonel Marzah said, "and his friends." He added with a smirk. He went to the far right corner, placed his hand against the wall, and moved down the wall until he found what he needed. "Hold my light." Colonel Marzah pushed into the wooden wall and moved a hidden door. Inside the small room, Russell saw several tables, maps on the walls, and several filing cabinets. Colonel Marzah went right to the middle drawer and opened the file cabinet. He rapidly looked at several files, grabbed stacks of paper, and left. They closed the hidden door.

Within the massive Sapo forest, General Abbdas opened the metal box and emptied the contents. The amount of blood diamonds was running low. He counted the five small sacks. Each sack contained one hundred diamonds ranging in size from small stones to several carats. He arrived at Sapo with over sixty bags of diamonds but keeping an army in exile paid and fed was expensive. The intimidation for anyone trying to pan for gold in the old river bed had yielded more than he thought but still not enough. He needed to send Koroma back to Sierra Leone, yet he had not heard from him in over a month since he departed for Monrovia. Sumarka looked inside the partially opened door. General Abbdas laid out all of the documents and photos. He smiled as he looked at the photos of him dressed in his best uniform and chest full of medals. Charles Taylor stood beside him congratulating him. He looked at the pictures of his family at Blue Lake in the interior of Liberia and thought of the fun times that was until his family was killed by the rebels as they approached Monrovia. He left Colonel Marzah in charge of the defense of Monrovia as he grieved and buried his family. He opened an envelope that was labeled 'Presidential Eyes Only' across the top in red ink. Inside he pulled out several photos of the president and a scantily clad supermodel. There were several documents and signatures that he reviewed and placed back into the envelope.

At the BTC compound, the Deputy Minister had the keys to the bungalows and he had the rooms opened before Russell arrived. Dust, dirt, and stale air lingered in the rooms. Colonel Marzah and Ike seemed pleased with the accommodations while Russell knew his men would not be happy. There was no generator to power the bungalow, but that mattered little as none of the air conditioners worked. There was a small lock box safe in one room that could hold the ammunition. The weapons would have to be hidden. Fortunately, he saw the windows were all barred and the front door was the only access point and seemed solid.

Ike and Colonel Marzah moved in while Russell went back to the Cape Hotel. Russell looked at the papers from the Presidential Palace.

Over a beer on the stone patio, Russell read several of the seized documents. He looked out over the beach below. The umbrellas and chairs were perfectly arranged. Local workers outnumbered the foreigners who relaxed by a ratio of three to one, yet more than a dozen Liberians waited outside of the yellow rope. They patiently waited to sell trinkets, paintings, and anything to a foreigner.

Within a few moments, Francesca arrived and did not say a word. Russell stared at this beautiful lady who gave him so much attention. He put the papers in a shipping envelope and would mail the documents to Freetown.

"Why are you here?" Russell asked.

"To make a difference." Francesca replied as she pointed her arm outward toward the other tables. "Like many of the foreigners here. I want to save lives." They talked over dinner, however, Russell felt there was something not right about her.

After dinner, Russell took Francesca to the piano bar. As they sat on a large couch in the corner under candlelight, they observed the many comings and goings of the NGO community, diplomats, local dignitaries, Lebanese, and many foreigners. Several diplomats from Egypt, France, and Germany were in heated discussions. They quieted when the new Minister of Finance came close to join the group. Liberia had embarked on a campaign to have the international community forgive the five billion dollars of debt held by foreign lenders. The new Liberian government operated on a cash base system and had not been able to operate a deficit. The local currency was weakened by inflation. The US greenback remained the primary currency. The economies existed: one where locals fought to survive every day and the other inflated by the infusion of foreigners. A local Liberian could never shop at the exclusive Abbu Jabbi market that had the freshest foods. Local guards stood outside with arm-length clubs to ensure beggars did not assault the customers. Foreigners fought through the throngs of one legged or one armed beggars who asked for handouts.

Russell walked Francesca toward her room and she pushed him against the wall. She kissed him hard on the lips before she entered her room and closed the door. Francesca was a master at manipulation.

CHAPTER 13

General Abbdas sat at his makeshift desk and reviewed the inventory of ammunition and explosives. He let his men keep their own weapons, but he held a majority of the ammunition. The weapons were needed to maintain the sense of fear among the gold sifters. He needed to take action against anyone who refused to pay protection. Abbdas' biggest fear was someone might roll a hand grenade under his bed while he slept. He could not inject discipline upon this rogue army, many of these men were wanted for atrocities. Undoubtedly, he knew some of his men were clinically insane, yet they were his best killers. The men who successfully hunted were rewarded with liquor. Prior to the army of exiles and dysfunctional murderers moved in, Sapo was plentiful with small and large animals. In the past two years, hundreds of animals had been shot to feed his exiled army. Giraffes, West African elephants, chimps, water buffalos, and kudos were all shot indiscriminately. Sumarka was a good cook and could take any bush meat and make a fine meal. The general was pleased with his bush wife, yet he still beat her sometimes, always in front of his men that demonstrated his power. Sumarka walked around the camp with her baby on her back. She buried her other child the day before and had no time to grieve. The child coughed heavily and spat up blood. There was no medicine in the camp and she could not ask to leave for the nearest village to find a doctor. She was a bush wife - she had no rights.

About a hundred miles away, the Cape Hotel's restaurant was busy. The dinner crowd was a sorted mix of foreigners and new Congo Liberians who had returned. Meals were served with precision and Tareek kept tight control over the staff. Uncle Anwar had invested a lot of money over the past six months. The kitchen, tables, chairs, and the bar were updated. The wine list was expanded to include many South African and Chilean vintages. Hummus and warm Lebanese bread filled the tables and patrons gobbled the food as they waited for the main course. The patrons dined on fresh grouper, tuna, and sought after giant local lobsters. The Lebanese chefs were absolutely superb, but could never work in a New York restaurant, as they had no sense of urgency. In

Lebanon, dinner was an event, not just a meal. Tareek made sure his staff walked and worked the tables to keep the guests entertained. When Tareek saw Chad sitting at the bar and not working, he confronted him. "What are you doing?"

"I don't work here anymore," replied Chad abruptly to his former boss. "You do not control me."

"What are you talking about?"

"I am not working for Anwar. I work for Rajik now."

Chad watched Feeatu. She moved elegantly around the tables and held the tray of dinners above her head. At thirty years old, she had a perfect figure, honed by years of manual labor. She owned no car and walked everywhere. She lived in a small enclave outside of Monrovia called Sinkhor, which was not destroyed by the civil war. Feeatu renovated a small shack for herself and her three boys. She wished more of a life for them and pushed them to attend school. She did not want her boys to end up like the thousand other young men who lived on Monrovia's streets. Her husband's death left her without anything. She worked ten hours a day. The tips she made kept her boys secure, alive, and content.

At the corner table, the Al-Qaeda operative, Rashad, watched Feeatu from a distance. He directed Chad to remain close to Feeatu. Rashad watched from a distance as he continued to eat his dinner by himself. No one recognized him and he was glad. Feeatu's husband was an important link to smuggled rough, untraceable diamonds from the Sierra Leone border to Monrovia. Feeatu's husband would wait days as young RUF boys walked thirty miles over the toughest terrain to avoid military patrols. On both sides of the border, the UN established regular patrols to combat the illegal diamond flow. Rashad surmised that Feeatu had the diamonds buried somewhere.

Russell and the Gunnys ventured out to the casino and left Stone at the Cape Hotel, as he was more interested in getting acquainted with the woman he saved from drowning. The casino parking lot was crowded with dozens of white SUVs, all sorts of NGO, government, and contractor vehicles. Along the outside wall, Russell saw a dozen local ladies lined up. They waited for something. The poker, dice, and roulette tables were crowded. Several Chinese had bet stacks of chips on the roulette numbers. Across the board, chips were stacked along the number lines and on the numbers. The Chinese man gambled heavily and won a small fortune. Cheers erupted. Rajik came out from the control room. He motioned to the pit boss. The Peruvian lady took over control of the wheel from the local. As eyes focused on placing the bets across the numbers, the small white ball was changed out. Only a few chips rested on double zero. The next number rolled was double zero. The Chinese man was not concerned and bet heavily again. The next double zero brought several sighs of disbelief. The Peruvian pit boss turned over control back to the local. Russell placed chips on the table and lost along with everyone else.

Russell found the private gambling room. He held up a wad of cash and the large bouncers allowed him to enter. Across the room, he saw the Al-Qaeda operative known as Rashad. He recognized him from the photo and the scar on his forehead. For a moment, he wondered what type of scene he would create if he just beat him, yet he knew the mission was priority. He found a seat at the poker table. He looked across the table and saw his friend from Barcelona who watched the game. He bet more, looked up, and she disappeared. The Gunnys were actively engaged at the poker table and enjoyed the free drinks. Russell watched them for several moments and went to the bathroom. He heard the door open, but did not turn around. Outside the security guard was pleased to have a crisp one hundred dollar bill and informed the men that the bathroom was broken and they had to go downstairs. Before he could zip up his pants, an arm came around his waist and he felt her movement. He was taken by surprise.

"What are you doing?" Russell inquired.

"Falling for you." The female Mossad agent whispered in his ear.

Russell was aroused and pleased to oblige her desire. He felt something strong for her. He did not know why, but whatever it was, his feelings were significantly different than what he had for Kristin. The passion he had for his former fiancé was more programmed with compatibility exams administered in direct questioning by her father. In the end, he saw the light and walked away from her and her father. The beauty from Barcelona now had her legs wrapped around him as she sat on the sink counter. She was pleased and held his face in her hands while she kissed him. Her life was many identities and she lived on the edge. Love was not allowed, yet she yearned for more than the life of a Mossad agent. She cleaned up and walked out. Major Tom Russell, a decorated Marine officer, walked back to the poker table. He felt violated, yet he could not inform the Gunnys.

At the Cape Hotel, the bar was not crowded, which was unusual for a Friday night. Rajik wondered if the NGO community must have gotten ill from the food, some disease outbreak, or just trying to pocket some of the money that they were getting from their contracts. Rajik watched the few patrons and observed who was present and more importantly, who was absent. Rashad dropped a piece of paper on Rajik's table as he sat down. Rajik opened the note and then burned it in the ashtray. Rashad had recruited Chad for his special project without Rajik's knowledge and Rajik was not pleased. He knew Rashad would be more than willing to die for his cause, but needed Chad to help complete his exit strategy.

Russell walked into the Cape Hotel lobby and saw Francesca sitting by the downstairs bar on an oversized leather couch. She still wore the sleeveless dress and her brown skin showed well in the lighting. He walked up to her. He wanted to kiss her shoulders, but did not as to raise attention. A kiss in public would bring unwanted attention. He looked at her necklace charm and asked to see it. She passed it and he read the inscription, 'For the lack of guidance a nation falls, but many advisors make victory sure' and looked at the photo. "Your family?" She nodded. From her body movement, he did not ask more. He thought the inscription unusual, but again knew better not to press her for information. She had something on her mind.

"What do you want?" Francesca asked.

"I'll take a beer." He said.

"No, I mean what do you want of me?" She was deceptive.

"I don't know what you are asking?" He did not know what she wanted; something did not seem right about her.

"What do you want me to do? Should I see you no more?" He knew what she was saying. He knew eyes were on them, some chuckles heard behind his back.

"I live a complicated life." She laughed lightly as she sipped her beer and thought this man had no idea what a complicated life meant. She was undercover for months at a time. She tracked and killed the enemies of Israel. She killed terrorists. She was not supposed to fall in love. She was a well-trained Mossad agent. "Do you go back to America soon?"

"No, not soon." Russell said and he paused for a long moment. "I don't know how long I will be in Liberia."

"Why are you here?"

"That's complicated." Russell wanted to tell her. He needed to talk to someone. Over the past few days, the camp they had been using was blown up; his British mentor had been sent out of country; the Deputy Minister thwarted an assassination attempt; and someone put a bullet an inch from his head that blasted a Colombian drug runner apart.

"Do you like what you do?" She asked inquisitively.

"I do. I've done things that mattered."

"Like what?" She needed to know more about him, anything that could be used. She would have his finger prints sent to Tel Aviv tonight lifted from the drinking glass he once held.

"I've saved lives in mountains as part of a rescue team. What about you, being a doctor ... that's pretty important."

"Saving a life is important." She did not want to tell him that most of the time she had to perform interrogations and her doctor skills helped inflict the severest pain imaginable. He could sense she was not telling him the full story. He purchased a bottle of Jack Daniels and went to his room. He needed to sort out what went wrong and what the hell he was going to do. Russell was finished with the undercover work; finished with the deceit; frustrated he could not tell her more; and he needed to get a haircut before he surprised the Nigerian general.

In the morning, Russell and Stone found the only barbershop in town. The Lebanese barber juggled the cigarette in his mouth, coughed several times, and held the razor blade against his neck. Luckily, he saw the barber install a fresh new blade out of the package out of fear of getting HIV. The barber was only about forty, but it appeared he already had lung cancer based upon the hard-digestive coughs emitting from his interior. The Arabic hookah pipes in the corner were on full blast. The newly arrived Lebanese businessmen gobbled down the tobacco and puff out most of the tar into the air for all to enjoy. Most Liberians did not smoke because they could not afford the cost; however, for the local boys who cleaned the shop, second hand smoked infiltrated their lungs.

Afterwards, Russell took Stone to the BTC compound to visit the Nigerian general. He dreaded the meeting to inform him that the British Colonel got blown up. The Nigerian was not expecting any visitors. The Nigerian never turned on the air conditioner when he was alone. He sat in his executive chair and reviewed the equipment status reports for all of the equipment the US government purchased for the new Liberian army. The aid knocked on the door and announced his visitors.

"My friends... how are you?" The general greeted the two Marine officers with solid handshakes and was surprised that they learned how to shake hands the Liberian way. After the pleasantries, Russell got down to business.

"Colonel Kitson had to leave Liberian."

"Why was that?"

"Well, it's hard to explain." He looked at the general to gauge his response. "The camp was attacked and there was an explosion." The general gasped and Russell sensed his concern. "But he's ok. He was airlifted out on a UN flight to London."

"Did you catch those responsible?"

"No, no we didn't." Russell handed the general several of the papers he removed from the Presidential Palace.

"Where did you obtain these?"

"You don't want to know." Russell responded. The general raised his right eyebrow to him. He was not used to junior officers speaking to him that way. At this point, Russell did not care about offending anyone. He was on a fast approaching timeline before the rainy season and things could turn for the worse if Charles Taylor came back to power.

"If these documents are legitimate, this paints a very bad picture against Mr. Taylor." The Nigerian said. Russell had hoped the general would draw a similar conclusion. Charles Taylor found sanctuary in Nigeria, yet the loophole in the Accra Peace Accord never stated anything about being charged for crimes against humanity in Sierra Leone. The documents clearly showed Charles Taylor directed General Abbdas to recruit, train, and use child soldiers. Taylor did not trust any teenagers in Liberia and worried the rebels would infiltrate the Presidential Palace and assassinate him just like Doe killed Tolbert. In the last months before exile, Taylor became extremely paranoid and would not allow anyone under the age of thirty in the Presidential Palace. Taylor ordered Abbdas to Sierra Leone and recruit former RUF children soldiers, who were some of the most brutal, carnivorous killers ever witnessed on the African continent.

The meeting helped Russell refocus. He needed to get his team out of the Cape Hotel. Russell stopped at the bungalows and found the Gunnys cleaning weapons. The Deputy Minister walked the two hundred yards from his office to the bungalows and embraced Russell.

"These bungalows will be a safe place for us to operate out of. Russell said as he pointed to the bars on the outside of the windows. Charles Taylor had the added security feature installed just in case he needed to hide somewhere. The images of Doe walking up the hill to kill President Tolbert in his sleep haunted Taylor.

"You'll be safe here." The Deputy Minister pointed to the local men who walked near the fall wall. "I hired more security guards."

"Would you mind if Ike took over your personal security?" Russell pointed to Ike and had him shake hands with the Deputy Minister. Ike had never met someone in such a high position of government and was very impressed. "Ike operated the Black Beret camp and needs a job."

"Agreed." The Deputy Minister heard about Kitson's injuries. More importantly, the Minister had no clue about proper security and welcomed the idea. He had kept a low profile since the assassination attempt, yet he was still vulnerable. At his father's palm oil plantation, the mansion renovation plans progressed beyond his wildest dream. He pulled more and more money out of the bag that helped put food on the table for the line of men who showed up for work every day. Unemployment in the countryside was near eighty percent. There were no jobs. Basic human survival equated to men and women scavenging and harvesting anything that would grow. Men journeyed all day into the deep jungle in search for food. Any animal within sight was killed. Bush meat became a delicacy for the starving.

The vehicles were loaded within thirty minutes. Weapons were wrapped in blankets and wooden boxes contained large amounts of ammunition. The Gunnys searched the vehicle left by the intruders and could not find any documentation to show the origin. Rozelli was worried it would be recognized and took a hammer to the front and back panels. He called it a little decorative touch, New York style. The two land rovers departed BTC compound toward Robertsport. The team was complete again with the four Marines, Ike, the Liberian Lieutenants, and now Colonel Marzah joining the team. They drove across the main streets of Monrovia and crossed over the bridge to Bushrod Island, named after Bushrod Washington, a relative of George Washington. Major Russell looked out the window at the crowded market scene and now knew why he was here. The purest sense of why he was here rested within the smallest faces he saw - the children. Despair and lawlessness ruled their world. They needed some hope for a future and if he contributed just one small part that would help repair him. It was not about him, the team, or hell even the mission. It was about giving these children a future. If that meant killing someone, he considered the possibilities.

At the Cape Hotel, Tareek replayed the audio. He could not tell what was being said. He tried to balance the signal and could not filter the surrounding noise. She became impatient and pushed her way into the control knobs. She moved and adjusted the filter to expound the words. "You need to fear Al-Qaeda" were the words Rashad spoke to Rajik. The Mossad agent knew it was now a totally different game. Her beautiful looks would not serve well toward manipulating Rashad. Her orders gave her considerable latitude. Mossad followed terrorists who wanted to inflict Israel harm. Mossad operations in Africa had been covert, yet there had been major operations such as the raid on Entebbe Airport in Uganda in 1976 that freed hundreds of Israeli citizens from certain death. The only concern Tel Aviv would have was her partnership with a Lebanese.

Several miles away and at the Taylor compound, Rashad remained in his private room. He did not want to go back downstairs and hear Chucky's rambling on how the Americans were out to get him. Rashad was paid a good amount of money to blow up things up. He looked at photos and thought of the targets. The Cape Hotel had layered security. The front gate had two guards, roving patrols, video surveillance, yet there were no visible weapons. The UN embargo restricted weapons, yet Rashad knew Anwar had weapons hidden. He circled a street behind the hotel where he would place a car bomb.

CHAPTER 14

Workers at the Robertsport mansion made significant progress in the past two weeks. Russell was impressed, yet he wished that the five thousand kilowatt generator had arrived. The generator building was renovated and a new ten thousand gallon fuel tank installed. In Liberia, generators were a premium commodity. The Deputy Minister invested thirty thousand dollars on the generator, but it would not arrive for another month on a cargo vessel. The new roads to harvest palm oil had just started and the Gunnys took advantage of the numerous knocked down trees to build an obstacle course. They orchestrated a crew of twenty local men to help construct the bunkers, walls, and overhangs needed to make it challenging. Russell was impressed about the new job creation program in Robertsport. So much attention had been placed on the women, many abused, yet no NGO wanted to provide jobs to former child soldiers drugged by the RUF.

The white UN vehicle caught Russell by surprise as it stopped at the main entrance gate three hundred feet down the road and turned into the compound. UN forces were not officially allowed outside of Monrovia alone, yet he saw dozens of UN vehicles at the beach. He wondered if someone was trying to get intelligence on his operation.

"Greetings my friend." General Abdurallah stepped out of the vehicle with another Nigerian in uniform. "You recall Brigadier General Addu." Russell greeted the officer properly with a quick salute. Even not in uniform, he sensed the Nigerians appreciated the military courtesy and respect. The one star Nigerian general was at the house party at the Club beer factory. "We must discuss some concerns." They went inside and Russell took them upstairs. Two local guards stood at the door. The bedroom was converted into an operations center. Several tables were connected in the middle with maps spread out. Photos lined the wall.

"UNMIL does not know about your mission."

"My boss in Germany told me New York knew." Russell felt something wrong about Addu. He sensed mistrust, greed, dishonesty, yet he refrained from speaking a single word.

"Yes, but New York never talked to us." the one star Nigerian general replied. "The SRSG does not receive much information from

New York, it is frustrating." Russell knew the SRSG stood for Special Representative to the Secretary General of the UN; basically, she called the head of the UN directly when there were issues. All UN military forces in Liberia reported to the SRSG and no actions were authorized unless the SRSG personally approved the orders. In the UN, there existed a significant level of mistrust for the military forces, regardless of country of origin.

"We have a mission." Russell stated firmly and really did not care about the UN's inability to properly task and communicate. He had his mission. "Sir, I don't know what to tell you. Africa Command gave me orders."

"Yes, I understand. What I am saying is perhaps we can serve both of our needs." Over the next hour, the one star Nigerian general laid out the UN Mission in Liberia's problems. At points, Russell dropped his mouth open in awe wondering how inept the UN staff was. In the end, they agreed that the American team would 'bag and tag' General Abbdas and bring him to UN headquarters for questioning. Russell would place a delayed detonator bomb at the site of any stockpiled weapons and ammunition in preparation for the UN to send in troops to clear out Sapo National Forrest. The one star Nigerian general relayed how upset the local governors became over the illegal logging performed by the Russian mafia. The unannounced guests left and Russell was pleased he did not have to entertain them.

Russell needed to clear his head. The mission would be difficult enough without added threat of the Russian mafia. The Marines dressed in military boots and bush clothes. The Lieutenants wore their new army uniforms while Ike wore his street clothes and flip-flops. In the daylight, they practiced moving and ducking in and around the palm trees. For several hours, they maneuvered through the new obstacles the Gunny's created. Sweat poured from all possible pours. Ike kept up and passed the Marines several times. Flip-flops did not slow him down. Afterwards the Marines went to the beach and stripped off their clothes. They jumped into the surf and caught the attention of several NGOs who rested under the palm tree shade. Several Liberians tried to surf. Stone watched.

Russell sat at the surfside bar on the edge of the beach. He saw Britney's older sister who sat with a table five feet away. He did not want to get into a conversation with her. She had several NGO contractors reviewing a new USAID contract document and it appeared everyone followed her wishes. He thought she resembled a Pied Piper and tried to push the NGO community around. Russell walked past them and did not speak a word. Outside on the beach, he saw about a dozen local girls and boys picking up discarded plastic water bags that washed ashore. The children brought the plastic bags to the local female sewing coop started by former Liberian women who had the fortune of attending Harvard and now gave back. The Liberian women were all brutalized during the civil war and the therapy of sewing by hand helped them cope. Several female Harvard graduates raised money, purchased sewing machines, and personally carried five sewing machines to Robertsport as there was no reliable mail system. Russell purchased a dozen bags to bring home and was amazed at the quality made from discarded trash. Russell showed the bags to the rest of the team on the beach.

"These international organizations are not helping." Rageone said. "There is no stability here."

"They're doing the best they can, under the circumstances." defended Stone as he saw a different side to the operations from his my new little friend.

"They don't care for us. A German lady called me a baby killer when she found out that I served in Iraq." Rozelli responded.

"Yeah and then he told her at least he did not kill six million Jews." Rageone blurted out.

"That's good for international relations," retorted Stone.

"There's a lot that needs to happen in this country and the first thing is better security. Let's not forget why we are here." Russell reminded then who was in charge and left. As he walked up the beach, a small albino boy about three feet tall and about seven years old emerged from behind an old destroyed boat, which was beached. Russell did not want to scare him as he heard albino children were very afraid and they had reason to be deathly afraid of strangers. Albinos had the recessive gene, a natural tragedy. In the secret society that underpinned Liberia and all of West Africa, witch doctors believed the bones from albinos held special medicinal purposes. Kidnapped albinos were kept alive for as long as they could as their limbs were sawed off for ritual healing events. It would not be uncommon for an entire skeleton of an albino to be used by the witch doctors. He read in the Gazette that twenty-two albino children disappeared in rural Nimba County two weeks ago. Many albinos moved to the city for protection. He wondered if this boy was part of that refugee movement. Against all of his instincts, he handed the boy a crisp fifty dollar bill, more money than his family earned in a month. Russell did not want the money as Hezbollah had touched it.

The Robertsport mansion was crowded with workers and Ike was back at work inspecting his security guards. The Gunnys developed detailed intelligence assessments on Charles Taylor and his beloved son Chucky. They outlined plans to conduct a snatch and grab operation.

"Here is the intel report on Charles Emmanuel, otherwise known as Chucky." Rozelli said, "Here is an undated photo I was able to find."

"He makes Hitler look like a choir boy." interjected Rageone.

"We know he is here but how and when is he trying to bring his father back to power?" Russell asked as he tried to get his team focused.

"Based upon what Koroma told us," Rozelli said, "An Al-Qaeda bomb expert is in country to teach the rebels how to make IEDs."

"How are they going to get the explosives?" Russell pondered aloud. "We need to inspect the port."

The port of Monrovia was under tight UN control and containers were regularly inspected. By UN mandate, no weapons were allowed within Liberia and the penalties were very severe. The Lebanese controlled most of the import business that helped prioritize what hotels, restaurants, casinos, and shops they would fill with the freshest food. Broken refrigerated containers were left on the dock and contents sent to the Red Light district for sale. No one cared about botulism. Five hundred meters down the road was the old Liberian Coast Guard base. The new army had not formed a Coast Guard, and the contactors supporting equipping and training the new army used the old base as needed. Six hundred squatters who resided on the base for over three years since Taylor's fall were pushed out.

Rajik needed to get out of Liberia quickly as he knew the Colombians were not pleased with the loss of over one hundred million dollars of cocaine and they would be coming looking for him. Perhaps, Rashad would help him get set up in the Congo. The international calls that he surmised were from FARC contacts went unanswered. He had no explanation. It was his arrangement, his negotiation, his threats to the Deputy Minister, and his security men that lost the four thousand kilograms of cocaine. He knew the Colombians would be unhappy about the cocaine, yet more upset that their plans to utilize a fragile West African nation as a means to smuggle cocaine became known.

Big Carl never knew what one hundred thousand dollars looked like, and he surely did not know what ten kilos of cocaine looked like either, but he was happy to take both. Three twenty foot zodiacs powered up to the sandy beach and over a dozen men who wore complete black outfits emerged. They carried AK47s and if their biceps could be seen, Big Carl would have seen the letters RUF scrawled by razor blades into their black skin. They had cold steel eyes and were hard-core murderers who joined Al-Qaeda. Former child soldiers had no future outside of violence and Liberia was a fertile recruitment area for Al-Qaeda. Five wooden boxes were lifted out of the black rubber boats and loaded in the truck. Big Carl was amazed at how fast the men moved.

Big Carl closed the suitcase filled with money and smiled at Rajik. As Big Carl turned toward his vehicle, Rajik took the opportunity and stuck an eight-inch knife into his left kidney. Big Carl stumbled and fell as he reached his hand toward the wound. He tried to think back to his military training but that was so long ago. He tried to swing his arm at Rajik but he was out of shape and in pain. Rajik stepped forward and stabbed him in the throat. The shock, anguish, and pain overtook Big Carl's face. Rashad laughed and walked over to kick the American several times in the head. Rajik pulled up Big Carl's shirt and used a surgical razor to rip open his entrails. He wanted to make sure the wild dogs got a hold of him so his body could not be identified.

In a deserted building that used to be the Department of Defense under the Samuel Doe regime, the Deputy Minister looked across the room at the other new Congo Ministers who came back to Liberia. Each of them worked hard to get the new Liberian government established. Several of the older Supreme Court judges sat in the corner and observed the ceremony. The Deputy Minister held the glass of blood up to the light and was disgusted. A secret society, one of a few that had endured throughout the years in Liberia took hold of the government. New Congo members must undergo a modified more westernized ritual of cutting underneath both arms as not to be visible. Gone were the human sacrifices. In keeping with voodoo heritage, poro became as one of the common practices that called for human genitalia mutilation. Heart men were another aspect of the secret society. Freemasons remained secret even more as there was a real internal society threat from heart men and witch doctors. The sanctity of the Liberian society was in jeopardy. Screams emitted from women covered in a pale white clay paste over their entire body. White lines and circles crisscrossed their naked torso. Masks were worn by them hoping to capture some of the 'juju' spiritual connection. The sixteen tribes were represented and the Deputy Minister could make out the designs for the Mandingo tribe who were one of the most feared from the north near the border of Guinea and Sierra Leone. The texture of the masks evoked fear. Some had jutting teeth that once belonged to either a man or large bush animal. Splotches of grizzled hair hang from the top of the masks. Eye sockets were chiseled holes and the weathered notches from a blunt tool resemble deep scared wrinkles. Juju was something all Liberians feared yet desired; a chance to be stronger than your enemy. The dances became more creative and vibrant. Feet lifted faster and faster in rhythm of the deep drum strikes. The high shrieks emitted chilling his spine. He did not want to be tarnished as a non-believer and drank more of the blood.

From the Cape Hotel, Feeatu rode in the back seat of a taxicab. She made good tips over dinner service. The large Frenchman liked her and even rubbed his hand along her backside. She did not complain and would have slept with him for a few dollars. She did not consider herself a prostitute like the young women who waited outside the Cape Hotel's main gate. Each lady was dressed in her best clothes and claimed that she was HIV free and clean from disease. Feeatu was pleased with the freedom of being in a cab by herself. She treated herself to purchase the entire fare. Most taxis were packed tight with as many riders as possible. She sunk her body in the old leather seat that smelled like a sewer. She did not care; she was exhausted and rubbed her feet. The taxi brought her several miles out of Monrovia, which was the scene of major fighting during the civil war. The burned out hulks of buildings were home to many families. Feeatu walked from Tubman Boulevard where the taxi cab dropped her off. Feeatu's home was on the fence-line of Spriggs Payne Airport that the UN used for military cargo planes. Often she looked out at the piles of supplies that arrived and were offloaded and wondered when she would get her aide. It never came. The only aid she would obtain was by back breaking work. She did not approve of her husband's criminal activity smuggling blood diamonds and certainly did not want her boys growing up to be thugs. She sent them to school, yet they were corrupted several times to quit school to make a few dollars peddling goods in Red Light district. Each time, she became furious and lectured for hours on importance of school, something she never had even as a little girl. She attended services at St. Peter's Lutheran Church down the street. She said many prayers in the remembrance ceremony for the souls of the six hundred parishioners who sought refuge and were murdered by the ATU.

At the Robertsport mansion, Russell sat on the front porch. He missed his mentor and drank several gin and tonics in his honor. He recalled the most important thing he told him, 'nothing is what is appears to be in Africa.' It was Valentine's Day and he reflected back to two years prior. He was still overcoming the mental anguish of Iskandariyah when the Redskin football cheerleaders arrived. He had just returned from Iskandariyah and sat on top of his armored jeep. The vehicle was littered with shrapnel marks from the explosion. He remembered the view of scantily clad women who danced around under flood lights. He remembered the mass chaos that ensued when indirect fire 107 millimeter Chinese rockets rained into the camp. He watched the surreal events unfold something probably not seen since Vietnam.

"What are you thinking about?" Francesca said. She took him by surprise as he was deep in thought.

"How did you know where I was?" Russell asked.

"Not hard." She could not tell him that Cellcom, his internet cell phone provider, was owned by an Israeli company that happened to provide full tracking and wiretaps.

"Are you hungry?" Russell inquired and she nodded.

Ike had a nice meal prepared from a goat that was found in the plantation field. Ike chased the animal for a mile before he was able to club it to death. The Gunnys were interested in their new guest, mostly they checked out her legs. She gave the rehearsed Doctors Without Borders resume and all of the wonderful things she did in Liberia. She talked about HIV, malaria prevention, snake bites, and diseases as if she were actually involved. Russell was impressed by the rehearsed tirade, yet he became more suspicious. After a few bottles of wine, he did not want her to drive the two hours back to the Cape Hotel. He had no clue that she maintained a bush shack five miles down the road where she did all of her practice firing. In the bedroom, she refused to take her shirt off, but gladly tossed the shorts in the corner.

"What's this charm?" Russell inquired as he reached over to hold it in the air. He inspected the necklace.

"My father gave this to me." Francesca said.

He looked on the back and asked. "What does the inscription say?"

"It is an old proverb that says, 'For lack of guidance a nation falls, but many advisors make victory sure.' It was a proverb my mother liked." She did not mention that her mother gave her the charm that held the seal of the Israeli Institute for Intelligence and Special Operations, basically the Mossad.

Stone had skipped dinner with the team and dined in a shack on the beach with his little blonde. He was pleased with the dinner and the smiles he received. He knew that he had her. As they walked back to the wood framed tents, she pointed to the Lebanese men who screamed and danced around a beach bonfire as loud music radiated.

"They do this every weekend." She said with disgust.

"What?" Stone asked.

"The loud music, screaming, and partying." She continued. "It's like Lebanese gone wild."

"Do you want me to go and talk to them?" Stone gave her a serious look and she knew he would tear them apart if she told him yes.

"No," she laughed. "Be serious, don't cause trouble."

"Alright," As they sat on the bed to talk, Stone had difficultly listening as the noise got louder. "Does this go on for long?"

"All night." She replied. "They stay up partying until daylight and then drive back to Monrovia. They come here every Saturday night and on Sunday there is a pile of beer bottles, empty liquor bottles, and just trash left all over this beautiful beach."

"Really." Stone added, "I'll be right back."

"No, don't go and cause trouble." She pleaded.

"I'm not. I forgot my pajamas. I need to run up to the mansion." Stone vaulted up the hill as if he was back on the Oklahoma University football team. Inside the mansion, he went to the arms room that was guarded by Ike's security men and departed with a small bag. He remained in the tree line that was relatively close to the beach. He pulled out the CS gas canisters and lined the five canisters on a log. He nearly removed all of the pins and prepared for the onslaught. He pulled the pins and tossed one after another over a hundred feet. He made sure that he staggered the location and took into account the breeze off of the ocean to flow the gas toward the bonfire. The Lebanese stopped laughing and within seconds, there were shouts of pain. The Lebanese men ran back and forth in several directions, some ran into one another and fell. Stone kept low to the ground and laughed at the sight that unfolded in front of him.

"What was the noise?"

"Nothing, a little present I had for them." Stone smiled.

"Really. Where are your pajamas?"

"Sorry, forgot them."

"So did I." She pulled back the covers that revealed a naked body with several descriptive tan lines. Captain Stone, a Marine with a purpose, did not take long to get undressed but took longer to find the bed in the dark. He attempted to crawl into the mosquito net that rested over top of them and ripped it from the ceiling. They both laughed.

Chapter 15

The morning sun brought beautiful sunshine across the crashing waves and the sandy beach. Vivacious sounds erupted around Robertsport. Children ran and shouted on their way to the one room church. The loud speakers emitted unrecognizable sounds as the preacher screamed into the microphone. Cheers over shadowed the loud speaker that riddled every ear within a one mile radius. Russell rolled over and tried to cover his head with the pillow, but she grabbed his pillow and covered her head. After a few minutes, he surrendered and got out of bed. He closed the windows to give her some peace. He walked outside and immediately stepped on and destroyed a large snail. His bare foot was nicked by the shell. Some of the largest snails in the world resided in Liberia. He saw a dozen more snails that crawled along the sidewalk in the morning dew.

The young albino boy waved at Russell as he walked along the shops in Robertsport. He did not know what the boy was saying based upon his thick bush dialect. Britney walked up and heard the boy speak. She informed Russell that the boy said we had the same skin. Russell nodded, held the albino's boy hand firmly, and shook his hand several times.

"Yes, we have the same skin." Russell said as he acknowledged the boy. "What's your name?"

"James...me name James." The albino boy ran off on a chore that Ike gave him. Over the past week, Ike hired more and more locals to support operations at the mansion.

"We tried to keep the albino children safe, but that has not worked well." Britney was sincere in her statement. She had a tear in her eye. "They took five boys in the middle of the night from the orphanage." She pointed down the street. "Nobody would do anything."

"Why were they taken?"

"Sadistic rituals that date back a hundred years."

"Is that why the Peace Corps is here?"

"Among other things, but my primary job is to help the orphanage school get started. We don't make much money, but I would not want to be anywhere else in the world."

"And your sister?"

"She's a control freak and took charge trying to get Robertsport renovated. The town has great potential." He nodded agreement that this sanctuary could rival any Hawaiian island paradise.

Russell looked at the outside of the mansion with all of the construction that transpired. The outside gardens needed a complete overhaul. The brick path toward the large oak tree was repaved. The lawn was mowed with a large riding lawnmower that Rageone had to show Ike how to operate. Russell guessed that the Deputy Minister did not want a line of boys swing machetes all day to cut the grass. Everyone was very pleased with Ike's performance and the Deputy Minister gave him more and more latitude to operate the compound. Ike's best find was an older woman named Sara who told Ike that she used to work at the mansion many years ago and before the civil war. She knew the mansion well and cleaned every room with extreme vigor. Russell enjoyed the songs that continuously came from Sara as she cleaned. Sara made a large breakfast buffet. Russell went back upstairs with a breakfast tray for his guest.

"Where did you go?" Francesca inquired. The female Mossad watched intently as Russell walked into the room.

"Out front, I was talking with the albino boy."

"James?" She asked.

"Yes."

"He's a nice boy. His mother left him at the orphanage down the street and no one saw her again." She and every foreigner who arrived in Robertsport knew his story of survival.

"That's got to be tough."

"Albino children are considered bad luck, outcasts." Francesca said. "It is very sad."

"I heard that they're taken by witchdoctors and tortured to death for their bones." Russell pointed out.

"Sadistic." Francesca confirmed. "We need to take care of that." Russell looked at her with an inquisitive stare. He did not know what to think. Something inside of him made he believe she was not telling him something. This beautiful lady seemed insulated.

The Gunnys were at the beach trying to surf. Several Liberian boys had better success as they tackled the waves on the long boards. The foreigner surf crowd enjoyed teaching the locals and they cheered them on. The morning revealed the pile of empty bottles and trash left by the Lebanese, yet everyone was very content to clean up as they had a very restful night that was after Stone dropped five CS gas canisters on their little bonfire party. Russell and his new Mossad girlfriend walked down the beach arm in arm. A vacation promoter could have taken a photo of the couple and readers would have commented how lovely they looked. Russell was content and the best part was he did not think about the upcoming mission. After they returned from their walk and found Stone and his new little girlfriend as they rested under the shade of several palm trees. They borrowed the twenty foot powerboat owned by Uncle Anwar out of the marina and spent the afternoon fishing. The fishing pole bent over quickly and the fish nearly pulled it out of her hands. Within seconds, Stone grabbed the fishing pole from Britney and he handled the fish. Over the next forty minutes, he landed an eighty kilogram marlin over six feet long from fin to nose. After the fish stopped fighting and bouncing on the boat, Russell removed his knife and sliced out an eight-inch chunk of fish. He further cut the piece into smaller sections for sushi. The boat landed at the marina and crowds of boys ran to see the catch. Ike cooked the fresh fish on an open fire. Sara cooked casaba and rice. The Gunnys laid out fresh bread they purchased from a local family. They opened several bottles of wine and everyone toasted. The Deputy Minister would have been impressed by the dinner crowd. The Saturday dinner party was a magnificent event and went well into the night.

At the Cape Hotel, the Sunday breakfast buffet feast was magnificent. Tareek closely managed the most important event of the week at the Cape Hotel. Tareek could readily handle the eighty hotel guests, who demanded everything imaginable at all times of day. Tareek was exhausted, especially as Uncle Anwar was on vacation in Detroit with Ghasson. Perched on top of five floors overlooking most of Monrovia beach front and tattered buildings, Tareek sat in a lounge chair on the rooftop balcony. The war ended and everyone knew who was on what side. Now, he did not know who to trust. The US Embassy compound with the ambassador's residence formerly the British Embassy overlooked the point. He could see the heavy guard force and wondered if that was enough to protect the Cape Hotel. The streets had been more active in the past three months since President Ellen took oath and more UN forces flowed into Monrovia.

Roads in Monrovia alternated between under construction and under full-scale digging to get to the foundation. Only the locals could understand the sewer flow and where not to go. The syrup brown water with speckles of feces bobbing was stagnant. Recent heat from the emerging sun did not have an impact on evaporating any of the water. The stench of red clay mud mixed with human pollution overwhelmed Tareek, yet the locals hanged tough and thrived in the tumultuous heat. They had to survive. Tareek walked down the street. He stopped on the corner. A little girl came up to him. She was nervous as she wanted to ask him something. In a young frail voice, she asked Tareek, "Will my arm grow back?" She raised her right arm that was chopped off. He stepped back for a moment. Tareek continued toward the market, the Monday morning one legged beggars were ready for an assault. The beggars had not eaten yet and were eager for money, what they called a little 'small, small'. Hands touched him and covered him as he pushed through the crowd. He had no wallet and if he did, it would have been taken. The only possession Tareek carried was Marsa's charm around his neck. He reached up and held the necklace to make sure it was in place.

Tareek saw rage and pain in the whites of the local men's eyes. Rage for crimes they witnessed and pain for the life they had been forced to live as the aftermath of major civil war. Tareek was athletic and physically fit, he aggressively moved through the pack. He swung his arms in wide motions up and down. The one legged bandits had some mercy for the foreigners; however, they had very little compassion for the Lebanese as they managed most of the commerce in Liberia and made stacks of money off of the backs of Liberians. Tareek never asked the Cape Hotel employees about their family situations. He never asked them how they survived the two civil wars. He never asked them where they lived. He chastised them when they smelled, but never provided them soap. He paid them cheap salaries, a minuscule amount compared with the one hundred and forty dollars the foreigners paid per night. Tareek sweated as he walked around Monrovia. He saw a part of the city that he was not used to. Roads and sidewalks did not exist in this area of the city as rumbled hulks of buildings barely stood, yet held many families. He passed the cemetery and walked faster as he heard the worst of the city's criminals lived in the crypts. The criminals pushed aside the corpses after stealing what they could and moved into the stone boxes.

Tareek walked briskly toward the bridge that connected Bushrod Island to Monrovia. Underneath he saw men in several dugout canoes who paddled hard against the current, fishing lines lingered over the side. Garbage floated and littered the water. He looked back toward Monrovia's skyline. The Dukor Hotel was completely bare and below the nearly destroyed hotel was Wave Tops bar that would be filled with foreigners at sunset. Tareek wondered what he was doing in Monrovia. Uncle Anwar invited him to Liberia. He missed his dead daughter Marsa, his wife, and his family. Their deaths constantly resonated in his thoughts. Hezbollah rolled freely throughout the Beirut mountainside. Druze kept them at bay and the Christian Druze hatred the Islamic fanatics. Tareek found himself partnering with a Mossad agent. He never expected that he would need her or let alone trust her. His high tech surveillance equipment found her out and proved essential maintaining accurate intelligence. Everyone who was someone came to the Cape Hotel at one point or another. Tareek held more information than he provided to Uncle Anwar, the godfather Ghasson, and the rest of the Lebanese community. Tareek had never killed anyone, let alone hurt anyone. Hatred and revenge infiltrated his mind and he needed to keep a handle on his emotions. The Cape Hotel was his protectorate and if he started a war with Hezbollah, his life would be expendable.

Later in the afternoon, Russell went to Monrovia with Ike to purchase supplies. The roads were severely muddy from the recent rain. He looked up ahead and saw a commotion. The van was sideways in the dirt road and the tires were spinning in the red, clayish mud.

"Idiots," Russell spoke out loud. On the hillside, he saw eight Chinese soldiers trying to pull the van from the rear axle out of the mud.

The driver pressed frantically on the accelerator and the van swayed left and right violently as smoke spewed from the rear tires. Russell told Ike to keep going. As they approached, several of the Chinese soldiers motioned to help pull them out. Without even thinking about it, Russell gave them the international peace sign - the middle finger of his left hand. Russell knew the Chinese business and government motives in Liberia. He also knew the Chinese businessmen wanted to take everything they possibly could for the cheapest price. Only Chinese workers were allowed in the mining camps, no Liberians were hired. At the abandoned Liberian Coast Guard base, smugglers brought in illegal Chinese immigrants on rubber zodiacs from container ships offshore. The Chinese imported most of their own food or established their own farms. China's government viewed Liberia as an economic engine and constructed one of the largest embassies in Africa. Thousands of Chinese workers on vacation from the remote iron camps had descended on Liberia like locust. To make matters more complicated, an engineer battalion from the Chinese Peoples Republic army worked under the UN mandate. Over a thousand Chinese soldiers set up camp outside of Monrovia. Russell did not trust the Chinese motives in Africa.

At the Cape Hotel, the restaurant was busy. For the third day in a row, the large overweight Frenchman gave Feeatu extremely good tips. She rubbed her hand across his back and offered to go upstairs with him. The foreigner approved. She snuck out of the Sunday brunch for thirty minutes and earned twenty dollars. After work, she treated herself to a taxi ride by herself. Chad followed Feeatu in his car. He kept a close watch on the car painted with yellow house paint. There were a lot of cars painted yellow to resemble taxi cabs. UN police routinely stopped all sorts of vehicles for illegal cab fares, but if a vehicle was painted yellow, the driver was rarely stopped. The taxi cab halted at the church that was the scene of the Sinkhor massacre. The road beyond was impassable with deep rooted potholes the size of craters, no vehicles traveled down the road, not even trucks. Feeatu stopped and looked as she exited the vehicle. Something in her mind told her that there was a threat close. She had solid survival instincts. She was one of the lucky few as she was never raped or physically assaulted. Nearly eighty percent of the women who remained in Liberia during the two brutal civil wars were raped multiple times. Child soldiers ruled the country side in places where there was no justice except tribal justice. Feeatu walked quickly and stopped fifty feet down the road. Whoever watched her could not drive down the broken road.

Chad assessed the road and was scared. Local men watched him. They came closer to the car as he sat watching Feeatu move down the road. Chad had worked with the locals and seen the beggars outside the Cape Hotel's main gate, but he never been in their neighborhoods. A boy with one arm knocked on the window and asked if he could clean the windshield. Chad waved him off. He was scared. He wanted to be back inside the Marshall compound with Rajik's security. Chad knew the Lebanese who owned the Abbu Jabbi market, and they were mugged. Locals targeted the Lebanese and were pleased to beat them as they felt the crooked Lebanese had a monopoly on the hotels, restaurants, and markets and made most of the money in Liberia.

At the Taylor compound, the sinister son walked the halls impatiently. Chucky was outraged at the incompetence of his father's lawyers. His father was being considered for indictment as a war criminal in Sierra Leone for recruiting child soldiers, providing them heroine, teaching them how to kill, and financing the RUF for their civil war that raged a few miles away on the other side of the border. Chucky had to routinely meet with Koroma in the Kono mine district to discuss strategy on both sides of the border. Sometime during the late 1990s, he wondered if he would get caught sneaking back and forth across the border. Sierra Leone could not invade Liberia as their military had to deal with the RUF, but they could have complained to the UN and the British. Chucky was pleased when the RUF attacked Freetown as they captured the city for several days. He already drafted an alliance with Koroma's help for Liberia and the new government of Sierra Leone. Based upon the draft agreement, the Charles Taylor regime and the new Koroma regime would control a majority of the world's rare elements, especially diamonds. De Beers and the rest of the European Diamond Cartel were not going to let that happen.

"Where's Koroma?" Chucky asked.

"We don't know ... nobody knows." responded Rajik. He tired of being Chucky's whipping boy, servant.

"Did he go back to Sierra Leone? He could not have. He's wanted for war crimes." Chucky talked out loud to himself. He was already drunk. Rajik did not respond. Chucky continued. "Where's Rashad? I have not seen him. I'm paying a lot of money for them to be here. Where are they?" Rajik shrugged his shoulders. He did not want to be there. Chucky looked at the gold plated 45 caliber pistol on the desk. He picked it up and fired a shot in the wall. "Find me Koroma...And get me Rashad." Rajik did not reply as he walked out. Rajik needed to distance himself from Chucky who sat on the couch waving the pistol. Chucky knew he had to remain hidden or he would be detained by the UN. He talked to his own lawyer by phone in the states. His lawyer heard the US was trying to charge Chucky for war crimes. There was a 1994 Federal Law passed that stated American citizens would be charged for crimes against humanity committed outside of the United States. Chucky knew that the UN had information on his activities as the ATU's leader. He was proud of his 'Demon Forces' and looked at several pictures of his men who stood on dead bodies as they held bloody hearts in the air.

After returning back to Robertsport, Russell was exhausted, both physically and mentally. They had spent hours traversing the obstacle course created by the Gunnys. His weeks in West Africa seemed like years. Russell thought about Colonel Kurtz, a fictitious combination of Joseph Conrad's Heart of Darkness. Russell found himself going deeper and deeper into Liberian society. Every day he learned more and became frustrated by the lack of progress in the post-war country. The surge in Iraq was in full steam and billions of dollars in reconstruction money poured into Iraq, a country that did not have the historical ties to America like Liberia. Many Liberians call America big brother and some were even as bold to state Liberia was the fifty-first state. However, the lack of donor money hindered progress.

Russell went to the operations room. Two of Ike's guards sat in chairs outside to keep some semblance of security. Ike had hired twelve men to secure the mansion at a cost of seven hundred dollars a week. The men appreciated the work. The Deputy Minister kept money flowing into Robertsport and the mansion. The Deputy Minister did not care about the source of the drug money from the FARC and wanted to make a difference. He freely passed dollars to the children who swarmed his vehicle when they saw him arrive in Robertsport. He paid for the local school house overhaul. Over the past month, he spent nearly a hundred thousand of the three hundred thousand he took from the FARC. Every time the Deputy Minister arrived at the Robertsport and saw the crowd of NGO and UN vehicles at the beach, he became more and more disgusted at the lack of progress in his country. He did not have the luxury to rest. Moreover, he escaped an assassination attempt while foreigners lounged in luxury on the pristine Robertsport beach.

Russell looked at the maps, the briefs, and photos. He needed the raw intelligence and the Gunny's did a great job as they laid out the mission. Everything rested on taking out General Abbdas. He had the key information on Charles Taylor's attempt to come back to power. He was worried about the offer by the UN to enter, kill, and arrest rebels in Sapo. He did not put much credibility in the UN forces and when he talked to Colonel Crevace in Germany, the colonel did not put much credibility either on the UN's ability to properly execute the Sapo mission. Russell was confident his team could capture and extract General Abbdas. He inspected the body harness he perfected during rescue missions in the Seattle Mountains. Russell was more concerned about the fall out. Would his intrusion into Sapo cause the rebels to respond? The rainy season approached and Russell needed to pull the trigger to start the Sapo mission.

CHAPTER 16

The Gunnys filled the boat full of equipment and extra fuel. Uncle Anwar's twenty foot boat was loaded down and rode low in the water. Seven men, equipment, weapons, ammunition, and two extra fifty-five gallon fuel drums overfilled the boat. Movement by water was the best option to get to Sapo National Forest. Greenville was the only port in close proximity to Sapo. The Russian mafia controlled most of the port, even with UN presence. The Russians illegally cut timber and made a lot of money. Russell was pleased that his team was on the move again. On this mission, he added three with Ike and the two Liberian Lieutenants to help. Over the past week, they trained heavily on tactics, hand and arm movements, and night vision goggles. Russell understood Ike's combat experience based upon what the British colonel told him. Ike conducted his own deep range patrol into Sierra Leone and took out a RUF rebel camp of nearly sixty. Ike had been tested, and Russell was confident in his abilities. However, Russell was concerned how the Liberian Lieutenants would perform in direct combat operations.

"Are you ready?" Russell asked Lieutenant Johnson. They sat in the front of the boat looking toward the coastline and beautiful beaches.

"Yes, sir. These are bad men in our country."

"The other Prince Johnson could be there." He wanted to test the Lieutenant and see what his reaction would be. The Lieutenant stopped admiring the scenery of his native land.

"Then I will kill him." Lieutenant Johnson said and walked away. Lieutenant Forleh waited a moment.

"Sir, Lieutenant Johnson is very competent."

"Is he related to the thug Prince Johnson?" Russell still had a concern over Lieutenant Prince Johnson III. When he first heard the name Prince, he thought of African royalty, but that was far from the truth. There was no royalty in Liberia, only social hierarchy from the educated freed slaves who returned to Africa compared to the bush tribes they found. Prince Johnson had murdered former Liberian president Samuel Doe in broad daylight and even cut out his heart.

"He says no. If he is a relative of Prince Johnson, I believe him when he says that he would kill him."

170

"Were you here during the civil war?"

"No, my family went to Guinea." Forleh said. "We lived in a refugee camp for almost three years."

"Did your father serve in the military?"

"He did, most men did." Forleh added. "Liberia has always been at war. Men, women, and children fight in Liberia."

"Perhaps, we can finally make peace stay here." Russell said.

"Maybe," Forleh said. He stopped for a moment to reflect. "I hope so. There has been too much war here."

The ocean spray crashed over the bow. Several were required to remain up front in the boat to provide better ballast. The Lieutenants looked sick and Russell sent them back to the rear. Stone joined him up front. The sound of the boat slamming onto the water echoed and they could not hear anything but the loud concussion of the boat's noise. Stone pointed toward the horizon. They could see the illegal fishing trawler. It slowly drifted along less than a mile away. They could see the large nets rise out of the water. Liberia's territorial waters stretched out twenty-two nautical miles from its shore, yet they had no capacity to patrol, interdict, or stop illegal fishing. Russell read an editorial that proclaimed Liberia lost twenty-six million dollars a year from illegal fishing. The major culprits were the Chinese. Russell was not surprised. He looked into the long-range scope and saw the Chinese flag on the large trawler. Illegal fishing cost Liberia millions of dollars, yet they could not enforce any maritime laws.

The boat made the journey down the coast to Greenville in eight hours. Rozelli maintained a steady speed of fifteen knots in the open ocean. The weather cooperated, yet the sea state bounced them around in the twenty foot boat pretty heavily. Greenville port was in complete disrepair. Monrovia's port had received a considerable amount of international donor funding. Other ports along the coast did not have any sustained security. Greenville, Harper, and the other small towns along the coast were not under complete UN control and any improvements would be stolen or sacked. The pier was trashed. The boat yard was consumed by piles of logs illegally removed from Sapo National Forest. The Russian mafia ran the port and filled ships headed back to Europe with cheap timbers. Money was funneled into the legitimate import business. Payoffs and intimidations were rampant. Rozelli powered the boat toward the far end of the port that Ike scouted after their recon trip to Sapo. The Lieutenants would remain with the boat and they covered the engines with an old tarp once they cooled. One would remain awake at all times and Russell was specific that if they had not returned in thirty-six hours to abandon the boat and make their way back to BTC by any means. Ike started the truck that he purchased for five hundred cash and left it in the town's market near the only hotel in town where at least there was some security. The foreigners caught the attention of many of the locals. The duffle bags were slung over their shoulders and weapons concealed. Each Marine had a two foot machete underneath their shirts, ready to be unleashed.

Deep inside Sapo National Forest, General Abbdas had not heard from Koroma for several days. He was concerned. Abbdas checked his phone again and again. He called Koroma's number - nothing. He even dared to venture close to Greenville in case the cell phone coverage was an issue, but the satellite phone he possessed worked fine. He had kept his rebel army together in one place since they departed Monrovia for Sapo. It had been three years in exile. He guessed about 1,800 troops remained with him, but he could not be sure. The rainy season approached. He needed to train his men on bomb making procedures so he could bring guerilla warfare to the streets of Monrovia. His men could easily infiltrate the city and cause havoc. The most important target would be the new President Ellen and he wanted to take her alive, yet he knew his men more than likely would kill her.

Across the table sat several of his officers. The general sat patiently as they read their weekly report on troops, equipment, weapons, and gold. He was pleased with the recent gold harvests as more water pumps were brought to strip mine the surrounding hillsides. His men could see their general was visibly upset. Sumarka made the major mistake of accidently dropping his drink. General Abbdas pressed Sumarka's hand on the table and looked into her eyes. His eyes became wider. The whites of his eyes showed more than his pupils. He crossed his eyes in a devilish manner and twisted his neck back and forth. He looked like a wild man. The others sat still and did not move. General

Abbdas kept his eyes trained on her. His other hand lifted a ten inch bush knife out from its sheath on his leg. The overhead swinging motion startled her and she attempted to pull her hand back, but she was unsuccessful. The knife's blade penetrated her hand and lodged into the wood table. Joyous laughter erupted from the rebels. Sumarka fell to her knees in pain and could not pull her hand back. Her other arm was not strong enough to remove the knife. General Abbdas laughed and leaned in close to her, "Where do you think you are going?"

"Please... please. I will not be able cook for you." Her pleading had changed his attitude. He had slammed the knife so hard into the table that it took a hard pull to eject the blade. Sumarka's abuse and pain had increased. She could not take anymore. She already lost one child and did not want to lose another. She could withstand abuse but did not want her baby to grow up as another abused bush wife.

For the rest of the afternoon General Abbdas walked throughout the camp. He had become more paranoid. He checked the lock on the ammunition room twice. He removed the boards that he used to conceal the hiding place of the secret metal box. The bags of rough diamonds were moved several times and counted. Sumarka observed his paranoid nature and was more scared. General Abbdas yelled out for the other bush wife. Sumarka could not understand what he said as he pointed to the bags of gold, perhaps he believed she stole from him. He pulled out his pistol and shot the other bush wife in the head. Sumarka froze. She did not move, even after he yelled for her to come in and clean up the mess. After ten minutes, Sumarka came in and removed the body by dragging her in a blanket. Sumarka buried the other bush wife behind the latrine shed. She sent her child down the path with everything she could carry to find a distant relative who was also a captured bush wife from the same village. She had hard enough time taking care of her baby and the general. She could not afford any more beatings for anything wrong the other children did.

Feeatu was late and needed to get to work. Her boys sat at the only table in the shack. One of the table's legs was missing and several concrete bricks held the table at the correct height. The boys needed to catch up on their homework in the morning light. There was no electricity and

Feeatu could not afford the two dollars required for new batteries for a flashlight. She kept her boys dressed well with the second hand clothes that she purchased in the Red Light district. Additionally, several neighbors provided scraps of clothes that did not fit their children anymore. The church had nothing to spare, yet Feeatu and her boys survived. Many Liberians lived in far worse conditions. With her job as a waitress at the Cape Hotel, she made five dollars a day and sometimes up to ten dollars a day in tips, if the foreigners were at all generous. Seven days a week she worked. Slowly she spent more and more money to fix and build upon the shack her family lived in. The abandoned building needed a new roof on the second floor so they lived on the first floor only. The concrete ceiling of the second floor served as the roof. She was cautious, as a squatter, the owners or someone claiming to be the owner could come at any time and force her out. She would be no resistance for a group of men who wanted the building. Her neighbors were squatters as well and they united more and more every day to keep their shacks and the area safer. Feeatu patted each of her boys on the head before leaving. The oldest boy was twelve. She thought he was such a good young man, the guardian of his brothers age nine and seven. Feeatu stepped on the stone block near the corner to make sure it was in place. Underneath was a tin can with nearly four hundred dollars in cash; more than she would have made in a year if she stayed working the family's farm in Banga. Her husband left her with no cash, only hidden diamonds that he stole from the RUF that remained buried in Banga.

As Feeatu walked down the road, the Lebanese man behind her moved quickly. He grabbed her from behind and tossed her in the back door of the first SUV. Neighborhood men saw the abduction and ran toward the vehicle that already sped down the street. Rashad held a knife against her throat as Chad wrestled her down. Feeatu fought hard until she was knocked out from the back of a pistol. Chad knew where to take her. The drive to Banga took over two hours. They passed through Red Light district and were caught up in the chaos of fifty thousand locals who shopped in a tight, confined area. Rashad knew the diamonds were in Banga near the farm, but he never saw the concealed hiding spot.

The village elders looked very hard and stared at the white men exiting the vehicles. A young child no more than three started screaming and crying. The screaming child was comforted by the elders. "She is scared. She has never seen a white man before." Feeatu said. Rashad chuckled as he pointed toward Chad's white skin. Chad heard natives were confused by white men and equated white men to 'juju' and death. They had to cross several stream beds that were not so small from the recent heavy rains. In another month, they would not even be able to cross as the rainy season would dump more than ten inches of rain a day in this area.

"It should be around this area." Feeatu pointed reluctantly. They had walked along the river bank and into the woods where several large Cyprus trees hung overhead. They crossed thru the casaba field. Feeatu walked toward the large bolder that was out of the norm. She pointed toward the ground.

"Dig." Rashad tossed the shovel near her and pointed the AK47 at her head. Feeatu was in good shape and dug quickly. Within five minutes, the shovel made contact with a metal container. She dug around the metal box and pulled it out. The green ammunition box was sealed with rust as she tried to open it. Rashad pushed her aside and hit the box with the butt stock of the AK47. He swung several times and the metal box opened on the ground. A pile of rough diamonds spilled in the dirt. Chad immediately fell to the ground to grab them and place them into a cloth bag. There must have been nearly a thousand rough diamonds in the metal box.

Not far away, Francesca looked through the rifle's scope and held her left hand in the air. She followed at a distance and was ready to strike. Her Mossad training taught her to create the distraction as she would not be able to hit the six targets. She counted down slowly on her hand by closing her fingers into the palm. Her thumb was last and as she pulled it into her palm, Tareek started running toward the bolder. The first shot ripped into chest of one of the RUF soldiers. The gunshot sound was muffled by the silencer. The sight of blood caused Rashad to drop to the ground. Chad was oblivious as he tried to scoop up the pile of rough diamonds into the bag. The firing became more deliberate and slower as she took up a stronger, more supported firing position. Tareek moved through the bush quickly and was able to cross the stream perpendicularly onto the other side within several seconds. Tareek did not waste time as he moved deeper into the woods so he could come directly behind the bolder. He pulled a large knife out of the sheath. Running through the trees, he was fortunate not to see many leaves that would warn Rashad. She positioned her shots to the left of the bolder. She had them pinned down. Chad finally realized that they were under attack and nestled his chubby body under the bolder. Tareek leaped forward about eight feet from the target, pulled the knife into attacking position, and let it sink into the RUF soldier's back. The force of the thrust coupled with his weight knocked the air out of RUF soldier who rolled to his side in agony. The RUF soldier was dead in seconds. With a quick motion, Tareek pulled this knife from the RUF soldier and tossed it at Chad who ducked. The knife bounced off of the large bolder. Tareek grabbed Feeatu and they ran back toward the river bed. Bursts of fire from the AK47 rained near them. They both fell into the water and Tareek pulled Feeatu toward the other side. He pulled and partially dragged her for another twenty yards deeper into the woods. As he stopped behind a tree, he looked into her open eyes. Feeatu was already dead.

At the entrance of Sapo National Forest, Ike parked the beat up vehicle. Several white NGO vehicles were present for those hard-core adventurers who did not believe the reports that stated Liberia was still unstable. Russell hoped he would not have to rescue any captured NGOs. Inside the main walking path, they marched quickly for almost six hours without any rest stops. The mark on the large Cyprus tree signaled the trail's location. Ike directed the team up the path for another hour until the night overcame the jungle. They waited until well after midnight before they moved again. As they walked down the path, weapons were raised along their shoulders as the team moved quickly down the path in the dark. The infrared red dots on the trees were easily picked up with the night vision goggles. Rozelli took lead and Rageone picked up the rear. The entire team moved with small gaps between team. Each member had multiple infrared markers across their bodies, on the back and front of helmets, arms, legs, and torso. Russell was very pleased on their movement. Within an hour, they were at the final hold point. Unless a target was spotted, the only one allowed to speak was team leader, Russell, and he did not utter a word. Everyone knew not to fire their weapon unless absolutely necessary. Rozelli pulled out the high resolution night scope that light up the night and could accurately provide distance to targets. He held the twenty inch scope for a minute and passed it down the line for each member to look. He took one last look for a longer time when it was passed back to him. As point man, it was his responsibility to get team to the mark. He tapped the man next to him who happened to be Russell and he passed the tap down the line. Their movement was slower and delicate. The team compressed their spacing and moved tight across the field. Weapons were raised and pointed in multiple directions looking for targets. Safeties were off and fingers pointed straight out along the trigger to prevent unwanted shots.

The floor boards creaked as they moved onto the balcony. Russell entered first. General Abbdas swung his knife toward Russell and he blocked it, twisted the arm that flew at him, and plunged the knife into the general's chest. He placed a hand over the general's mouth and cushioned his fall to limit noise. He flashed a light into his face and realized he just killed their high value target. The team moved into the room and watched their mission go down the toilet. Stone remained outside hooked up on the headset and microphone.

"What are we going to do now?" whispered Stone. The door opened slowly and Rozelli nearly fired his weapon. He flashed the moon beam on the side of his weapon into Sumarka's face. She was scared, yet relieved. Rozelli put her face down on the floor with arms spread as he checked for weapons.

"Do you understand me?" Rozelli whispered into her ear and she nodded. "I am going to let you up, if you remain quiet. Do you understand?" She nodded.

"Who are you?" Russell looked at the local woman.

"Bush wife, me taken from me village."

"We are looking for papers, information." Russell asked. "Do you understand me?" She nodded and went over toward the bed. She pulled up a loose board and pointed to the metal box. Rageone was the explosive expert on the team and inspected for any trip wires. Once he confirmed it was safe, he opened the box. He passed several papers to

Russell. In the flashlight, he emptied a black bag and saw gold sparkle in his palm. There were twelve black bags and he removed them. Several tin canisters were filled with rough diamonds and he gave the thumbs up sign as he looked inside. Russell opened the confiscated manila envelope marked 'Presidential Eyes Only' across the top. He reviewed the documents and recognized the woman in the photos.

"Where are the explosives?" Russell asked her. She did not understand. He made a big boom hand motion. "Bombs, weapons." She pointed toward the back door. Russell motioned for Rageone to go with her and set the explosive charges.

Ike laid out the harness and rolled General Abbdas onto it. Ike cleaned up the blood the best he could. Rageone returned with Sumarka. He whispered to Russell that he wired the door and set the explosive timer for five hours, which would be around sunrise. Russell was skeptical that UN helicopters and troops would move into Sapo on time, but he kept his word to the one-star Nigerian general. The Gunny's carried the harness out of the building.

"Boss, wha du her?" Ike asked Russell.

"She has to come with us or they will kill her." Russell knew he had the latitude to get the job done. He confiscated a treasure trove of documents and had one dead former Liberian general. If the woman or baby became too much, he could drug them. Sumarka understood what she was told and grabbed her baby. The few things she possessed remained. She gladly left the building that had been her torture chamber for the past three years.

Meanwhile at the Taylor compound, Chucky had sobered up for his main event. He grew his beard out and gone was his wig and other disguises. He looked into the car mirror before he entered the Cape Hotel lobby. Two of the RUF soldiers followed in trace. As he walked into the piano bar on the rooftop of the Cape Hotel, everything stopped – the music, the conversations, the pouring of drinks – everything stopped. Chucky smiled like a high profile celebrity who walked the red carpet. He caught their attention and the next move shocked them even more as he walked across the room and joined Rajik's table. Utter shock overcame their faces as they saw the man in charge of the demon forces reenter their lives. Many of the newly arrived NGOs had no idea what Chucky looked like in person. Everyone immediately turned and pointed in his direction. Tareek watched the video feed from the office and taped the conversation between Chucky and the Hezbollah operative.

CHAPTER 17

Within Sapo National Forest, the morning explosion occurred precisely on time, as designated. Several miles away, Russell heard the riveting sound. They were still on the path, slowed by the weight of the limp body in the harness. The jungle canopy shielded the plume of smoke. The overhead surveillance airplane took photos and marked the spot. Just as Russell thought, the UN bureaucracy stalled any movement of UN troops into Sapo National Forest. As they walked out of the jungle to the rangers' station, Russell observed no backup support of UN vehicles or personnel. As he speculated, no one came.

The Lieutenants were pleased to see the team return. The Lieutenants had only one problem and lifted the tarp that revealed a dead Russian, a mafia lookout. Someone would be looking for him soon. The Gunnys took one arm and leg of the dead general and tossed him onto the boat before any locals or Russian mafia saw anything. The box of papers was a treasure trove of information and Russell could not wait. While the boat bounced in the waves, Russell opened the manila folder and looked at the documents closer. He reviewed the pictures taken at a dinner party in South Africa in 1997. In several photos were Charles Taylor and British super model Naomi Campbell. Several documents had Campbell's signatures that showed she accepted five large rough diamonds from Charles Taylor's assistant. Once Russell told the team what he had found, the Gunnys were extremely livid that Campbell accepted blood diamonds and commented how they would take extreme pleasure talking to her if she ever visited Manhattan. Ike was confused why everyone was so excited that she took diamonds. Russell tried to explain why Campbell should have stood up for all of the repressed Africans who farmed and died in the blood diamond camps. Ike could not understand as everyone stole from Africa. Russell became frustrated trying to explain. The boat picked up speed as it cleared the port of Greenville. The water was calm and Rozelli accelerated the craft up a cruise speed of about fifteen knots.

By morning, the boat had arrived on the outskirts of Monrovia. Russell dialed the personal number for Brigadier General Addu. Russell did not inform him that the high value target was dead and would rather surprise him. The only landmark Rozelli knew in the dark was the Presidential Palace. He halted the engine thirty feet from the beach and the tide carried the boat onto the beach. Several white UN vehicles were positioned along the road next to the beach below the Presidential Palace.

"He's dead." Russell lifted the blanket and showed General's Abbdas' face.

"Indeed." Addu stated coldly. "It does not make things easier." The Nigerian officer stared intently at the corpse. "We needed information to put Charles Taylor on trial." Russell handed him the papers and photos. "What are these?"

"It should be enough information to charge Taylor with war crimes." Russell seemed confident and believed in what he read. "The photos are quite revealing. It appears President Taylor had a quite interesting relationship with a British supermodel."

"Indeed." Addu looked at the partially nude photos of the super model who received blood diamonds from Charles Taylor.

The one star Nigerian general pointed to Sumarka and asked in a stern voice. "Who is she?"

"Bush wife, kidnapped from her village. We'll take care of her." Addu nodded. He wanted nothing to do with helping her. Russell could tell he was displeased.

"Was there anything else?" Addu inquired.

"The explosion went off well, if that is what you mean."

"Diamonds." Addu got to the point. "Did you find diamonds?"

"No, there wasn't any there." Russell knew there was no physical means to trace rough diamonds from any of the conflict zones. He wondered why the general wanted the diamonds. "We found several bags of gold dust." He handed the bags to the Nigerian general and he was pleased to take them. Russell surmised the general had a UN boss who he needed to report to. The entire international community seemed so engrossed in the rebel's rare earth elements. Russell wondered if the UN had checks in place to make sure no blood diamonds were smuggled out. Something about Addu did not rest well with Russell. He wondered if Addu actually had called in a strike on Sapo or were they his patsy.

The Nigerian general neither thanked them nor bid farewell. It appeared they had created a tremendous amount of paperwork for him to explain how Abbdas died. Russell speculated that he would be blamed by name in Addu's official UN correspondence. Ike pushed the boat off the sand bar and jumped into the front. As they moved slowly away from the base of the Presidential Palace, Russell opened one of the tins that contained the rough diamonds. The team looked at him and he smiled back at them as he poured the contents into the ocean. He repeated the action several more times. "Given back to Mother Earth," Russell spoke out loud. The Gunnys shook their heads in disbelief as he discarded nearly five million dollars in rough, untraceable diamonds.

The Robertsport mansion was dark atop the hill. A few candles flickered in the window. Sara had stayed awake and waited. She had no idea when they would return or what night. For the past two nights, she slept in the chair in the middle of the entry room and tonight she waited. The crying sound of a baby startled Sara and she opened the main door.

"Careful, heart men out tonight." Sara spoke in her thick bush accent.

"What happened?" Russell shouted as he grabbed her arm.

"Heart men cum n take James." Sara spoke. Upon hearing the news, Ike was visibly upset. Ike became fond of James and promised the albino child nothing would happen to him. Without a word, Ike grabbed the machete behind the door and left. Russell did not like the looks of this. Albino children were considered child witches and the witch doctors believed they must exercise the demons out of the albino children before taking their bones out from them. The bones were mashed into dust used in a spiritual ceremony to chase away evil spirits.

Within ten minutes, Ike and Russell found the area they thought James was taken. It was easy to find. Screams emitted from the bush hut, several men standing outside were covered in white clay paste over their entire body. White lines and circles crisscrossed their naked torso. Ike and Russell moved toward the back of the grass hut and quietly cut a large opening. They peered inside. Masks were worn by everyone. Some masks had jutting teeth that once belonged to either a man or large bush animal. Splotches of grizzled hair hung from the masks. Eye sockets were chiseled holes and the weathered notches from a blunt tool resemble deep scarred wrinkles. As they watched, the dances became more vibrant. Russell cocked a round in the chamber. There were no UN security personnel within fifty miles in any direction.

Ike used the machete to cut a hole in the back of the grass hut. They slowly peeled back the straw. Candles illuminated the interior of the large hut, which spanned thirty feet. Russell watched the ceremony underway and surmised the hut must have been the ritual location for the local witch doctor. In the center of a pentagram drawn in the dirt was the village witch doctor. Each of the man's hands possessed a knife. The mask he wore was painted with white designs and marks. Dead long hair jutted from the top and sides of the mask. Through the mask's eye sockets, Russell saw whites of his eyes and knew this was no prank, trick, or artificial ceremony. They were going to kill James. The sounds became louder as hands hit the drums harder and harder. Chilled screams emanated from the masks. Women danced faster and jumped higher. Abrupt silence arrived as the witch doctor held up his arms. Two large men dragged James and tied him between two posts in the middle of the pentagram. Russell waited for the witch doctor to make his move. Russell was nervous. He could tell Ike was ready to jump into the middle of the hut. He could not wait any longer.

"Drop the knife." Russell shouted as he pushed his body into the small opening. He extended the pistol. He did not wait for a response and he would not repeat himself. The first round that he fired took the knife out of the witch doctor's right hand and ripped a huge hole into his palm. The witch doctor dropped the other knife to hold his hand. One of the large men who tied James to the post stepped forward and Russell was not going to allow him another step. The second round that he fired went into the man's right shoulder. In several seconds, the large man fell. Russell pointed the pistol at the forehead of the other large man. The witch doctor screamed something. Russell could not understand his native dialect. Ike understood him and shouted back to him and the others in the ceremony. Ike cut James loose and held him close to his side. Ike shouted at the witch doctor in his native tongue. Russell could tell what Ike said and felt like he just entered a standoff.

"Get on the ground, on the ground," shouted both Gunnys as they came through the front hatch. Rageone swung the butt of his machine gun into the belly of the other witch doctor. The force put him down quickly. Stone did not provide a verbal command and gave a flying drop kick with his size twelve foot shoe to the center of the witch doctors chest. The force of the impact knocked the witch doctor out of the pentagram. His mask flew in the corner. Stone pulled out his digital camera and started taking photos. He pulled off the other masks and took photos of the rest of the crowd. Stone tossed the masks in the middle of the room into a pile.

"What took you so long?" Russell joked, now that the situation was under control.

"Sir, you didn't wait for us." Rozelli replied.

"I was in a hurry to make sure Ike did not do anything crazy."

"Well I had to get my camera." Stone said. He continued to take photos and even asked the witch doctor to smile. "I saw this when I lived in Nigeria. They hide behind their masks to scare, intimidate, and murder." Stone added. "Once they are exposed, they lose their power."

"They generate fear to stay powerful." Russell considered.

"These men are evil and will kill in the name of juju," replied Stone, who witnessed the horrors of tribalism in his native Nigeria.

"Now they will not cause us any troubles." Russell said as he watched the Gunnys push everyone outside. Russell looked at his men and yelled, "Burn the place." Stone torched the grass hut with a flare.

Down the street from the Robertsport mansion, the small concrete building resided less than two hundred yards from the road. With the thick, unkempt brush, the small building was isolated and served the female Mossad agent well. She liked to use the remote building for firing practice and interrogation. Tonight was her fifth interrogation in the past five months. The other four provided solid raw intelligence on Hezbollah operations and Rajik's growing power in Liberia. She never released her prisoners, bodies were buried in back.

"Who are you working for?" She pulled back his sleeves and saw the RUF tattoo scrawled into his bicep. Tareek held the flash light into his face. The small block building had a spotlight in the center of the room, but he believed the light in the eyes would scare him more. She allowed Tareek to do what he wished, as she knew he was not skilled in interrogations.

"Who are you working for?" still she received no answer. She had patience and all night to conduct her unorthodox interrogation. Mossad agents were trained to deliver three interrogations tactics; the first haphazard and usually involved immediate bullet holes in the subject; the second involved a considerable amount of physical abuse and pain; and the third involved experimental hypnotic drugs that regularly resulted in death. She trained on all three and was not predisposed to either except when she tried the hypnotic drugs, her subjects died within an hour. She liked the second technique as she always received a good physical workout.

"If you tell us what I need to know," Francesca paused, "You live." She looked into his eyes. "If not, well." She pulled on a pair of black rubber gloves. "Let's just say it will be painful."

On the porch of the Robertsport mansion, Russell and Stone shared several beers in the warm night. "We did well tonight." Major Russell clanked beers with Captain Stone. "You were right on point as always." Russell offered to his subordinate. Within a few moments, the Gunnys arrived with more cold beers. Russell congratulated them as well on the haphazard mission rescuing James.

"Where's Ike?" inquired Russell.

"He's taking care of Sumarka and James," Stone responded.

"It's like he has his own family here," Rageone offered.

"You heard what happened to his family?" Everyone did. Russell felt compelled to state the obvious. They drank a few more club beers, the local brew and watched the flames begin to die down in the distance. The grass hut fire spread somewhat and engulfed dead palm leaves and other dried brush. The rainy season was still several weeks away.

Inside Monrovia, the Freemason building sat idle, windows covered with plywood, furniture gone, toilet fixtures gone, everything pretty much gone. The one hundred and fifty year old marble blocks that comprised the walls and floors remained in place. For the past ten years, the mansion sat idle, nothing moved inside, except tonight. The Deputy Minister told the presidential guards to wait by the vehicle. They would not be allowed inside. If someone wanted to assassinate him inside, he would not be able to stop them. The Deputy Minister gained more confidence every day.

Liberian Freemasons had ties back to colonial America and many of the signatures for the Declaration of Independence were Freemasons. African American Freemasons were part of the American Revolution and provided much needed information on British movements at Lexington and Concord. Freed slaves were common in the far northern states during America's Revolution. When conservative socialists wanted to experiment sending freed slaved back to Africa in the 1840s, the Freemasons were part of the first returning colonists. Over the decades, the Freemasons became more than a secret society. The organization became the bedrock for development of Liberia, similar to America. Under the Tolbert regime in the 1970s, the Freemasons thrived and were embedded in much of Liberian society. When Doe murdered President Tolbert in his sleep, the Freemasons went underground. Although Doe regularly had his picture taken with American President Reagan and touted his hatred of communism, the Freemasons knew Doe was a butcher, a cannibal, a sadistic human being. When Doe was killed by Prince Johnson, the Freemans believed the arrival of Charles Taylor would restore Freemasons to previous grandeur. After Taylor started to use child soldiers and filled them full of heroin as much as they could consume, the Freemasons went back underground.

The Deputy Minister of Defense was pleased to see the turnout. His Freemason brothers came out in force, word spread quickly that action had to be taken. "My brothers, my countrymen, my friends, we cannot let Charles Taylor come back to power," said the Deputy Minister. A thirty-nine degree Freemason, one of the highest ranks, hobbled as he stood. The elder gentleman who remained in Monrovia throughout the two civil wars clapped loudly. "We may not all agree on the new president, but we must give her a chance." The Deputy Minister paused for a moment. "I have received reports that Taylor has hired former RUF soldiers." The Deputy Minister heard cheers from the crowd and he continued. "American Special Forces are here and they killed General Abbdas." Applause erupted from the crowd. The thirty-nine degree Freemason looked at the Deputy Minister while he spoke and smiled widely. The Freemasons were thrilled that Adolphus Urey came back to Liberia, assumed his father's role in the Freemasons, and found his destiny. "We cannot let Charles Taylor come back to power," the Deputy Minister paused, "at all costs."

Back in Robertsport, Russell could not sleep. He did not know what kept him awake as hundreds of thoughts scrambled around in his head. He dropped on the bed fully clothed with his gear, yet he could not fall to sleep. Not even the few club beers edged him to sleep. The Sapo mission was a resounding success. He killed a brutal thug who could have killed tens of thousands more. They saved a young mother from the tortuous existence as a bush wife. Something inside him told him that there was an immediate threat. Russell walked downstairs. The regular security guard was absent from his post at the front door. Russell slowly opened the front door and rapidly moved through the small opening and into the darkness. The moon was covered by clouds and a slight rain started. Russell pulled his knife from the sheath wrapped onto his right ankle. He could only see several feet in front. He stepped on the side walk. On his second step, he crushed a large snail with his boot. The noise was soft but in the dead of night, he thought it sounded like a cannon going off. He moved onto the grass. He spotted movement at the corner of the house and stopped. He wondered if the man could be one of Ike's roving guards. He crouched and crept closer. The dark clothes of the man told him that he was not one of Ike's men. His right foot knocked the back of the man's left knee and he wrapped his arms around the man's neck in a choke hold. The man grabbed for his eyes, but could not find them as Russell buried his head in the man's back. The intruder made several grunts and moans as he passed out. Russell checked for a pulse. The crackle of a snail shattered the night's silence ten feet away from him in the direction where the first intruder came from. Russell did not have time to authenticate the intruder's position. He hoped for the best as he threw the knife. A loud scream ignited and Russell placed his hand over the dying man's mouth to extinguish the noise. Within a minute, Ike was outside with a gun.

"Get the rest of the team," Russell said softly. Ike had the house awakened and the team was assembled with full gear and weapons within two minutes. The Gunnys did not require orders and ran to the middle of the lawn. The Gunnys dove and landed in prone positions. The night spotting scopes on the high-powered rifles were already turned on. They scanned the area out to one hundred meters in the pitch blackness. Ike went to the front gate and found two of his guards killed.

"Sir, look at the marks." Stone lifted the sleeve. "RUF."

"Take this one to the basement and lock him up." The Lieutenants tied up the intruder and dragged him inside.

"Sir, are they after us?" asked Stone.

"Don't know. We need to find if there are any more in the area. Get the vehicle." Russell said. His team moved quickly. The seasoned team did not need instructions. Rozelli climbed onto the vehicle's roof and climbed his belt into the roof brace. He had the machinegun chambered and ready. Rageone sat in the far back of the vehicle with the rear door open in case of a threat behind as they passed. Stone drove with the lights turned off, both inside and outside. Russell scanned the road with high-powered night vision scope. The submachine gun rested against his leg and the 45 caliber pistol rested on his chest in the holster.

"Something on the right at two hundred meters." Rozelli whispered into the headset.

"Negative, don't see anything." Russell responded.

Tareek found the interrogation painful to watch. The female Mossad agent was brutal. Blood flew across the room as she kept on hitting him. He hated the Hezbollah for what they did to Marsa and his family, yet he could not bring himself to the level of violence he now witnessed. He felt horrible that Feeatu was dead. He liked her. Her body remained wrapped in the back of the SUV. He wished that he had hit Chad with the knife and caused him pain. Uncle Anwar was still in America for two more weeks and Tareek wondered if that was too long to wait. He could go to the other Lebanese for help, yet they were all afraid of Rajik. Tareek breathed deeply several times to relax. He opened the door to go back inside.

"There." Stone said, "two hundred meters to the right."

"Got it," said Russell as he looked into the scope, "get ready to move." Stone stopped the vehicle by placing the gear in neutral and sliding into a small sand pile on the side of the road. He did not touch the brakes as the lights would give away their presence.

"Is there anybody living there?" Rozelli asked.

"Don't know." Russell believed the Deputy Minister owned all the way to the end of the road. "Could be squatters or could be a threat."

Tareek did not move as the Marines entered the room and pointed the machineguns in his face. Tareek dropped his weapon quickly. Russell lifted the chin of the man tied to the chair and looked at the bloody pulp face in front of him. All of a sudden Russell heard a familiar voice.

"Well hello Tom." The female Mossad agent said as she entered from the back door. Weapons were quickly pointed at her. Each Marine turned their eyes back to one another as they wondered if she were a threat. She walked in with her hands raised. Her black rubber gloves were covered with blood along with her shirt and arms. On her right hip, she wore a holster that contained a fifty caliber Desert Eagle pistol. On the other hip, she wore a twelve inch serrated knife. The straps from the pistol and knife kept her black trousers close to her thighs. Her hair was braided and rested on her left shoulder.

"What are you doing?" Russell asked and quickly added. "Who are you?"

"I'm conducting an interrogation." Francesca looked down at the RUF solider, "until I was rudely interrupted." She smiled. "Can I put my hands down now?" Francesca inquired. Once Russell nodded, she slowly moved her arms in front of her body into a martial arts stance.

"Who are you?" Rozelli asked.

"Mossad." She looked at each of their faces. "Israeli intelligence."

"We know all about the Mossad." replied Rozelli. From the tone in his voice, Russell could tell that Rozelli wanted to put a bullet hole in her. Russell waved his arm for everyone to lower their weapons, yet he kept his weapon trained on her. He did not know what to think. The girl he was falling for was somebody else entirely.

"Can I talk to you privately?" Francesca motioned for Russell to follow her outside. She noticed that Russell still had a pistol in his hand and for a moment, she considered making a strike to his groin and kicking the weapon out of his hand. But she kept her calm.

"Who the hell are you?"

"I told you Israeli intelligence."

"No, damn it listen. What is your name?"

"Francesca."

"Did you play me?" Russell asked.

"No, not at all. You were a luxury."

"What the hell does that mean?"

"A whimsical choice." Francesca smiled with those brilliant white teeth and added. "I like you."

"How can I trust you?"

"Don't be so over dramatic, Tom." Francesca said, "It's not like our two countries are at war. We are after the same thing."

"And what is that?"

"Peace, stability," Francesca replied. After a brief moment, she added, "And dead Al-Qaeda operatives."

"Somehow, I don't think you are telling me the full story."

"Well maybe, we can go back to your room and you can interrogate me." Francesca moved closer to and placed her hand on his chest. He pushed her away.

"No, hell no. You lied to me."

"Technically, I did not as I was under cover. And thank you for breaking into my interrogation."

"Who is that guy?"

"RUF. He killed one of the Cape Hotel's waitresses. Her body is in the truck." She pointed to the SUV in case he did not believe her. "We thought she was in danger so we watched her. Outside of her house, she was snatched by several RUF thugs and Chad from the Cape Hotel."

"Chad, I remember him from the restaurant. He had man boobs."

"Yes, that's him and he is now working with Rajik. We knew Feeatu's husband transported illegal diamonds that he received from the RUF in Sierra Leone. The RUF came for her and Chad helped."

"What a scumbag."

"Indeed. They found the diamonds buried near her village. They were going to kill her so I shot several of them as we tried a rescue mission. Unfortunately, Feeatu was shot."

"Did you recognize anyone else besides Chad?"

"No, just some RUF soldiers." Francesca did not tell him about Rashad and what Tel Aviv told her about Al-Qaeda operatives in Liberia. She had to get more information. She could not give him too much, at least she could not tell him yet.

"They tried to attack the mansion and I took one out and captured another."

"Is he still alive?" Francesca inquired. "I can interrogate him."

"Yes," Russell said. "And we will ask the questions."

"Fair enough." Francesca said. She held her hand up to shake. "Friends?"

"Perhaps." Russell looked at the fresh blood on the black rubber glove. "I haven't decided yet." She stepped closer and kissed his still lips. At first, he pushed her away. She kissed him again. Against every basic instinct of trust he had, he returned the kiss.

"What are you going to do with the bodies?"

"We'll bury the RUF in back, no one will miss him. We'll take Feeatu to a funeral home in Monrovia. Tareek said he would pay for it and take care of her three boys."

"We took out General Abbdas." Russell bragged on the success of his team's mission.

"Nice work." Francesca smiled. "He was a scumbag."

"Indeed. There's a lot of them here."

"So can we kiss and makeup?" Francesca smiled at Russell with those brilliant white teeth. Her face possessed a seductive look.

CHAPTER 18

At the new governmental office in Monrovia, the Deputy Minister waited to speak with the president. He sat in a plastic chair that was spray painted brown to cover up the dirt. It was the best chair in the waiting area. The president's office had to be moved down the street when an electrical fire erupted on the second floor of the Presidential Place. Fire destroyed a large portion of Charles Taylor's archives and the Deputy Minister believed the fire was deliberately set.

The Deputy Minister was concerned. Time was short and any further delays would cost many more lives. He knew the president would know what to do. Her own personal history in Liberia was filled with violence. Over twenty-five years before, she was the Minister of Finance for President Tolbert when Doe marched up the hill from BTC to the Presidential Palace. Ellen was told by the soldiers who arrested her that Doe killed President Tolbert in his bed. The next day Ellen was lined up along the back wall of BTC with ten other members of the Tolbert government. The other Ministers were mostly relatives of President Tolbert, except for Ellen. As the firing squad lifted their weapons to kill them, Lieutenant General Dubar intervened and demanded his former Master Sergeant Doe spare Ellen's life. She reflected back to her time under arrest for nine months in a small building next to the BTC compound. She lived on fish heads and rice and lost substantial weight; she was on the verge of near starvation.

The Deputy Minister looked at his notes. He wanted to be brief and to the point. They needed America's help to take out Charles Taylor before he returned to Liberia. The UN had been ineffective, and the Deputy Minister did not believe they could be trusted. Taylor had bribed many Nigerians in the past. America was Liberia's only hope toward building a stable future. He thought of his own father's murder and recommitted himself to bring about change for the better in this war-torn nation. He looked at his request for a Navy SEAL team and wondered if the Liberia president would approve his request to America. Russell walked out into the morning sunlight and saw Ike and Sara playing with Sumarka's baby on the lawn. Ike made several toys out of wood and Sara provided a blanket for the baby to play on. They let

Sumarka get some much-needed rest. Russell was amused at the two older Liberians who acted like typical grandparents as they fussed over the baby. James was upstairs safely asleep. Russell was pleased at the success of the rescue mission to save James. He liked James and hoped the Deputy Minister would not be upset as the number of occupants increased as he had remained in Monrovia. When Russell talked with the Deputy Minister on the phone, he was hesitant to leave the protection provided by the presidential security detail. He feared another assassination attempt. Russell thought everything was going fine until he received the call from Colonel Crevace in Germany.

"Major Russell, we have a slight problem," the Marine colonel said. There was concern in his voice and his tone shocked Russell back to the call he received from Crevace that sent him into Iskandariyah. Russell remembered the concern his boss had. The Iraqi Police had a problem controlling the surging protestors and Crevace asked Russell to go in with the army's 77th Scouts to only observe. He should have known Russell would not stand still as the bomb detonated and ripped apart two hundred and fifty bodies. Crevace knew Russell would take action and he could depend on him. Crevace secretly was concerned Russell would take far too much action and create an international incident if he was not careful.

"Go ahead Sir."

"Need you to prepare to move to Nigeria and take custody of former Liberian president Charles Taylor. Upon return to Liberia he will be brought under UN arrest and sent to Sierra Leone to face war crimes." Russell was silent as he thought of a hundred possibilities of what could go wrong.

"You are the only ones close enough," Crevace continued, "Can you support?"

Entering a foreign country to bring a known war criminal was daring. "Are we getting support in Nigeria?" He quickly considered Stone's background.

"Limited. The Nigerian government has promised to turn Taylor over but that is it. They will not take him out of Nigeria, we have to do that. There will be a US Air Force Gulfstream commercial jet arriving tomorrow to pick you up. You will be the on-scene commander."

Russell was glad the colonel did not say it looked like an easy mission. "We will definitely have a big problem with Chucky." Russell was very concerned with Chucky and his ATU thugs. And he heard Chucky was working with Hezbollah contacts.

"We have an answer to that. He will be charged in the US for crimes against humanity that he committed in Liberia. I'm not sure how State Department plans to get Chucky back to the states. With everything going on in the world, military aircrafts are not an option."

"I have an idea for that." said Russell as he quickly developed thoughts. "The 727 Gulfstream jet confiscated in the drug heist could possibly make it to the Caribbean. This plane would not have to stop along the route and get questioned by custom officials." Russell did not know where and if Chucky had friends helping his exiled father get back into power. He continued, "Chucky could be flown to a US friendly country in the Caribbean and then flown to Miami where he can be turned over to federal agents."

"Sounds like that is in the too hard to do category," responded Colonel Crevace.

"Not really. If you can get an Air Force crew down here to fly out the 727. We will bag and tag Chucky for movement." He thought of any potential law enforcement issues. "I can also send the Gunnys with him, just to make sure."

"Understood." The colonel who was three thousand miles away asked. "Can you get Taylor with just yourself and Captain Stone?"

"I think so, Stone is Nigerian and that will carry a lot of weight."

"Great, one plane tomorrow with an extra crew. Your Gunnys will bag and tag Chucky and escort him. Confirm mission."

"Mission confirmed." Russell thought that he should take one more look at the 727. There were a pile of cigarette butts. Russell thought that the plane may blow up midflight. If the internal fuel lines jerry-rigged off of the barrels remained sealed, it possibly would work.

The 727 Gulfstream rested on the flight line near the UN hangar where it was guarded by several Pakistani soldiers who wore blue helmets. The Marines approached and did not say a word as they walked up to the aircraft door and opened it. The airplane had been sealed up tightly for over two weeks and the good news was there were limited fumes from the fuel. They inspected the jerry-rigged barrel and fuel hose concoction the Columbians built. Remarkably, the engineers in Bogota spent a long time configuring the in-flight refueling system. A sealed hose system lay on the floor and linked to the external tanks. There were several digital fuel gauges and monitors.

"Looks like we will have a nice long flight." Rageone said in a half joking manner.

"We need to get some drugs to knock Chucky out." Rozelli replied as he already thought about how best to handle the mission. The Gunnys looked at the photos and studied the images. "We are going to need a distraction."

At the Taylor compound, Rajik brought two more local girls over for Chucky to assault. Rajik had induced the local girls with enough drugs so the pain would not hurt as much. He knew Chucky would beat them badly. Rajik looked on. He had to keep Chucky happy until his exit strategy was completed. Rashad laughed as Chucky slapped the first girl. Rashad laid the detonator devices across the table. He inspected the electronics in detail. The detonators were hidden inside a container of potatoes from Kinshasa. The container was loaded inside the boat, yet he knew the boat's overhead latches leaked. He removed the remote detonators from the bubble wrap. There was moisture inside the circuit. Rashad blew air across the circuit panel. Rashad always packed extra detonators for pretrial tests. The abandoned Voice of America site resided past Carrysburg and out of site. Rashad believed it would be the perfect location to train his RUF soldiers and test the equipment. Rashad opened the eight boxes that contained military grade C4 explosives. He kept the explosives inside. He had four of his men load the truck for the forty minute drive to the abandoned Voice of America site. Rashad looked at the two drugged up girls who watched him work the explosive equipment. He did not care that they witnessed his actions as he knew Chucky would kill them. Rashad loaded the boxes full of detonators and explosives into the black SUV.

The black SUV pulled out of the Taylor compound and Russell watched it closely. He could not risk an assault in the open street, worse a firefight. The best vantage point was across the street from the Taylor compound at the Coconut Grove Resort. The Gunnys kicked open the top floor door and scared to death the couple in bed. The man was an overweight foreigner while the woman was a local. The man thought for a moment that perhaps his wife sent him but quickly surmised the men with large rifles did not care about them as they were locked in the bathroom. The sniper night vision scopes were only accurate up to one hundred and fifty meters but during the daylight, the Gunnys could hit three hundred meters very accurately.

"Ready when you are," Rozelli said as he adjusted the scope.

"Standby," Russell said as he watched the guards. He looked at Stone as he leveled two launchers in both arms. They nodded to one another and Stone fired. Several illumination grenades popped out of the barrels into the darkness. Flares ignited two hundred feet in the air and drifted downward. The guards looked upward and the three guards took shots to the chest within seconds. The flares drifted with the wind as the parachutes clung to the air. Russell and Stone climbed the side wall with the grappling hook and knotted rope.

"Keep watch," Russell whispered in the headset as he climbed on top of the fifteen-foot wall.

"Understood," Rageone replied. Once a guard stepped out from the corner and pointed his AK47, Rageone fired. The bullet ripped through the guard's chest and dropped him.

"Two hundred feet," Rozelli whispered and added. "Left side of second building."

"Got him." Rageone replied. "Taking the shot on that distance." They both knew the silencer's weight affected the weapons handling and they knew accuracy was impacted with the greater distance. Rageone gripped the barrel tighter, breathed out, and gently pulled the trigger. The body in the scope fell to the ground.

"Clear," Rozelli said and added. "We will join you in two minutes."

Russell and Stone moved toward the main house and entered within seconds. They quickly looked at the empty basement rooms as they moved inside. They mastered the staircase with very few creaks and moans. In the main bedroom, they found someone asleep in the large bed and injected the needle before even checking who he was. With a quick flash of a red lens light, Russell confirmed the limp body was indeed Chucky Taylor.

Rajik awoke from the sight of the bright flare in the bedroom window. He moved to the back staircase and grabbed his AK47. He did not know who sent the flare in the night sky and surmised within a few seconds that it must have been the Americans. Rajik gained his senses and grabbed several magazines filled with ammunition.

As Russell and Stone dragged the body down the stairs, an AK47 erupted and splattered bullets along the wall. They let go of Chucky and sent him crashing down the staircase in a summersault motion. Stone jumped over the railing head first and landed flat on the floor. The new magazine inserted in the AK47 gave Rajik thirty more rounds. He placed the weapon on full automatic and let the rounds fly.

As Russell prepared to return fire, he heard an unusual weapon's sound. The fifty caliber Desert Eagle pistol sounded like a howitzer canon. Francesca fired round after round at Rajik. She sent fifteen rounds at him and reloaded. Rajik already ducked and ran out the back door. The Gunnys burst through the front door with weapons raised.

"Did you see him?" Francesca shouted. She was dressed in a complete black outfit that hugged her body tight.

"No one came toward us." Rozelli replied.

"Where the hell did you come from?" Russell asked.

"I've been following you." Francesca said. She looked at Russell and ran out the front door with Russell in pursuit.

Within a moment, Francesca spotted Rajik with her night vision scope. She sprinted after him like a leopard. Francesca zipped through traffic and crossed the busy street in seconds. Russell stopped for several speeding, out of control taxis and then crossed. Francesca spotted the security guard at the back door of Coconut Grove Resort's casino. As she approached, the guard moved toward her. She kicked him in the groin and dropped him. With rapid reflexes, Francesca moved inside the back poker room and raised the large Desert Eagle pistol. Without waiting, she shot two guards in the head as they turned toward her direction. She did not wait to be shot at. The sound of gunfire scared the crowd and many fell onto the floor for cover. Rajik hurried from his office with a bag of cash and fired a pistol in her general direction. She stopped behind an overturned table that held several frightened foreign white men. Russell saw she was trapped and he unloaded his sub-machinegun. Bullets ripped apart the wall that contained Rajik's office. Rajik dove back into his office and left out a secret passage behind the wall in the closet. After a few seconds of silence, Russell pointed toward the room and he covered while she moved forward. They both entered the office, but Rajik was already gone. They hurried out of the back door of the casino back toward the Taylor compound.

"I'm always saving you." Francesca shouted as they sprinted. In the distance, they heard UN police sirens. Russell believed that they had about three minutes to get out there.

"We had everything perfectly under control." Russell quipped.

"Sure, just like the drugs at the airport."

"That was you?" He asked and she smiled at him. Quickly, they returned back to the Taylor compound.

"What do you have?" Russell asked as he approached his team.

"Chucky, some documents, bag of counterfeit Liberian cash, and couple of dead local girls." Stone replied.

"What about a bomb?" Francesca asked.

"Nothing."

"No truck or explosive devices?" she asked further.

"None, like I said." responded Rozelli.

"Why?" Russell asked.

"I cannot tell you." Francesca stated coldly and added, "We need to take out Rajik."

Russell quickly conversed with Stone and gave him instructions to get Chucky out of the country at all costs, as he was going after Rajik. Ike and the Lieutenants had two vehicles parked at the outside gate. The Gunnys loaded Chucky in the back door. Russell took control of the vehicle with the female Mossad agent in the passenger seat. They went after Rajik. UN sirens shrieked louder as the vehicles became closer. Across the street, the crowd emptied the casino and ran toward their vehicles. A line of NGO white SUVs blocked the departure gate as each beeped their horns as they jockeyed for position. Sheer fear engulfed the foreigner's faces as violence returned to Monrovia.

Stone quickly got everyone to Roberts International Airport. On the flight line, the two US Air Force pilots already had the plane running and ready for takeoff. The extra crew of three personnel figured out the refueling lines and had all of the tanks topped off. Everybody packed inside Ike loaded the Gunnys gear.

"Where are we off to?" Rageone said jokingly as he slung the rifle off his chest.

"Trinidad." said one of the aircrew as they helped load bags.

"Where the hell is that?" Rozelli inquired.

"Caribbean," remarked the Air Force colonel who was not too pleased with the questions. "We leave in five minutes."

"Is Chucky going to be out the entire time?" Stone asked.

"I gave him about eight ccs, which should keep him out for six more hours." Rozelli said. "I don't want to give him another dose until he wakes up. Then I can give him enough to knock him out for the remaining trip." Rozelli looked at the ample of potion he concocted to make sure he had enough. After a moment, he placed it inside of his jacket.

"Miss u, haf gad trep." Ike said in his bush dialect. Ike walked inside the plane cabin. Ike leaned over to get one last look at Chucky Taylor, one of the most despised men in Liberia. Ike had seen the horrors of the Taylor regime firsthand. Ike spat in the face of the most notorious butchers in Liberian history.

CHAPTER 19

The road to Marshall was deserted, isolated from the chaos that gripped Monrovia. The town of Marshall was sparse with few inhabitants after the civil war. The Lebanese outnumbered the locals five to one. The fishing wire across the road was linked to two explosive charges on either side. Rajik knew they would come. Russell drove fast and the vehicle bounced hard from the uneven dirt road. He traveled faster than the road conditions normally allowed and swerved several times to regain control. The vehicle sped faster than Rajik had estimated. Rajik watched the vehicle hit the fishing wire. The explosive force from the bombs knocked the rear of the vehicle upward. The vehicle flipped and rolled several times. The front windshield smashed, glass became projectiles. The vehicle's roof crushed on top of them. Russell could only move slightly. Their weapons flew out of the vehicle as it rolled. They were trapped. Within a few seconds, a light shined in their faces.

"I should have killed you a long time ago." Rajik leveled the semi-automatic pistol toward the female Mossad agent's head and pressed the barrel against her temple. He pushed harder and harder until a mincing sound emitted from her mouth. "It takes me great pleasure to kill an Israeli." Rajik found Russell's sub-machinegun.

"They will know that it was you," Russell blurted, "and they will kill you."

"You Americans. You are so cowboys. No one will come looking for her and most definitely no one will come looking for you." Rajik pointed the pistol going back and forth between both of their foreheads, "get out."

Russell knew this guy would have no problems putting bullets in their heads. Rajik forced them to walk the two hundred yards to the Marshall compound. Chad smiled when he saw Rajik bring the prisoners. Russell contemplated making a run for it, but he was still somewhat dazed from the accident. Chad tied their hands together in front with duct tape and pushed them into the rear of the speed boat.

"Maybe my little friends will have something to talk to you about." Rajik said. Laughter emitted from Chad's chubby face. Rajik pointed the speed boat downstream and accelerated the engine. The current flowed toward the ocean, which helped the boat move quickly through the water. Russell had a hard time collecting himself as he was still dizzy from the crash. Up in front of the boat, Chad flashed the fifty thousand kilowatt light across the river. Up ahead was Monkey Island. Russell looked for the eyes of several dark sinister primates as Chad flashed the massive beam onto them.

Francesca twisted her body and pulled a slender, straight blade from the back of her boot and rolled back into position. Rajik and Chad did not notice her movement. She leaned back against the blade and put her weight onto it. The pain in her arms was great, yet she knew that would be the only way to cut into the duct tape. Rajik and Chad worked the anchor in front of the boat. Francesca was already off the boat's deck and had cut through Russell's binding tape with one swipe before they were seen. They nodded and both jumped into the water, ran, and splashed loudly as they charged toward shoreline. Fortunately, for them, Chad had limited reflexes and was unable to get his pistol out from his waistband. Rajik dropped the anchor line and hurled toward his AK47, which rested on front cushions. Rajik opened automatic fire. The spray of automatic weapons fire was wide and uncontrolled. The power of the weapon got away from him and bullets randomly splattered. Rajik rested his left arm on the front of the weapon to gain control. By the time he gained control, the prisoners were already in the brush. Regardless, Rajik ripped a full clip into the brush.

"Chad go!" ordered Rajik. Chad looked at him and wondered if he was serious. From the expression on Rajik's face, this was no time to question his new master. Chad waddled out of the boat and fell into the two feet of water face first. He levied the automatic pistol on the shoreline. He chugged to the shore, already out of breath. Within seconds, he was in a different world, something his body was neither accustomed with nor conditioned for.

The female Mossad agent and United States Marine moved quickly in the brush. They were both very physically fit. No words were spoken and hand signals communicated their next actions. As they knelt, Russell grabbed Francesca by the back of the neck, pushed his face into hers, and gave her a kiss. In response, she looked at him as if she was going to slap him for making such a gesture at this time.

Chad stumbled through the thick brush. They both heard Chad swear as he fell. Russell knew Chad was clumsy, yet he had a weapon and they did not. Chad gripped the pistol tight. He felt power in the weapon that protected him. He cursed Rajik for sending him onto the island, yet he feared him more. Chad breathed heavy.

The branches along the ground moved against the weight of the large black mamba. The grey snake gingerly moved back and forth and swayed its thirteen foot length from one side to another. Francesca saw the snake first. She positioned her two inside fingers toward her eyes to signal the threat. Russell acknowledged and remained still. Chad did not look down as he kept the pistol elevated chest high and did not see the snake. The black mamba snake lifted its body three feet off of the ground and lunged at Chad's chest. It injected a large painful bite. Chad winced and shrieked from the pain. He knocked the head of the snake with the pistol but it did not drop. Again, he hit it harder and fired toward the snake's body. The fourth shot struck the ten inch diameter snake's body. Chad became hysterical and ran toward the boat. With his exhaustive movements, the poisonous venom traveled faster in his blood system.

"Help me, help me." Chad screamed as he ran. Rajik saw blood on Chad's shirt and did not know what happened. Instinctively, Rajik opened fire, dumping a full magazine wildly into the shoreline. Rajik loaded another magazine and the next magazine went just as fast.

"Snake... snake bit me." Chad shouted. His body shook. Rajik watched the shoreline for any more movement for several minutes as his prodigy required immediate medical attention and more significantly, the anti-venom dose that was kept locked in the refrigerator.

"Help me. Please... help me." Chad whimpered.

"Wait," Rajik said. "They must die." Rajik kept his eyes on the shoreline and moved the spotlight back and forth. He held the AK47 in the other arm.

"Help me." Chad whimpered. "Please."

Rajik looked down at the jelly of a man who never exercised. Rajik was not impressed with Chad on his first combat assignment. He started the motor and shifted direction toward the compound upriver.

"They're gone." Russell said as he stood as he heard the engines.

"We are not off of the island yet." Francesca said as she held the blade in front of her, ready to strike. Russell turned as he heard something that moved behind him. As Russell turned, Francesca thrust the blade forward into the neck of a three foot chimpanzee that limped up behind them. During the attack, they did not hear the chimp move closer. Rajik's random fire wounded the chimp in the chest. It was enraged. She put the animal out of its misery.

"Move, now," Russell shouted. "This way." They both heard a large movement. The sound of breaking branches and heavy deep gurgling sounds that approached fast. Neither looked to see what chased them and knew whatever it was that it was big. Branches broke in their hands as they moved up and down the tangled branch limbs in the thick jungle canopy. The only paths were made by the primates and were close to the ground. Everything above waist height was a dense weave of growth that had been untouched for years, if not decades. Russell and Francesca pushed, grabbed, and clawed across the branches - both of them grunted from their labors. Behind them within arm's reach was the massive chimp infected with HIV. Out of the corner of her eye, Francesca sighted an opening ten feet away - a distant glimmer of light off of the water resonated in her eyes.

"Follow me," Francesca demanded. They twisted and contorted their bodies on top of the branches. The large chimp reached his muscled arm upward and clawed into the branches above as it attempted to grab body parts as they passed overhead. She did not grimace or stop as the large chimp temporarily held her leg. She kicked forward and lunged through an opening six feet above the water and fell into open space. Russell followed and landed on top of her. They rolled in the water. As they stood, they were brought face to face with the large male chimp that stood six feet tall. The large chimp held its ground as it was deadly fearful of the water although it was only several feet deep. They plunged their bodies into the shallow water and swam for their lives. With all of the splashing and their faces in the water, neither heard the blood gurgling sound that erupted from the beast's mouth as it banged its massive chest.

"We should move up the shoreline. The river will take us right out to the sea and then forget it," Russell said. The flow of the river was fast and even faster in rainy season. They walked along the shore in waist deep water and pushed through the water with every bit of strength. "If we get up another hundred feet, the current should take us diagonally across." Russell looked at the river for several moments and completed his calculations. He continued. "We should move farther, the riptide underneath is much faster." They did not talk for the next hour as they pulled their bodies forward on any branch or twig that jutted from the river bank offering some glimmer of hope that they would not drown.

"Look," Francesca said as she pointed her arm. Boat running lights moved down the river at a high rate of speed. The sound of the dual engine echoed as Rajik powered the boat at full throttle.

Russell saw the lights at the Marshall compound, which billowed out from the dark night. He found a log and pulled it from the shore line. They both held on and started kicking violently across the river. Within minutes, the sky opened up and heavy rain penetrated the night. They breathed hard. The voluminous rain showered upon them and nearly choked them. She could barely hang on and he held her arm. As fast as the rain started, it ceased. He kicked violently. Francesca was exhausted and almost fell off the log into the depths of the black river. Russell knew they did not have much distance, yet he could not see the shoreline in the dark cloudless night. However, he could see the lights from the Marshall compound. He did some quick geometry and guessed the current must have moved them about half a mile downstream. He kicked harder against the river's surface and in twenty minutes, they arrived at the shoreline. He dragged her out of the water. She was dead weight. Russell carried her for ten minutes down the road until she stopped him and wanted to walk. Russell held her tight as they hobbled forward.

They approached the Marshall compound in a slow manner as it appeared abandoned. There were no local guards, and the vehicles were missing, except for several motorcycles. Their professional assault instincts came back to them, even in their time of exhaustion. They surveyed the scene. Words were not spoken and hand signals were communicated between them. He mimicked to himself that they are actually getting very good working together. Once inside the main building, Russell grabbed a knife in the kitchen. Francesca did not wait and went through the rooms. The place was empty except for the body mass of Chad who failed his master. Slumped on the couch, Chad's shirt was ripped open, cut by a pair of scissors that rested on the carpet. Next to Chad was a snakebite kit. His right man boob was a mass of blackish skin that swelled. As she looked closer, Francesca saw the incision of black mamba teeth around Chad's right man boob. None of her medical training would help Chad as he breathed his final life away.

Russell started one of the motorcycles and with Francesca on back throttled it down the dirt road. The gas tank was empty and the engine died in five minutes. Russell pushed the motorcycle off the side of the road. He knew that they were still a thirty-minute ride from the main road, which led back to Monrovia. He knew that they should not go back to the Marshall compound. If they went forward into the darkness, he knew they risked robbery or death. He did not have time to decide as the female Mossad agent started to walk toward Monrovia. He quickly followed and caught up to her. After twenty minutes on the road, an elderly woman came up to them.

"No white people walk here at night." The elder local woman stated. There was a sense of concern in her voice. Russell assessed that she was peaceful and meant well. Russell and Francesca had no weapons except for a butcher's knife. They followed her up the path. After three hundred yards, they entered the center of a small camp with six bush huts scattered around the perimeter of the camp. Several men looked at them with suspicion and the elderly woman spoke something in bush dialect. One of the men offered them to sit by the fire and get warm. A young woman gave them a blanket to wrap themselves inside. The chill from the water had left them quickly as they huddled together. The man passed a plastic jug. Russell smelled it and knew the contents were palm wine.

"From the top of the tree?" Russell said as he pointed upward and the man nodded. He recalled how Captain Stone, the Nigerian forced him to drink palm wine several times. Stone warned him not to drink palm wine unless it was tapped from the top of the tree. Palm wine should be drunk the same day before fermentation. The horrible smell was just as bad as the taste. Russell toasted the jug in the air and took a large gulp. He handed it to the female Mossad agent.

"That's horrible." Francesca spat the liquid out.

"It does take getting used to and given the circumstances," Russell replied and he added. "Don't think we can complain." Francesca gave him a thoughtful look and took another sip. He took another big gulp and passed the bottle.

"This is my country and we must take it back." said the man who brought the palm wine. "You must remember that we are coming off of fourteen years of civil war and we cannot do it alone."

"I understand." Russell paused and looked at him closely. He continued, "Your English is good."

"I was taught by Christian Evangelists. The civil war was very hard on us. Rebels are not far from here. The UN keeps them away, but what happens when UN goes?"

"Liberia is building a new army."

"Samuel Doe was a military man and he started a coup." He paused and added. "Liberians cannot trust the army?"

"We have two Liberian officers working with us and they are committed to keeping Liberia safe." Russell understood the man's skepticism as it was widespread in Liberia. Mistrust of the military and anyone who carried a weapon for that matter was widespread. Horrific memories of the civil war and the brutality inflicted by child soldiers resonated in everyone's minds.

"Can they be trusted?" the elder man inquired.

"Yes." Russell said and he added. "They will become Liberia's greatest generation."

"What is that?"

"Greatest generation is what we had in America during the Second World War. We had an entire generation fight in war and survive to keep the peace."

"Yes, America our big brother," the man replied. "But America never came to stop our war."

"No, we didn't." Russell thought of how easy it would have been to stop the bloodshed of doped up child soldiers who wore wigs, yielded machetes, and raped thousands of women. Somalia was too close in the minds of many Americans. For the first time, he felt embarrassed that his country had let Liberia down.

"They killed everything, even all of the animals." He waived his arms in the air. "We had beautiful animals."

"I heard." Russell offered. "Liberia was very beautiful."

"My wife, my sisters, and even my daughters Sasha and Sandy were raped." The man started to cry. "I was not here." He paused for a few moments. "I'm a fisherman. I go fish and the rebels raided Marshall. They killed many. Babies were killed. Boys were taken to fight."

"I'm sorry." Russell was sincere.

"We men came back from fishing and found houses on fire, bodies...dead bodies. Blood was everywhere."

"War is violent and cruel." Russell did not know what to say.

"I pray to God that he will forgive me and what I have done."

"I'm sure he will."

"I hope so because without God we are all animals." The man looked directly into Russell's eyes for several awkward moments. "When the boys returned to kill more of us, I killed them... All of them." The elder man had rage in his eyes even several years later. He offered no further explanation as he departed.

The fire was stoked with several logs to give more heat and the cold guests appreciated it. The palm wine tasted horrible but their bellies felt warm from the alcohol. The smell almost made her sick, but she squeezed her nose to drink more. The elder woman pointed to a grass hut and said they could stay overnight. Both guests were tired and excused themselves.

"So much pain here." Francesca said as she nestled up against Russell to get body heat.

"It tears your heart out." Russell said quietly. "Whatever it takes, whatever it takes, we need to keep these people safe." He looked at her and Francesca was already asleep. Within ten minutes, she started to snore. Russell discovered that she snored more and more as he stayed with her. She told him that she was a real light sleeper and probably was when he was not around. Russell stuck the kitchen knife in dirt in case he needed it in the middle of the night. He kept one eye open on the entrance. Russell did not sleep.

Chapter 20

Russell was exhausted from lack of sleep. The morning rain drenched them as they walked away from Marshall. They were tired, hungry, and severely thirsty. Several motorbikes passed and did not stop. The road was in complete disarray after the rain storm. The clay and deep holes prevented vehicles from entering the road and they were surprised when an NGO vehicle stopped.

"Do you need a ride?" asked the Pied Piper of the NGO community.

"Anywhere would be fine."

"I recognize you. Your friend, the Nigerian, is trying to date my sister." Russell nodded at the comment. She continued, "Well that is just not going to work. It's a phase for her." She looked at the female Mossad agent and said, "Young girls do funny things in Africa...right?" They both smiled at one another. Russell just wanted a ride and did not want to get in a fight and tossed out of the vehicle. "My father will put an end to it if she continues to see him." Russell thought back to his former love, Kristin, and her father trying to put an end to their relationship. He remembered the constant berating comments about how he was not worthy enough for her. He wondered if the Pied Piper was against her sister being in an inter-racial relationship. He wanted to change the subject, as he was too damn exhausted to walk and wanted the ride.

"So what are you doing out here so early in the morning?"

"I received word from one of my NGOs that three women were kidnapped for female circumcision and taken into the bush. Isn't that barbaric?"

"It's their country." Russell replied.

"Excuse me?" The Pied Piper said with a high inflection.

"They have been performing rituals for hundreds of years. How can we invoke our will on them?"

"It's just barbaric. These women are taken against their will and we must put a stop to it." Russell sensed the ride was not going to be pleasant and the stop at the village even worse as this western NGO, aid worker tried to inform the villagers that they were barbarians.

"Have you talked to the new Liberian government?" Russell inquired. "They could talk to the villagers."

"They're all corrupt and worthless. We need to change things in this country now, instead of waiting and waiting and trying to get through the red tape. I am sick and tired of waiting. We need to make this country better."

"What about one of new Congo Ministers?" Russell inquired.

"No one will help us." The Pied Piper of the NGO community abruptly spoke. Everyone was quiet for the next ten minutes.

Up the road from Marshall were several smaller fishing villages. Families lived in somewhat isolation and made an existence out of fishing along the river. The bad road jolted him, but Russell was pleased not to be walking anymore. He wanted to go after Rajik, but knew that he had to make sure Chucky got sent out of the country. He needed rest and closed his eyes. He did not know how long he was out. As the vehicle stopped, he awoke and looked out. The village appeared deserted, almost sinister looking down the street. Within the walls of the thatched grass huts, he saw glimpses of small faces as they peered out. He could tell they were being watched.

"How are you going to get them out of here?" Russell asked the Pied Piper.

"We are going to take them." The local driver looked in the rear view mirror at Russell and he could tell that the local was not pleased with what was about to occur. Russell saw movements in the bush and knew they were in an ambush site.

"Let me talk to them." Francesca said. She pulled out her identification card for Doctors Without Borders. As she departed the vehicle, several men emerged with machetes.

"Wait." Russell directed the Pied Piper to remain in the vehicle. "She's a doctor." The female Mossad agent talked to the men for several moments and they pointed down the road. "They were taken into the bush." She said as she opened the door.

"They're probably dead by now. How screwed up is this country." The Pied Piper spoke. Russell held his tongue; after all, he needed the ride.

The driver drove the vehicle based upon his new instructions. After twenty minutes down the path that had no resemblance of a path, yet alone a road, they arrived at several wooden huts. The Pied Piper jumped out and Russell quickly followed as he hoped she would not create an international incident. Three women, all in their late teens, were wrapped up in blankets. Francesca checked each one for several moments. The frail, thin girl in the middle had a very high temperature.

"She needs medicine." Francesca said as he pointed to one of the girls. "Her infection is bad." The elder woman nodded and allowed her to leave. Russell picked up the young woman and put her in the vehicle.

The Pied Piper directed the driver toward the Wave Tops bar in Monrovia. Russell held the young girl on his lap while his girlfriend, the doctor and undercover Mossad agent, looked at her. The Pied Piper would not allow the young woman to be seen at JFK Hospital as everyone who went there, went there to die. When they reached the desolate street and abandoned looking building that contained the rooftop bar, Russell carried the girl who weighed no more than eighty pounds up the five flights of stairs. Several NGOs saw him and cleared a cushioned couch for the patient. The Pied Piper directed movements and found the medicine Francesca requested. The patient's arrival spoiled the afternoon mood at the bar.

Russell left Francesca as she attended to her patient. From Wave Tops veranda, he could see boats vibrate in the ocean. The heavy rains emerged and bombard the small dugout canoes. Violent waves tossed the canoes as the wind picked up. The small dots in the vast ocean were difficult to see. Russell counted fifteen boats at first and several more as the waves moved up and down. The near sideways rain pelted the men as they held onto their lives.

Russell spotted several NGO men who watched the boats from the veranda, under cover of the bamboo and tin roof. He wondered if they had actual jobs as it was midday and they were intoxicated. Russell looked back and watched his lovely doctor take care of her patient. Russell assessed that she was indeed a good physician. The Pied Piper gave instructions to several NGO females to go find a safe place to bring the patient, God forbid that she would be there during happy hour.

Russell wanted to get out of there. He gave one of the cook's in the kitchen fifty dollars to borrow his motorcycle. Russell sped down the street and swerved in and out of traffic. On back, Francesca held tight around his waist. The sideways, heavy rain soaked them. He could barely see in front of him and parked the motorcycle on the side of the building.

"I called my uncle for help," Stone said as he greeted them at the front door of the bungalow.

"Oh." Russell was too exhausted to think about the consequences of informing the richest man in Nigeria.

"I need a shower." The Israeli spy said as she pushed passed the men and entered the bathroom.

The Deputy Minister knocked on the door and entered. "Sir, how are you?" Russell asked.

"Fine, I heard a plane left late last night with Chucky onboard."

"And two of my men as escorts." Russell injected. "They are headed to Trinidad and will await a flight directly to Miami where Chucky will be arrested by US Marshalls for crimes against humanity."

"That is great news. What about the father?" The Minister inquired. "The former president?"

"A plane will arrive tonight to take us to Nigeria."

"Good, very good." The Deputy Minister said and he added. "General Abdurallah will travel with you to make sure that there are no problems in Nigeria."

"Boss, u eat?" Ike asked the Deputy Minister. Ike was pleased that he had a new boss. The Deputy Minister waived him off; however, Ike went to the kitchen to make food anyways.

"Well hello." Francesca said as she walked out of the bathroom. She had wrapped the towel tightly around her chest and the bottom of the towel barely covered her. She offered her hand to the Deputy Minister.

"I am Deputy Minister Urey."

"Yes, I know who you are."

"What is your name?" the Deputy Minister inquired.

"My name is Lieutenant Colonel Francesca Waszey of the Israeli Defense Force."

"Damn sir, she out ranks you," spouted Captain Stone with a smile on his face.

"She's Mossad." Russell chimed in.

"Really and what is Israeli intelligence doing here?" inquired the Deputy Minister.

"Keeping things safe. Now if you could excuse me so I can get dressed." She went into the bedroom and found some of Russell's clothes that he left there. The oversized sweat shirt and loose pants felt great on her body. She looked in the mirror and laughed out loud at her appearance. She lifted the sweat shirt and looked at her eight-inch scar. Maybe she would tell him how she got it. She wore the charm necklace that her father gave her when she was twelve years old. She tucked the necklace inside the sweatshirt.

The abandoned Voice of America site was the perfect location for explosive tests and Rashad had several bombs already built. He held class inside the large concrete building. Rajik provided the rest of his security team. He had no need to go back to the casino or the Marshall compound. He had fifty thousand dollars in cash. Rajik closely watched Rashad lock the black fabric bags filled with rough diamonds in a back room. One of his RUF soldiers stayed in the room at all times behind locked doors. On the wall, Rashad wrote several fabled Al-Qaeda slogans such as 'Death to America', 'Kill the Infidels', 'Death to Israel', and several others. Rashad wanted to expand the Al-Qaeda operations in West Africa. Rashad was disgusted when the RUF declared peace that ended the Sierra Leone civil war. He was part of the Freetown invasion as a teenager and was pleased with the massacre, death, and destruction. He partied for days and was so stoned he barely recalled how he was wounded and evacuated back to the Kono district. Rashad inspected the helicopter that they pushed underneath a metal overhang. If the Americans or UN had over flight or satellite coverage, they would not see the helicopter profile. Tonight they would have to find the final ingredient needed for their massive bomb.

At Roberts International Airport, the Air Force Gulfstream commercial jet was parked outside of the main terminal next to the large Brussels'

Airliner that overshadowed the smaller aircraft. They waited for thirty minutes for the general to arrive, he was late. Russell knew he had better wait or face the consequences.

"What did your uncle say?"

"We better talk before the general arrives," said Stone, "My uncle placed several of his men to watch Taylor. He had intel that some in the Obasanjo administration did not want to see Taylor indicted as a war criminal."

"Are you kidding me? Why?"

"Oil. There are substantial oil deposits off Liberia's shore. My uncle has a copy of the secret UN report." Russell looked surprised. "My uncle has vast resources."

"These new found oil deposits would be a direct conflict with what is in Nigeria."

"Not necessarily." Stone offered. "My uncle owns one of the largest oil companies in Nigeria and has drilling rights booked for a long time. Nigeria's global export would remain the same. The real issue is who in Liberia would try to negotiate the lease contracts. Let's just hope Liberia does not fall in the same fate as Nigeria did with the massive amount of overnight wealth from oil."

"I thought Nigeria's problems were more Christian versus Muslim."

"No, outsiders believe that. Nigeria's problems all stem from rapid wealth and generational hatred over land disputes."

"Why would Nigeria take Taylor in exile in the first place?"

"Members of the Nigeria cabinet may be trying to win favor with Taylor and perhaps have him run for the next Liberian election."

"Are you serious?"

"Charles Taylor remains very popular here." Stone replied. "If you recall, he had an entire propaganda machine and quoted Doctor Martin Luther King when he got tossed out in exile."

"We cannot let this scumbag come back to power."

"Gentlemen...how are you doing?" asked the large two-star Nigerian general as he boarded the plane. He squeezed into the airplane's seat.

Within a moment, the aircraft accelerated down the runway. The wheels bounced from several large potholes that were previous mortar impacts covered with dirt. The airplane ride was three hours in the small jet. The plane landed at the Nigerian capital city of Abuja. The Nigerian general waddled down the aisle and emerged from the aircraft. He was immediately greeted by several older men in suits. Russell could tell from the conversation that something was wrong. Stone did not wait and walked over to a blackened limousine. A well-dressed man in his sixties emerged and hugged him.

"Bad news," The Nigerian general said. "Very bad news."

"What is it?" Russell asked.

"Charles Taylor escaped."

"How the hell could that happen," Russell added, "Sir?"

"He was under house arrest. When they went to detain him, he was gone. Servants have no idea where he went." The general walked back to several Nigerian soldiers and shouted at them.

"Taylor's gone." Russell said to Stone as he returned.

"I know. He was tipped off that we were coming." Stone said as he winked. "There will be a helicopter landing here in five minutes."

"Where are we going?"

"Cameroon." Stone replied. Russell looked surprised but knew not to question his right-hand man. Stone was reliable and talented. Russell popped his head into the cockpit and told the pilots to remain in place for six hours. He asked for eight, but they agreed on six hours. As they walked toward the helicopter landing pad, Russell asked, "What about the general?"

"We had better leave him out of this. If there is a conspiracy in the cabinet, we should not place him in an awkward position to arrest Taylor."

The two-star Nigerian general looked perplexed as the two Marine officers boarded a helicopter and lifted off. One of the men standing next to the Nigerian general was already on a cell phone. The helicopter ride north to the border of Nigeria and Cameroon was almost an hour. In the darkness, Russell could see many lights on in this more developed country. Nigeria had emerged as an economic powerhouse.

"Any issues crossing international airspace?" Russell asked.

"From whom? Cameroon does not have an air force to speak of and there are no radars or missiles to shoot us down."

The helicopter landed five hundred yards from the border crossing at Gamboru, Cameroon. Stone talked to the pilots and the rotors continued to turn. There was considerable activity at the border post for the middle of the night. Russell was extremely impressed by Stone's connections. His uncle had vast wealth and resources. He wondered why he walked away from that lifestyle and remembered what he told him in Fallujah, Iraq about wanting to serve a higher calling.

"Where is he?" Stone asked one of the border guards and he pointed inside. The guards looked suspiciously at the white man, Russell. Inside the border officer was pleased to shake the hand of a relative of the richest man in Nigeria who needed a favor.

Russell looked into the cell and saw the former brutal leader slumped over in a chair. He looked tired. He was dressed in safari clothes and the guard officer pointed to the stacks of cash and two blocks of pure cocaine they found with him.

"What do we do with the others?" The guard officer asked.

"Not our concern." Russell replied. "Charge them with drug smuggling." He knew prosecuting for drug smuggling in Cameroon would get the death penalty. "Lift off in five minutes." directed Russell. Stone helped the Cameroon border officer place handcuffs on Charles Taylor who did not speak. Taylor seemed weak and frail, tired from his expeditious attempt to flee Nigeria.

As they landed back in Abuja, the Nigerian general assigned to help transform the new Liberian army was gone. He found another means of travel to get back to Monrovia. The US Air Force pilots were pleased to see the Marines return and ready to get out of Nigeria. Stone placed the former president in the middle of the twelve seat jet. Stone sat in front. Russell moved to the back and looked down at the former brutal dictator as he passed. Taylor did not utter a word. He had been captured and assessed his own fate.

On March 29, 2006, the Deputy Minister watched in the morning light as the small jet that contained a former brutal dictator landed at Roberts International Airport. As the door of the jet opened, Stone emerged with Taylor in handcuffs. Cameras from a dozen global news organizations captured the moment. What they did not see was the white man who stood behind Charles Taylor on the aircraft. And they surely did not hear Russell when he whispered in Charles Taylor's ear, "We got you, you son of a bitch." The Deputy Minister passed Charles Taylor over to UN officers who escorted him to a waiting UN helicopter that would take the former president to Freetown to face war crimes; specifically crimes against humanity for using child soldiers to wage war. The next day, March 30, 2006, Chucky Taylor was arrested in Miami as he was escorted by two Marine Gunnery Sergeants who were New York City cops and on loan to FBI's Counter Espionage Unit.

Chapter 21

Russell was excited by the capture of Charles Taylor and his bastard son, Chuck. The Deputy Minister was even more elated. He repeatedly thanked Russell and Stone for everything they did. He hugged Russell with a strong embrace. The Deputy Minister had an impending press conference with the president and had to hurry off, yet he took time to thank them multiple times. Ike waited patiently and had slept in the vehicle. He was pleased to see his friends return safe from the airplane flight. Ike had never been in an airplane and did not trust flying. The drive back to the Robertsport mansion took over four hours because of the recent heavy rains that damaged the dirt roads. They were exhausted. Russell walked into his bedroom and observed Francesca asleep in his bed. Francesca awoke when the door opened and placed her hand under the pillow. Russell did not have to see as he knew the Desert Eagle pistol was beneath the pillow he slept on.

"Why are you here?" Russell asked.

She pulled back the blanket to reveal a nightgown. "Didn't you miss me?"

"No, I've been busy." He sat on the bed. "We got Charles Taylor."

She reached up and gave him a big hug, "That's great." He did not push her off, but she could sense something was not right between them. Russell wanted answers as his mission was coming to an end.

"Why are you here? Are you tracking Hezbollah? Or are you tracking me?" Russell asked.

"We care about stability here and in Sierra Leone."

"Bullshit, level with me."

"Diamonds, we are here for the diamonds. An Israeli company called Fauvilla Diamond Exports purchased the Manga Egoli mine. Most of the world's legitimate diamonds now come from Sierra Leone. But what made it more concerning is that they believe they found what could be the largest diamond mine in the world."

"Where?" Russell asked.

"North of us. I cannot say where, but I can tell you that it is inside Liberia's borders." He remembered the articles on blood diamonds during the Sierra Leone civil war whereby Liberia exported billions of dollars in rough diamonds yet Liberia had no major diamond mines.

"I thought Liberia did not have diamonds."

"The issue has been getting to the diamonds. There is a new process developed in Israel that uses deep shafts and mechanized pipes to burrow into the kimberlite pipes." He remembered the geology report from Freetown about how diamonds were made. Volcanic activity millions of years ago erupted violently and created tubes in the earth's crust that reached several hundred miles into the earth. Kimberlite pipes were named for the diamond tubes found in Kimberly, South Africa.

"Is Israel tracking the illegal diamonds?"

"No, conflict diamonds make up only five percent of the diamond trade."

"Perhaps, but that equates to millions of dollars for Al-Qaeda and rebels."

"That's not our problem - that's yours." Francesca offered. "If America wants to become Africa's cop, that's your prerogative."

"Don't you feel for these people?" Russell inquired.

"I do, yet I learned a long time ago to keep the mission top priority. I don't make up the missions. I just carry them out." She lifted her shirt to reveal the eight-inch scar on left side.

"I thought Mossad agents were not supposed to have any identifiable marks."

"You're correct. That is why I always wear full bathing suits and long shirts." Francesca said.

"What happened?"

"I was in Paris," Francesca started. "On holiday after I passed my medical bar exam in Barcelona. However, in the Mossad, you are always on call. A mission went very wrong. I was sent in as the cleaner. Bodies were everywhere. I was told not to bring anyone out. Some were still alive, but I could not treat them, even as a certified doctor. They were beyond help. One of the dying men ignited a bomb. I took a large piece of shrapnel in my side. The place was overrun with cops within minutes. I had to crawl a thousand yards to get out of there. My handler would not come and get me because of the mess. I had to stitch myself up the best I could. I poured gun powder from a shell over the wound and ignited it on fire to seal the wound. I waited for two days for them to come find me. I was almost dead."

Russell sensed that she still lied about something. She did not tell him that her father wanted her tested to see if she could actually be tough enough to become a female Mossad agent. As a seasoned Mossad agent and director of Mossad operations, her father knew that female Mossad agents had much harder assignments than their male counterparts.

Russell fell onto the bed and passed out. He was exhausted. When he woke up, she was gone. Russell went into the command room. He poured over the raw intelligence and maps of Sierra Leone. The UN pulled out a majority of its forces seven months ago and the Sierra Leone army operated in the countryside. He was concerned if they had to explain their presence. The British General in Freetown would not understand. The Lome Peace Accord signed four years ago ended the hostilities between the Kabbah's government and the RUF. Soon after, Nigerians and British soldiers landed under the Economic Community of West Africa States Monitoring Group (ECOMOG). Soon after, Koroma was indicted by Special Court in Freetown.

Russell looked at the history of the Kimberly Process, signed in Kimberly, South Africa, where large diamonds were discovered in the 1800s. Kimberly became the perfect location to show all that was bad from diamonds. The local myth identified the Kimberly mine as the largest hand-dug hole in history. The Boer wars started over territory disputes between British and Dutch settlers and an all-out guerrilla war ensued. Africans died by the thousands. De Beers had its origins in Kimberly and their hands were not free of the blood to gain control of diamonds. In the Kono district of Sierra Leone, hundreds of men and children searched the gravel pits and hoped for a major find. Rough diamonds were sold to local merchants and transported to Freetown for polishing and export. The average black market price for a carat of rough diamond went for two hundred dollars while the diamond fetched thousands of dollars in America or the UK. The Kimberly Process required certification from known diamond suppliers and forbade companies to purchase rough diamonds from areas where conflict diamonds have originated. However, only a portion of the world had signed the Kimberly Process, many of the former Soviet states never signed and transnational actors such as Al-Qaeda would never oblige.

Russell wondered if he could kill a child soldier. He saw the video clips of boys who jumped around, strung up on drugs and alcohol, as they repeatedly chanted *"shed the blood."* The photos of children standing over dead bodies haunted Russell. He wondered if he hesitated that if it would cost his life or any member of his team. Koroma told the Gunnys how mean spirited the children RUF soldiers were and how he felt scared among them. For nearly ten years, the RUF rebels disregarded peace negations. They kidnapped boys and trained them to kill. The indoctrination required heavy doses of heroin and repeated beatings. Koroma said he looked into their eyes and saw no soul. Russell cared more about the slaves kidnapped to operate the camp. If the RUF rebels shot at them, they would have to return fire. For Russell's team, there would be no medical evacuation or rescue mission if they were over powered or worse captured alive. By all rights, it was a suicide mission, yet something within told him he could not sit idly by. The camp would be broken up for the rainy season and the RUF rebels would merge back into the dense forest, not to be seen again for another six months. He questioned his decision to illegally enter Sierra Leone for hours. A more legitimate threat was the rebel army that hid in Sapo National Forest. They could attack Monrovia and cause considerable chaos, death, and destruction.

At the Firestone Plantation, Colonel Marzah was lonely and watched out for any movement around the camp. Within days, local scavengers overran the camp and took everything. The fence was gone, windows removed, wiring and scrap metal pulled from the rubble, and anything anyone else could possibly use. A dozen times, he walked down the hillside to feed the chimp. His former Black Beret camp was deadly quiet, except for the random scream by the chimp. The other chimps left, only Lucy remained. As the land rover approached the intersection of the dirt trail, Colonel Marzah saw the white man get out and walk up the hill.

"Colonel, how have you been?"
"Good, but it is so quiet now."

"If you did not hear the news, we got Charles Taylor and his son. Both will face war crimes."

"That is good, that is very good."

"I asked around and you appear to be one of the few honest men in Liberia."

"I always tried to do the right thing." Marzah replied.

"They want you to testify in Sierra Leone against Taylor, but we are going to need your help first."

They drove into the Black Beret camp one last time and Ike smiled as he saw Lucy running on top of the old kitchen building. Ike missed Lucy. He missed the British Colonel. Russell told Ike that it was ok to bring Lucy back to the mansion.

After they returned to the Robertsport mansion, Ike took the several hundred dollars Russell gave him and procured a beat up truck. They would take the black SUV that they received from the intruders at the Black Beret camp. The two vehicles would give them enough transport to move the equipment and the team north. The Deputy Minister already departed for Monrovia. He was still afraid to stay at the mansion by himself, especially as he thought assassins roamed.

"Will you be here when I return?" Russell looked at Francesca.

"You're certain that you are coming back alive?" Francesca smirked. She was not good at farewells and was upset that he put her in this position. She had always been the one with the exit strategy and the first to leave. She kept to the Mossad rules. Never get close. Never let them see her weak, and never - absolutely never fall in love.

"You're damn right I am coming back." He kissed her farewell.

Francesca stepped back and slapped him enough to get his attention, "Until I see you again, I guess." She turned and walked back into the mansion to get her things.

The vehicle loading was in the final stages. Russell told Ike that he would be right back. As he walked into the bedroom, Francesca turned and swung her right arm toward his face. Russell blocked the arm shot with a quick jab and hooked her arm. Her feet tried to sweep his, but he was able to block the move. He tossed her on the bed and they both laughed. The moves took less than twenty seconds and for the next ten minutes she laid her head on his chest - no words were spoken.

Ike drove the first vehicle with Lieutenant Johnson in the passenger seat. Russell moved into the back seat with Colonel Marzah. The tinted rear windows helped conceal the white man's presence. They drove north on the one lane road through Maakando and Magima. Both were small towns and their presence generated mild interest. As they drove deeper into Liberia's vast wilderness, they encountered the border town of Bouma. Locals stopped and looked at them closely. Ike found the directions to the contact's house easy. The old man pushed open a rusted metal door that barely rested on the traction bar for the former UN food warehouse. The building was in utter decay and had not been used since the Sierra Leone refugee crisis.

The team moved out quickly. On the small path, Russell saw the large snake. The king cobra would not move from the path, this was its territory and it felt threatened. Russell waved his hand toward Stone. They both stopped and watched the king cobra as it raised three feet in the air. Russell knew the cobra could strike up to ten feet and they were definitely within firing range for the venomous creature. The immediate thought in his head was no anti-venom for one hundred miles in any direction; even if the hospitals in Monrovia had the antidotes. There were only six in the entire country. His thoughts froze him more than the immediate threat. The movement behind the snake caught his eyes as Lieutenant Forleh chopped the tail with his machete that caused the snake to immediately spin its fanged head around. As the snake turned, Lieutenant Johnson swung his machete and took the king cobra's head off. Both Liberian officers smiled at their accomplishment. Ike went over and picked up the snake meat. After a long day's hike, they camped. Ike was pleased with the kill as he cooked the snake above burning logs. The rain started and nearly destroyed the fire. Hastily, they hung ponchos above the fire far enough not to be burned from the flames. Everything was soaked. The ponchos provided little protection in the fierce driving rain. Each ate portions of the cooked snake and tried to get some rest in the downpour. Russell came close to getting hypothermia and the feeling scared the hell out of him. He stood up and started moving. He woke everyone up as they needed to start moving. The threat of hypothermia was real. By midday, they were exhausted. The sun warmed up and the humidity made the jungle unbearable. The jungle canopy kept the wind out and the dead air drove the humidity to an unbearable level. Even with the green camouflage paint, he was still the whitest man within several hundred miles and Russell loved it.

They walked deeper into the bush. His head was dizzy from dehydration. For two days they walked. He had sweats and bad chills. The heavy chilling rain followed by abrupt periods of scorching sunshine confused his body. The incredible humidity generated within seconds penetrated all of his pours. The once solid green pattern of camouflage paint on his face disintegrated. He realized that they were deep in the bush and no one would see them anyways. Regardless, any local would know upon sight as to how he walked that he was a foreigner. Ike waived for them to stop, the major road was several hundred feet ahead. They would have to wait until late night to cross. Ike stripped off all of his gear and made his way toward the contacts house in the village of Wonde. Ike came back before nightfall with the bad news that none of the contact's vehicles worked. They would have to march the next twenty miles deeper into the bush. They pushed themselves as they knew the rainy season would arrive soon and the rebels would vacate for refuge in the Gola Forest. Older people and infants that held the rebels up would be shot or stabbed. All left to die.

The GPS coordinates showed that the camp was above Widaro and near a major river. The map did not show the smaller streams. Koroma was positive on the GPS coordinates and was more than happy that his life would be spared. Of course that was until Ike kidnapped Koroma and brought him back to his town to be burned alive. Koroma probably wished that he had a better death from old age in a comfortable prison cell. Russell concentrated as best as he could. It was the fourth day of hard rain and he could not even remember what day of week it was. Days blurred together with lack of sleep. When the rain lightened, thunder echoed loud and fierce. Every time he attempted to close his eyes, he was startled by the tumultuous thunder that crackled.

"What are we going to do when we get there?" Lieutenant Forleh asked as they all sat under large tree to rest.

"Kill em all." responded Ike.

"Those who surrender will not be shot," Russell responded. "We can tie them up and leave them for the local police." Ike looked mad and

Russell wondered if giving Ike a loaded AK47 and five extra full magazines was a good idea. He recalled what the British Colonel said about Ike when we went across Sierra Leone border and took out an entire RUF camp all by himself. He wondered if Ike actually liked killing the RUF.

"I don't know about Ike." Stone offered as they looked at the map together.

"We'll keep an eye on him." Russell said. "If he gets out of control and starts killing everyone, we may have to take him out." Russell knew they were already breaking several international treaties and probably some arcane US law that stated military personnel will not on their own terms invade a foreign country and attack a RUF rebel camp. However, Russell would not accept any war crimes under his command for shooting civilians and prisoners.

"How much farther?" Colonel Marzah asked. He might have been a colonel in the Liberian army but the Lieutenants were far better at basic land navigation and troop leading skills.

"We should be within range in another hour. Keep quiet and move slowly." Russell told the team.

Russell and Stone moved forward to observe the camp from a nearby hill. They crawled over a hundred yards just in case RUF rebels walked around the camp for security. Each had a knife pulled and ready to take out any lookouts. Fortunately, they did not encounter any. From the vantage point, they had good observations. The RUF camp was small, barely noticeable except for little kids running around playing in the water. At first, Russell thought they stumbled upon a village, but then he saw men, women, and children tied together with rope as they walked on a path. The camp was hardly noticeable from the ground and definitely not noticeable from the air. He counted over twenty RUF rebels who carried AK47 rifles. They wore baseball hats turned around backward. Some wore red and blonde female wigs. Russell did not see any watch towers. The blood diamond slaves were kept in a corralled area that had rusty barbed wire around it. The best option he could think of was direct frontal assault.

"Are you ready?" Each one nodded back to the Russell. The six of them spread out on line. Russell stayed in the center and he placed

Stone on the far right. On the other end, he placed Ike. He knew they would be able to hold their own. Closer to him were the two Lieutenants and Colonel Marzah.

The first RUF soldier looked puzzled as Russell put a round in the middle of his chest. It took him only a moment to die and fall over. They walked directly forward and fired conservatively. They aimed only at the RUF. The shock of the attack took the RUF rebels completely off guard as they scrambled for their weapons.

"You're free." Russell said as he pulled open the barbed wire gate to let the captives free. They did not understand. "Run...RUN!" Russell shouted. They moved as fast as they could. Some of the women tried to get all of their belongings and babies. Russell made sure that they were not in the line of fire.

Several of the child soldiers started to fire back. Some hid behind trees. Their marksmanship ability was absolutely horrible as many rounds ripped into the foliage far from their intended targets. Russell could see that many of them were firing on full automatic without even looking at their targets. Their high rate of fire helped empty the weapons. The child soldiers were easy shots. As Russell looked throughout the camp, many of the diamond captives already departed. A few women with young babies remained as they cowered over protecting their little ones. As Russell walked over to a grass hut, a rebel came from behind the building and tried to fire his weapon. The weapon jammed and the child soldier looked confused.

"Drop the weapon." Russell could have shot him. The child soldier tried to fire the weapon again and cursed at it. As Russell tied to negotiate, Ike came up behind and hit the child over the head with the end of his AK47. The force knocked the boy unconscious.

CHAPTER 22

The team spent an hour as they collected twelve dead RUF bodies, weapons, and ammunition. Koroma provided a detailed description of the rebel leader, but Russell did not find his body. Russell wondered if he would return soon. The rebel leader's grass hut was packed with pornographic magazines, liquor, and used syringes. Ike dug in the dirt floor of the leader's hut, something he learned on his previous attack into Sierra Leone. After ten minutes, he unearthed metal tin cans full of rough diamonds. He handed the cans to Russell who walked out of the grass hut and passed the cans among the several mothers who remained. He also opened his wallet and gave them all of the cash he had. Stone did the same. The women collected as much as they could carry and walked away from their terror. Russell watched them as they hurried out of the camp. The bush wives carried their babies born in captivity. The RUF child soldiers were half the age of the women.

Stone took charge of the prisoners. Ike and Lieutenant Forleh had to carry the rebel child who Ike knocked out in a makeshift stretcher. Lieutenant Johnson led the prisoners down the path in front toward the main road. Russell and Colonel Marzah moved into the woods, just in case the rebel leader returned and discovered his camp under attack. Russell stayed connected with the others on the wireless headset that could reach up to five hundred meters. As the team extended themselves in the jungle canopy, Russell heard the regular ten minute radio checks. The last one was inaudible as they were out of communication range. Twenty minutes had passed and Russell was worried. A few moments later, Stone returned. Russell made sure they did not fire on one another.

"Wish you could've seen it." Stone laughed, "Ike found a can of red spray paint in one of the huts and painted RUF all over them. It will take a lot of scrubbing to get that off."

"Where did you leave them?"

"Close to the side of the road." Stone replied. "We placed a large log in the center of the road to stop the police. The Lieutenants can tie some great knots. Those murderers are not going anywhere."

Ike obtained some gasoline from the rebel leader's generator and poured fuel on the dead bodies, weapons, and ammunition. Around the bodies, Stone placed several grenades. Russell looked down at the bodies. He saw open white eyes that looked back at him in death. He saw biceps with the letters RUF scrawled with dull razor blades. Young boys who recruited and trained as child soldiers were stacked like wood. Charles Taylor kept them drugged, funded, and equipped to kill. These children lost their souls a long time ago and only know how to kill, rape, and brutalize any living human. Russell saw in their dead eyes the reason why Charles Taylor needed to go to jail for the rest of his life.

The team moved into the bush away from the RUF camp. Russell walked thirty feet, pulled the pin on the incendiary grenade, tossed it at the pile, and ran as fast as he could. The loud explosions rang in the air as he ran toward the rest of the team. He passed to the front and the rest followed him as they ran as fast as they could. Explosions ripped into the jungle's solitude.

The reciprocal trip was easier to take from the wave points Russell entered into the GPS. Russell pushed the team to get out of the area, at least close enough to the Liberian border, just in case they ran into an inquisitive Sierra Leone border patrol. Rain poured heavy upon them. At times, they could not breathe, yet they trudged forward, step after painful step. Russell pushed them beyond exhaustion. He was accustomed to forced hikes. On the Seattle Mountain rescue team, he was always in front breaking new trails in the snow as the rescue team hiked near vertical slopes to find stranded and injured climbers. He was driven. Rain would not stop his team; they needed to get out of there.

The Robertsport mansion finally received the generator and had power. The team had been gone for four days and it was a pleasant site to see lights on within the mansion. Russell was not surprised as he saw no sign of his Mossad agent. Russell had no means to contact her as she had refused to provide a cell phone number. Sumarka hugged Ike and welcomed everyone back. Sara came downstairs and started cooking right away, even though the men told her that they were too tired to eat. Sara would not listen. The mansion looked fabulous. The Deputy Minister splurged on new fixtures. Sara spent days cleaning. The Deputy Minister had not been back since the assassination attempt and they were eager to show him everything fixed up. Russell took all of the intelligence, photos, paper work from the command room and burned it. Their missions were complete and it was time to relax, or so he thought.

On a road that led from the large UN base into Monrovia, the makeshift police stop on Tubman Boulevard confused the Pakistani driver as he approached. He made a comment to the other Pakistani soldier as the police officer approached. Rashad wore the police uniform that he had stripped from the dead police officer he shot an hour before. Rashad looked like a policeman and passed as a local with his dark complexion. As he approached the fuel truck, Rashad pulled the pistol and placed the gun to the Pakistani driver's head. He pulled the trigger. Quickly, he pointed at the other Pakistani soldier and shot him in the belly. Rashad watched him wither in pain. After a few seconds, he placed a round in the middle of his chest. Blood spurted from the hole and he watched the man take his last breath. The UN five thousand gallon truck was hijacked within two minutes.

In Monrovia, Tareek smiled at the lovely doctor and female Mossad agent as she walked into the Cape Hotel's roof top piano bar. She was dressed in a long black dress. She ate in her old room as she could not bring herself to go back into the restaurant and not see Feeatu work the tables. She liked Feeatu, as did many patrons. Tareek moved Feeatu's boys to the room in back of the kitchen. He needed someone to take the boys. Liberian orphanages refused as the boys were too old as they already overflowed with young, more adoptable children. She thought of asking the Deputy Minister if he would mind if Ike or Sara could take care of the boys at the Robertsport mansion. There was plenty of space and it was in the country. If the boys remained in Monrovia, there were too many distractions, crooks, and violence that would consume them and ruin their lives. There were only several old relatives back at Feeatu's village. All of the younger relatives were either dead or whereabouts unknown. The Mossad agent felt guilty that her shots were not deadlier and several lived to escape and kill Feeatu as she ran. The activity in the piano bar was surprisingly quiet as they walked in. The large local man at the piano sang, *"The world will welcome new lovers, as time goes by."* Strands from the piano lingered in her ears. What was she doing with this American and how would her father react. Her father was not only a retired general who fought and was decorated in the Arab Israeli war, but he was also a Mossad agent.

Russell was easy to spot as he exited the vehicle. Francesca lowered her sunglasses and stared at him from the balcony outside of the piano bar. He looked upwards as he sensed he was being watched.

"I'm falling for you." Russell said as he approached her on the balcony. The panoramic view in front of him was something out of a movie with flowing waves and a beautiful woman.

"You shouldn't. I am not someone who stays in one place." Francesca said as a matter of fact. She had a hard life as a Mossad agent and her life was constantly in jeopardy.

"I want to be with you." Russell wanted to say forever, but that scared him to death.

"No, you don't. The life I have chosen, there are men, very bad men, who want to kill me."

"I understand all that and I can deal with that. "

"Are you sure?"

"Yes, but there is one thing." Russell said. She looked at him and nodded. "I need to know your real name." She was not surprised and had to deal with this question many times before. Each time she was able to provide preplanned cover names with no expression on her face to tell she was lying. This time was different. Now, for the first time in her life she had strong feelings for someone. "My family name is Waszey."

"Waszey," He paused. "Is that Polish?"

"My father raised me." She continued without acknowledging the compliment. "My mother was killed in Tel Aviv."

"I'm sorry." He did not need to know the circumstances but he surmised her mother died at the hands of Israel's enemies.

"As you know now, I am a Lieutenant Colonel in the Israeli Defense Force, but you do not have to salute me or call me ma'am."

"Thank you."

"You are very welcome. So, where do we go from here?" she asked. His immediate thought was back to his room, but that would not help the situation and surely create more gossip in the party.

"I don't know." He repeated himself in a softer more uncertain tone. "I don't know."

Russell followed in his vehicle. He did not want to be stranded on the side of the road or left in Monrovia without a means to escape. He became more paranoid based upon the questions and eyes and the party. He did not know how many of Rajik's thugs were left alive. Tareek was standing at the bar. "Is there a place we can talk?" The two walked into Tareek's office. Russell speculated that Tareek had the entire place wired, but did not know to what extent. The eight video screens cycled through numerous cameras strategically located.

"I need your help saving someone's life."

"If you have not observed from your few months here human life does not mean much in Monrovia." Tareek replied sarcastically.

"I have seen that."

"What do you want?"

"I want you to tell Hezbollah that there is an Israeli intelligence officer in Monrovia." He pointed to the bar as she stood out in the white sequence dress. "I love her."

"Love is a precarious position in Monrovia." Tareek offered.

"She is going to die in Monrovia."

"So what of it, I will die in Monrovia."

"You lost your family. Don't let their death blind you." Russell said and added. "I heard about Feeatu's death...I'm sorry."

"Another victim of blood diamonds." Tareek said point blank.

"We can make a difference here and finally make this place safe." Russell said. Tareek thought about that for a moment. He recalled the little amputee girl, a victim as a baby, asked him if her arm would grow back. Russell continued. "I know you don't care about the business, but you must care about the Liberians. They have suffered tremendously."

"I know they have." Tareek said. "We have all suffered from war." Tareek walked away in an abrupt manner.

Russell requested the hotel driver to drive Francesca and him to Wave Tops bar for the sunset view. Russell looked out the vehicle window and observed men who stood in the sewer holes and dug-out dirt with their hands. Teenage boys hustled with anything that could move something: a wheel barrel, a cart, or their young hardened backs. Mothers, no more than children themselves, carried little babies draped on their lower back nestled with a cloth wrap. On their heads were goods for sale. Old men hobbled with age, yet still functioned carrying and moving whatever needed to be sold. Wheelchair occupants, if anyone would call the contraptions wheelchairs, pedaled with their arms. Some of the contraptions were just pieces of steel and two tires linked together for movement. They considered themselves lucky so they would not have to crawl. Their legs were battered or taken during the brutal ravages of two civil wars. Russell saw an elderly woman dressed in a beautiful dress. She moved slowly with the cane. Her right leg was gone. She hobbled with the aid of the cane and moved the best that she could. For a brief moment, Russell connected with the elderly lady's eyes and she smiled at him. In the pain of her walk, he sensed a glimmer of happiness in her. Russell guessed that she had lost her leg in a brutal fashion, yet she was now free and seemed happy. Russell wondered how Liberians survived the civil war's brutality, however they endured.

Wave Tops bar was crowded with NGOs, construction workers from the new US Embassy under development, Chinese officials, Lebanese, Russian mafia, and several new Congo Ministers. The party scene from the poolside at the Cape Hotel had shifted to watch sunset at Wave Tops bar. Russell ordered a gin and tonic. The owners who were more part time surfers than bar managers were behind the counter and served up some powerful concoctions. Russell recognized the guy from the Robertsport scene and they bonded. The bar owner wanted to open a surf school for Liberians in Robertsport. Russell told him that was a great idea. Russell looked out over the balcony and saw the packed tin roofs on Bushrod Island. On most charity pamphlets for giving to Liberian causes, the tin roof tops were in the photos. Over two hundred thousand locals packed into a two mile square area. NGOs and many white foreigners had never entered as the threat toward robbery and mugging were very real, even during the daylight. Children played soccer on the beach. Naked children tried to jump into the crashing waves; however, out of fear they ran back before the surf hit them. Again and again, they repeated their actions. Russell looked back toward the city and could see the remnants of Hotel Dukor, which loomed over the city and Wave Tops.

"We are having a charity raffle tonight." The Pied Piper of the NGO community interrupted his peaceful sunset. "We are going to give away a free trip to Accra, which is in Ghana." No shit, Russell thought to himself. "The money goes to a great cause. We are starting a sewing coop near the Vomoma House."

"I thought there was one there started by a Harvard Business School graduate who was Liberian." Russell replied as he had heard that the battered women made fabulous outfits that was also served as therapy for their oppression from horrific events during the civil war.

"No this is different." The NGO replied in an abrupt manner. "This one will make handbags."

"You know I heard about her and what she did in just several months, truly remarkable." Francesca said as she could sense Russell wanted to get under the Pied Piper's skin.

"This female coop will make designer bags and we will have some international models come here to show them off."

"Like Naomi Campbell." Russell replied.

"Perhaps, we don't know just yet."

"Do you know Naomi Campbell accepted blood diamonds from Charles Taylor?" Russell stated as a matter of fact.

"That's absurd. She has been a strong advocate for human rights and AIDs awareness."

"Sure, but I don't really care because she accepted blood diamonds." The Pied Piper swung her hand toward Russell's face to slap him, but the female Mossad agent who was trained in deadly hand to hand combat caught it in mid-air and twisted her hand around her back. Francesca whispered into her ear and pushed her away. The Pied Piper of the NGO community did not bother them for the rest of the night.

"What did you say to her?"

"She never said thank you for saving the woman who had the circumcision. I told her that if she did not stop bothering us, I would give her one."

"A circumcision?"

"A lot of women in Africa have one." Francesca replied. "It's been a tradition for decades, if not centuries. I really don't know what the big deal is, but I guess that was enough for her to piss her pants." She pointed to the wet spot on the back of the Pied Piper's legs.

"You're too much." Russell laughed. "She's probably off to go warn everyone about me now."

"And probably talk to that nice German lady who called one of your men a baby killer." They both laughed at the trials and tribulations of the expat community. Sunset revealed magnificent orange, red, and yellow colors in the cloud bank. They looked out toward the beach in front of West Point and saw over a hundred children play.

The Robertsport mansion was full of activity as Liberian high society arrived to see the mansion and its grounds restored to former grandeur. Over two hundred people enjoyed the afternoon cookout and live music. Several of the American Embassy personnel arrived and looked at Russell with considerable suspicion as they had heard the U.S. Ambassador was not pleased about the mission to grab Taylor. Two older men, American contractors, came up to Russell. They asked if he was involved in the drug bust and capturing Charles Taylor and his bastard son. Russell looked at them without blinking and denied any involvement. As he walked around the grounds, he felt a constant watch on him from both the foreigners and locals. Someone must have talked or speculated about his actions. Sara found the Deputy Minister as he arrived and asked him if he remembered her. He did not. She pointed to the large oak tree down the walkway on the ridgeline and told him that was where his father along with her husband and other men from the village were shot. The Deputy Minister dropped to the ground and cried. A crowd surrounded the man who possessed dual citizenship between America and Liberia. An older Liberian, a man who was the highest Freemason, thirty-nine-degree, placed his hand on his shoulder and told the Deputy Minister that Liberia was his home.

CHAPTER 23

It was close to midnight when Russell returned to the Cape Hotel. He was pretty drunk and glad to have a driver. Russell looked down the street and saw some of the same diplomats with their black license plates as they stumbled to their cars. There were no drunken driving enforcement and prosecution would be out of the question, yet Russell wondered how the diplomats would feel if they killed a local. Laws were hard to enforce in the post-civil war society.

Francesca's hotel room was larger than the one Russell had when he stayed at the Cape. The room was reserved for the Liberian president and other foreign dignitaries when they visited. The plush interior was a far cry from what the locals experienced. Russell felt guilty for only a moment as he crashed on the king sized bed. As Francesca changed into a silky nightgown, Russell was out stone cold. The ten minutes that she took to prepare herself was too long for him. He snored loud. Francesca changed again into a black outfit and opened the third floor window. She tossed the knotted rope out the window. Before she climbed out, she took one last look at her passed out lover. She needed to clear her head and she needed to get more intelligence on Rajik. Her vehicle was the lone car on the road in the early hours. The turning mark was the unused green wheat harvesters, courtesy of US taxpayers. She turned down a desolate road and found the safe house. It looked empty, but she could not be sure. Francesca scaled the side of the concrete building with the aid of suction cup gloves and knee pads. She was inside within seconds. The Desert Eagle was raised and ready to fire. The room was empty. She found pictures of Monrovia posted and spread on the wall with Arabic writing. She took pictures and departed. Within an hour, she climbed back into her hotel room window, changed outfits, crawled back into bed, and snuggled next to her man.

Russell awoke in the morning in a daze. Francesca was already on the balcony and enjoyed a hot coffee. As he walked out, Russell sensed that his new love interest was pissed at him for some reason, probably because he crashed hard. He saw a pile of clothes in the corner and a knotted rope. He knew better than to ask. Francesca went to the shower and he used that as an opportunity to get out of there. Russell needed to work on his after action report. He definitely did not want an Israel spy watch over him while he completed it. He caught a local cab ride to the BTC compound and went into the bungalow to think about what transpired in the past four months in order to complete his report.

The bungalow offered Russell solitude. There were no radios or televisions, just silence. The first thing Russell did was open his journal to see what he wrote. Inside his notebook cover, he read the anonymous quote the Brigadier General Canteberry gave him in Freetown nearly five months ago. *'Doped up soldiers robed in the spoils of war – dresses, wigs, construction helmets, and swimming goggles – fired on civilians and rival factions with equal disdain.'* He now understood why the two civil wars became incredibly violent as the rule of law was not followed. RUF child soldiers were guilty for rampant violence. Heroin and other potent drugs were induced into the boys who were exploited to commit atrocities. Their young brains were unable to discriminate what was right and wrong as they murdered the innocent.

Russell started writing his report but became lost in thought. He wondered how he would explain his time in Liberia. He looked out the back window. The large metal green door stood out. As in most of the metal doors by the seaside, heavy dents of rust pocketed the large metal green door. The thought of the firing squad that carried out their orders from a madman named Master Sergeant Samuel Doe. Bullet holes were still visible. As the bullets ripped through the Tolbert family, they riddled the cement wall adjacent to the large green door. White wash paint never covered the murder squad's actions as the Tolberts were shot in cold blood. The only victim to escape was President Ellen Johnson-Sirleaf.

Russell gazed at the skyline. The sun was bright for a change. The break in clouds temporary halted the rainy season and brought nice weather for a change. As he opened the window, he could hear waves crash and he smelled the poignant sea salt air. The sun emitted warmth and the hypnotic sounds from crashing waves made him reflect that he could be in Hawaii, except he was still in Monrovia. He looked at the large green door again and recalled something he read about President Doe as he celebrated the first anniversary of the Tolbert regime's execution. A lavish party tent was erected by the large green door.

Underneath there were fine covered dining tables and a well-stocked bar. At the time of the anniversary of the execution, the large green door thrust open and President Doe walked onto the beach as if he was General MacArthur returning to retake the Philippines in World War II. President Doe hosted a lavish celebration all night with many foreign dignitaries. Everyone praised Doe to include Americans who thought the spread of Soviet Union communism was the imminent threat in Africa. The foreign dignitaries enjoyed the party. Later that same night, none were invited to the cannibalistic ritual later in the basement of the Presidential Palace where Doe had taken a bite from a dead man's heart. The man was a distant Tolbert relative and Doe wanted the juju power from the man's heart.

Russell continued to write his report into the late hours. He needed a break from Francesca and more importantly needed the sleep. His legs remained sore from hiking into and out of Sierra Leone as they assaulted the remote RUF camp. He went to sleep before midnight, but was awakened by the all night revival church. The sounds were cacophonic. The vibrations from the sound rattled the old brick. Arcane voices shouted in no apparent rhythm of sound. The jubilation continued without rest until four in the morning. Harrowing voices were amplified by speakers. Russell hugged another pillow against his ears.

In the morning, a heavy rain erupted. The earth shattering rain sounded like a freight train. At first, he heard several drops and then hundreds and within twenty seconds, thousands of rain drops hammered the bungalow's tin roof. The sideways rain chilled the air and drenched everything. Water quickly piled up to over six inches on the front lawn. Gusts of wind from the storm blew palm trees over at severe angles. Coconuts were expelled with the force. Branches flew into the air. Rain penetrated the tin roof through many holes and Russell watched the water drip down the concrete walls. He covered the computer and tried to get back to sleep. The deafening sound penetrated every sense, muscle, and bone in his body. He could not rest.

Russell went back to his report. *The main principle of any counter-insurgency doctrine is human-centric operations,'* he wrote in the computer. He recalled several comments made by the British Colonel and quoted him in the report as he often said, *'Nothing is what it appears to be in Africa.'* He remembered Kitson's comments on Africa counter-insurgency operations as well as the primary African theorists such as Trinquer, Callwell, and Kenyatta. Russell focused on what the underlining problems were with the security situation in Liberia. The disenfranchised, former military were provided a few hundred dollars and told to drop off their weapons for fifty dollars. The former Liberian soldiers signed an agreement not to wage war on the new government. Unemployment approached eighty percent. If the former Liberian soldiers had a job, the money they made was minuscule to survive. The two economies, one of the poor Liberian and the second inflated by foreigners' travel allowances made Liberia's economy a train wreck. He read several reports on post-civil war economic reconstruction. Signs throughout Monrovia highlighted to pay your taxes to help Liberia move forward, yet the locals know if they paid money it went into the pockets of some government official. Wide distrust existed. The tax rate remained thirty-five percent. The tax payment did not include any bribes needed to keep your place from being looted, sometimes by the local police. In the Red Light district market, no one paid taxes and commerce progressed. Everything imaginable was sold. Forks and spoons were considered necessities in many western countries were called luxury items in war-torn Liberia.

The rain stopped and he took a moment to walk outside. He observed the damage. The small shacks outside BTC had tin roofs blown off. The locals were soaked and there was no way to get dry. For Liberians, the rainy season was the cold time of year and they huddled under overhangs with old blankets. In a four month period, Liberia would experience over twenty-two feet of rain, most of it arrived in torrential downpours like the one he just endured. Liberia was the second wettest spot on the planet. He pondered how Liberia would move forward. Russell thought back to his background. He had walked in the presence of audacious wealth. For a fleeting moment, his mind raced back to that summer in the Hamptons. He thought of the wild parties and chance encounters of being in the same bar as a Hampton celebrity. In the trips around the quaint Hampton villages and rows of billionaire summer playground beach cottages, he peered into the lifestyle. Pug noses of snobby children pointed to the air. Parents believed their perfect children would become the next Hamptons elite. For generations, military service had taken the most obnoxious, undisciplined, poor or rich snob and forged them into something. Humility was something he learned in the humid summer days along the water at Annapolis and in the woods of Quantico. He never wanted to return to the Hamptons again and committed himself to never walking the perfectly aligned streets with fifteen-foot hedges bringing privacy to summer occupants.

Russell returned to BTC compound. The red, white, and blue paint cascaded across bricks accented the Liberian flag, which rested above on the fifty foot flag pool. A slight breeze moved the flag and he looked up and saw the Liberian flag, the one large star resided in the middle of the blue, red and white stripes spread along the canvas. He felt the heritage back to colonial America and the freed slaves who came to Liberia with hope. He recalled the Liberian motto, *'The love of Liberty brought us here.'* He finished the report and brought the laptop back to Robertsport to send on the satellite link.

Meanwhile at the abandoned Voice of America compound, the explosion ripped apart the old car and sent metal flying across the field. Rashad was pleased with the results. The high-powered C4 explosive worked well and he was equally impressed with the remote detonators that he built. He was concerned that moisture in the container damaged the electronics. Rashad handed out submachine guns from one of the wooden boxes. The new recruits he solicited from Rajik were pleased to shoot the weapons. Rashad believed he could recruit them into Al-Qaeda and gain a foothold in Liberia.

"Make sure each man has enough ammo," Rashad said to several of his terrorists. Rashad had each man line up and he inspected their weapons, disguises, and gear. Rashad was pleased with his terrorist cell and believed he would get a promotion out of this assignment. Perhaps, he would take his fight to Sierra Leone.

Rajik watched him closely to see how he controlled his terrorist cell. Rajik liked the large amount of money and jewels that the Al-Qaeda operative possessed. Rajik wanted wealth and would do anything to get it. He was not going back to Beirut to sit on a mountainside post and wait for the Israelis to attack. Rajik liked the easy money he made from the casino, yet he could not go back there now. Besides, he had heard the UN closed the casino down. He needed to get out of Liberia and he believed Al-Qaeda would be his ticket.

In the morning, Russell headed north out of Monrovia toward his favorite beach community in Robertsport. Russell was pleased to be back at the Deputy Minister's mansion. The waves cascaded across the beach and the palm trees dipped in the sea breeze. Local men were busy as they raked the beach and cleaned up garbage that floated ashore during the night's heavy storm. He was pleased to be able to get some much needed peace compared to the all night revival at the church outside the BTC compound and noise from rain that smashed against the bungalow's tin roof. Russell reviewed his final report one more time and pressed the enter button to launch it to Colonel Crevace in Germany on a secured satellite link. He would surely receive a phone call on his report and realized his controversial comments about the UN and NGO support would be removed. His report outlined how the trouble started: Doe killed Tolbert; Prince Johnson killed Doe; Taylor took over; and Taylor was pushed out after a fourteen-year span at the expense of four hundred thousand Liberian lives. He noted Ike kidnapped Koroma and his tribe conducted a ritualistic healing by burning Koroma alive. Russell accepted responsibility for placing a knife in General Abbdas' chest in self-defense. To help the Charles Taylor indictment, he remarked on the documents he turned over to the UN, the photos of a supermodel with blood diamonds, and he summarized Colonel 'zigzag' Marzah's ability to provide factual testimony.

The only absent part from his report was his intrusion into Sierra Leone on hard intelligence provided by Koroma to take out a blood diamond camp whereby they freed over a hundred captives. He was disgusted that Rajik escaped and was worried that Rashad still ran loose in Liberia. Russell saw Rashad only once at the casino and wished that he had taken care of him then. Russell wanted Al-Qaeda out of Liberia, preferably in body bags. He passed his concerns onto the Deputy Minister and he promised to talk to the Freemasons about the Al-Qaeda threat. The Deputy Minister informed him that many of the important community leaders had come out of hiding to join the Freemason movement. Both concurred that the UN would be ineffective dealing with Rajik and Rashad.

Ike, the Lieutenants, and Captain Stone loaded all of the weapons and gear borrowed from Sierra Leone. The three IMATT land rovers were lined up and cleaned. Ike liked keeping the vehicles cleaned. James scrubbed the tires with a wet sponge. Stone gave James a bush hat to wear in order to keep the sun off of his sensitive skin. Russell inventoried the communication gear, night vision goggles, weapons, grenades, and ammunition. The mission came to an end and they would fly out tomorrow night from Roberts International Airport, or so they thought. The three land rovers were followed by the hijacked SUV they brought from the Firestone Plantation. At the Bo-waterside border crossing, British troops were present. They inventoried and properly received all of the equipment. Brigadier General Canteberry who was the British General in charge of the Sierra Leone mentoring mission was present. He provided Russell an update on Colonel Kitson's wounds, which was good news to Russell that the British Colonel would be fine. Canteberry could tell something changed within Russell, Africa got under his skin.

"Colonel, thank you." Russell told Colonel Marzah.

"Thank you sir, you have made a difference."

"I hope so. What are you going to tell the War Crimes Committee?" asked Russell.

"The truth," Colonel Marzah said, "Charles Taylor was a cannibal and butcher. Several times, he ordered me to kill prisoners. Taylor feasted on humane intestines and body parts."

"How do you know?"

"I was one of his battalion commanders and I protected Taylor to keep him in power. He relied upon me to keep his horrible regime operating. I wished that I did not support Taylor."

"And the child soldiers?" Russell asked as he wanted to know.

"Taylor ordered me to Sierra Leone to hire RUF child soldier to fight in Liberia. I brought boxes full of heroin needles and gave them money to buy drugs. Every trip, I came back with tin cans full of blood diamonds that I bought with drug money."

"It's a vicious circle."

Colonel Marzah had seen a lot of death. He felt heavy despair and huddled over. "It's all my fault. I should have killed Taylor a long time ago. I had the chance. I could have ended the civil war with one bullet. I wish that I killed Taylor."

"No, it would have been worse. Taylor's crazy son would have taken over and he was more sadistic."

He sobbed some more, "I could've killed him too."

"You can't kill them all." Russell said with a laugh to lighten the mood and Colonel Marzah wiped his face. He laughed slightly.

"I guess you're right, but it would have been fun to put a bullet in them both. I really despised that little bastard son. He was a real pain to deal with."

"Well he is going away for a very long time." Russell said.

"So will Charles Taylor."

"Indeed, so will the biggest butcher of them all." Russell waved farewell as Colonel Marzah drove off. He would have a long tough road ahead of him coming to grips with the brutality and testimony against his former president and Commander in Chief. He will be demonized by the press and Taylor's lawyers.

Sara made everyone a large meal of local lobsters, fresh fish, and casaba. Ike caught the lobsters earlier in the cove with the fishing net and chopped the heads off with a machete. Liberian lobsters were different from New England as they did not have claws. The heads had to be removed before cooking. Ike passed the Liberian pepper. Russell still refused to try any as he had a plane to catch tomorrow night. The Liberian Lieutenants laughed as Russell passed on the hot pepper sauce. Stone loaded up on the pepper sauce and placed large amounts on the lobster meat. Sumarka hustled between the seats to fill drinks and provided more food. Her baby rested on her back in satchel cloth. The baby was awake and cried. She named the baby Ellen after the president and first African woman leader in the history of the continent. Everyone liked her choice. Lucy disrupted the meal as she ran, jumped onto table, and grabbed a plantain. Ike chased her and everyone laughed boisterously.

"What did your uncle say?" Russell asked Stone as they sat on the porch. They enjoyed several Club beers.

"He was not pleased with the Nigerian cabinet. President Obasanjo is getting older and there are some who view him as weak."

"Really," Russell paused, "Could there be a potential coup?"

"Perhaps, but not likely. Nigeria had its fill of military coups." Stone reflected on his personal life. "I remember being on vacation as a teenager and hiding in a bunker at my uncle's beach house. We did not know if we would escape the country or not."

"It's good to have an escape strategy." Russell said.

"Violence and cruelty were common threads in Africa's past. I hope the future is more certain and stable. But it only takes one out of control general or dictator to unravel the peace."

"Are you going to return to Nigeria?"

"I am, after this mission, tomorrow night when you fly out. I need to find out what happened to my father."

"Does your uncle know?"

"No, or at least he told me no." Stone paused for a moment and added. "I believe him. He's never lied to me."

"How much are you worth?"

Stone took a moment to think about the response. He knew his friend was disgusted with audacious wealth and had issues with his previous fiancé's father. Stone's money remained in a trust as the single and sole heir of his father's holdings in the family business. Stone never asked for a penny and made his way through Oklahoma University on football scholarship and the kindness of the Stone family whose last name he adopted. He looked at Major Russell and responded to his question. "With the real estate, bonds, business ventures, holdings, trust fun, the last tally was about one hundred and eighty."

"Million?"

"Ya, million." Stone replied in a quiet manner.

"Shit, now I really do not like you." They both laughed. "Do you know your girlfriend's sister does not think you are good enough for her, or at least her daddy?"

"I suspected as much. She told me that I was a phase for her, an African experience. Whatever that meant."

"Does either of them know your real family name?"

"No and I would like to keep it that way."

"And of course." Russell said and inquired further. "Britney has no idea what you are worth?"

"Absolutely not." Stone had prided himself on what he had accomplished in his life to date without the wealth.

CHAPTER 24

Rashad yearned for a massive explosion that would be filmed for propaganda. He sought an aerial view to film the destruction. More importantly, he needed a backup remote detonator if the driver failed to have the jihadist courage at the final moment. In preparation for the mission, the helicopter was pulled out from under the overhang at the abandoned Voice of America site. A few feet away, RUF soldiers painted over the numbers on the white UN five thousand gallon fuel truck. Rashad chose the lightest skin RUF killer who possibly would pass for a Pakistani soldier. The Sierra Leone soldiers had much darker skin, but one had a lighter complexion. Rashad purchased a uniform in Red Light district. Many of the uniforms from the nations that supported the UN effort in Liberia were stolen and sold on the black market. Rashad crawled on top of the fuel truck and inspected the remote detonator. Rashad made sure all of the rough diamonds were loaded and secured in the first vehicle. After the attack, they would drive north to Guinea and make their way to Mali to deliver the diamonds to an Al-Qaeda leader.

Rajik watched the preparation events unfold before him and believed that he entered a runaway freight train on a collision course. He needed to get away from Rashad and the rest of his insane jihad fighters. Most importantly, he needed to get out of Liberia. Rashad jumped down from the fuel tanker and made a long distance call to Yemen. After several moments, Rashad gave a wave to everyone that the mission was a go. The jihadists loaded up and departed the abandoned Voice of America compound, a location that once preached freedom during the cold war to squelch communism. The helicopter lifted off forty minutes afterwards.

Ike drove Russell and Stone to Monrovia. As they entered the Cape Hotel gate, Russell saw Francesca in the parking lot. She was dressed in tight black pants and a black shirt. Her hair was tied tightly in a braid and she wore a bush hat. She loaded the final piece of luggage. Ike dropped Russell off and departed toward Wave Tops bar.

"Are you leaving?" Russell asked as he stepped closer.

"My cover is blown," Francesca said as she looked at him. He could tell that she was upset. "My truck is packed with everything I have." He looked in back and saw several rocket launchers and boxes of ammunition that stuck out from underneath the tarp, which covered most of the back. He noticed that she painted over top of the Doctors Without Borders sign on the doors.

"Where you going?"

"Far from here." Her cell phone rang. Francesca conversed in Hebrew and shot a glance at Russell. He had never heard her speak her native tongue.

"What's wrong?" Russell sensed a change in her.

"Get in." She said as she slammed the rear hatch shut. They both jumped in the vehicle. Francesca accelerated and blasted the vehicle out the front gate of the Cape Hotel at a fast pace. "There's a truck bomb moving toward Monrovia."

"How do you know?"

"An Israeli company owns one of the cell phone companies here and the other one we tapped into." Francesca gave him a nonchalant stare and added. "Basically, we have monitored every call coming into and out of Liberia for the past six months. And I found a pile of surveillance photos in a safe house."

"Is it Rashad?" Russell asked, yet she did not reply. Russell wanted to get more intelligence reports on Al-Qaeda operations in Africa and Rashad's name kept coming up again and again. Langley thought he was a low level operative but something did not sit right with Russell. He believed there was something more at stake. Russell had a feeling in his gut that he needed to take out Rashad immediately.

The vehicle bounded over the haphazardly paved road that the Chinese did not complete. The vehicle slammed into the massive potholes that still remained, and Russell found himself pressed against the dashboard. He lifted the weapon to check the safety mechanism. Fortunately, he had placed the Uzi on safe.

"Is Rashad behind this?" Russell asked. He observed a clear stretch of road where they could have a conversation without bouncing all over the vehicle.

"Yes and our friend Rajik is with him." Francesca did not waste time as she sped the vehicle. She slammed on the horn to alert everyone to move and fast. Russell looked in back of the vehicle and observed a missile launcher in the crate. He surmised this was no ordinary mission.

"Do you know their target?" Russell inquired. Francesca looked at Russell, a man whom she had shared many intimate moments in the past four months. Russell sensed something was severely wrong. Her facial expression was stone cold.

"Your embassy." Francesca replied.

The Al-Qaeda jihadist dressed as a Pakistani soldier had a difficult time driving the big fuel tanker down the dirt roads that had been washed out from the recent storms. Several times, he drove on the side of the road and ran over logs. Rajik hoped the vehicle would not explode from all of the bouncing around, especially as he was in the explosive blast radius. Rajik looked in the back of the SUV and saw the box filled with over a thousand rough diamonds. The jihadist driver watched him in the rear view mirror suspiciously. Once the fuel tanker got on the main road, Rajik's vehicle pulled out in front to guide the truck bomb.

Francesca saw the white UN fuel truck in the other direction and shifted the steering wheel. Tires screeched as she braked and turned the vehicle around. Locals flung their bodies out of the way. Within two minutes, she pulled up behind. She did not see another vehicle that emerged from behind. The Al-Qaeda jihadist sped a black SUV as he had observed the white woman driving. Bullets blew out the back window. Glass fragments bombarded the interior of the vehicle. Francesca swerved the vehicle as Russell tried to get a clear shot. Russell fired widely. His second shot went wide left as did the third and fourth shots.

The SUV driver pulled his arm back to concentrate more on the slippery road. The syrup brown water covered the main street from the morning's heavy rain. The vehicle swerved and splashed in the brown water. The driver kept the vehicle steady as he fired at the foreigners again. Bullets ripped into the metal doors.

As Francesca shifted the vehicle from one side of the road to the other, she accelerated toward the fuel tanker. As the black SUV moved up alongside on the right, Francesca shifted the steering wheel and crashed against the other vehicle. Not knowing what laid beneath the darkened water on the road, the SUV driver made a fatal mistake and plowed four feet deep into an open sewer drain. The vehicle came to an abrupt stop as the front filled the hole and the rear of the vehicle lifted off the ground. When the wheels came to rest, the black SUV listed on its side. Russell observed blood was smeared across the windshield from the driver's face.

Francesca accelerated the truck at fast as it would move in the syrupy water. She jumped the vehicle over the curb. The vehicle hit dry pavement and skidded. She missed several local ladies who walked with reed woven baskets on their heads. She frightened them and caused the baskets to tumble onto the pavement. Within seconds, Francesca pulled up alongside of the fuel tanker again.

Russell gave her a whimsical stare as he made up a plan on the fly. He thought about what would happen if he fired the Uzi into the fuel truck. More than likely, he concluded it would blow up and kill a lot of the locals. Russell slung the Uzi over his head and climbed out the vehicle's window. He stood upon onto the hood as Francesca moved to the rear of the fuel truck. He jumped onto the back ladder on the fuel tanker. She waited an extra second to make sure that he was on board. The other SUV in front of the fuel truck with Rajik on board turned around and headed directly toward her. Francesca quickly swerved the vehicle to the right to get out of collision course. She jumped the curve and plowed through a bush hut. Locals dove for cover as she slammed the horn. She swerved back onto the road.

Rajik gripped the door handle and screamed as they almost struck the vehicle in front of them. The jihadist in the front passenger seat passed Rajik a pistol. Rajik placed his gun out the window and shot at the man on the tanker and then realized he could blow them all up. He concentrated his next shot on the other vehicle. He recognized her and was surprised to see she was still alive after Monkey Island.

Russell walked gingerly as if a surfer in completion on a heavy wave as he moved forward on top of the tanker. Russell concluded the best course of action and emptied the Uzi into the top of the cab. Bullets ripped into the metal roof and killed the impersonator. The vehicle maintained a straight line as the driver slumped forward.

247

All of sudden, Russell felt a sting in top of his right shoulder as a bullet pierced his clothes. He looked up in time and witnessed a helicopter moving overhead at a high rate of speed. Russell fell onto the roof and kicked out the passenger's window. He pushed the dead driver's body out the door and grabbed the wheel. The driver's limp body hit the pavement and bounced. Francesca ran over the body as she sped up along the right side to get in front of the tanker.

For over a mile, the vehicles played a deadly cat and mouse game as bullets were repeatedly fired. Russell drove toward the old Liberian Coast Guard base. Francesca slowed down and pointed her arm out the window to signal him to keep going forward. She got out of the vehicle and pulled a rocket launcher out of the back. As Rajik's jihadist driver turned the corner, Francesca launched the rocket, missed the fast moving vehicle, and blasted a wall apart. The vehicle swerved and crashed.

Rajik wasted no time and crawled out the broken rear window. He grabbed the box filled with rough diamonds. Rajik stopped a local cab driver, pressed the pistol against the man's head, and took the vehicle. Although Rajik was over a hundred feet away, Francesca still shot at him with her Desert Eagle pistol. The sound of the canon echoed. The round impacted the taxi's back window and blew it out. Francesca jumped into her vehicle and began chase.

As Russell drove down the five hundred yard jetty, he saw the helicopter overhead. The pilot swerved back and forth. He heard rounds penetrate the truck's metal roof. Russell worked the rope he found in the front seat around the steering wheel. There was an AK47 that he used to keep the pedal pressed to the floor.

High above, Rashad worked the remote detonator. He pressed it again and again. He opened the batteries, reinserted them, and shook the detonator. Again and again, he pressed the keypad with no success.

Once the rope was taug, Russell jumped from the fast moving truck. Russell rolled onto the dirt and fell into the water. The truck bomb continued down the jetty. Before the vehicle crashed into the ocean, the detonator worked and triggered a massive explosion. The fire ball consumed the sky and pushed the helicopter backward. Russell did not wait to see what the helicopter pilot would do once he regained control.

Russell sprinted fast toward the road. Several locals had stopped to witness the humongous fireball. Russell tossed a man several hundred dollars and purchased his motorbike on the spot. Russell sped toward Monrovia and the only sanctuary place he considered, the U.S. Embassy.

The helicopter spun back in Russell's direction. The sound of helicopter blades thundered as the aircraft came overtop him. The helicopter passed low, about twenty feet off the ground. The helicopter's side door was open and Russell recognized Rashad. There was a traffic jam up ahead. Russell jumped the motorbike across the curb and into oncoming traffic. Machine gun fire erupted and ripped apart a cement truck next to him as he sped past. Russell accelerated the motorbike and moved back and forth in between traffic. He crossed over the bridge connecting Monrovia to Bushrod Island.

Up ahead, the Hotel Dukor loomed over top of Monrovia. He accelerated to the top of the hill and arrived at the front of the hotel. He slammed on the brakes and skidded into one of the large cement towers reaching upward to hold the mammoth weight of the old circular restaurant above. He heard the helicopter as it hovered and saw two men jump twenty feet to the ground. As he entered the staircase, he heard several shots fired in his vicinity. He rushed up the stairs and gagged at the viral smell of rotten urine. His military boots thumped hard against the tiled steps. Squatters emerged from the darkened rooms to see what the loud commotion was and only caught a fleeting glimpse of Russell as he sky-rocketed his body to the fifteenth floor. A flimsy plywood door held intruders at bay. With one giant kick, he knocked the makeshift door off its hinges. A local security contractor protecting the cellular transmission towers on top was startled. Fear quickly covered his face. The only thing Russell could think of quickly was corny and sounded every more corny after he said it, "American Marine, everything's ok." The middle age man, who was probably former AFL, nodded. "Everything will be ok." Russell stated calmly. They both heard the noise. Russell pointed toward the staircase and said, "You'd better get out of here."

Russell did not see the helicopter but he heard it overhead. He weaved his way through the deserted roof top bar and ran to the other side of the roof. The helicopter hovered closer and he saw it out of the right side of his eye. Muzzle flashes signaled rounds headed his way and ricochets forced him to dive for cover behind the bar. Heavy volleys of machinegun fire ripped apart the legendary twelve foot high mahogany placards that displayed various wildlife scenes.

The helicopter banked hard left and moved over top of the hotel. Russell did not have time to think. He grabbed the military sack that they had previously stowed from the team's rappel training. He quickly put on the heavy canvas gloves and belt harness. With sheer instinct, he made several loops with the rope. He anchored the rope around the concrete pillar and tossed it over the side of the hotel's wall. The rope unfurled two hundred feet below. Russell heard men as they approached on the staircase. With utmost sped, Russell ran past the antiquated dance floor and watched the helicopter as it emerged. Without giving them a chance for a shot, he leaped off the side of the building face forward in a straight downward Australian style rappel. Russell ran down the wall and pushed his arm forward to let the rope pass through the harness as he completed the rappel. The shooters did not have a clear shot and the helicopter floated closer to the ground. Russell ran until all of the rope exited the harness. Within five seconds, he was free.

The two men looked over the wall and did not desire to follow. The men ran back down the staircase. Over two hundred feet below, Russell ran at full speed toward the desolate building that contained Wave Tops bar. He vaulted the five level staircases and was completely out of breath when he saw Stone.

"Did you see that explosion?" Stone asked. Russell pointed toward the doorway and tried to catch his breath.

"They're coming." Russell said as he panted heavily between breathes. "We have to go." Stone grabbed Britney and started toward the doorway until machine gun ripped the floor apart. With one arm, Stone tossed Britney behind the bar. Bullets shattered liquor bottles. The helicopter hovered at level height of the veranda. Russell saw Rashad as he pointed the machine gun at him. Russell stood still. There was no place to hide. Rashad had Russell dead, but someone else intervened.

From several hundred feet away, a projectile missile was launched at the intended target. The explosive force initially lifted the helicopter higher in the air. Fire engulfed inside the aircraft. Russell saw

Rashad as he dropped the weapon and tried to climb out. The helicopter shifted left, fell straight below, and exploded. The fireball from the aircraft's fuel drifted up toward the fifth floor balcony. Russell rushed and looked over the edge at the burning hulk. Out toward the bridge, he saw her. On top of a vehicle, the female Mossad agent waved. Francesca's vehicle was sideways and had stopped all traffic. She quickly jumped into the vehicle and accelerated away from Monrovia. She needed to get rid of the weapons and vehicle. Mossad agents operated undercover and Francesca was exposed.

Stone emerged from behind the bar counter with blood on his shirt, some of it was his and some was Britney's. They both took ricochet shots in their legs. Stone pressed his hands against her right thigh while blood seeped out of his own wound. He disregarded his injury to help the woman he fell for. Russell tossed several bar towels to soak up the blood. Stone grabbed the blender and ripped the electrical cord from the device. He wrapped the wire tight over top of the towels against Britney's wound. The look on her face was complete and utter shock.

Russell heard the sound of men as they raced up the stairs. The two jihadists charged into the room. Russell waited behind the door and pounced on them like a lion. He knocked the weapon out of the first one's hands with a bamboo stick he had grabbed. The second one tried to fire but was pushed back by the collision from the other jihadist. Stone hobbled forward with all of his strength. He leveled his fist across the face of one jihadist and dropped him. Russell swung the bamboo stick several times and knocked out the second. Within moments, they had tied them up for the local UN police to deal with. Russell looked around at Wave Tops bar that was completely blown apart and had a bad feeling the NGO community would not be pleased at their onetime sanctuary.

Russell was out of money and informed the taxi driver that he would pay him later. The driver saw the blood on Stone and Britney and had sympathy. He drove them to the Jordanian Medical Hospital and parked the car to get paid. Russell lied to the UN guards and said they were victims of the explosion that happened earlier at the Liberian Coast Guard base. The Jordanian surgeons were more inquisitive of the gunshot fragments. Russell was informed that both of them would have to be airlifted to Germany for surgery. Russell used Britney's phone and called her older sister. The Pied Piper of the NGO community screamed in the phone at Russell and hung up. Russell bid farewell to his Captain America who was already drugged, incoherent, and on his way out.

The traffic on the bridge from Bushrod Island was stalled. The black Mercedes luxury sedan with tinted windows waited. Colonel Chan from the People's Republic of China rolled down the window and watched the helicopter explode. He smiled widely as chaos had arrived once again to Liberia and China would be in a great position to help restore order. There were over a thousand troops outside Monrovia and Beijing would send more. The Chinese colonel kept solid surveillance on all of the foreigners and knew which Liberian Ministers were the best to bribe. He was pleased with the utter disorder that evolved in front of his eyes. When he returned to the Chinese Embassy, he would review the phone and communication transcripts. The indiscreet water tower held two powerful aperture array antennas for surveillance. The Chinese had tracked all communications within Liberia.

Rajik saw the explosion down the shoreline and powered his speedboat faster to get out of the area. Rajik looked down at the wooden box filled with nearly a thousand rough diamonds and smiled at his ticket out of Liberia. He steered the motor boat south toward Cote D'Ivoire. Rajik planned to hold course along the coastline to get as far away as possible.

The taxi cab driver had waited for Russell and brought him back to BTC. Russell had money hidden in his dresser and gave the man several crisp one hundred dollar bills, which Russell had won at the casino. He considered all of his winnings from the casino as Hezbollah money and did not want it. Russell phoned Colonel Crevace in Germany and gave him a verbal debrief. Colonel Crevace was pleased they had stopped a truck bomb, yet very upset the UN had not done more to protect Liberia and maintain security.

Russell poured a heavy scotch drink. The heavy rain penetrated the night. The BTC security guards were bundled within the towers and guard shack. Russell placed the large rough diamond on the table and took several photos. He rested his thumb next to it as no one would doubt he possessed a forty carat rough diamond. The British Colonel mentioned that it would be worth about half a million dollars. The pink tone to the diamond looked beautiful, and Russell admired the reflections of the lamp as he held the diamond overhead. He carried the diamond all over Liberia, Nigeria, and Sierra Leone. No one would ever suspect someone would be so naïve to carry an expensive stone. In the simplicity of carrying the stone, he fooled everyone.

Russell turned off the bungalow's light and opened the door. He did not want anyone to see him depart. The parade field was muddied from the intense rain. He walked to the center of the field and looked up at the Liberian national flag. The rainy wind pushed the flag hard and it fluttered heavily. Russell fell to his knees and dug a foot hole in the dirt with his knife. He took out the forty carat rough, untraceable diamond from his pocket. He said a short prayer for the souls who may have died finding this gem and buried the large rough diamond in a heavy downpour. He gave the diamond back to Mother Earth. After all the violence he had witnessed firsthand for the rough diamonds, he could not bring himself to keep it. Russell wanted to put faith in the Kimberly Process; however, he knew many former Soviet bloc countries and Al-Qaeda would not abide by the agreement. The abuse and knowledge of blood diamonds would have to be eradicated.

The hard rain deafened all noise. Francesca knocked hard on the door to make sure he knew someone was there. Slowly, he opened the door as he held a sharp butcher knife behind his back. She smiled at him with those brilliant white teeth. He pulled Francesca close and gave her a big hug, not just for saving his life, but because he really missed her.

"Why did you come back?" Russell asked.

"I wanted to see you."

"But you're in danger. Hezbollah knows you are here."

"I know," Francesca said, "But it does not matter anymore." She took off her shirt. She was self-conscious about her scar. He looked at her scar in the light. The indention of the wound was several centimeters and the skin that grew back after she burned herself was not normal, something out of a horror movie. He leaned forward and kissed her scar to make her understand that he felt her pain. She tackled him onto the bed and they wrestled, laughed, and pulled the bed net off of the ceiling.

Several hours later, he awoke and heard her snore next to him. Russell laughed slightly to himself and rolled back to sleep. If Francesca would snore beside him, Russell thought he must have done something right in their relationship to make her believe she was in a secure place.

In the early hours before dawn, Francesca slithered out of bed. Russell neither noticed nor moved. Russell was out cold and did not feel the needle Francesca had injected into his neck. The medicine placed him into a deep sleep. After five minutes, she checked his vitals. Francesca collected all of her things, cleaned down the room of all fingerprints as a matter of habit, kissed him on the forehead, and departed the bungalow. The prior night she had cleaned out her vehicle and wiped it down completely. She considered blowing the vehicle up; however, she knew it would create attention. She left the keys in the ignition.

A rubber boat landed behind BTC compound, on the same beach where former Master Sergeant Doe tossed the bodies from the murdered Tolbert regime. As the small boat bounced across the waves, Francesca looked back toward the bungalow and thought of Russell. Her infatuation was against everything the Mossad trained her, yet she did not care. Francesca hated the helpless feeling, yet she yearned for him. She did not know when she would see him, if ever, especially after her father discovered what happened in Liberia. Her father would find out about her love interest with the American.

Her father had developed American assets when he was assigned to the Israeli Consulate in Washington, DC. As a teenager growing up in Alexandria, Virginia, Francesca was trained at an early age to manipulate. She did not want her father to get information on Russell. She was determined to keep his name out of her reports. She knew Tel Aviv would track him for the rest of his life. As the rubber boat arrived at the non-descript container ship, she was happy to be out of Liberia. She opened the necklace charm to see the small photo of herself and her mother who died weeks later from a Hamas bomb blast in Tel Aviv. She read the inscription, *'For lack of guidance a nation falls, but many advisors make victory sure.'* Her Mossad assignments had taken her all over the world under many aliases. Francesca looked back toward Liberia and already missed Tom Russell.

Chapter 25

Russell awoke not knowing what time it was. The sedative that Francesca injected into his vein had worn off. He never felt the small prick from the needle when she stuck him. Her training as a Mossad agent and physician taught her well. Russell looked upward and saw the bed net was hung back from the ceiling. Little ropes reached up to the rusty nails, which protruded from white beams. Russell wrestled his exit from the bed net and made his way into the kitchen for water.

"Francesca?" Russell shouted. He grabbed his head and shouted again. "Francesca?" No one answered. How long was he out? Russell had no clue. He heard loud sounds from the church and realized that it was Sunday morning. He must have slept for entire day.

The only thing Francesca left was a letter on the table. Russell read the short note, crumpled the letter, and tossed it in the trashcan. After a minute, he returned and retrieved the paper wad. He gently folded it on the table and read it again. It was a simple note, addressed to no one. *'Don't try to find me, it cannot be, we cannot be.'*

Russell needed to get out of the bungalow and jumped into the vehicle. He headed toward Robertsport one last time. As he parked near the mansion, he looked out toward the ocean. Waves lavished over the speckled white sand. He remembered what the British Colonel told him about Africa, *"Once you get it in your blood, it is hard to get it out."* Russell felt his time in Liberia forever changed him. He thought of Liberia's struggle for peace and continued independence as the longest lasting independent nation on the African continent.

Russell handed Ike the keys for the hijacked vehicle that they had obtained from the Black Beret camp. There were no stolen vehicle reports in the war-torn country. Ike asked Russell if he wanted to go with him to bring Lucy to her new home. Lucy had gained twenty pounds and eight inches since she was purchased off the Monrovia streets. Ike motioned to the canoe; however, Russell did not want to spend the entire day paddling. Russell drove over to the marina, and they borrowed Uncle Anwar's speedboat. Russell turned the boat up into the river that connected the large Fisherman's Lake. He cruised deep into the lake toward Massatin Island, which was used as a sanctuary during the war.

"Ike, are you sad to see Lucy go?"

"Ya boss, Ike sad. Lucy gud chimp." Ike held Lucy on his lap. The chimp was scared by the boat engine noise.

"I have to leave Liberia, but I will be back someday."

"Ya boss. U cum back." Ike paused. He lifted his machete and waved it in the air. "Ike keep u sav." Russell knew Ike meant it.

Russell thought of his mentor and missed the British Colonel. In the two months he had spent with the British Colonel, Russell learned more about counter-insurgency operations in Africa than in his entire life, especially since the Dark Continent had a plethora of sinister wars.

Russell stopped the speedboat at Massatin Island. From the shore, he saw the old, decayed wooden buildings. Once upon a time, these shacks provided a safe haven. At one point, the island was populated by two hundred locals who fled the brutal fighting. Ike hugged Lucy one last time. Russell was surprised to see Lucy provide a reciprocal hug, near human characteristics. As they pulled the boat away, Ike waved farewell. Russell knew it was the right decision to put Lucy on the island. In another year, Lucy would be over a hundred pounds and would be able to tear the face off of a grown man.

In his new vehicle, Ike drove Russell back to Monrovia one last time. As Ike parked the vehicle inside the Cape Hotel, Russell handed Ike a thick envelope full of money. He had discretionary money to fund the operation and thought of no one more deserving. Ike looked at the money, about three thousand dollars and quickly raised his head to make sure no one watched him. Russell saw several tears flow down Ike's face. The Liberian man who was named after the great American general and former president had witnessed a significant amount of violence in his lifetime.

"Ike miss bossman." Ike mustered only a few words.

Uncle Anwar and Ghasson returned from their trip to Detroit. Tareek briefed them in detail on the madness that occurred since they departed. Tareek told them how Chad joined Hezbollah and died from a snake bite. Tareek informed them how Feeatu was killed by Rajik and no one knew his whereabouts. Ghasson promised that the entire Lebanese community would be on the lookout for him, all eighty thousand. Local papers talked of UN Special Forces who fought Al-Qaeda terrorists in the streets. There were pictures of the burned out helicopter and many speculated that it crashed. There were more pictures of a burning fuel tanker. The UN covered up the hijacking and claimed the vehicle caught fire accidently, and the driver courageously drove the fuel tanker down the jetty to prevent any injuries.

As Russell walked up to them, Uncle Anwar and Ghasson stood and welcomed Russell. They both told him to come back anytime. They knew what Russell and his team did and appreciated his help keeping Liberia safe and indirectly helping to protect their financial interests. Uncle Anwar offered Russell a complimentary meal. The chef in the corner with his large chef's top hot grilled up fresh fish. Russell filled his plate and sat in the last corner table in the far end, a two person table. As Russell ate, he looked out through the plate glass window to the beautiful beach below. Russell shoveled large piles of food into his mouth until he suddenly stopped. Outside the Cape Hotel entrance gate, a young mother with a baby on her back begged for food as westerners passed. He surmised that she must have had lost her tongue as she moved her hand back and forth to her mouth to signal that she was hungry.

"May I join you?" He looked up and saw the Pied Piper of the NGO community. "My sister is fine. My father wants me to leave."

"I heard she was fine. Stone is fine. Everybody is fine."

"You should take this more seriously." The Pied Piper injected. "She could have been killed."

"Over four hundred thousand have died in Liberia. Bodies are found in Monrovia every day. Your sister will be fine."

"How can you be so cruel?"

"It's reality." Russell replied coldly.

"Not my reality." She blasted back at him. "Liberia will be secure once we educate the former child soldiers."

"I doubt that." Russell offered. "Many of them are beyond help. I have seen the rage in their eyes. Most have post-traumatic stress and require significant counseling and more than likely will never come."

Russell looked at his food and suddenly lost his appetite. He looked out the window, and saw someone who could use some help.

"Excuse me." Russell said in the same polite tone that he was trained to use at Annapolis during the many formal dinner events.

Russell took his plate and walked out of the restaurant. He walked up to the young mother and gave her the entire plate. The young mother looked surprised. He told her several times that it was alright to take the plate. At the same time, Russell discreetly slipped a fifty dollar bill into her palm. She looked even more surprised. She mumbled something inaudible. Russell saw that her tongue was torn out, probably to ensure not to tell who had raped her. Down the street, Russell saw Eric and he waved to him. Eric brought a bucket of water with him and was ready to wash a vehicle. Russell pulled out several hundred dollar bills that he had won gambling at the Coconut Grove Casino. The bills were crisp and Eric thought that for a moment the money was not real. Russell nodded to him to accept the money. Russell did not want any of the Hezbollah money. Eric grabbed the new money and stuffed the bills into his underwear. Russell watched with admiration as Eric screamed in delight and yelped loudly as he ran down the street.

Russell observed Tareek in the distance and wanted to thank him. As he approached, he observed Tareek direct some of the local boys to rake the beach.

"Thank you for everything you have done." Russell said and offered his hand. "I hope we have made Liberia more peaceful."

"We have common goals: you and I," Tareek said, "We both want peace."

"Agreed."

"Do you want a drink?" Tareek asked, "Gin and tonic?"

"Club beer would be fine. I've had more gin and tonic to last a lifetime. I need to go back to Iraq to dry out." Tareek looked at him quizzically as he did not understand military members do not drink in war zones. They sat down on the lounge chairs.

"When do you leave Liberia?" Tareek inquired.

"Tonight. Deputy Minister Urey will take me."

"Good." Tareek said. "It will be nice to see him again. I need to talk to him about Featu's boys. It would be so much better if they lived outside of Monrovia. The orphanages would not take them, no matter how much money I gave them. They are overloaded as more families cannot afford to keep their babies."

"I can talk to him." Russell offered. "He may be able to help."

"Thank you. Did they ever find out who wanted to assassinate him?"

"I believe it was Rajik based upon how the drug deal went down." Russell paused for a moment and added. "No one has seen Rajik."

"Rajik is scum." Tareek spat. "He's not like the rest of us."

"I know that."

"No, I don't think you do. Let me explain. Hezbollah and Hamas are terror groups and they keep us in line by fear and reprisals. Very few Lebanese stand up against them as they will be killed, their families killed, their friends killed. We came here to make a new life."

"I hope you can find peace here." Russell knew what happened to Tareek's family. Russell reached to shake his hand. "My friend." Tareek was choked up as he thought about his little Marsa.

Russell enjoyed the scene as the waves crashed hard on the beach. The sun was covered by clouds as the rainy season fast approached. The beach cove was a hot spot for foreigners, and Tareek made sure the beach was manicured daily. It became an oasis in the midst of filth and raw sewage from the city's inhabitants.

The Deputy Minister pulled into the Cape Hotel and was treated like a rock star. Uncle Anwar and Ghasson shook his hand and welcomed him. Foreigners pointed to the man who became the most valuable addition to the new Liberian government. The Monrovia newspapers touted the Deputy Minister as a modern hero of Liberia for the drug bust and the capture of Charles Taylor. As part of the new Congo group who reemerged from exile in America, the Deputy Minister maintained dual passports and he occasionally thought about leaving. However, every day he gained more and more confidence that he would restore peace and stability in Liberia.

Russell looked out the window as the Deputy Minister drove him to the airport. Monrovia looked no better than eight months ago when Russell first arrived. A sudden burst of hard rain drove everyone to seek cover. The torrents of water flowed down the streets as haphazard rivers.

The Deputy Minister drove through the stagnant water in the middle of the road and passed two taxis that stalled in the water. Russell looked on the side of Tubman Boulevard and saw one of the underlining examples of why donations had not worked to bring Liberia back into the modern century. The large green harvester trackers and trailers sat idle. Hundreds of thousands of dollars had been spent on the large wheat harvesters. The purchase was poorly communicated as wheat crops never grew in Liberia. Russel heard more examples of egregious contracts as foreigners lived plush lifestyles in secure compounds outside the city.

Russell did know if he would ever see Francesca again and wondered where she was right now. Was she on a mission for the Mossad? Did she have to put her good looks to use manipulating some poor schmuck? Was Francesca her real name? Russell did not know and worse he could not get her out of his mind. He opened the envelope left on the table. *'Don't try to find me, it cannot be, we cannot be.'* The words scrawled on the page infuriated him.

The rain gained strength as a precursor to what would happen during the rainy season. The wiper blades were on full. They passed the idle Presidential Palace and Russell hoped President Ellen Johnson-Sirleaf would never occupy the building that possessed so many demons. In front of the Ministry of Foreign Affairs, the large Liberian flag fluttered in the breeze. One brilliant white star resided in the middle of the blue backdrop with five red and six white stripes, close to America's flag. Living in Africa taught Russell humility. Africa would forever be in his blood. He was forever changed by his time living in Liberia.

"Are you sad to leave?" The Deputy Minister asked.

"I am, but I need to get back to my life."

"Maybe someday you will return." The Deputy Minister said. "I have my father's home in Robertsport. You are more than welcome to come and stay with me."

"That would be nice." Russell wondered if the Deputy Minister would remain alive. The Columbian drug lords must have been very upset losing a key drug route through Liberia and four thousand kilos worth an estimated street value of one hundred million U.S. dollars.

At the airport, the chaos of bodies moving back and forth stopped traffic several hundred feet from the terminal. The Deputy Minister pushed a button on the dashboard that ignited a red light in front and a loud police siren. The wave of bodies slowly parted as he pushed the vehicle forward. Several Liberian police officers arrived and pushed into the crowd. The Deputy Minister drove the government vehicle directly in front of the terminal. Outside of the terminal, Russell observed two Liberians Lieutenants who stood straight in their formal dress uniform. Each stood still with a perfect hand salute as Major Russell jumped out of the vehicle. He bid farewell to Lieutenants Davidson Forleh and Prince Johnson III. Russell informed them that they were the future of not only the new Liberian military but their fledgling nation.

As Russell headed into the terminal, an elderly woman stopped five feet outside of the terminal, dropped to the ground, and kissed the concrete. Joyous screams erupted as relatives saw the elderly woman who had just arrived from America. In other greetings, locals hugged white Europeans. Many foreigners slowly reappeared since the civil war had ended. Soon after the greetings with their Liberian friends, tears erupted down their white cheeks, probably sorrow for leaving them behind as the rebels overran their orphanage, church, or missionary.

On the plane, Russell went right to sleep. He was beyond exhaustion. The drone of the engines did not keep him awake. The twenty-hour flight was horrific and maybe someday there would be a more direct route to America. After eight solid hours of sleep, the plane arrived in Brussels. Russell was shocked by the brilliance of the architecture and cleanliness. He spent an hour in the nicest bathroom he had seen in five months. Russell had time to waste on his six hour layover. His senses were overwhelmed with the magnificence of wealth as he observed the spectacular artwork strung throughout the airport. He had departed one of the poorest nations on the planet and now arrived at one of the wealthiest. Russell sat down and placed his head in his hands. He closed his eyes to better grasp what he had just encountered.

Russell pondered Charles Taylor's fate as he was indicted in Sierra Leone from Hague's World Court for crimes against humanity.

Evidence showed Taylor would be tried for exporting of blood diamonds, recruiting child soldiers, and waging war. He opened up his notebook to the first page and read the inscriptions he wrote five months before. The first one was anonymous, *'Doped up soldiers robed in the spoils of war – dresses, wigs, construction helmets, and swimming goggles – fired on civilians and rival factions with equal disdain.'* He contemplated how far Liberia had come from two significant civil wars and wondered if this fledgling society could stay off the cusp of another war with armed, rival factions still sitting in Guinea and Cote D'Ivoire. The other quote was much older, *'The love of Liberty brought us here'* and is the inscription on Liberia's crest with a sailing schooner traveling the ocean to bring freed slaves back to Africa, a test of society that has endured. He reflected upon what the British colonel stated, *'Nothing in Africa is what it appears to be.'*

And what would happen in Sapo National Forest? Water pumps sent volumes of water and stripped out topsoil in search for gold. Hillsides disappeared and would permanently scar Sapo. West African elephants, pygmy hippos, chimps, and other wildlife were slaughtered to feed the growing number of squatters. The rebel army freely existed in Sapo and waited for word to start an insurgency. Russell believed the intelligence reports that stated several thousand of Charles Taylor thugs entered Sapo. Many of the squatters were war criminals who had existed on the out strings of society. They demanded protection money from the gold diggers and kidnapped young girls for bush wives. Russell knew Al-Qaeda had arrived in Liberia and Rashad's death would not stop them. Al-Qaeda camps throughout Africa were fueled by new recruits who happened to be former child soldiers.

Russell thought of America's history, a test of democracy that endured: sometimes at odds during America's civil war. The nation endured racial and gender inequality, civil rights movement, and war protests. America's little brother Liberia had emerged from two civil wars during 1990 to 2003 that left over 400,000 dead and one million Liberians exiled out of an overall population of only three million. He thought of all of the Liberians he met and hoped they would find sustained peace in their lives. Liberia would forever be in his thoughts and prayers.

What Russell did not know was his dossier was requested by Langley's Deputy Director of Africa Operations. By the end of the day, the Pentagon had released military orders to send Russell on his next assignment to Africa, specifically the Democratic Republic of the Congo. Langley was pleased by Russell's handling of the fast pace, dynamic operation and wanted him as a CIA operative. What Langley did not know was Russell had strong feelings for a female Mossad agent left out of the reports.

In Tel Aviv, Francesca stared at the reports in front of her. The past eight hours of questioning by Mossad leadership had been grueling. Her father had been the harshest interrogator; he wanted Russell dead. But she thought she could turn the American into a spy for Israel and that appealed to them. What she did not tell them—her father would have issued Russel's immediate sanction no matter his potential value—was that she suspected she was pregnant.

Read the next books in the series:

CRISIS IN THE CONGO

Russell was sent back in Africa to track down illegal Uranium shipments that originated out of the Congo. Quickly, he discovered a nation haunted by its past as a former Belgian colony and the brutality of a ruthless thirty-two-year reign by Joseph Mobutu. Russell is shocked after the arrival of his former girlfriend, an Israeli Mossad agent. With the assistance of several retired CIA operatives, Russell managed to navigate through corrupt officials and extreme danger. Russell cheats death and strikes a blow against an international arms syndicate after he eliminated a large stockpile of high grade Uranium destined for the black market.

THE EBOLA ODYSSEY

With his African expertise, Russell was sent back to Liberia and stopped a sinister plan hatched by Hezbollah operatives who weaponized Ebola and sought to strike Tel Aviv. In this high-stakes operation, Russell discovered a lesser known group of former KGB officers, called Voctrad that sold the 1960s era Ebola weapon technology. Russell navigated his way through a society ravaged by abject poverty and the horrors of a fourteen-year civil war. Russell escaped danger with the assistance of his British liaison from MI6 and the mother of his child who happened to be an Israeli Mossad agent. As the world's most deadly virus spread like a raging forest fire, Russell found himself in a deadly match with Voctrad, Hezbollah, and an Al-Qaeda terrorist cell.